BEST KEPT SECRET

ALSO BY JEFFREY ARCHER

NOVELS

Not a Penny More, Not a Penny Less

Shall We Tell the President?   Kane and Abel

The Prodigal Daughter   First Among Equals

A Matter of Honour   As the Crow Flies   Honour Among Thieves

The Fourth Estate   The Eleventh Commandment

Sons of Fortune   False Impression

The Gospel According to Judas
(*with the assistance of Professor Francis J. Moloney*)

A Prisoner of Birth   Paths of Glory

Only Time Will Tell   The Sins of the Father

SHORT STORIES

A Quiver Full of Arrows   A Twist in the Tale

Twelve Red Herrings   The Collected Short Stories

To Cut a Long Story Short   Cat O' Nine Tales

And Thereby Hangs a Tale

PLAYS

Beyond Reasonable Doubt   Exclusive   The Accused

PRISON DIARIES

Volume One – Belmarsh: Hell

Volume Two – Wayland: Purgatory

Volume Three – North Sea Camp: Heaven

SCREENPLAYS

Mallory: Walking Off the Map   False Impression

JEFFREY ARCHER

THE CLIFTON CHRONICLES

VOLUME THREE

BEST KEPT SECRET

MACMILLAN

First published 2013 by Macmillan
an imprint of Pan Macmillan, a division of Macmillan Publishers Limited
Pan Macmillan, 20 New Wharf Road, London N1 9RR
Basingstoke and Oxford
Associated companies throughout the world
www.panmacmillan.com

ISBN 978-0-230-74824-8 HB
ISBN 978-0-230-77086-7 TPB

1 3 5 7 9 8 6 4 2

A CIP catalogue record for this book is available from
the British Library.

Typeset by SetSystems Ltd, Saffron Walden, Essex
Printed and bound by CPI Group (UK) Ltd, Croydon, CR0 4YY

Visit **www.panmacmillan.com** to read more about all our books
and to buy them. You will also find features, author interviews and
news of any author events, and you can sign up for e-newsletters
so that you're always first to hear about our new releases.

TO

SHABNAM AND ALEXANDER

My thanks go to the following people
for their invaluable advice and help with research:

Simon Bainbridge, Robert Bowman, Eleanor Dryden,
Alison Prince, Mari Roberts and Susan Watt

THE BARRINGTONS

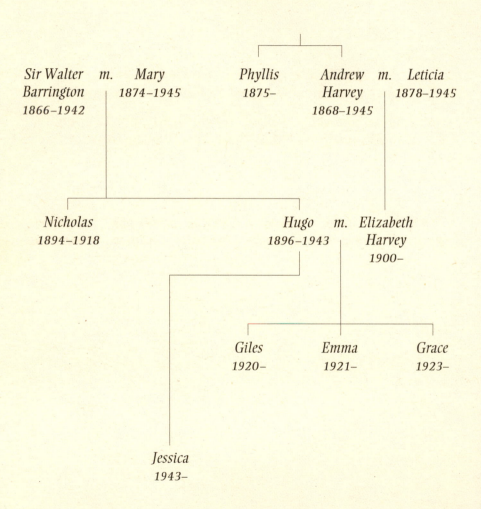

Sir Walter   m.   Mary   Phyllis   Andrew   m.   Leticia
Barrington   1874–1945   1875–   Harvey   1878–1945
1866–1942   1868–1945

Nicholas   Hugo   m.   Elizabeth
1894–1918   1896–1943   Harvey
                                               1900–

                         Giles   Emma   Grace
                         1920–   1921–   1923–

Jessica
1943–

THE CLIFTONS

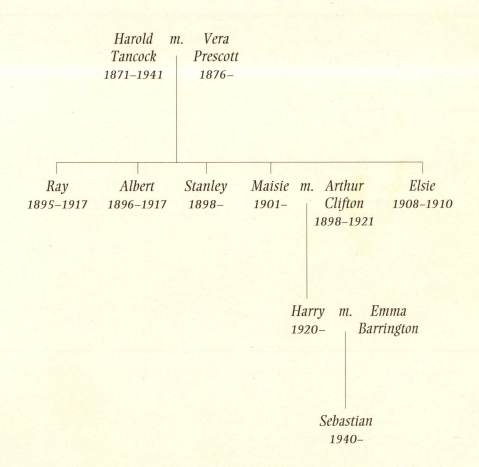

Harold *m.* Vera
Tancock Prescott
1871–1941 *1876–*

Ray   Albert   Stanley   Maisie *m.* Arthur   Elsie
1895–1917 *1896–1917* *1898–* *1901–*   Clifton   *1908–1910*
                                              1898–1921

Harry *m.* Emma
1920–   Barrington

Sebastian
1940–

PROLOGUE

BIG BEN STRUCK four times.

Although the Lord Chancellor was exhausted, and drained from what had taken place that night, enough adrenalin was still pumping through his body to ensure that he was quite unable to sleep. He had assured their lordships that he would deliver a ruling in the case of Barrington versus Clifton as to which of the young men should inherit the ancient title and the family's vast estates.

Once again he considered the facts, because he believed that the facts, and only the facts, should determine his final judgment.

When he'd begun his pupillage some forty years before, his pupilmaster had advised him to dismiss all personal feelings, sentiment or bias when it came to making a judgment on either your client or the case before you. The law was not a profession for the faint-hearted or the romantic, he stressed. However, after abiding by this mantra for four decades, the Lord Chancellor had to admit he'd never come across a case that was so finely balanced. He only wished F.E. Smith was still alive, so he could seek his advice.

On the one hand . . . how he hated those clichéd words. On the one hand, Harry Clifton had been born three weeks before his closest friend, Giles Barrington: fact. On the other hand, Giles Barrington was unquestionably the legitimate son of Sir Hugo Barrington and his lawfully wedded wife, Elizabeth: fact. But that didn't make him Sir Hugo's first born, and that was the relevant point of the will.

1

On the one hand, Maisie Tancock gave birth to Harry on the 28th day of the ninth month after she'd admitted having a dalliance with Sir Hugo Barrington while they were on a works outing to Weston-super-Mare. Fact. On the other hand, Maisie Tancock was married to Arthur Clifton when Harry was born, and the birth certificate stated unequivocally that Arthur was the father of the child. Fact.

On the one hand ... the Lord Chancellor's thoughts returned to what had taken place in the chamber after the House had finally divided and the members had cast their votes as to whether Giles Barrington or Harry Clifton should inherit the title and *all that therein is*. He recalled the Chief Whip's exact words when he announced the result to a packed House.

'Contents to the right, two hundred and seventy-three votes. Non-contents to the left, two hundred and seventy-three votes.'

Uproar had broken out on the red benches. He accepted that the tied vote had left him with the unenviable task of having to decide who should inherit the Barrington family title, the renowned shipping line, as well as property, land and valuables. If only so much hadn't rested on his decision when it came to the future of these two young men. Should he be influenced by the fact that Giles Barrington wished to inherit the title and Harry Clifton didn't? No, he should not. As Lord Preston had pointed out in his persuasive speech from the opposition benches, that would create a bad precedent, even if it was convenient.

On the other hand, if he did come down in favour of Harry ... he finally dozed off, only to be woken by a gentle tap on the door at the unusually late hour of seven o'clock. He groaned, and his eyes remained closed while he counted the chimes of Big Ben. Only three hours before he had to deliver his verdict, and he still hadn't made up his mind.

The Lord Chancellor groaned a second time as he placed his feet on the floor, put on his slippers and padded across to the bathroom. Even as he sat in the bath he continued to wrestle with the problem.

Fact. Harry Clifton and Giles Barrington were both colour

blind, as was Sir Hugo. Fact. Colour blindness can only be inherited through the female line, so it was nothing more than a coincidence, and should be dismissed as such.

He got out of the bath, dried himself and pulled on a dressing gown. He then slipped out of the bedroom and walked down the thickly carpeted corridor until he reached his study.

The Lord Chancellor picked up a fountain pen and wrote the names 'Barrington' and 'Clifton' on the top line of the page, under which he began to write the pros and cons of each man's case. By the time he'd covered three pages in his neat copperplate hand, Big Ben had struck eight times. But still he was none the wiser.

He put down his pen and reluctantly went in search of sustenance.

The Lord Chancellor sat alone, eating his breakfast in silence. He refused even to glance at the morning newspapers so neatly laid out at the other end of the table, or to turn on the radio, as he didn't want some ill-informed commentator to influence his judgment. The broadsheets were pontificating on the future of the hereditary principle should the Lord Chancellor come down in favour of Harry, while the tabloids only seemed interested in whether or not Emma would be able to marry the man she loved.

By the time he returned to the bathroom to brush his teeth, the scales of Justice still hadn't come down on either side.

Just after Big Ben chimed nine, he slipped back into his study and went over his notes in the hope that the scales would finally tilt to one side or the other, but they remained perfectly balanced. He was going over his notes yet again when a tap on the door reminded him that, however powerful he imagined he was, he still couldn't hold up time. He let out a deep sigh, tore three sheets off the pad, stood up, and continued reading as he walked out of his study and down the corridor. When he entered the bedroom he found East, his valet, standing at the foot of the bed waiting to perform the morning ritual.

East began by deftly removing the silk dressing gown before

3

helping his master on with a white shirt that was still warm from ironing. Next, a starched collar, followed by a finely laced neckerchief. As the Lord Chancellor pulled on a pair of black breeches, he was reminded that he'd put on a few pounds since taking office. East then assisted him with his long black and gold gown before turning his attention to his master's head and feet. A full-bottomed wig was placed on his head before he stepped into a pair of buckled shoes. It was only when the gold chain of office that had been worn by thirty-nine previous Lord Chancellors was draped on his shoulders that he became transformed from a pantomime dame into the highest legal authority in the land. A glance in the mirror, and he felt ready to walk on stage and play his part in the unfolding drama. Just a pity he still didn't know his lines.

The timing of the Lord Chancellor's entrance and exit from the North Tower of the Palace of Westminster would have impressed a regimental sergeant major. At 9.47 a.m. there was a knock on the door and his secretary, David Bartholomew, entered the room.

'Good morning, my lord,' he ventured.

'Good morning, Mr Bartholomew,' the Lord Chancellor replied.

'I am sorry to have to report,' said Bartholomew, 'that Lord Harvey died last night, in an ambulance on his way to hospital.'

Both men knew this was not true. Lord Harvey – Giles and Emma Barrington's grandfather – had collapsed in the chamber, only moments before the division bell had sounded. However, they both accepted the age-old convention: if a member of either the Commons or the Lords died while the House was in session, a full inquiry as to the circumstances of his death had to be set up. In order to avoid this unpleasant and unnecessary charade, 'died on his way to hospital' was the accepted form of words that covered such eventualities. The custom dated back to the time of Oliver Cromwell, when members were allowed to wear swords in the chamber, and foul play was a distinct possibility whenever there was a death.

The Lord Chancellor was saddened by the death of Lord Harvey, a colleague he both liked and admired. He only wished that his secretary had not reminded him of one of the facts he had written in his neat copperplate hand below the name of Giles Barrington; namely, that Lord Harvey had been unable to cast his vote after he'd collapsed, and had he done so, it would have been in favour of Giles Barrington. That would have settled the matter once and for all, and he could have slept soundly that night. Now he was expected to settle the matter once and *for all*.

Below the name of Harry Clifton, he had entered another fact. When the original appeal had come before the Law Lords six months before, they had voted 4–3 in favour of Clifton inheriting the title and, to quote the will . . . *and all that therein is*.

A second tap on the door, and his train bearer appeared, wearing another Gilbert and Sullivan-esque outfit, to signal that the ancient ceremony was about to begin.

'Good morning, my lord.'

'Good morning, Mr Duncan.'

The moment the train bearer picked up the hem of the Lord Chancellor's long black gown, David Bartholomew stepped forward and thrust open the double doors of the stateroom so his master could set off on the seven-minute journey to the chamber of the House of Lords.

Members, badge messengers and house officials going about their daily business stepped quickly to one side when they spotted the Lord Chancellor approaching, making sure his progress to the chamber was unimpeded. As he passed by, they bowed low, not to him, but to the Sovereign he represented. He proceeded along the red-carpeted corridor at the same pace as he had done every day for the past six years, in order that he would enter the chamber on the first chime when Big Ben struck ten in the forenoon.

On a normal day, and this was not a normal day, whenever he entered the chamber he would be met by a handful of members who would rise politely from the red benches, bow to the Lord Chancellor and remain standing while the bishop on duty conducted morning prayers, after which the business of the day could commence.

But not today, because long before he reached the chamber, he could hear the murmur of chattering voices. Even the Lord Chancellor was surprised by the sight that greeted him when he entered their lordships' house. The red benches were so packed that some members had migrated to the steps in front of the throne, while others stood at the bar of the House, unable to find a seat. The only other occasion on which he remembered the House being so full was when His Majesty delivered the King's Speech, in which he informed members of both Houses of the legislation his government proposed to enact during the next session of Parliament.

As the Lord Chancellor walked into the chamber, their lordships immediately stopped talking, rose as one and bowed when he took his place in front of the Woolsack.

The senior law officer in the land looked slowly around the chamber to be met by over a thousand impatient eyes. His gaze finally settled on three young people who were seated at the far end of the chamber, directly above him in the Distinguished Strangers' Gallery. Giles Barrington, his sister Emma and Harry Clifton wore funereal black in respect for a beloved grandfather and, in Harry's case, a mentor and dear friend. He felt for all three of them, aware that the judgment he was about to make would change their whole lives. He prayed it would be for the better.

When the Right Reverend Peter Watts, Bishop of Bristol – how appropriate, the Lord Chancellor thought – opened his prayer book, their lordships bowed their heads, and didn't lift them again until he'd uttered the words, 'In the name of the Father, the Son and the Holy Ghost.'

The assembled gathering resumed their places, to leave the Lord Chancellor the only person still on his feet. Once they'd settled, their lordships sat back and waited to hear his verdict.

'My lords,' he began, 'I cannot pretend that the judgment you have entrusted me with has proved easy. On the contrary, I confess it to be one of the most difficult decisions I've had to make in my long career at the bar. But then it was Thomas More who reminded us that when you don these robes you must be willing to make decisions that will rarely please all men. And indeed, my lords, on three such occasions in the past, the Lord Chancellor, having delivered his judgment, was later that day beheaded.'

The laughter that followed broke the tension, but only for a moment.

'However, it remains my duty to remember,' he added after the laughter had died down, 'that I am answerable only to the Almighty. With that in mind, my lords, in the case of Barrington versus Clifton, as to who should succeed Sir Hugo Barrington as his rightful heir and be granted the family title, the lands and all that therein is . . .'

The Lord Chancellor once again glanced up towards the gallery, and hesitated. His eyes settled on the three innocent young people in the dock, who continued to stare down at him. He prayed for the Wisdom of Solomon before he added, 'Having considered all the facts, I come down in favour of . . . Giles Barrington.'

A buzz of murmuring voices immediately erupted from the floor of the House. Journalists quickly left the press gallery to report the Lord Chancellor's ruling to their waiting editors that the hereditary principle remained intact and Harry Clifton could now ask Emma Barrington to be his lawfully wedded wife, while the public in the visitors' gallery leant over the balcony railings to see how their lordships would react to his judgment. But this was not a football match, and he was not a referee. There would be no need to blow a whistle, as each member of their lordships' house would accept and abide by the Lord Chancellor's ruling without division or dissent. As the Lord Chancellor waited for the clamour to subside, he once again glanced up at the three people in the gallery most affected by his decision to see how they had reacted. Harry, Emma and Giles still stared expressionlessly down at him, as if the full significance of his judgment had not yet sunk in.

After months of uncertainty, Giles felt an immediate sense

of relief, although the death of his beloved grandfather removed any feeling of victory.

Harry had only one thought on his mind as he gripped Emma firmly by the hand. He could now marry the woman he loved.

Emma remained uncertain. After all, the Lord Chancellor had created a whole new set of problems for the three of them to consider that he wouldn't be called on to solve.

The Lord Chancellor opened his gold-tasselled folder and studied the orders of the day. A debate on the proposed National Health Service was the second item on the agenda. Several of their lordships slipped out of the chamber, as business returned to normal.

The Lord Chancellor would never admit to anyone, even his closest confidant, that he had changed his mind at the last moment.

HARRY CLIFTON
AND
EMMA BARRINGTON

1945–1951

1

'THEREFORE IF ANY MAN *can show any just cause why these two people may not lawfully be joined together in holy matrimony, let him now speak, or else hereafter for ever hold his peace.'*

Harry Clifton would never forget the first time he'd heard those words, and how moments later his whole life had been thrown into turmoil. Old Jack, who like George Washington could never tell a lie, had revealed in a hastily called meeting in the vestry that it was possible that Emma Barrington, the woman Harry adored, and who was about to become his wife, might be his half-sister.

All hell had broken loose when Harry's mother admitted that on one occasion, and only one, she had had sexual intercourse with Emma's father, Hugo Barrington. Therefore, there was a possibility that he and Emma could be the offspring of the same father.

At the time of her dalliance with Hugo Barrington, Harry's mother had been walking out with Arthur Clifton, a stevedore who worked at Barrington's Shipyard. Despite the fact that Maisie had married Arthur soon afterwards, the priest refused to proceed with Harry and Emma's wedding while there was a possibility it might contravene the church's ancient laws on consanguinity.

Moments later, Emma's father Hugo had slipped out of the back of the church, like a coward leaving the battlefield. Emma and her mother had travelled up to Scotland, while Harry, a desolate soul, remained at his college in Oxford, not knowing what to do next. Adolf Hitler had made that decision for him.

Harry left the university a few days later and exchanged his academic gown for an ordinary seaman's uniform. But he had been serving on the high seas for less than a fortnight when a German torpedo had scuppered his vessel, and the name of Harry Clifton appeared on the list of those reported lost at sea.

'Wilt thou take this woman to thy wedded wife, wilt thou keep thee only unto her, as long as you both shall live?'

'I will.'

It was not until after the end of hostilities, when Harry had returned from the battlefield scarred in glory, that he discovered Emma had given birth to their son, Sebastian Arthur Clifton. But Harry didn't find out until he had fully recovered that Hugo Barrington had been killed in the most dreadful circumstances, and bequeathed the Barrington family another problem, every bit as devastating to Harry as not being allowed to marry the woman he loved.

Harry had never considered it at all significant that he was a few weeks older than Giles Barrington, Emma's brother and his closest friend, until he learned that he could be first in line to inherit the family's title, its vast estates, numerous possessions, and, to quote the will, *all that therein is*. He quickly made it clear that he had no interest in the Barrington inheritance, and was only too willing to forfeit any birthright that might be considered his, in favour of Giles. The Garter King of Arms seemed willing to go along with this arrangement, and all might have progressed in good faith, had Lord Preston, a Labour backbencher in the Upper House, not taken it upon himself to champion Harry's claim to the title, without even consulting him.

'It is a matter of principle,' Lord Preston had explained to any lobby correspondents who questioned him.

'Wilt thou have this man to thy wedded husband, to live together after God's ordinance, in the holy estate of matrimony?'

'I will.'

Harry and Giles had remained inseparable friends through-out the entire episode, despite the fact that they were officially set against each other in the highest court in the land, as well as on the front pages of the national press.

Harry and Giles would both have rejoiced at the Lord Chancellor's decision had Emma and Giles's grandfather Lord Harvey been in his seat on the front bench to hear the ruling, but he never learned of his triumph. The nation remained divided by the outcome, while the two families were left to pick up the pieces.

The other consequence of the Lord Chancellor's ruling was, as the press were quick to point out to their rapacious readers, that the highest court in the land had ordained that Harry and Emma were not of the same bloodline, and therefore he was free to invite her to be his lawfully wedded wife.

'With this ring I thee wed, with my body I thee worship, and with all my worldly goods I thee endow.'

However, Harry and Emma both knew that a decision made by man did not prove beyond reasonable doubt that Hugo Barrington was not Harry's father, and as practising Christians, it worried them that they might be breaking God's law.

Their love for each other had not diminished in the face of all they had been through. If anything, it had grown stronger, and with the encouragement of her mother, Elizabeth, and the blessing of Harry's mother Maisie, Emma accepted Harry's proposal of marriage. It only saddened her that neither of her grandmothers had lived to attend the ceremony.

The nuptials did not take place in Oxford, as originally planned, with all the pomp and circumstance of a university wedding, and the inevitable glare of publicity that would accompany it, but at a simple, register office ceremony in Bristol, with only the family and a few close friends in attend-ance.

Perhaps the saddest decision that Harry and Emma reluctantly agreed on was that Sebastian Arthur Clifton would be their only child.

2

HARRY AND EMMA left for Scotland to spend their honeymoon in Mulgelrie Castle, the ancestral home of Lord and Lady Harvey, Emma's late grandparents, but not before they had left Sebastian in Elizabeth's safe keeping.

The castle brought back many happy memories of the time they'd spent a holiday there just before Harry went up to Oxford. They roamed the hills together during the day, rarely returning to the castle before the sun had disappeared behind the highest mountain. After supper, the cook having recalled how Master Clifton liked three portions of broth, they sat by a roaring log fire reading Evelyn Waugh, Graham Greene and, Harry's favourite, P. G. Wodehouse.

After a fortnight, during which time they encountered more Highland cattle than human beings, they reluctantly set out on the long journey back to Bristol. They arrived at the Manor House looking forward to a life of domestic tranquillity, but it was not to be.

Elizabeth confessed that she couldn't wait to get Sebastian off her hands; tears before bedtime had occurred once too often, she told them as her Siamese cat, Cleopatra, leapt up on to her mistress's lap and promptly fell asleep. 'Frankly, you haven't arrived a moment too soon,' she added. 'I haven't managed to complete *The Times* crossword once in the past fortnight.'

Harry thanked his mother-in-law for her understanding, and

he and Emma took their hyperactive five-year-old back to Barrington Hall.

◄○►

Before Harry and Emma were married, Giles had insisted that as he spent the majority of his time in London carrying out his duties as a Labour Member of Parliament, they were to consider Barrington Hall as their home. With its ten-thousand-book library, expansive park and ample stables, it was ideal for them. Harry could write his William Warwick detective novels in peace, while Emma rode every day, and Sebastian played in the spacious grounds, regularly bringing strange animals home to join him for tea.

Giles would often drive down to Bristol on Friday evenings in time to join them for dinner. On Saturday morning he would conduct a constituency surgery, before dropping into the dock workers' club for a couple of pints with his agent, Griff Haskins. In the afternoon, he and Griff would join 10,000 of his constituents at Eastville Stadium to watch Bristol Rovers lose more times than they won. Giles never admitted, even to his agent, that he would rather have spent his Saturday afternoons watching Bristol play rugby, but had he done so Griff would have reminded him that the crowd at the Memorial Ground was rarely more than two thousand, and most of them voted Conservative.

On Sunday mornings, Giles could be found on his knees at St Mary Redcliffe, with Harry and Emma by his side. Harry assumed that for Giles this was just another constituency duty, as he'd always looked for any excuse to avoid chapel at school. But no one could deny that Giles was quickly gaining a reputation as a conscientious, hard-working Member of Parliament.

And then suddenly, without explanation, Giles's weekend visits became less and less frequent. Whenever Emma raised the subject with her brother, he mumbled something about parliamentary duties. Harry remained unconvinced, and hoped that his brother-in-law's long absences from the constituency would not eat into his slim majority at the next election.

One Friday evening, they discovered the real reason Giles had been otherwise engaged for the past few months.

He had rung Emma earlier in the week to warn her that he was coming down to Bristol for the weekend, and would arrive in time for dinner on Friday. What he hadn't told her was that he would be accompanied by a guest.

Emma usually liked Giles's girlfriends, who were always attractive, often a little scatty and without exception adored him, even if most of them didn't last long enough for her to get to know them. But that was not to be the case this time.

When Giles introduced Virginia to her on Friday evening, Emma was puzzled by what her brother could possibly see in the woman. Emma accepted that she was beautiful and well connected. In fact Virginia reminded them more than once that she'd been Deb of the Year (in 1934), and three times that she was the daughter of the Earl of Fenwick, before they'd even sat down for dinner.

Emma might have dismissed this as simply being nerves, if Virginia hadn't picked at her food and whispered to Giles during dinner, in tones she must have known they could overhear, how difficult it must be to find decent domestic staff in Gloucestershire. To Emma's surprise, Giles just smiled at these observations, never once disagreeing with her. Emma was just about to say something she knew she would regret, when Virginia announced that she was exhausted after such a long day and wished to retire.

Once she had upped and departed, with Giles following a pace behind, Emma walked through to the drawing room, poured herself a large whisky and sank into the nearest chair.

'God knows what my mother will make of the Lady Virginia.'

Harry smiled. 'It won't matter much what Elizabeth thinks, because I have a feeling Virginia will last about as long as most of Giles's other girlfriends.'

'I'm not so sure,' said Emma. 'But what puzzles me is why

she's interested in Giles, because she's clearly not in love with him.'

—◄o►—

When Giles and Virginia drove back to London after lunch on Sunday afternoon, Emma quickly forgot about the Earl of Fenwick's daughter as she had to deal with a far more pressing problem. Yet another nanny had handed in her notice, declaring that it had been the last straw when she'd found a hedgehog in her bed. Harry felt some sympathy for the poor woman.

'It doesn't help that he's an only child,' said Emma after she'd finally got her son to sleep that night. 'It can't be fun having no one to play with.'

'It never worried me,' said Harry, not looking up from his book.

'Your mother told me you were quite a handful before you went to St Bede's school, and in any case, when you were his age, you spent more time down at the docks than you did at home.'

'Well, it won't be long before he starts at St Bede's.'

'And what do you expect me to do in the meantime? Drop him off at the docks every morning?'

'Not a bad idea.'

'Be serious, my darling. If it hadn't been for Old Jack, you'd still be there now.'

'True,' said Harry, as he raised his glass to the great man. 'But what can we do about it?'

Emma took so long to reply that Harry wondered if she'd fallen asleep. 'Perhaps the time has come for us to have another child.'

Harry was so taken by surprise that he closed his book and looked closely at his wife, unsure if he'd heard her correctly. 'But I thought we'd agreed . . .'

'We did. And I haven't changed my mind, but there's no reason why we shouldn't consider adoption.'

'What's brought this on, my darling?'

'I can't stop thinking about the little girl who was found in my father's office the night he died' – Emma could never bring herself to say the word killed – 'and the possibility that she might be his child.'

'But there's no proof of that. And in any case, I'm not sure how you'd find out where she is after all this time.'

'I was thinking of consulting a well-known detective writer, and seeking his advice.'

Harry thought carefully before he spoke. 'William Warwick would probably recommend that you try and track down Derek Mitchell.'

'But surely you can't have forgotten that Mitchell worked for my father, and didn't exactly have our best interests at heart.'

'True,' said Harry, 'and that's exactly why I would seek his advice. After all, he's the one person who knows where all the bodies are buried.'

◄○►

They agreed to meet at the Grand Hotel. Emma arrived a few minutes early and selected a seat in the corner of the lounge where they could not be overheard. While she waited, she went over the questions she planned to ask him.

Mr Mitchell walked into the lounge as the clock struck four. Although he'd put on a little weight since she'd last seen him, and his hair was greyer, the unmistakable limp was still his calling card. Her first thought was that he looked more like a bank manager than a private detective. He clearly recognized Emma, because he headed straight for her.

'It's nice to see you again, Mrs Clifton,' he ventured.

'Please have a seat,' Emma said, wondering if he was as nervous as she was. She decided to get straight to the point. 'I wanted to see you, Mr Mitchell, because I need the help of a private detective.'

Mitchell shifted uneasily in his chair.

'When we last met, I promised I would settle the rest of my father's debt to you.' This had been Harry's suggestion. He said

18

it would make Mitchell realize she was serious about employing him. She opened her handbag, extracted an envelope and handed it to Mitchell.

'Thank you,' said Mitchell, clearly surprised.

Emma continued, 'You will recall when I last saw you we discussed the baby who was found in the wicker basket in my father's office. Detective Chief Inspector Blakemore, who was in charge of the case, as I'm sure you remember, told my husband the little girl had been taken into care by the local authority.'

'That would be standard practice, assuming no one came forward to claim her.'

'Yes, I've already discovered that much, and only yesterday I spoke to the person in charge of that department at City Hall, but he refused to supply me with any details as to where the little girl might be now.'

'That will have been at the instruction of the coroner following the inquest, to protect the child from inquisitive journalists. It doesn't mean there aren't ways of finding out where she is.'

'I'm glad to hear that.' Emma hesitated. 'But before we go down that path, I need to be convinced that the little girl was my father's child.'

'I can assure you, Mrs Clifton, there isn't any doubt about that.'

'How can you be so sure?'

'I could supply you with all the details, but it might cause you some discomfort.'

'Mr Mitchell, I cannot believe that anything you could tell me about my father would surprise me.'

Mitchell remained silent for a few moments. Eventually he said, 'During the time I worked for Sir Hugo, you'll be aware that he moved to London.'

'Ran away on the day of my wedding, would be more accurate.'

Mitchell didn't comment. 'About a year later, he began living with a Miss Olga Piotrovska in Lowndes Square.'

'How could he afford that, when my grandfather had cut him off without a penny?'

'He couldn't. To put it bluntly, he was not only living with Miss Piotrovska, but living *off* her.'

'Can you tell me anything about this lady?'

'A great deal. She was Polish by birth, and escaped from Warsaw in 1941, soon after her parents were arrested.'

'What was their crime?'

'Being Jewish,' said Mitchell without feeling. 'She managed to get across the border with some of the family's possessions, and made her way to London, where she rented a flat in Lowndes Square. It wasn't long after that that she met your father at a cocktail party given by a mutual friend. He courted the lady for a few weeks and then moved into her apartment, giving his word that they would be married as soon as his divorce came through.'

'I said nothing would surprise me. I was wrong.'

'It gets worse,' said Mitchell. 'When your grandfather died, Sir Hugo immediately dumped Miss Piotrovska, and returned to Bristol to claim his inheritance and take over as chairman of the board of Barrington's shipping line. But not before he'd stolen all of Miss Piotrovska's jewellery as well as several valuable paintings.'

'If that's true, why wasn't he arrested?'

'He was,' said Mitchell, 'and was about to be charged when his associate, Toby Dunstable, who had turned King's evidence, committed suicide in his cell the night before the trial.'

Emma bowed her head.

'Would you rather I didn't continue, Mrs Clifton?'

'No,' said Emma looking directly at him. 'I need to know everything.'

'Although your father wasn't aware of it when he returned to Bristol, Miss Piotrovska was pregnant. She gave birth to a little girl, who is named on the birth certificate as Jessica Piotrovska.'

'How do you know that?'

'Because Miss Piotrovska employed me when your father could no longer pay my bills. Ironically, she ran out of money just as your father inherited a fortune. That was the reason she travelled down to Bristol with Jessica. She wanted Sir Hugo to know he had another daughter, as she felt it was his responsibility to bring the girl up.'

'And now it's my responsibility,' said Emma quietly. She paused. 'But I've no idea how to go about finding her, and I was hoping you could help.'

'I'll do whatever I can, Mrs Clifton. But after all this time, it won't be easy. If I come up with anything, you'll be the first to hear,' the detective added as he rose from his seat.

As Mitchell limped away, Emma felt a little guilty. She hadn't even offered him a cup of tea.

◄○►

Emma couldn't wait to get home and tell Harry about her meeting with Mitchell. When she burst into the library at Barrington Hall, he was putting down the phone. He had such a huge grin on his face that all she said was, 'You first.'

'My American publishers want me to do a tour of the States when they launch the new book next month.'

'That's wonderful news, darling. At last you'll get to meet Great-aunt Phyllis, not to mention Cousin Alistair.'

'I can't wait.'

'Don't mock, child!'

'I'm not, because my publishers have suggested you join me on the trip, so you'll be able to see them too.'

'I'd love to go with you, darling, but the timing couldn't be worse. Nanny Ryan has packed her bags, and I'm embarrassed to say that the agency's taken us off their books.'

'Perhaps I could get my publishers to agree to Seb coming along as well.'

'Which would probably result in all of us being deported,' said Emma. 'No, I'll stay at home with Seb, while you go off and conquer the colonies.'

Harry took his wife in his arms. 'Pity. I was looking forward to a second honeymoon. By the way, how did your meeting with Mitchell go?'

◄○►

Harry was in Edinburgh addressing a literary lunch when Derek Mitchell phoned Emma.

'I may have a lead,' he said, not giving his name. 'When can we meet?'

'Ten o'clock tomorrow morning, same place?'

No sooner had she put the phone down than it rang again. She picked it up, to find her sister on the other end of the line.

'What a pleasant surprise, Grace, but knowing you, you'll have a good reason for calling.'

'Some of us have full-time jobs,' Grace reminded her. 'But you're right. I rang because last night I attended a lecture given by Professor Cyrus Feldman.'

'The double Pulitzer Prize-winner?' said Emma, hoping to impress her sister. 'Stanford University, if I remember correctly.'

'I'm impressed,' said Grace. 'More to the point, you'd have been fascinated by the talk he gave.'

'He's an economist, if I recall?' said Emma, trying to keep her head above water. 'Hardly my field.'

'Or mine, but when he spoke about transport . . .'

'Sounds riveting.'

'It was,' said Grace, ignoring her sarcasm, 'especially when he touched on the future of shipping, now that the British Overseas Airways Corporation is planning to start a regular air service from London to New York.'

Emma was suddenly aware of why her sister had rung. 'Any hope of getting a transcript of the lecture?'

'You can do better than that. His next port of call is Bristol, so you can go along and hear him in person.'

'Perhaps I could have a word with him after the lecture. There's so much I'd like to ask him,' said Emma.

'Good idea, but if you do, be warned. Although he's one of those rare men whose brain is bigger than his balls, he's on his fourth wife, and there was no sign of her last night.'

Emma laughed. 'You're so crude, sis, but thanks for the advice.'

—◦—

Harry took the train from Edinburgh to Manchester the following morning and, after addressing a small gathering in the city's municipal library, agreed to take questions.

The first was inevitably from a member of the press. They rarely announced themselves, and seemed to have little or no interest in his latest book. Today it was the turn of the *Manchester Guardian*.

'How is Mrs Clifton?'

'Well, thank you,' Harry replied cautiously.

'Is it true you're both living in the same house as Sir Giles Barrington?'

'It's quite a big house.'

'Do you feel any resentment about the fact that Sir Giles got everything in his father's will, and you got nothing?'

'Certainly not. I got Emma, which is all I ever wanted.'

That seemed to silence the journalist for a moment, allowing a member of the public the chance to jump in.

'When will William Warwick get Chief Inspector Davenport's job?'

'Not in the next book,' said Harry with a smile. 'I can assure you of that.'

'Is it true, Mr Clifton, that you've lost seven nannies in less than three years?'

Manchester clearly had more than one newspaper.

In the car on the way back to the station, Harry began to grumble about the press, although the Manchester rep pointed out that all the publicity didn't seem to be harming his sales. But Harry knew that Emma was becoming concerned about the endless press attention, and the effect it might have on Sebastian once he started school.

'Little boys can be so brutal,' she'd reminded him.

'Well, at least he won't be thrashed for licking his porridge bowl,' said Harry.

◄o►

Although Emma was a few minutes early, Mitchell was already seated in the alcove when she walked into the hotel lounge. He stood up the moment she joined him. The first thing she said, even before she sat down, was, 'Would you like a cup of tea, Mr Mitchell?'

'No, thank you, Mrs Clifton.' Mitchell, not a man for small talk, sat back down and opened his note book. 'It seems the local authority has placed Jessica Smith—'

'Smith?' said Emma. 'Why not Piotrovska, or even Barrington?'

'Too easy to trace, would be my bet, and I suspect the coroner insisted on anonymity following the inquest. The local authority,' he continued, 'sent a Miss J. Smith to a Dr Barnardo's home in Bridgwater.'

'Why Bridgwater?'

'Probably the nearest home that had a vacancy at the time.'

'Is she still there?'

'As far as I can make out, yes. But I've recently discovered that Barnardo's is planning to send several of their girls to homes in Australia.'

'Why would they do that?'

'It's part of Australia's immigration policy to pay ten pounds to assist young people's passage to their country, and they're particularly keen on girls.'

'I would have thought they'd be more interested in boys.'

'It seems they've already got enough of them,' said Mitchell, displaying a rare grin.

'Then we'd better visit Bridgwater as soon as possible.'

'Hold on, Mrs Clifton. If you appear too enthusiastic, they might put two and two together and work out why you're so interested in Miss J. Smith, and decide you and Mr Clifton aren't suitable foster parents.'

'But what reason could they possibly have to deny us?'

'Your name for a start. Not to mention that you and Mr Clifton weren't married when your son was born.'

'So what do you recommend?' asked Emma quietly.

'Make an application through the usual channels. Don't appear to be in a rush, and make it look as if they are taking the decisions.'

'But how do we know they won't turn us down anyway?'

'You'll have to nudge them in the right direction, won't you, Mrs Clifton.'

'What are you suggesting?'

'When you fill in the application form, you're asked to put down any preferences you might have. It saves everyone a lot of time and trouble. So if you make it clear that you're looking for a girl of around five or six, as you already have a son who's a little older, it should help narrow the field.'

'Any other suggestions?'

'Yes,' replied Mitchell. 'Under religion, tick the box marked no preference.'

'Why will that help?'

'Because Miss Jessica Smith's registration form states mother Jewish, father unknown.'

3

'How did a limey ever get the Silver Star?' asked the immigration officer at Idlewild as he studied Harry's entry visa.

'It's a long story,' said Harry, thinking it might not be wise to tell him that the last time he'd set foot in New York he'd been arrested for murder.

'Have a great time while you're in the States.' The officer shook Harry by the hand.

'Thank you,' said Harry, trying not to look surprised as he passed through immigration and followed the signs to the baggage claim area. As he waited for his suitcase to appear, he once again checked his arrival instructions. He was to be met by Viking's chief publicist, who would accompany him to his hotel and brief him on his schedule. Whenever he visited a city in Britain, he was always accompanied by the local sales rep, so he wasn't quite sure what a publicist was.

After retrieving his old school trunk, Harry made his way towards customs. An officer asked him to open the trunk, made a cursory check, then chalked a large cross on the side before ushering him through. Harry walked under a huge semi-circular sign that declared *Welcome to New York*, above a beaming photograph of the mayor, William O'Dwyer.

Once he emerged into the arrivals hall, he was greeted by a row of uniformed chauffeurs holding up name cards. He searched for 'Clifton' and, when he spotted it, smiled at the driver and said, 'That's me.'

'Good to meet you, Mr Clifton. I'm Charlie.' He grabbed

Harry's heavy trunk as if it was a briefcase. 'And this is your publicist, Natalie.'

Harry turned to see a young woman who had been referred to on his instructions simply as 'N. Redwood'. She was almost as tall as him, with fashionably cut blonde hair, blue eyes, and teeth straighter and whiter than any he'd ever seen, except for on a billboard advertising toothpaste. If that wasn't enough, her head rested on an hourglass figure. Harry had never come across anything like Natalie in post-war, ration-book Britain.

'Nice to meet you, Miss Redwood,' he said, shaking her hand.

'And it's good to meet you, Harry,' she replied. 'Do call me Natalie,' she added as they followed Charlie out of the concourse. 'I'm a huge fan. I just love William Warwick, and have no doubt your latest book is going to be another winner.'

Once they reached the kerb, Charlie opened the rear door of the longest limousine Harry had ever seen. Harry stood aside to allow Natalie to get in first.

'Oh, I do love the English,' she said as he climbed in beside her, and the limo joined a stream of traffic making its slow progress into New York. 'First, we'll be going to your hotel. I've booked you into the Pierre, where you have a suite on the eleventh floor. I've left just enough time in your schedule for you to freshen up before you join Mr Guinzburg for lunch at the Harvard Club. By the way, he's looking forward to meeting you.'

'Me too,' said Henry. 'He published my prison diaries, as well as the first William Warwick novel, so I've a lot to thank him for.'

'And he's invested a great deal of time and money to make sure *Nothing Ventured* gets on to the bestseller list, and he asked me to brief you fully on how we plan to go about that.'

'Please do,' said Harry as he glanced out of the window to enjoy sights he'd last seen from the back of a yellow prison bus that was taking him off to a jail cell rather than a suite at the Pierre Hotel.

A hand touched his leg. 'There's a lot we have to cover

before you see Mr Guinzburg.' Natalie handed him a thick blue folder. 'Let me start by explaining how we intend to go about getting your book on to the bestseller list, because it's very different from the way you do things in England.'

Harry opened the folder and tried to concentrate. He'd never before sat next to a woman who looked as if she'd been poured into her dress.

'In America,' Natalie continued, 'you've only got three weeks to make sure your book hits the *New York Times* bestseller list. If you don't make it into the top fifteen during that time, the bookstores will pack up their stock of *Nothing Ventured* and return them to the publisher.'

'That's crazy,' said Harry. 'In England once a bookseller has placed an order, as far as the publisher is concerned the book is sold.'

'You don't offer bookstores a sale or return option?'

'Certainly not,' said Harry, shocked by the idea.

'And is it also true that you still sell books without offering a discount?'

'Yes, of course.'

'Well, you're going to find that's the other big difference over here, because if you do make it into the top fifteen, the cover price will automatically be halved, and your book will be moved to the back of the store.'

'Why? Surely a bestseller should be prominently displayed at the front of the shop, even in the window, and certainly not be discounted.'

'Not since the advertising boys discovered that if a customer comes in looking for a particular bestseller, and they have to go to the back of the store to find it, one in five customers buys two more books on their way to the sales counter, while one in three picks up another one.'

'Clever, but I'm not sure that will ever catch on in England.'

'I suspect it will only be a matter of time, but at least you'll now appreciate why it's so important to get your book on the list as quickly as possible, because once the price is halved, you're likely to stay in the top fifteen for several weeks. In fact, it's harder to get off the list than to get on. But if you fail, *Nothing Ventured* will have disappeared from the bookshelves a month today, and we will have lost a great deal of money.'

'I get the message,' said Harry as the limousine passed slowly over Brooklyn Bridge and he was reunited with yellow cabs and their cigar-stub-smoking drivers.

'What makes it even tougher is that we have to visit seventeen different cities in twenty-one days.'

'We?'

'Yes, I'll be holding your hand throughout the trip,' she said casually. 'I usually stay in New York and allow a local publicist in each city to look after visiting authors, but not this time, because Mr Guinzburg insisted I wasn't to leave your side.' She lightly touched his leg again, before turning a page of the folder on her lap.

Harry glanced at her, and she gave a coquettish smile. Was she flirting with him? No, that wasn't possible. After all, they'd only just met.

'I've already got you booked on to several of the major radio stations, including the *Matt Jacobs Show*, which has eleven million listeners every morning. No one's more effective than Matt when it comes to moving books out of the stores.'

Harry had several questions he would like to have asked, but Natalie was like a Winchester rifle, a bullet was fired every time you raised your head.

'Be warned,' she continued, not drawing breath, 'most of the big shows won't give you more than a few minutes – it's not like your BBC. "In depth" is not a concept they understand. During that time remember to repeat the title of the book as often as possible.'

Harry began to turn the pages of his tour schedule. Each day seemed to begin in a new city, where he would appear on an early-morning radio show, followed by countless broadcast and print interviews before dashing off to the airport.

'Do all your authors get this kind of treatment?'

'Certainly not,' said Natalie, the hand back on the leg again. 'Which brings me to the biggest problem we have with you.'

'You have a problem with me?'

'We sure do. Most of the interviewers will want to ask you about your time in prison, and how an Englishman came to win the Silver Star, but you must always switch the subject back to the book.'

'In England, that would be considered rather vulgar.'

'In America, vulgar is what gets you on to the bestseller list.'

'But won't the interviewers want to talk about the book?'

'Harry, you must assume that none of them will have read it. A dozen new novels land on their desks every day, so you'll be lucky if they've read more than the title. It'll be a bonus if they even remember your name. They've only agreed to have you on their shows because you're an ex-con who won the Silver Star, so let's turn that to our advantage and plug the book like crazy,' she was saying as the limousine drew up outside the Pierre Hotel.

Harry wished he was back in England.

The driver leapt out and opened the boot as a hotel porter walked across to the car. Natalie led Harry into the hotel and across the lobby to the reception desk, where all he had to do was show his passport and sign the registration form. Natalie appeared to have prepared the way of the Lord.

'Welcome to the Pierre, Mr Clifton,' said the desk clerk as he handed him a large key.

'I'll see you back here in the lobby –' Natalie checked her watch – 'in an hour. Then the limo will take you to the Harvard Club for your lunch with Mr Guinzburg.'

'Thank you,' said Harry, and watched as she walked back across the lobby and disappeared through the revolving doors and out on to the street. He couldn't help noticing that he wasn't the only man whose eyes never left her.

A porter accompanied him to the eleventh floor, showed him into his suite and explained how everything worked. Harry had never stayed in a hotel that had a bath *and* a shower. He decided to make notes so he could tell his mother all about it when he returned to Bristol. He thanked the porter, and parted with the only dollar he had.

The first thing Harry did, even before unpacking, was to pick up the phone by the bed and place a person-to-person call to Emma.

'I'll call you back in around fifteen minutes, sir,' said the overseas operator.

Harry stayed too long in the shower, and once he had dried himself on the largest towel he'd ever seen, he had only just started to unpack when the phone rang.

'Your overseas call is on the line, sir,' said the operator. The next voice he heard was Emma's.

'Is that you, darling? Can you hear me?'

'Sure can, honey,' said Harry, smiling.

'You sound like an American already. I can't imagine what you'll be like after three weeks.'

'Ready to come back to Bristol would be my bet, especially if the book doesn't get on to the bestseller list.'

'And if it doesn't?'

'I may be coming home early.'

'That sounds good to me. So where are you calling from?'

'The Pierre, and they've put me in the biggest hotel room I've ever seen. The bed could sleep four.'

'Just make sure it only sleeps one.'

'It's got air-conditioning, and a radio in the bathroom. Mind you, I still haven't worked out how to turn everything on. Or off.'

'You should have taken Seb with you. He would have mastered it by now.'

'Or taken it apart and left me to put it back together again. But how is the boy?'

'He's fine. In fact he seems more settled without a nanny.'

'That's a relief. And how's your search for Miss J. Smith coming along?'

'Slowly, but I've been asked to go for an interview at Dr Barnardo's tomorrow afternoon.'

31

'That sounds promising.'

'I'm meeting Mr Mitchell in the morning, so I know what to say and, perhaps more important, what not to say.'

'You'll be fine, Emma. Just remember it's their responsibility to place children in good homes. My only worry is how Seb will react when he finds out what you're up to.'

'He already knows. I raised the subject with him last night just before he went to bed, and to my surprise he seemed to love the idea. But once you involve Seb, a separate problem always arises.'

'What is it this time?'

'He expects to have a say when it comes to who we pick. The good news is that he wants a sister.'

'That could still be tricky if he takes against Miss J. Smith and sets his heart on someone else.'

'I don't know what we'll do if that happens.'

'We'll just have to convince him somehow that Jessica was his choice.'

'And how do you propose we do that?'

'I'll think about it.'

'Just remember not to underestimate him. If we do, it could easily backfire.'

'Let's talk about it when I get back,' said Harry. 'Must rush, darling, I have a lunch appointment with Harold Guinzburg.'

'Give him my love, and remember, he's another man you can't afford to underestimate. And while you're at it, don't forget to ask him what happened to—'

'I haven't forgotten.'

'Good luck, darling,' said Emma, 'and just make sure you get yourself on to that bestseller list!'

'You're worse than Natalie.'

'Who's Natalie?'

'A ravishing blonde who can't keep her hands off me.'

'You're such a storyteller, Harry Clifton.'

◄○►

Emma was among the first to arrive at the university's lecture theatre that evening to hear Professor Cyrus Feldman lecture on the topic, *Having won the War, has Britain lost the peace?*

She slipped into a place at the end of a row of raked seats about halfway back. Long before the appointed hour the room was so packed that latecomers had to sit on the gangway steps, with one or two even perched on windowsills.

The audience burst into applause the moment the double Pulitzer Prize-winner entered the auditorium, accompanied by the university's vice chancellor. Once everyone had resumed their places, Sir Philip Morris introduced his guest, giving a potted history of Feldman's distinguished career, from his student days at Princeton, to being appointed the youngest professor at Stanford, to the second Pulitzer Prize he'd been awarded the previous year. This was followed by another prolonged round of applause. Professor Feldman rose from his place and made his way to the podium.

The first thing that struck Emma about Cyrus Feldman, even before he began to speak, was how handsome the man was, something Grace had omitted to mention when she'd called. He must have been a shade over six foot, with a head of thick grey hair, and his suntanned face reminded everyone which university he taught at. His athletic build belied his age, and suggested he must spend almost as many hours in the gym as in the library.

The second he began to speak, Emma was captivated by Feldman's raw energy, and within moments he had everyone in the auditorium sitting on the edge of their seats. Students began furiously writing down his every word, and Emma regretted not bringing a notepad and pen along with her.

Speaking without notes, the professor nimbly switched from subject to subject: the role of Wall Street after the war, the dollar as the new world currency, oil becoming the commodity that would dominate the second half of the century and possibly beyond, the future role of the International Monetary Fund, and whether America would remain fixed to the gold standard.

When his lecture came to an end, Emma's only regret was that he'd scarcely touched on transport, with just a passing mention of how the aeroplane would change the new world order, both for business and tourism. But like a seasoned pro, he reminded his audience that he'd written a book on the subject. Emma wouldn't be waiting for Christmas to get hold of a copy. It made her think about Harry, and hope his book tour was going as well in America.

Once she'd purchased a copy of *The New World Order*, she joined a long queue of those waiting to have their copies signed. She had nearly completed the first chapter by the time she reached the front of the line, and was wondering if he might be willing to spare a few moments to expand his views on the future of the British shipping industry.

She placed the book on the table in front of him, and he gave her a friendly smile.

'Who shall I make it out to?'

She decided to take a chance. 'Emma Barrington.'

He took a closer look at her. 'You wouldn't by any chance be related to the late Sir Walter Barrington?'

'He was my grandfather,' she said proudly.

'I heard him lecture many years ago on the role of the shipping industry should America enter the First World War. I was a student at the time, and he taught me more in one hour than my tutors had managed in a whole semester.'

'He taught me a lot too,' said Emma, returning his smile.

'There was so much I wanted to ask him,' added Feldman, 'but he had to catch the train back to Washington that night, so I never saw him again.'

'And there's so much I want to ask you,' said Emma. 'In fact, "need" would be more accurate.'

Feldman glanced at the waiting queue. 'I guess this shouldn't take me more than another half hour, and as I'm not catching the train back to Washington tonight, perhaps we could have a private chat before I leave, Miss Barrington?'

4

'AND HOW IS my beloved Emma?' asked Harold Guinzburg after he'd welcomed Harry to the Harvard Club.

'I've just spoken to her on the phone,' said Harry. 'She sends her love, and was disappointed that she wasn't able to join us.'

'Me too. Please tell her I won't accept any excuses next time.' Guinzburg guided his guest through to the dining room and they took their seats at what was clearly his usual corner table. 'I hope you're finding the Pierre to your liking,' he said as a waiter handed them both menus.

'It would be fine, if only I knew how to turn the shower off.'

Guinzburg laughed. 'Perhaps you should ask Miss Redwood to come to your rescue.'

'If she did, I'm not sure I'd know how to turn her off.'

'Ah, so she's already subjected you to her lecture on the importance of getting *Nothing Ventured* on to the bestseller list as quickly as possible.'

'A formidable lady.'

'That's why I made her a director,' said Guinzburg, 'despite protests from several directors who didn't want a woman on the board.'

'Emma would be proud of you,' said Harry, 'and I can assure you that Miss Redwood has warned me of the consequences should I fail.'

'That sounds like Natalie. And remember, she alone decides if you return home by plane or row boat.'

Harry would have laughed, but he wasn't sure his publisher was joking.

'I would have invited her to join us for lunch,' said Guinzburg, 'but as you may have observed, the Harvard Club does not allow women on the premises – don't tell Emma.'

'I have a feeling you'll see women dining in the Harvard Club long before you spot one in any gentlemen's club on Pall Mall or St James's.'

'Before we talk about the tour,' said Guinzburg, 'I want to hear everything you and Emma have been up to since she left New York. How did you win the Silver Star? Has Emma got a job? How did Sebastian react to meeting his father for the first time? And—'

'And Emma insisted that I don't go back to England without finding out what's happened to Sefton Jelks.'

'Shall we order first? I don't care to think about Sefton Jelks on an empty stomach.'

◄○►

'I may not be catching the train to Washington, but I'm afraid I do have to get back to London tonight, Miss Barrington,' said Professor Feldman after he'd signed the last book. 'I'm addressing the London School of Economics at ten tomorrow morning, so I can only spare you a few minutes.'

Emma tried not to look disappointed.

'Unless . . .' said Feldman.

'Unless?'

'Unless you'd like to join me on the journey to London, in which case you'd have my undivided attention for at least a couple of hours.'

Emma hesitated. 'I'll have to make a phone call.'

Twenty minutes later, she was sitting in a first-class railway carriage opposite Professor Feldman. He asked the first question.

'So, Miss Barrington, does your family still own the shipping line that bears their illustrious name?'

'Yes, my mother owns twenty-two per cent.'

'That should give the family more than enough control, and that's all that matters in any organization – as long as no one else gets their hands on more than twenty-two per cent.'

'My brother Giles doesn't take a great deal of interest in the company's affairs. He's a Member of Parliament and doesn't even attend the AGM. But I do, professor, which is why I needed to speak to you.'

'Please call me Cyrus. I've reached that age when I don't want to be reminded by a beautiful young woman just how old I am.'

Grace had been right about one thing, thought Emma, and decided to take advantage of it. She returned his smile before asking, 'What problems do you envisage for the shipbuilding industry during the next decade? Our new chairman, Sir William Travers—'

'First-class man. Cunard were foolish to let such an able fellow go,' interrupted Feldman.

'Sir William is considering whether we should add a new passenger liner to our fleet.'

'Madness!' said Feldman, thumping the seat beside him with a clenched fist, causing a cloud of dust to billow up into the air. Before Emma could ask why, he added, 'Unless you have a surplus of cash that you need to dispose of, or there are tax advantages for the UK shipping industry that no one's told me about.'

'Neither, that I'm aware of,' said Emma.

'Then it's time for you to face the facts. The aeroplane is about to turn passenger ships into floating dinosaurs. Why would any sane person take five days crossing the Atlantic Ocean, when they can do the same journey in eighteen hours by plane?'

'More relaxing? Fear of flying? You'll arrive in better shape?' suggested Emma, recalling Sir William's words at the AGM.

'Out of touch and out of date, young lady,' said Feldman. 'You'll have to come up with something better than that if you're going to convince me. No, the truth is that the modern businessman, and even the more adventurous tourist, wants to cut down on the time it takes to reach their destination, which in a very few years will sink, and I mean sink, the passenger liner business.'

'And in the long term?'

'You haven't got that long.'

'So what do you recommend we do?'

'Invest any spare cash you have in building more cargo vessels. Planes will never be able to carry large or heavy items like motor cars, plant machinery or even food.'

'How do I convince Sir William of that?'

'Make your position clear at the next board meeting,' said Feldman, his fist once again banging on the seat.

'But I'm not on the board.'

'You're not on the board?'

'No, and I can't see Barrington's ever appointing a woman director.'

'They don't have any choice,' said Feldman, his voice rising. 'Your mother owns twenty-two per cent of the company's stock. You can demand a place on the board.'

'But I'm not qualified, and a two-hour train journey to London, even if it is with a Pulitzer Prize-winner, isn't going to solve that problem.'

'Then it's time to get qualified.'

'What do you have in mind?' asked Emma. 'Because there isn't a university in England that I'm aware of that has a business degree on its curriculum.'

'Then you'll have to take three years off and join me at Stanford.'

'I don't think my husband or my young son would think much of that idea,' replied Emma, breaking her cover.

This silenced the professor, and it was some time before he said, 'Can you afford a ten-cent stamp?'

'Yes,' said Emma tentatively, not sure what she was letting herself in for.

'Then I'll be happy to enrol you as an undergraduate at Stanford in the fall.'

'But as I explained—'

'You stated, without reservation, that you could afford a ten-cent stamp.'

Emma nodded.

'Well, Congress has just passed a bill that will allow American military who are serving overseas to sign up for a business degree without actually having to attend classes in person.'

'But I'm not an American, and I'm certainly not serving overseas.'

'True,' said Feldman, 'but hidden in the bill's small print you'll find, under special exemptions, the word "Allies", which I'm pretty sure we can take advantage of. That is, assuming you're serious about the long-term future of your family's company.'

'Yes, I am,' said Emma. 'But what will you expect of me?'

'Once I've registered you as an undergraduate at Stanford, I'll send you a course reading list for your freshman year, along with tape-recordings of every lecture I give. On top of that, I'll set you an essay to write each week, and return it to you once I've marked it. And if you can afford more than ten cents, we could even talk on the phone from time to time.'

'When do I start?'

'This fall, but be warned, there are assessment tests every quarter that decide if you should be allowed to continue on the course,' he was saying as the train pulled into Paddington station. 'If you're not up to it, you'll be dropped.'

'You're willing to do all that because of one meeting with my grandfather?'

'Well, I confess I was rather hoping you might join me for dinner at the Savoy tonight so we can talk about the future of the shipbuilding industry in greater detail.'

'What a nice idea,' said Emma, giving him a kiss on his cheek. 'But I'm afraid I bought a return ticket, and I'll be going home to my husband tonight.'

◄○►

Even if Harry still couldn't work out how to turn on the radio, at least he'd mastered the hot and cold taps in the shower.

Once he was dry, he selected a freshly ironed shirt, a silk tie Emma had given him for his birthday, and a suit his mother would have described as Sunday best. A glance in the mirror, and he had to admit he wouldn't have been considered in vogue on either side of the Atlantic.

Harry stepped out of the Pierre on to 5th Avenue just before eight and began walking towards 64th and Park. It only took him a few minutes before he was standing outside a magnificent brownstone house. He checked his watch, wondering what was fashionably late in New York. He recalled Emma telling him she'd been so nervous at the thought of meeting Great-aunt Phyllis that she'd walked around the block before summoning up enough courage to climb the steps to the front door, and even then she only managed to press the bell marked 'Tradesmen'.

Harry marched up the steps and banged firmly with the heavy brass knocker. As he waited for the door to be answered, he could hear Emma remonstrating with him – *Don't mock, child*.

The door opened and a butler wearing a tailcoat, who was clearly expecting him, said, 'Good evening, Mr Clifton. Mrs Stuart is waiting for you in the drawing room. Would you care to follow me?'

'Good evening, Parker,' Harry replied, although he'd never seen the man before. Harry thought he detected the flicker of a smile as the butler led him down the corridor to an open lift. Once he'd stepped inside, Parker closed the grille, pressed a button and didn't speak again until they reached the third floor. He pulled open the gate, preceded Harry into the drawing room and announced, 'Mr Harry Clifton, madam.'

A tall, elegantly dressed woman was standing in the middle of the room, chatting to a man Harry assumed must be her son.

Great-aunt Phyllis immediately broke away, walked across to Harry and, without a word, gave him a bear hug that would have impressed an American linebacker. When she finally released him, she introduced her son Alistair, who shook Harry warmly by the hand.

'It's an honour to meet the man who ended Sefton Jelks's career,' said Harry.

Alistair offered a slight bow.

'I also played a small part in that man's downfall,' sniffed Phyllis, as Parker handed her guest a glass of sherry. 'But don't get me started on Jelks,' she added, as she ushered Harry towards a comfortable chair by the fire, 'because I'm far more interested to hear about Emma, and what she's been up to.'

Harry took some time bringing Great-aunt Phyllis up to date on everything Emma had done since she'd left New York, not least because she and Alistair kept interrupting him with questions. It wasn't until the butler returned to announce dinner was served that they moved on to a different subject.

'So how are you enjoying your visit?' asked Alistair as they took their seats round the dining table.

'I think I preferred being arrested for murder,' said Harry. 'Far easier to deal with.'

'That bad?'

'Worse in some ways. You see, I'm not much good at selling myself,' admitted Harry as a maid placed a bowl of Scotch broth in front of him. 'I'd rather hoped the book might speak for itself.'

'Think again,' said Great-aunt Phyllis. 'Just remember, New York isn't an offshoot of Bloomsbury. Forget refinement, understatement and irony. However much it's against your better nature, you'll have to learn to sell your wares like an East End barrow boy.'

'I'm proud to be England's most successful author,' said Alistair, raising his voice.

'But I'm not,' said Harry, 'by a long chalk.'

'I've been overwhelmed by the American people's reaction to *Nothing Ventured*,' said Phyllis, joining in the charade.

'That's only because no one's read it,' protested Harry, between mouthfuls.

'Like Dickens, Conan Doyle and Wilde, I'm confident the United States will turn out to be my biggest market,' added Alistair.

'I sell more books in Market Harborough than I do in New York,' Harry said as his soup bowl was whisked away. 'It's patently obvious that Aunt Phyllis ought to take my place on the book tour, and I should be sent back to England.'

'I would be only too delighted to do so,' said Phyllis. 'It's just a pity I don't have your talent,' she added wistfully.

Harry helped himself to a slice of roast beef and far too many potatoes, and it wasn't long before he began to relax as Phyllis and Alistair regaled him with tales of Emma's exploits when she'd turned up in New York in search of him. It amused him to hear their version of what had taken place, and only served to remind him just how lucky he'd been to end up sleeping in the next bed to Giles Barrington when he first went to St Bede's. And if he hadn't been invited to tea at the Manor House to celebrate Giles's birthday, he might never have met Emma. Not that he'd even glanced at her at the time.

'You do realize you'll never be good enough for her,' said Phyllis as she lit a cheroot.

Harry nodded, appreciating for the first time why this indomitable lady had turned out to be Emma's Old Jack. If they had sent her off to war, he thought, Great-aunt Phyllis would surely have come home with the Silver Star.

When the clock struck eleven, Harry, who might have had one brandy too many, rose unsteadily from his chair. He didn't need reminding that at six the next morning Natalie would be standing in the hotel lobby, waiting to whisk him off for his first radio interview of the day. He thanked his hostess for a memorable evening, and for his trouble received another bear hug.

'Now, don't forget,' she said, 'whenever you're interviewed, think British, act Yiddish. And if you ever need a shoulder to cry on, or a half-decent meal, just like the Windmill Theatre we never close.'

'Thank you,' said Harry.

'And when you next speak to Emma,' said Alistair, 'do remember to send our love, and be sure to chastise her for not accompanying you on this trip.'

Harry decided this wasn't the moment to tell them about Sebastian and what the doctors described as his hyper-active problem.

The three of them somehow squeezed into the lift, and Harry received one last hug from Phyllis, before Parker opened the front door and he was cast back on to the streets of Manhattan.

'Oh hell,' he said after he'd walked a short way down Park Avenue. He turned and ran back to Phyllis's house, up the steps and banged on the front door. The butler didn't appear quite as quickly this time.

'I need to see Mrs Stuart urgently,' said Harry. 'I hope she hasn't gone to bed.'

'Not that I'm aware of, sir,' said Parker. 'Please, follow me.' He led Harry back down the corridor and into the lift where once again he pressed the button for the third floor.

Phyllis was standing by the mantelpiece puffing away on her cheroot when Harry made his second entrance. It was her turn to look surprised.

'I'm so sorry,' he said, 'but Emma will never forgive me if I return to England without discovering what's happened to that lawyer who foolishly underestimated her.'

'Sefton Jelks,' said Alistair, looking up from his seat by the fire. 'The damn man finally resigned as senior partner of Jelks, Myers and Abernathy, albeit somewhat reluctantly.'

'Shortly afterwards, he disappeared off to Minnesota,' added Phyllis.

'And he won't be returning in the near future,' said Alistair, 'as he died some months ago.'

'My son is a typical lawyer,' said Phyllis, stubbing out her cheroot. 'He only ever tells you half the story. Jelks's first heart attack warranted a small mention in the *New York Times*, and it was only after the third that he received a short and not very flattering paragraph at the bottom of the obituary page.'

'Which was more than he deserved,' said Alistair.

'I agree,' said Phyllis. 'Although it gave me considerable pleasure to discover that only four people attended his funeral.'

'How do you know that?' asked Alistair.

'Because I was one of them,' said Phyllis.

'You travelled all the way to Minnesota just to attend Sefton Jelks's funeral?' said Harry in disbelief.

'I most certainly did.'

'But why?' demanded Alistair.

'You could never trust Sefton Jelks,' she explained. 'I wouldn't have been truly convinced he was dead until I'd seen his coffin being lowered into the ground, and even then I waited until the gravediggers had filled in the hole.'

◄○►

'Please have a seat, Mrs Clifton.'

'Thank you,' said Emma as she sat down on a wooden chair and faced the three governors, who were in comfortable seats behind a long table on a raised dais.

'My name is David Slater,' said the man in the centre, 'and I'll be chairing this afternoon's meeting. Allow me to introduce my colleagues, Miss Braithwaite and Mr Needham.'

Emma tried to make a rapid assessment of the three invigilators she was facing. The chairman wore a three-piece suit, an old school tie she recognized, and looked as if this wasn't the only board he chaired. Miss Braithwaite, who sat on his right, was dressed in a pre-war tweed suit and thick woollen stockings. Her hair was done up in a bun, leaving Emma in no doubt that she was a spinster of this parish, and the set of her lips suggested she didn't smile that often. The gentleman on the chairman's left was younger than his two colleagues, and reminded Emma that it was not so long ago that Britain had been at war. His bushy moustache suggested the RAF.

'The board has studied your application with interest, Mrs Clifton,' began the chairman, 'and with your permission, we would like to ask you a few questions.'

'Yes, of course,' said Emma, trying to relax.

'How long have you been considering adoption, Mrs Clifton?'

'Ever since I realized I couldn't have another child,' replied

Emma, without adding any details. The two men smiled sympathetically, but Miss Braithwaite remained po-faced.

'You state on your application form,' continued the chairman, looking down at his papers, 'that you would prefer to adopt a girl aged around five or six. Is there any particular reason for that?'

'Yes,' said Emma. 'My son Sebastian is an only child, and my husband and I felt it would be good for him to be brought up with someone who hasn't had all the advantages and privileges he has taken for granted since birth.' She hoped her reply hadn't sounded too rehearsed, and could have sworn the chairman placed a tick in a box.

'Can we assume from your answer,' said the chairman, 'that there are no financial restrictions that might hinder you bringing up a second child?'

'None whatsoever, Mr Chairman. My husband and I are comfortably off.' Emma noticed this elicited another tick.

'I only have one more question,' said the chairman. 'You stated in your application that you would consider a child from any religious background. May I ask if you are affiliated to any particular church?'

'Like Dr Barnardo,' said Emma, 'I am a Christian. My husband was a choral scholar at St Mary Redcliffe.' Looking directly at the chairman, she added, 'Before he went on to Bristol Grammar School, where he ended up as the senior chorister. I was educated at Red Maids' School, before winning a scholarship to Oxford.'

The chairman touched his tie, and Emma felt things couldn't be going much better, until Miss Braithwaite tapped her pencil on the table. The chairman nodded in her direction.

'You mentioned your husband, Mrs Clifton. May I enquire why he isn't with you today?'

'He's in the United States on a book tour. He'll be returning in a couple of weeks' time.'

'Is he often away?'

'No. Very rarely in fact. My husband is a writer by profession, so he's at home most of the time.'

'But he must need to visit a library occasionally,' suggested Miss Braithwaite, with what might have passed as a smile.

'No, we have our own library,' said Emma, regretting the words the moment she'd uttered them.

'And do you work?' Miss Braithwaite asked, making it sound like a crime.

'No, although I assist my husband in any way I can. However, I consider being a wife and mother a full-time job.' Although Harry had recommended this line, he knew only too well that Emma didn't believe it, and she now believed it even less after meeting Cyrus Feldman.

'And how long have you been married, Mrs Clifton?' persisted Miss Braithwaite.

'Just over three years.'

'But I see from your application form that your son Sebastian is eight years old.'

'Yes, he is. Harry and I were engaged in 1939, but he felt it was his duty to sign up even before war had been declared.'

Miss Braithwaite was about to ask another question, when the man on the chairman's left leant forward and said, 'So you were married soon after the war ended, Mrs Clifton?'

'Sadly not,' said Emma, looking at a man who only had one arm. 'My husband was badly wounded by a German landmine only days before the war ended, and it was some time before he was fit enough to be discharged from hospital.'

Miss Braithwaite still appeared unmoved. Emma wondered, could it be possible that . . . she decided to take a risk she knew Harry would not have approved of.

'But, Mr Needham,' she said, her eyes not leaving the man with one arm, 'I consider myself to be among the lucky ones. My heart goes out to those women whose husbands, fiancés and sweethearts did not return to their families, having made the ultimate sacrifice for their country.'

Miss Braithwaite bowed her head, and the chairman said, 'Thank you, Mrs Clifton. Someone will be in touch with you in the near future.'

5

Natalie was standing in the lobby waiting for him at 6 a.m. She looked just as crisp and perky as she had done when she'd left him the day before. Once they were seated in the back of the limousine, she opened the inevitable folder.

'You begin the day being interviewed by Matt Jacobs on NBC, the highest-rated breakfast show in the country. The good news is that you've been given the prime slot, which means you'll be on some time between seven forty and eight a.m. The not-so-good news is that you're sharing it with Clark Gable, and Mel Blanc, the voice of Bugs Bunny and Tweetie Pie. Gable's promoting his latest movie, *Homecoming*, in which he stars alongside Lana Turner.'

'And Mel Blanc?' said Harry, trying not to laugh.

'He's celebrating a decade with Warner Brothers. Now, taking into account sponsors' breaks, I estimate you'll be on air for four to five minutes, which you must think of as 240 to 300 seconds. I cannot stress enough,' continued Natalie, 'how important this show is for launching our whole campaign. You won't be doing anything bigger in the next three weeks. This could not only get you on to the bestseller list but, if it goes well, every major show across the country will want to book you.'

Harry could feel his heartbeat rising by the second.

'All you have to do is find any excuse to mention *Nothing Ventured*,' she added as the limousine drew up outside the NBC studios at the Rockefeller Center.

Harry couldn't believe the sight that greeted him when he stepped out on to the pavement. The narrow entrance that led to the front of the building had been fenced off and was crammed on both sides with screaming fans. As Harry made his way through the crowds of expectant onlookers, he didn't need to be told that 90 per cent of them had come to see Clark Gable, 9 per cent Mel Blanc, and possibly 1 per cent . . .

'Who's he?' someone shouted as Harry hurried past.

Perhaps not even 1 per cent.

Once he was safely inside the building, a floor walker escorted him to the green room and briefed him on timings.

'Mr Gable will be on at seven forty. Mel Blanc will follow him at seven fifty, and we're hoping to get you on by seven fifty-five in the run-up to the news.'

'Thank you,' said Harry as he took a seat and tried to compose himself.

Mel Blanc bounced into the green room at 7.30, and looked at Harry as if he was expecting to be asked for an autograph. Mr Gable, accompanied by his entourage, followed a few moments later. Harry was surprised to see the screen idol dressed in a dinner jacket and carrying a glass of whisky. Gable explained to Mel Blanc that it wasn't an early morning drink, because he hadn't been to bed. Laughter followed him as he was whisked away, and Harry was left alone with Mel.

'Listen carefully to Gable,' said Mel as he sat down next to Harry. 'The minute the red light goes on, no one, including the studio audience, will realize he's had anything to drink but orange juice, and by the time he comes off, everyone will want to see his new movie.'

Mel turned out to be right. Gable was the ultimate professional, and the title of his new film got a mention at least every thirty seconds. And although Harry had read somewhere that he and Miss Turner couldn't stand each other, Gable was so gracious about his co-star that even the most cynical listener would have been convinced they were bosom pals. Only Natalie didn't look pleased, because Gable overran his slot by forty-two seconds.

During the ad break, Mel was escorted up to the studio. Harry learnt a great deal from Mel's performance, during which Sylvester, Tweety Pie and Bugs Bunny were all given an outing. But the thing that most impressed him was that when Matt Jacobs asked what was clearly the final question, Mel just went on talking, and stole another thirty-seven seconds of his precious time.

During the next ad break, it was Harry's turn to be led up to the guillotine, where he knew his head was about to be removed. He sat down opposite his host and smiled nervously. Jacobs was studying the inside flap of a copy of *Nothing Ventured* that looked as if it had never been opened before. He glanced up and returned Harry's smile.

'When the red light goes on, you'll be on the air,' was all he said before turning to the first page. Harry checked the second hand of the studio clock: four minutes to eight. He listened to an advertisement for Nescafé, as Jacobs scribbled down a couple of notes on a pad in front of him. The ad ended with a familiar jingle, and the red light went on. Harry's mind went blank, and he wished he was at home having lunch with Emma, even facing a thousand Germans at Clemenceau ridge, rather than 11 million Americans enjoying their breakfast.

'Good morning,' said Jacobs into his microphone, 'and what a morning it's been. First Gable, then Mel, and we end this hour of the breakfast show with a special guest from Great Britain, Harry' – he quickly checked the book's cover – 'Clifton. Now, before we talk about your new book, Harry, can I confirm that the last time you set foot in America you were arrested for murder?'

'Yes, but it was all a misunderstanding,' spluttered Harry.

'That's what they all say,' said Jacobs with a disconcerting laugh. 'But what my eleven million listeners will want to know is, while you're here, will you be getting together with some of your old convict buddies?'

'No, that's not the reason I'm in America,' began Harry. 'I've written a—'

'So Harry, tell me about your second impression of America.'

'It's a great country,' said Harry. 'New Yorkers have made me feel so welcome, and—'

'Even the cab drivers?'

'Even the cab drivers,' repeated Harry, 'and this morning I got to meet Clark Gable.'

'Is Gable big in England?' asked Matt.

'Oh yes, he's very popular, as is Miss Turner. In fact I can't wait to see their new film.'

'We call them movies over here, Harry, but what the hell.' Jacobs paused, glanced up at the second hand on the clock, and said, 'Harry, it's been great having you on the show, and good luck with your new book. After a few words from our sponsors, we'll return at the top of the hour with the eight o'clock news. But from me, Matt Jacobs, it's goodbye, and have a great day.'

The red light went off.

Jacobs stood up, shook hands with Harry and said, 'Sorry we didn't get more time to talk about your book. Loved the cover.'

◄◦►

Emma sipped her morning coffee before opening the letter.

Dear Mrs Clifton,

Thank you for attending the board meeting last week. I am pleased to inform you that we would like to take your application to the next stage.

Emma wanted to ring Harry immediately but knew it was the middle of the night in America, and she wasn't even sure which city he was in.

We have several suitable candidates for you and your husband to consider, a number of whom are residing in our homes at Taunton, Exeter and Bridgwater. I will be

happy to send information on each child, if you would be
kind enough to let me know which home you'd prefer to
visit first.
  Yours sincerely,
            Mr David Slater

One call to Mitchell confirmed that Jessica Smith was still at
Dr Barnardo's in Bridgwater, but was hoping to be amongst
those going to Australia. Emma checked her watch. She would
have to wait until noon before Harry could be expected to ring
and she could tell him the news. She then turned her attention
to a second letter which had a ten-cent stamp on it. She didn't
need to check the postmark to know who had sent it.

◄◌►

By the time Harry arrived in Chicago, *Nothing Ventured* had
come in at number 33 on the *New York Times* bestseller list,
and Natalie was no longer placing a hand on his leg.

'No need to panic,' she reassured him. 'The second week is
always the most important. But we've got a lot of work to do if
we're going to make it into the top fifteen by next Sunday.'

Denver, Dallas and San Francisco took them almost to the
end of the second week, by which time Harry was convinced
that Natalie was among those who hadn't read the book. Some
of the prime-time shows dropped Harry at the last minute, and
he started to spend more and more of his time in smaller and
smaller book stores signing fewer and fewer copies. One or two
proprietors even refused to let him do that because, as Natalie
explained, they couldn't return signed copies to the publisher
as they were considered damaged goods.

By the time they touched down in Los Angeles, *Nothing
Ventured* had crept up to number 28 on the bestseller list and,
with only a week to go, Natalie couldn't mask her disappointment. She began to hint that the book just wasn't moving out
of the shops fast enough. That became even more apparent the
following morning when Harry came down to breakfast and
found someone called Justin sitting opposite him.

51

'Natalie's flown back to New York overnight,' Justin explained. 'Had to meet up with another author.' He didn't need to add, someone who's more likely to make it into the top fifteen of the bestseller list. Harry couldn't blame her.

During his final week, Harry zigzagged across the country, appearing on shows in Seattle, San Diego, Raleigh, Miami and finally Washington. He began to relax without Natalie by his side constantly reminding him about the bestseller list, and even managed to mention *Nothing Ventured* more than once during some of the longer interviews, even if it was only on local shows.

When he flew back into New York on the final day of the tour, Justin checked him into an airport motel, handed him an economy-class ticket for London, and wished him luck.

◄o►

Once Emma had filled in the Stanford application form, she wrote a long letter to Cyrus to thank him for making it all possible. She then turned her attention to a bulky package that contained profiles of Sophie Barton, Sandra Davis and Jessica Smith. It only took a cursory reading for her to realize which candidate Matron favoured, and it certainly wasn't Miss J. Smith.

What would happen if Sebastian agreed with Matron or, worse, decided he preferred someone who wasn't even on the shortlist? Emma lay awake wishing Harry would call.

◄o►

Harry thought about calling Emma, but assumed she would already have gone to bed. He began to pack so everything would be ready for the early morning flight, then lay down on the bed and thought about how they could convince Sebastian that Jessica Smith was not only the ideal girl to be his sister, but *his* first choice.

He closed his eyes, but there wasn't any hope of snatching even a moment's sleep while the air-conditioning thumped out a constant rhythm as if auditioning for a place in a Calypso band. Harry lay on the thin, lumpy mattress, and rested his head on a foam pillow that enveloped his ears. There certainly wasn't a choice between a shower and a bath, just a washbasin with constantly dripping brown water. He closed his eyes and reran the last three weeks, frame by frame, like a flickering black and white movie. There had been no colour. What a complete waste of everyone's time and money it had all been. Harry had to admit he just wasn't cut out for the author tour, and if he couldn't even get the book into the top fifteen after countless radio and print interviews, perhaps the time had come to pension off William Warwick along with Chief Inspector Davenport and start looking for a real job.

The headmaster of St Bede's had hinted quite recently that they were looking for a new English teacher, although Harry knew he wasn't cut out to be a schoolmaster. Giles had graciously suggested, on more than one occasion, that he should join the board of Barrington's so that he could represent the family's interests. But the truth was, he wasn't family, and in any case, he'd always wanted to be a writer, not a businessman.

It was bad enough living in Barrington Hall. The books still hadn't earned enough money to buy a house worthy of Emma, and it hadn't helped when Sebastian had asked him quite innocently why he didn't go out to work every morning, like every other father he knew. It sometimes made him feel like a kept man.

Harry climbed into bed just after midnight, even more desperate to call Emma and share his thoughts with her, but it was still only five in the morning in Bristol, so he decided to stay awake and ring her in a couple of hours' time. He was just about to turn off the light when there was a gentle tap on the door. He could have sworn he'd left the *Do Not Disturb* sign on the handle. He pulled on his dressing gown, padded across the room and opened the door.

'Many congratulations,' was all she said.

He stared at Natalie, who was holding up a bottle of champagne and wearing a tight-fitting dress with a zip down the front that didn't need an invitation to pull it.

'What for?' said Harry.

'I've just seen the first edition of Sunday's *New York Times*, and *Nothing Ventured* has come in at number fourteen. You've made it!'

'Thank you,' said Harry, not quite grasping the significance of what she was saying.

'And as I've always been your biggest fan, I thought you might like to celebrate.'

He could hear Great-aunt Phyllis's words ringing in his ears: *You do realize you'll never be good enough for her.*

'What a nice idea,' said Harry. 'Just give me a moment,' he added, before walking back into the room. He picked up a book from a side table and returned to join her. He took the bottle of champagne from Natalie and smiled. 'If you've always been my biggest fan, perhaps it's time you read this,' he said, handing her a copy of *Nothing Ventured*. He quietly closed the door.

Harry sat on the bed, poured himself a glass of champagne, picked up the phone and booked an overseas call. He'd almost finished the bottle by the time Emma came on the line.

'My book's crept on to the bestseller list at number fourteen,' he said, slurring his words.

'That's wonderful news,' said Emma, stifling a yawn.

'And there's a ravishing blonde standing outside in the corridor holding a bottle of champagne, and she's trying to break my door down.'

'Yes, of course there is, darling. By the way, you'll never believe who asked me to spend the night with him.'

6

THE DOOR WAS OPENED by a woman in a dark blue uniform with a starched white collar. 'I'm Matron,' she announced.

Harry shook hands, then introduced his wife and son.

'Why don't you come through to my office,' she said, 'then we can have a chat before you meet the girls.'

Matron led the three of them down a corridor that was plastered with colourful paintings.

'I like this one,' said Sebastian, stopping at one particular painting, but Matron didn't respond, clearly believing children should be seen and not heard.

The three of them followed her into her office.

Once the door was closed, Harry began by telling Matron how much they'd all been looking forward to the visit.

'As I know the children have,' she replied. 'But first I must explain a few of the home's rules, as my only interest is the well-being of the children.'

'Of course,' said Harry. 'We're in your hands.'

'The three girls you have shown an interest in, Sandra, Sophie and Jessica, are currently in an art lesson, which will give you a chance to see them interacting with other children. When we join them it is important that we allow them to continue their work, because they must not feel they are taking part in a competition. That can only end in tears, and might well have long-term repercussions. Having been rejected once, they don't need to be reminded of that experience. If the children see families walking around, of course they know you're thinking about adoption. Why else would you be here? What they mustn't find out is that you are only considering two or three of them. And of course, once you've met the three girls, you may still want to visit our homes in Taunton and Exeter before you make up your minds.'

Harry would have liked to tell Matron that they'd already decided, although they hoped it would look as if it was Sebastian who made the final choice.

'So, are we ready to join the art class?'

'Yes,' said Sebastian, leaping up and running to the door.

'How will we know who's who?' asked Emma, rising slowly from her seat.

Matron scowled at Sebastian before she said, 'I will introduce several of the children to you, so none of them feel they are being singled out. Before we join them, do you have any questions?'

Harry was surprised that Sebastian didn't have a dozen, but simply stood by the door impatiently waiting for them. As they walked back down the corridor towards the art class, Sebastian ran ahead.

Matron opened the door to the classroom, and they entered and stood quietly at the back. She nodded to the master in charge, who said, 'Children, we have been joined by some guests.'

'Good afternoon, Mr and Mrs Clifton,' said the children in unison, several of them looking round, while others carried on painting.

'Good afternoon,' said Harry and Emma. Sebastian remained uncharacteristically silent.

Harry noticed that most of the children kept their heads bowed and appeared somewhat subdued. He stepped forward to watch a boy painting a football match. He obviously supported Bristol City, which caused Harry to smile.

Emma pretended to be looking at a picture of a duck, or was it a cat, while she tried to work out which of the children was Jessica, but she was none the wiser by the time Matron joined her and said, 'This is Sandra.'

'What a wonderful painting, Sandra,' said Emma. A huge grin appeared on the girl's face, while Sebastian bent down and took a closer look.

Harry walked across and began chatting to Sandra, while Emma and Sebastian were introduced to Sophie.

'It's a camel,' she said confidently, before either of them could ask.

'Dromedary or Bactrian?' asked Sebastian.

'Bactrian,' she replied equally confidently.

'But it's only got one hump,' said Sebastian.

Sophie smiled, and immediately gave the animal another hump. 'Where do you go to school?' she asked.

'I'll be going to St Bede's in September,' Sebastian replied.

Harry kept an eye on his son, who was clearly getting on well with Sophie, and feared he'd already made up his mind, but then suddenly Sebastian switched his attention to one of the boys' paintings, just as Matron introduced Harry to Jessica. But she was so engrossed in her work she didn't even look up. However hard he tried, nothing would break the girl's concentration. Was she shy, even petrified? Harry had no way of knowing.

Harry returned to Sophie who was chatting to Emma about her camel. She asked him if he preferred one hump or two. While Harry considered the question, Emma left Sophie and strolled across to meet Jessica, but, like her husband, she couldn't get a word out of the girl. She began to wonder if the whole exercise was going to end in disaster with Jessica going to Australia while they ended up with Sophie.

Emma moved away and began chatting to a boy called Tommy about his erupting volcano. Most of his paper was covered in deep red flames. Emma thought that Freud would have wanted to adopt this child, as he daubed even more blobs of red paint on to the canvas.

She glanced across to see Sebastian chatting to Jessica while staring intently at her painting of Noah's Ark.

At least she seemed to be listening to him, even if she didn't look up. Sebastian left Jessica and gave Sandra's and

Sophie's paintings one more look, then went and stood by the door.

A few minutes later, Matron suggested they all return to her office for a cup of tea.

After she had poured three cups and offered them each a Bath Oliver biscuit, she said, 'We will quite understand if you want to go away, give it some thought and perhaps return later, or visit one of our other homes, before you come to a final decision.'

Harry remained resolutely silent, as he waited to see if Sebastian would show his hand.

'I thought all three girls were quite delightful,' said Emma, 'and found it almost impossible to choose between them.'

'I agree,' said Harry. 'Perhaps we should do as you suggest, go away and discuss it between ourselves and then let you know how we feel.'

'But that would be a waste of time if we all want the same girl,' said Sebastian, with a precocious child's logic.

'Does that mean you've made up your mind?' asked his father, realizing that once Sebastian had revealed his choice, he and Emma could outvote him, although he accepted that might not be the best way for Jessica to begin her life at Barrington Hall.

'Before you decide,' said Matron, 'perhaps I should supply a little background information on each of the three children. Sandra has been by far the easiest to keep under control. Sophie is more gregarious but a bit of a scatterbrain.'

'And Jessica?' asked Harry.

'She's undoubtedly the most talented of the girls, but lives in a world of her own and doesn't make friends easily. I would have thought of the three, Sandra might well suit you.'

Harry watched as Sebastian's frown turned into a scowl. He switched tactics.

'Yes, I think I agree with you, Matron,' said Harry. 'My choice would be Sandra.'

'I'm torn,' said Emma. 'I liked Sophie, bubbly and fun.'

Emma and Harry stole a quick glance at each other. 'So

now it's up to you, Seb. Will it be Sandra or Sophie?' asked Harry.

'Neither. I prefer Jessica,' he said, then jumped up and ran out of the room, leaving the door wide open.

Matron rose from behind her desk. She clearly would have had words with Sebastian if he'd been one of her charges.

'He hasn't quite got the hang of democracy yet,' said Harry, trying to make light of it. Matron headed for the door, looking unconvinced. Harry and Emma followed her down the corridor. When Matron entered the classroom, she couldn't believe her eyes; Jessica was unpinning her picture and handing it to Sebastian.

'What did you offer her in exchange?' Harry asked his son as Sebastian marched past him clutching on to Noah's Ark.

'I promised her that if she came to tea tomorrow afternoon, she could have her favourite food.'

'And what is her favourite food?' asked Emma.

'Hot crumpets covered in butter and raspberry jam.'

'Would that be all right, Matron?' asked Harry anxiously.

'Yes, but perhaps it would be better if all three of them came.'

'No thank you, Matron,' said Emma. 'Jessica will be just fine.'

'As you wish,' said Matron, unable to mask her surprise.

As they drove back to Barrington Hall, Harry asked Sebastian why he'd chosen Jessica.

'Sandra was quite pretty,' he said, 'and Sophie was lots of fun, but I'd have been bored with both of them by the end of the month.'

'And Jessica?' asked Emma.

'She reminded me of you, Mama.'

◄o►

Sebastian was standing by the front door when Jessica came to tea.

She climbed the steps, clinging on to Matron with one hand and clutching one of her paintings in the other.

'Follow me,' declared Sebastian, but Jessica remained on

59

the top step as if glued to the spot. She looked petrified, and wouldn't budge until Sebastian returned.

'This is for you,' she said, handing over her painting.

'Thank you,' said Sebastian, recognizing the picture he'd spotted on the wall in the corridor at Dr Barnardo's. 'Well, you'd better come in, because I can't eat all the crumpets on my own.'

Jessica stepped tentatively into the hall, and her mouth opened wide. Not because of the thought of crumpets, but at the sight of real oil paintings with frames hanging on every wall.

'Later,' promised Sebastian, 'otherwise the crumpets will get cold.'

As Jessica walked into the drawing room, Harry and Emma rose to greet her, but once again she couldn't take her eyes off the pictures. She eventually sat down on the sofa next to Sebastian, and transferred her longing gaze to a pile of sizzling hot crumpets. But she didn't make a move until Emma handed her a plate, followed by a crumpet, followed by a knife, followed by the butter, followed by a bowl of raspberry jam.

Matron scowled as Jessica was about to take her first bite.

'Thank you, Mrs Clifton,' Jessica blurted out. She devoured two more crumpets, each accompanied by a 'Thank you, Mrs Clifton'.

When she turned a fourth down with 'No thank you, Mrs Clifton', Emma wasn't sure if she would have liked another one, or Matron had instructed her not to eat more than three.

'Have you ever heard of Turner?' asked Sebastian, after Jessica had finished her second glass of Tizer. She bowed her head and didn't reply. Sebastian stood up, took her by the hand and led her out of the room. 'Turner's quite good actually,' he declared, 'but not as good as you.'

'I just can't believe it,' said Matron as the door closed behind them. 'I've never seen her so at ease.'

'But she's hardly uttered a word,' said Harry.

'Believe me, Mr Clifton, you've just witnessed Jessica's version of the Hallelujah Chorus.'

Emma laughed. 'She's quite delightful. If there's a chance of her becoming a member of our family, how do we go about it?'

'It's a long process, I'm afraid,' said Matron, 'and it doesn't always end satisfactorily. You could begin by having her here for the occasional visit and, if that goes well, you might consider what we call a weekend leave. After that, there's no turning back, because we mustn't set up false hopes.'

'We'll be guided by you, Matron,' said Harry, 'because we certainly want to give it a try.'

'Then I'll do everything I can,' she replied. By the time she'd drunk her third cup of tea and even managed a second crumpet, Harry and Emma had been left in no doubt what was expected of them.

'Where can Sebastian and Jessica have got to?' asked Emma, when Matron suggested that perhaps they should be on their way.

'I'll go and look for them,' Harry was saying, when the two children came bursting back into the room.

'Time for us to go home, young lady,' said Matron as she rose from her place. 'After all, we must be back in time for supper.'

Jessica refused to let go of Sebastian's hand. 'I don't want any more food,' she said.

Matron was lost for words.

Harry led Jessica into the hall and helped her on with her coat. As Matron walked out of the front door, Jessica burst into tears.

'Oh no,' said Emma. 'And I thought it had all gone so well.'

'It couldn't have gone better,' whispered Matron. 'They only start crying when they don't want to leave. Take my advice, if you both feel the same way, fill in the forms as quickly as possible.'

Jessica turned around and waved before she climbed into Matron's little Austin 7, tears still streaming down her cheeks.

'Good choice, Seb,' said Harry, placing an arm around his

son's shoulders as they watched the car disappear down the drive.

◄○►

It was to be another five months before Matron left Barrington Hall for the last time and headed back to Dr Barnardo's on her own, another of her waifs and strays happily settled. Well, not so happily, because it was not long before Harry and Emma realized that Jessica had problems of her own that were every bit as demanding as Sebastian's.

Neither of them had paused to consider that Jessica had never slept in a room on her own, and on her first night at Barrington Hall she left the nursery door wide open and cried herself to sleep. Harry and Emma became used to a warm little object climbing into bed between them not long after she woke in the mornings. This became less frequent when Sebastian parted with his teddy bear, Winston, handing the former prime minister over to Jessica.

Jessica adored Winston, second only to Sebastian, despite her new brother declaring somewhat haughtily, 'I'm far too grown up to have a teddy bear. After all, I'll be going to school in a few weeks' time.'

Jessica wanted to go to St Bede's with him, but Harry explained that boys and girls didn't go to the same school.

'Why not?' Jessica demanded.

'Why not indeed,' said Emma.

When the first day of term finally dawned, Emma stared at her young man, wondering where the years had gone. He was dressed in a red blazer, red cap and grey flannel shorts. Even his shoes shone. Well, it was the first day of term. Jessica stood on the doorstep and waved goodbye as the car disappeared down the drive and out of the front gates. She then sat down on the top step and waited for Sebastian to return.

Sebastian had requested that his mother didn't join him and his father on the journey to school. When Harry asked why, he replied, 'I don't want the other boys to see Mama kissing me.'

Harry would have reasoned with him, if he hadn't recalled his first day at St Bede's. He and his mother had taken the tram from Still House Lane, and he'd asked if they could get off a stop early and walk the last hundred yards so the other boys wouldn't realize they didn't own a car. And when they were fifty yards from the school gates, although he allowed her to kiss him, he quickly said goodbye and left her standing there. As he approached St Bede's for the first time, he saw his future classmates being dropped off from hansom cabs and motor cars – one even arrived in a Rolls-Royce driven by a liveried chauffeur.

Harry had also found his first night away from home difficult, but, unlike Jessica, it was because he'd never slept in a room with other children.

But the alphabet had been kind to him, because he ended up sleeping in a dormitory with Barrington on one side and Deakins on the other. He wasn't as lucky when it came to his dormitory prefect. Alex Fisher slippered him every other night of his first week, for no other reason than Harry was the son of a dock labourer, and therefore not worthy of being educated at the same school as Fisher, the son of an estate agent. Harry sometimes wondered what had happened to Fisher after he left St Bede's. He knew that he and Giles had crossed paths during the war when they'd served in the same regiment at Tobruk, and he assumed Fisher must still live in Bristol, because he'd recently avoided talking to him at a St Bede's Old Boys' reunion.

At least Sebastian would be arriving in a motor car, and as a day bug he wouldn't suffer the Fisher problem, because he would be returning to Barrington Hall every evening. Even so, Harry suspected that his son wasn't going to find St Bede's any easier than he had, even if it would be for completely different reasons.

When Harry drew up outside the school gates, Sebastian jumped out even before he'd had time to pull on the brakes. Harry watched as his son ran through the gates and disappeared into a melee of red blazers in which he was indistinguishable from a hundred other boys. He never once looked back. Harry accepted that *the old order changeth, yielding place to new.*

He drove slowly back to Barrington Hall and began to think about the next chapter of his latest book. Was it time for William Warwick to be promoted?

As he approached the house, he spotted Jessica sitting on the top step. He smiled as he brought the car to a halt. But when he climbed out, the first thing she said was, 'Where's Seb?'

◄○►

Each day, while Sebastian was away at school, Jessica retreated into her own world. While she waited for him to return home she would pass the time by reading to Winston about other animals, Pooh Bear, Mr Toad, a white rabbit, a marmalade cat called Orlando, and a crocodile that had swallowed a clock.

Once Winston had fallen asleep, she would tuck him up in bed, return to her easel and paint. On and on. In fact, what Emma had once considered the nursery had been converted by Jessica into an art studio. Once she had covered every piece of paper she could lay her hands on, including Harry's old manuscripts (he had to keep his new ones locked up), with pencil, crayon or paint, she turned her attention to redecorating the nursery walls.

Harry didn't want to curb her enthusiasm, far from it, but he did remind Emma that Barrington Hall wasn't their home, and perhaps they ought to consult Giles before she escaped from the nursery and discovered how many other pristine walls there were in the house.

But Giles was so smitten with the new arrival at Barrington Hall that he declared he wouldn't mind if she repainted the whole house inside and out.

'For heaven's sake, don't encourage her,' begged Emma. 'Sebastian has already asked her to repaint his room.'

'And when are you going to tell her the truth?' Giles asked as they sat down for dinner.

'We can't see that there's any need to tell her yet,' said Harry. 'After all, Jessica's only six, and she's hardly settled in.'

'Well, don't leave it too long,' Giles warned him, 'because she already looks upon you and Emma as her parents, Seb as her brother, and calls me Uncle Giles, while the truth is she's my half-sister, and Seb's aunt.'

Harry laughed. 'I think it will be some time before she can be expected to grasp that.'

'I hope she never has to,' said Emma. 'Don't forget, all she knows is that her real parents are dead. Why should that change, while only the three of us know the whole truth?'

'Don't underestimate Sebastian. He's already halfway there.'

7

HARRY AND EMMA were surprised when they were invited to join the headmaster for tea at the end of Sebastian's first term, and quickly discovered it was not a social occasion.

'Your son's a bit of a loner,' declared Dr Hedley, once the maid had poured them a cup of tea and left the room. 'In fact he's more likely to befriend a boy from overseas than one who's lived in Bristol all his life.'

'Why would that be?' asked Emma.

'Boys from far-flung shores have never heard of Mr and Mrs Harry Clifton, or his famous uncle Giles,' explained the headmaster. 'But, as is so often the case, something positive has come out of it because we've become aware that Sebastian has a natural gift for languages that in normal circumstances might have been missed. In fact, he is the only boy in the school who can converse with Lu Yang in his native tongue.'

Harry laughed, but Emma noticed that the headmaster wasn't smiling.

'However,' Dr Hedley continued, 'there may be a problem when it comes to Sebastian sitting his entrance exam for Bristol Grammar School.'

'But he came top in English, French and Latin,' said Emma proudly.

'And he scored one hundred per cent in maths,' Harry reminded the headmaster.

'True, and all very commendable, but unfortunately, at the same time, he languishes near the bottom of his class in history, geography and natural sciences, all of which are compulsory subjects. Should he fail to reach the pass mark in two or more of these, he will automatically be rejected by BGS, which I know would be a great disappointment for both of you, as well as his uncle.'

'Great disappointment would be an understatement,' said Harry.

'Quite so,' said Dr Hedley.

'Do they ever make exceptions to the rules?' asked Emma.

'I can only recall one case in my tenure,' said the headmaster, 'and that was for a boy who had scored a century every Saturday during the summer term.'

Harry laughed, having sat on the grass and watched Giles score every one of them. 'So we'll just have to make sure he realizes the consequences of dropping below the pass mark in two of the compulsory subjects.'

'It's not that he isn't bright enough,' said the headmaster, 'but if a subject doesn't appeal to him, he quickly becomes bored. The irony is, with his talent for languages, I predict he'll sail into Oxford. But we still have to make sure he paddles into BGS.'

◄○►

After a little coaxing from his father, and some considerable bribery from his grandmother, Sebastian managed to climb a few places off the bottom in two of the three compulsory subjects. He'd worked out that he was permitted to fail one, and chose natural sciences.

By the end of Sebastian's second year, the headmaster felt confident that with a little more effort the boy would obtain the necessary pass mark in five of the six exam subjects. He too had given up on natural sciences. Harry and Emma were beginning to feel more hopeful, but still tried to keep Sebastian up to the mark. And indeed, the headmaster might have proved right in his optimistic assessment, had it not been for two incidents that occurred during Sebastian's final year.

8

'IS THAT YOUR father's book?'

Sebastian looked at a pile of novels stacked neatly in the window of the bookshop. A sign above them read, *Nothing Gained by Harry Clifton, 3s 6d. The latest adventure of William Warwick*.

'Yes,' said Sebastian proudly. 'Would you like one?'

'Yes, please,' said Lu Yang.

Sebastian strolled into the shop, followed by his friend. A table near the front was piled high with his father's latest hardback, surrounded by paperbacks of *The Case of the Blind Witness* and *Nothing Ventured*, the first two novels in the William Warwick series.

Sebastian handed Lu Yang a copy of each of the three books. They were quickly joined by several of his classmates, and he gave each of them a copy of the latest book, and in some cases the other two as well. The pile was rapidly diminishing when a middle-aged man charged out from behind the counter, grabbed Sebastian by the collar and dragged him away.

'What do you think you're doing?' he shouted.

'It's all right,' said Sebastian, 'they're my father's books!'

'Now I've heard everything,' said the manager as he marched Sebastian, who was protesting with every stride, towards the back of the shop. He turned to an assistant and said, 'Call the police. I caught this thief red-handed. Then see if you can retrieve the books his friends ran off with.'

The manager shoved Sebastian into his office and dumped him firmly on to an old horsehair sofa.

'Don't even think about moving,' he said as he left the office, closing the door firmly behind him.

Sebastian heard a key turning in the lock. He stood up, walked across to the manager's desk and picked up a book, then sat back down and began reading. He'd reached page nine, and was getting to quite like Richard Hannay, when the door opened and the manager returned with a triumphant smirk on his face.

'There he is, chief inspector, I caught the lad red-handed.'

Chief Inspector Blakemore tried to keep a straight face when the manager added, 'Had the gall to tell me the books belonged to his father.'

'He wasn't lying,' said Blakemore. 'That's Harry Clifton's boy.' Looking sternly at Sebastian, he added, 'But that's no excuse for what you did, young man.'

'Even if his father is Harry Clifton, I'm still short one pound and eighteen shillings,' said the manager. 'So what do you intend to do about that?' he added, pointing an accusing finger at Sebastian.

'I've already contacted Mr Clifton,' said Blakemore, 'so I don't think it will be long before that question is answered. While we wait for him, I suggest you explain the economics of bookselling to his son.'

The manager, looking a little chastened, sat down on the corner of his desk.

'When your father writes a book,' he said, 'his publishers pay him an advance, and then a percentage of the cover price for each copy sold. In your dad's case, I would guess that would be around ten per cent. The publisher also has to pay his salesmen, the editorial and publicity staff, and the printer, as well as any advertising and distribution costs.'

'And how much do you have to pay for each book?' asked Sebastian.

Blakemore couldn't wait to hear the bookseller's reply. The manager hesitated before saying, 'Around two-thirds of the cover price.'

Sebastian's eyes narrowed. 'So my father only gets ten per cent on each book, while you pocket thirty-three per cent?'

'Yes, but I have to pay rent and rates for these premises, as well as my staff's wages,' said the manager defensively.

'So it would be cheaper for my father to replace the books rather than pay you the full amount of the cover price?'

The chief inspector wished Sir Walter Barrington was still alive. He would have enjoyed this exchange.

'Perhaps you could tell me, sir,' continued Sebastian, 'how many books need to be replaced.'

'Eight hardbacks and eleven paperbacks,' said the manager, as Harry walked into the office.

Chief Inspector Blakemore explained to him what had happened, before adding, 'I won't be charging the boy for shoplifting on this occasion, Mr Clifton, just issuing him with a caution. I'll leave it to you to make sure, sir, that he doesn't do anything as irresponsible again.'

'Of course, chief inspector,' said Harry. 'I'm most grateful, and I'll ask my publishers to replace the books immediately. And there will be no more pocket money for you, my boy, until every penny has been paid back,' he added, turning to face Sebastian.

Sebastian bit his lip.

'Thank you, Mr Clifton,' said the manager, and added a little sheepishly, 'I was wondering, sir, as you're here, if you'd be kind enough to sign the rest of the stock?'

◄o►

When Emma's mother Elizabeth went into hospital for a check-up, she tried to reassure her daughter that there was nothing to worry about, and told her she wasn't to tell Harry or the children because it would only make them anxious.

It certainly made Emma anxious and, as soon as she returned to Barrington Hall, she phoned Giles at the House of Commons, and then her sister in Cambridge. They both dropped everything and caught the next train to Bristol.

'Let's hope I'm not wasting your time,' said Emma after she'd picked them up from Temple Meads.

'Let's hope you *are* wasting our time,' Grace replied.

Giles appeared preoccupied and stared out of the window as they continued their journey to the hospital in silence.

Even before Mr Langbourne had closed the door to his office, Emma sensed the news wasn't going to be good.

'I wish there was an easy way to tell you this,' the specialist said once they'd sat down, 'but I'm afraid there isn't. Dr Raeburn, who's been your mother's GP for several years, carried out a routine check-up, and when he got the results of his tests, he referred her to me in order that I could carry out a more detailed examination.'

Emma clenched her fists, something she used to do as a schoolgirl whenever she was nervous or in trouble.

'Yesterday,' continued Mr Langbourne, 'I received the results from the clinical lab. They confirmed Dr Raeburn's fears: your mother has breast cancer.'

'Can she be cured?' was Emma's immediate response.

'There is no cure at present for someone of her age,' said Langbourne. 'Scientists are hoping for a breakthrough at some time in the future, but I fear that won't be soon enough for your mother.'

'Is there anything we can do?' asked Grace.

Emma leant across and took her sister's hand.

'During this time, she will need all the love and support you and the family can give her. Elizabeth is a remarkable woman, and after all she has been through, she deserves better. But she's never once complained – not her style. She's a typical Harvey.'

'How long will she be with us?' asked Emma.

'I fear,' said Langbourne, 'that it will be a matter of weeks, rather than months.'

'Then there's something I have to tell her,' said Giles, who hadn't spoken until then.

◄○►

The shoplifting incident, as it came to be known at St Bede's, turned Sebastian from a bit of a loner into something of a folk hero, and boys who previously wouldn't have bothered with him invited him to join their gangs. Harry began to believe this might be a turning point, but when he told Sebastian that his grandmother only had a few weeks to live, the boy crept back into his shell.

Jessica had begun her first term at Red Maids'. She worked far harder than Sebastian, but didn't come top in any subject. The art mistress told Emma it was a pity that painting wasn't a recognized subject, because Jessica had more talent at the age of eight than she herself had shown in her final year at college.

Emma decided not to repeat this conversation to Jessica but to allow the child to discover for herself just how talented she was in the fullness of time. Sebastian regularly told her she was a genius, but what did he know? He also thought Stanley Matthews was a genius.

A month later, Sebastian failed three of his mock papers, taken only weeks before the BGS entrance exams. Neither Harry nor Emma felt they could chastise him while he was so distressed about his grandmother's condition. He would accompany Emma to the hospital every afternoon after she picked him up from school, climb on to his grandmother's bed and read to her from his favourite book until she fell asleep.

Jessica painted a new picture for Granny every day, and dropped it off at the hospital the following morning before Harry took her on to school. There were only a few blank spaces left on the walls of her private gallery by the end of term.

Giles missed several three-line whips, Grace countless tutorials, Harry endless deadlines, and Emma sometimes failed to reply to Cyrus Feldman's weekly letters. But it was Sebastian who Elizabeth most looked forward to seeing every day. Harry couldn't be sure who benefited more from the experience, his son or his mother-in-law.

◄○►

It didn't help that Sebastian had to take his exam for Bristol Grammar School while his grandmother's life was ebbing away.

The outcome was as the headmaster of St Bede's had predicted, mixed. His Latin, French, English and maths papers were of scholarship level, while he barely made the pass mark in history, failed narrowly in geography, and scored just 9 per cent in his natural sciences paper.

Dr Hedley called Harry at Barrington Hall moments after the results had been posted on the school notice board.

'I'll have a private word with John Garrett, my opposite number at BGS,' he said, 'and remind him that Sebastian scored a hundred per cent in Latin and maths, and will almost certainly be scholarship material by the time it comes for him to go to university.'

'You might also remind him,' said Harry, 'that both his uncle and I were at BGS, and his grandfather, Sir Walter Barrington, was chairman of the governors.'

'I don't think he'll need reminding,' said Hedley. 'But I will point out that Sebastian's grandmother was in hospital while he was taking the exams. All we can do is hope he backs my judgement.'

He did. Dr Hedley called Harry at the end of the week to say that the headmaster of BGS would be recommending to the board that, despite Sebastian failing two of the set papers, he should still be offered a place at BGS for the Michaelmas term.

'Thank you,' said Harry. 'That's the first good news I've had in weeks.'

'But,' Hedley added, 'he reminded me that in the end it will be the board's decision.'

◄○►

Harry was the last person to visit his mother-in-law that night, and was just about to leave when Elizabeth whispered, 'Can you stay for a few more minutes, my dear? There's something I need to discuss with you.'

'Yes, of course,' said Harry, sitting back down on the edge of the bed.

'I spent the morning with Desmond Siddons, our family

lawyer,' Elizabeth said, stumbling over each word, 'and I wanted to let you know that I've executed a new will, because I can't bear the thought of that dreadful woman Virginia Fenwick getting her hands on any of my possessions.'

'I don't think that's a problem any longer. We haven't seen or heard from Virginia for weeks, so I assume it's all over.'

'The reason you haven't seen or heard from her for weeks, Harry, is because she wants me to believe it's all over. It's not a coincidence that she disappeared from the scene only days after Giles learned I didn't have long to live.'

'I'm sure you're overreacting, Elizabeth. I don't believe even Virginia could be that callous.'

'My dear Harry, you always give everyone the benefit of the doubt because you have such a generous nature. It was a lucky day for Emma when she met you.'

'It's sweet of you to say so, Elizabeth, but I'm sure that given time—'

'That's the one thing I don't have.'

'Then perhaps we should ask Virginia to come and visit you?'

'I've made it clear to Giles on several occasions that I'd like to meet her, but each time I've been rebuffed with more and more unlikely excuses. Now, why do you think that is? Don't bother to answer, Harry, because you'll be the last person to work out what Virginia's really up to. And you can be sure she won't make her move until after my funeral.' A flicker of a smile crossed Elizabeth's face before she added, 'But I still have one card up my sleeve, which I don't intend to play until I've been lowered into my grave, when my spirit will return like an avenging angel.'

Harry didn't interrupt Elizabeth as she leant back and, with all the energy she could muster, removed an envelope from under her pillow. 'Now listen to me carefully, Harry,' she said. You must be sure to carry out my instructions to the letter.' She gripped his hand. 'If Giles should contest my latest will—'

'But why would he do that?'

'Because he's a Barrington, and Barringtons have always

been weak when it comes to women. So, if he should contest my latest will,' she repeated, 'you must give this envelope to the judge who is selected to decide which member of the family will inherit my estate.'

'And if he doesn't?'

'You must destroy it,' said Elizabeth, her breathing becoming shallower by the second. 'You are not to open it yourself, or ever let Giles or Emma know of its existence.' She tightened her grip on his hand, and whispered almost inaudibly, 'Now you must give me your word, Harry Clifton, because I know Old Jack taught you that should always be enough.'

'You have my word,' said Harry, and placed the envelope in an inside pocket of his jacket.

Elizabeth relaxed her grip, and sank back on the pillow, a contented smile on her lips. She never did discover if Sydney Carton escaped the guillotine.

◄○►

Harry opened the post while he was having breakfast.

Bristol Grammar School,
University Road,
Bristol

July 27th, 1951

Dear Mr Clifton,

I am sorry to inform you that your son, Sebastian, has not been . . .

Harry leapt up from the breakfast table and walked across to the telephone. He dialled the number at the bottom of the letter.

'Headmaster's office,' announced a voice.

'May I speak to Mr Garrett?'

'Who's calling, please?'

'Harry Clifton.'

'I'll put you through, sir.'

'Good morning, headmaster. My name is Harry Clifton.'

'Good morning, Mr Clifton. I've been expecting your call.'

'I can't believe the board came to such an ill-founded decision.'

'Frankly, Mr Clifton, neither could I, especially after I'd pleaded your son's case so vehemently.'

'What reason did they give for turning him down?'

'That they mustn't be seen to be making an exception for an old boy's son when he'd failed to obtain the pass mark in two compulsory subjects.'

'And that was their only reason?'

'No,' replied the headmaster. 'One of the governors raised the matter of your son being cautioned by the police for shoplifting.'

'But there's a perfectly innocent explanation for that incident,' said Harry, trying not to lose his temper.

'I don't doubt there is,' said Garrett, 'but our new chairman couldn't be swayed on the matter.'

'Then he'll be my next call. What's his name?'

'Major Alex Fisher.'

GILES BARRINGTON

1951–1954

9

GILES WAS DELIGHTED although not surprised to find that the parish church of St Andrew's, where Elizabeth Harvey had been married, and her three children baptised and later confirmed, was packed with family, friends and admirers.

The Reverend Mr Donaldson's tribute reminded everyone how much Elizabeth Barrington had done for the local community. Indeed, he said, without her generosity, the restoration of the church tower would not have been possible. He went on to tell the congregation just how many people, far beyond these walls, had benefited from her wisdom and insight when she was patron of the cottage hospital, and of the role she had played as head of her family, following the death of Lord Harvey. Giles was relieved, as no doubt were most of those present, that the vicar made no reference to his father.

Reverend Donaldson ended his eulogy with the words, 'Elizabeth's life was cut short by her untimely death at the age of fifty-one, but it is not for us to question the will of our Lord.'

After he had returned to his pew, Giles and Sebastian each read a lesson, 'The Good Samaritan' and 'The Sermon on the Mount', while Emma and Grace recited verses by their mother's favourite poets. Emma chose Shelley:

> *Lost angel of a ruined paradise!*
> *She knew not 'twas her own, – as with no stain*
> *She faded, like a cloud which had outwept its rain.*

While Grace read from Keats:

Stop and consider! life is but a day;
A fragile dew-drop on its perilous way
From a tree's summit; a poor Indian's sleep
While his boat hastens to the monstrous steep . . .

As the congregation filed out of the church, several people asked who the attractive woman on Sir Giles's arm was. Harry couldn't help thinking that Elizabeth's prediction was already coming to pass. Dressed entirely in black, Virginia was standing at Giles's right hand as the pall-bearers lowered Elizabeth's coffin into the grave. Harry recalled his mother-in-law's words: *I still have one card up my sleeve.*

After the burial service had been completed, the family and a few close friends were invited to join Giles, Emma and Grace at Barrington Hall for what the Irish would have called a wake. Virginia moved deftly from mourner to mourner, introducing herself as if she were already the lady of the house. Giles didn't seem to notice, and if he did, clearly didn't disapprove.

'Hello, I'm Lady Virginia Fenwick,' she said when she met Harry's mother for the first time. 'And where do you fit in?'

'I'm Mrs Holcombe,' Maisie replied. 'Harry's my son.'

'Oh, yes, of course,' said Virginia. 'Aren't you a waitress or something?'

'I'm the manager of the Grand Hotel in Bristol,' Maisie said, as if dealing with a tiresome customer.

'Of course you are. But then, it will take me a little time to get used to the idea of women working. You see, the women in my family have never worked,' Virginia said, quickly moving on before Maisie could respond.

'Who are you?' asked Sebastian.

'I'm Lady Virginia Fenwick, and who are you, young man?'

'Sebastian Clifton.'

'Ah yes. Has your father finally managed to find a school that will take you?'

'I'll be going to Beechcroft Abbey in September,' countered Sebastian.

'Not a bad school,' replied Virginia, 'but hardly top drawer.

My three brothers were all educated at Harrow, as the past seven generations of Fenwicks have been.'

'Where did you go to school?' asked Sebastian, as Jessica came rushing across to him.

'Have you seen the Constable, Seb?' she asked.

'Little girl, don't interrupt me when I'm speaking,' said Virginia. 'It's frightfully rude.'

'Sorry, miss,' said Jessica.

'I'm not "miss", you should always address me as Lady Virginia.'

'Have you seen the Constable, Lady Virginia?' asked Jessica.

'I have indeed, and it compares favourably with the three in my family collection. But it's not in the same class as our Turner. Have you heard of Turner?'

'Yes, Lady Virginia,' said Jessica. 'J. M. W. Turner, possibly the greatest watercolourist of his age.'

'My sister's an artist,' said Sebastian. 'I think she's just as good as Turner.'

Jessica giggled. 'Excuse him, Lady Virginia, as Mama often reminds him, he does have a tendency to exaggerate.'

'Clearly,' said Virginia, leaving them to go off in search of Giles, as she felt it was time for the guests to leave.

Giles accompanied the vicar to the front door, which was taken as a sign by the remainder of the guests that the time had come for everyone else to depart. When he closed the door for the last time, he breathed a sigh of relief, and returned to the drawing room to join the family.

'Well, I think that went as well as could be expected in the circumstances,' he said.

'One or two of the hangers-on treated it more like a feast than a wake,' said Virginia.

'Would you mind, old chap,' Giles said, turning to Harry, 'if we dressed for dinner? Virginia feels strongly about that sort of thing.'

'One can't afford to let standards slip,' volunteered Virginia.

'My father couldn't have let them slip much further,' said Grace, which caused Harry to stifle a laugh. 'But I'm afraid you'll have to count me out. I have to get back to Cambridge as I have a supervision to prepare. In any case,' she added, 'I came dressed for a funeral, not a dinner party. Don't bother to show me out.'

◄○►

Giles was waiting in the drawing room when Harry and Emma came down for dinner.

Marsden poured them each a dry sherry, then left the room to check that everything was running to schedule.

'A sad occasion,' said Harry. 'Let's drink to a great lady.'

'To a great lady,' said Giles and Emma, raising their glasses as Virginia swept into the room.

'Were you talking about me, by any chance?' she asked, without any suggestion of irony.

Giles laughed, while Emma could only admire the magnificent silk taffeta gown that swept away any memories of Virginia's mourning weeds. Virginia touched her diamond and ruby necklace to make sure Emma hadn't missed it.

'What a beautiful piece of jewellery,' said Emma on cue, as Giles handed Virginia a gin and tonic.

'Thank you,' said Virginia. 'It belonged to my great-grandmother, the Dowager Duchess of Westmorland, who bequeathed it to me in her will. Marsden,' she said, turning to the butler, who had just returned, 'the flowers in my room are beginning to wilt. Perhaps you could replace them before I retire this evening.'

'Certainly, m'lady. When you are ready, Sir Giles, dinner is served.'

'I don't know about you,' said Virginia, 'but I'm famished. Shall we go through?' Without waiting for a reply, she linked arms with Giles and led them all out of the room.

During the meal, Virginia regaled them with stories about her ancestors, making them sound like the backbone of the British Empire. Generals, bishops, cabinet ministers, and of course a few black sheep, she admitted – what family doesn't have one or two of those? She hardly drew breath until the dessert had been cleared, when Giles dropped his bombshell. He tapped his wine glass with a spoon to ensure he had everyone's attention.

'I have some wonderful news to share with you,' he announced. 'Virginia has paid me the great honour of consenting to be my wife.'

An uneasy silence followed, until Harry eventually said, 'Many congratulations.' Emma somehow managed a weak smile. As Marsden uncorked a bottle of champagne and filled their glasses, Harry couldn't help thinking that Elizabeth had only been in her grave for a few hours before Virginia had fulfilled her prophecy.

'Of course, once we're married,' said Virginia, touching Giles gently on his cheek, 'there are bound to be a few changes around here. But I can't imagine that will come as much of a surprise,' she said, smiling warmly at Emma.

Giles appeared so bewitched by her every word that he simply nodded his approval whenever she came to the end of a sentence.

'Giles and I,' she continued, 'plan to move into Barrington Hall soon after we're married, but as a general election is on the cards, the wedding will have to be put off for a few months, which should give you more than enough time to find somewhere else to live.'

Emma put down her glass of champagne and stared at her brother, who didn't meet her gaze.

'I'm sure you'll understand, Emma,' he said, 'that we'd like to begin our married life with Virginia as the mistress of Barrington Hall.'

'Of course,' said Emma. 'Frankly, I'll be only too happy to return to the Manor House, where I spent so many happy years as a child.'

Virginia glared at her fiancé.

'Ah,' Giles eventually managed. 'I had intended to give Virginia the Manor House as a wedding present.'

Emma and Harry glanced at each other, but before either of them could speak, Virginia said, 'I have two elderly aunts, both of whom have recently been widowed. It will be so convenient for them.'

'Giles, have you even considered what might be convenient for Harry and me?' asked Emma, staring directly at her brother.

'Perhaps you could move into one of the cottages on the estate?' suggested Giles.

'I don't think that would be appropriate, my darling,' said Virginia, taking his hand. 'We mustn't forget that I plan to have a large household, in keeping with my position as the daughter of an earl.'

'I have no desire to live in a cottage on the estate,' said Emma, spitting out the words. 'We can afford to buy our own home, thank you.'

'I'm sure you can, my dear,' said Virginia. 'After all, Giles tells me Harry is quite a successful author.'

Emma ignored the comment and, turning to her brother, said, 'How can you be so sure that the Manor House is yours to give away?'

'Because some time ago, Mama took me through her will line by line. I'd be only too happy to share its contents with you and Harry if you think it might help you plan for the future.'

'I really don't think it's appropriate to discuss Mama's will on the day of her funeral.'

'I don't want to appear insensitive, my dear,' said Virginia, 'but as I'll be returning to London in the morning, and will be spending most of my time preparing for the wedding, I think it would be best to sort out these matters while we're all together.' She turned to Giles, and gave him the same sweet smile.

'I agree with Virginia,' said Giles. 'No time like the present. And I can assure you, Emma, Mother has made more than adequate provision for both you and Grace. She has left you ten thousand pounds each, and divided her jewellery equally between you. And she's left Sebastian five thousand, which he'll inherit when he comes of age.'

'Such a fortunate child,' said Virginia. 'She's also given her Turner of *Lock at Cleveland* to Jessica, but it will remain in the family until she's twenty-one.' In that one sentence, Virginia revealed that Giles had shared the details of his mother's will with his fiancée, before bothering to tell either Emma or Grace. 'Most generous,' continued Virginia, 'remembering that Jessica is not even a member of the family.'

'We look upon Jessica as our daughter,' said Harry sharply, 'and treat her as such.'

'Half-sister, I think would be more accurate,' said Virginia. 'And we mustn't forget that she's a Barnardo's orphan, as well as being Jewish. I suppose it's because I come from Yorkshire that I have a tendency to call a spade a spade.'

'And I suppose it's because I come from Gloucestershire,' said Emma, 'that I have a tendency to call a scheming bitch a scheming bitch.'

Emma rose from her place and marched out of the room. For the first time that evening, Giles looked embarrassed. Harry was now certain that neither Giles nor Virginia was aware that Elizabeth had executed a new will. He chose his words carefully.

'Emma's a little overwrought following the funeral. I'm sure she'll have recovered by the morning.'

He folded his napkin, bade them goodnight and left the room without another word.

Virginia looked at her fiancé. 'You were magnificent, Bunny. But I have to say, what a touchy lot your family are, though I suppose that's only to be expected after all they've been through. However, I fear it doesn't augur well for the future.'

10

'THIS IS THE BBC Home Service. Here is the news, and this is Alvar Lidell reading it. At ten o'clock this morning, the prime minister, Mr Attlee, requested an audience with the King and asked His Majesty's permission to dissolve Parliament and call a general election. Mr Attlee returned to the House of Commons, and announced that an election would be held on Thursday, October twenty-fifth.'

The following day, 622 members packed their bags, cleared their lockers, bade farewell to their colleagues and returned to their constituencies to prepare for battle. Among them was Sir Giles Barrington, the Labour candidate for Bristol Docklands.

◄○►

Over breakfast one morning during the second week of the campaign, Giles told Harry and Emma that Virginia would not be joining him in the run-up to the election. Emma didn't attempt to hide her relief.

'Virginia feels she might even lose me votes,' admitted Giles. 'After all, no member of her family has ever been known to vote Labour. One or two may have supported the odd Liberal, but never Labour.'

Harry laughed. 'At least we have that in common.'

'If Labour were to win the election,' said Emma, 'do you think Mr Attlee might ask you to join the Cabinet?'

'Heaven knows. That man plays his cards so close to his chest even he can't see them. In any case, if you believe the polls, the election is too close to call, so there's not much point in dreaming about red boxes until after we know the result.'

'My bet,' said Harry, 'is that Churchill will scrape home this time. Mind you, only the British could kick a prime minister out of office after he'd just won a war.'

Giles glanced at his watch. 'Can't sit around chatting,' he said. 'I'm meant to be canvassing in Coronation Road. Care to join me, Harry?' he said with a grin.

'You must be joking. Can you see me asking people to vote for you? I'd turn off more people than Virginia.'

'Why not?' said Emma. 'You've handed in your latest manuscript to the publisher, and you're always telling everyone first-hand experience is more worthwhile than sitting in a library checking endless facts.'

'But I've got a busy day ahead of me,' protested Harry.

'Of course you have,' said Emma. 'Now let me see, you're taking Jessica to school this morning and, oh yes, you're picking her up this afternoon and bringing her home.'

'Oh all right. I'll join you,' said Harry. 'But strictly as an observer, you understand.'

◄o►

'Good afternoon, sir, my name is Giles Barrington. I hope I can count on your support at the general election on October twenty-fifth?' he said as he stopped to chat to a constituent.

'You certainly can, Mr Barrington. I always vote Tory.'

'Thank you,' said Giles, quickly moving on to the next voter.

'But you're the Labour candidate,' Harry reminded his brother-in-law.

'There's no mention of the parties on the ballot paper,' said Giles, 'only the candidates' names. So why disillusion him? Good afternoon, my name is Giles Barrington, and I was hoping—'

'And you can go on hoping, because I won't be voting for a stuck-up toff.'

'But I'm the Labour candidate,' protested Giles.

'Doesn't stop you being a toff. You're as bad as that Frank Pakenham fellow, a traitor to your class.'

Harry tried not to laugh as the man walked away.

'Good afternoon, madam, my name is Giles Barrington.'

'Oh, how nice to meet you, Sir Giles. I've been a great admirer of yours ever since you won the MC at Tobruk.' Giles bowed low. 'And although I would normally vote Liberal, on this occasion you can rely on me.'

'Thank you, madam,' said Giles.

She turned to Harry, who smiled and raised his hat. 'And you needn't bother raising your hat to me, Mr Clifton, because I know you were born in Still House Lane, and it's disgraceful that you vote Tory. You're a traitor to your class,' she added before marching off.

It was Giles's turn to try not to laugh.

'I don't think I'm cut out for politics,' said Harry.

'Good afternoon, sir, my name is—'

'—Giles Barrington. Yes, I know,' the man said, refusing Giles's outstretched hand. 'You shook hands with me half an hour ago, Mr Barrington, and I told you I'd be voting for you. But now I'm not so sure.'

'Is it always this bad?' asked Harry.

'Oh, it can be far worse. But if you place your head in the stocks, don't be surprised if there are people who are only too happy to throw the occasional rotten tomato in your direction.'

'I would never make a politician,' said Harry. 'I take everything too personally.'

'Then you'll probably end up in the House of Lords,' said Giles, coming to a halt outside a pub. 'I think a quick half pint is called for, before we return to the battlefield.'

'I don't think I've been in this pub before,' said Harry, looking up at a flapping sign with a Volunteer beckoning them in.

'Me neither. But come the day of the election, I'll have had a drink in every hostelry in the constituency. Pub landlords are always happy to express an opinion.'

'Who'd want to be a Member of Parliament?'

'If you have to ask that question,' said Giles as they entered the pub, 'you'll never understand the thrill of fighting an election, taking your seat in the House of Commons and playing a role, however minor, in governing your country. It's like war without the bullets.'

Harry headed for a quiet alcove in a corner of the pub, while Giles took a seat at the bar. He was chatting to the barman when Harry returned to join him.

'Sorry, old fellow,' said Giles. 'I can't hide away in a corner. Have to be seen at all times, even when I'm taking a break.'

'But there are some confidential matters I was hoping to discuss with you,' said Harry.

'Then you'll just have to lower your voice. Two half pints of bitter, please, barman,' said Giles. He settled back to listen to what Harry had to say, in between being slapped on the back and told by several customers – not all of them sober – how to run the country, and called everything from 'sir' to 'you bastard'.

'So, how's my nephew getting on at his new school?' asked Giles after he'd drained his glass.

'Doesn't seem to be enjoying Beechcroft any more than he did St Bede's. I've had a word with his housemaster, and all he said was that Seb's very bright, and almost certain to be offered a place at Oxford, but still doesn't make friends easily.'

'I'm sorry to hear that,' said Giles. 'Perhaps he's just shy. After all, no one loved you when you first went to St Bede's.' He turned back to the barman. 'Two more halves, please.'

'Coming right up, sir.'

'And how's my favourite girlfriend?' asked Giles.

'If you're referring to Jessica,' said Harry, 'you'll have to join a long queue. Everybody loves that little girl, from Cleopatra to the postman, but she only loves her dad.'

'When will you tell her who her real father is?' said Giles, lowering his voice.

'I keep asking myself that question. And you don't have to tell me I'm storing up trouble for the future, but I never seem to find the right time.'

'There won't ever be a right time,' said Giles. 'But don't

leave it too long, because one thing's certain, Emma will never tell her, and I'm fairly certain Seb's already worked it out for himself.'

'What makes you say that?'

'Not here,' said Giles, as another constituent slapped him on the back.

The barman placed two half pints on the counter. 'That'll be ninepence, sir.'

As Harry had paid for the first round, he assumed it must be Giles's turn.

'Sorry,' said Giles, 'but I'm not allowed to pay.'

'Not *allowed* to pay?'

'No. A candidate is not permitted to buy any drinks during an election campaign.'

'Ah,' said Harry, 'at last I've found a reason for wanting to be an MP. But why, pray?'

'It might be thought I was trying to buy your vote. Goes back to the reform of the rotten boroughs.'

'I'd want a damn sight more than half a pint before I'd consider voting for you,' said Harry.

'Keep your voice down,' said Giles. 'After all, if my brother-in-law isn't willing to vote for me, the press are bound to ask, why should anyone else?'

'As this clearly isn't the time or the place for a conversation on family matters, is there any chance of you joining Emma and me for dinner on Sunday evening?'

'Not a hope. I have three church services to attend on Sunday, and don't forget, it's the last Sunday before the election.'

'Oh God,' said Harry, 'is the election next Thursday?'

'Damn,' said Giles. 'It's a golden rule that you never remind a Tory of the date of the election. Now I'll have to rely on God to support me, and I'm still not altogether sure which side he's on. I shall fall on my knees on Sunday morning at Matins, seek his guidance during Vespers and pray during evensong, and then hope the vote will end up two to one in my favour.'

'Do you really have to go to such extremes, just to win a few more votes?'

'Of course you do if you are contesting a marginal constituency. And don't forget, church services get far bigger turnouts than I ever manage at my political meetings.'

'But I thought the church was meant to be neutral?'

'And so it should be, but vicars will always tell you they have absolutely no interest in politics, while having few qualms about letting their parishioners know exactly which party they will be voting for, and often from the pulpit.'

'Do you want another half, as I'm paying?' asked Harry.

'No. I can't waste any more time chatting to you. You not only don't have a vote in this constituency, but even if you did, you wouldn't be backing me.' He leapt off his stool, shook hands with the barman and dashed out of the pub on to the pavement, where he smiled at the first person he saw.

'Good afternoon, sir. My name is Giles Barrington and I hope I can count on your support next Thursday at the general election.'

'I don't live in this constituency, mate, I'm down from Birmingham for the day.'

◄○►

On the day of the election, Giles's agent, Griff Haskins, told the candidate he felt confident the voters of Bristol Docklands would keep faith with their member and send him back to represent them in the House of Commons, even if it was with a slightly reduced majority. However, he was not convinced that the Labour Party would hold on to power.

Griff turned out to be right on both counts, because at three o'clock on the morning of 27 October 1951, the returning officer announced that after three recounts, Sir Giles Barrington was duly elected as the Member of Parliament for Bristol Docklands, with a majority of 414 votes.

Once all the results across the nation had come in, the Conservative Party ended up with an overall majority of 17

seats, and Winston Churchill once again found himself residing at No.10 Downing Street. The first election he'd won as
Conservative leader.

The following Monday, Giles drove up to London and took
his seat in the House of Commons. The chatter in the corridors
was that as the Tories only had a majority of 17, it wouldn't be
long before another election had to be called.

Giles knew that whenever that took place, with a majority
of only 414, he would be fighting for his political life, and if he
didn't win it could well be the end of his career as an MP.

11

THE BUTLER HANDED Sir Giles his post on a silver tray. Giles flicked quickly through it, as he did every morning, separating the long, thin, brown envelopes, which he placed to one side, from the white, square ones which he would open immediately. Among the envelopes that caught his attention that morning was a long, thin white one that bore a Bristol postmark. He tore it open.

He pulled out a single sheet of paper addressed *To Whom It May Concern*. Once he'd read it, he looked up and smiled at Virginia, who had joined him for a late breakfast.

'It will all be done and dusted next Wednesday,' he announced.

Virginia didn't look up from her copy of the *Daily Express*. She always began the morning with a cup of black coffee and William Hickey, so she could find out what her friends were up to, and which debutantes were hoping to be presented at court that year, and which had no chance.

'What will be done and dusted?' she asked, still not looking up.

'Mama's will.'

Virginia forgot all about hopeful debutantes, folded her newspaper and smiled sweetly at Giles. 'Tell me more, my darling.'

'The reading of the will is to take place in Bristol next Wednesday. We could drive down on Tuesday afternoon, spend the night at the Hall, and attend the reading the next day.'

'What time will it be read?'

Giles glanced at the letter once again. 'Eleven o'clock, in the offices of Marshall, Baker and Siddons.'

'Would you mind terribly, Bunny, if we drove down early on the Wednesday morning? I don't think I can face another evening being nice to your chippy sister.'

Giles was about to say something, but changed his mind. 'Of course, my love.'

'Stop calling me "my love", Bunny, it's dreadfully common.'

'What sort of day have you got ahead of you, my darling?'

'Hectic, as usual. I never seem to stop nowadays. Another dress fitting this morning, lunch with the bridesmaids, and then this afternoon I have an appointment with the caterers, who are pressing me on numbers.'

'What's the latest?' asked Giles.

'Just over two hundred from my side, and another hundred and thirty from yours. I was rather hoping to send out the invitations next week.'

'That's fine by me,' said Giles. 'Which reminds me,' he added, 'the speaker has granted my request to use the Commons' terrace for the reception, so perhaps we ought to invite him as well.'

'Of course, Bunny. After all, he is a Conservative.'

'And possibly Mr Attlee,' suggested Giles tentatively.

'I'm not sure how Papa would feel about the leader of the Labour Party attending his only daughter's wedding. Perhaps I could ask him to invite Mr Churchill.'

◄○►

The following Wednesday, Giles drove his Jaguar over to Cadogan Gardens and parked outside Virginia's flat. He rang the front doorbell, expecting to join his fiancée for breakfast.

'Lady Virginia has not come down yet, sir,' said the butler. 'But if you'd care to wait in the drawing room, I can bring you a cup of coffee and the morning papers.'

'Thank you, Mason,' Giles said to the butler, who had once confessed to him privately that he voted Labour.

Giles settled down in a comfortable chair, and was offered

a choice of the *Express* or the *Telegraph*. He settled on the *Telegraph*, because the headline on the front page caught his attention: Eisenhower announces he will stand for president. The decision didn't surprise Giles, although he was interested to learn that the general would be standing as a Republican, because until recently no one seemed quite sure which party he supported, after both the Democrats and the Republicans had made overtures to him.

Giles glanced at his watch every few minutes, but there was no sign of Virginia. When the clock on the mantelpiece struck the half hour, he turned his attention to an article on page seven, which suggested Britain was considering building its first motorway. The stalemate in the Korean War was covered on the parliamentary pages, and Giles's speech on a forty-eight-hour week for all workers and every hour beyond that being treated as overtime was quoted at length, with an editorial condemning his views. He smiled. After all, it was the *Telegraph*. Giles was reading an announcement in the court circular that Princess Elizabeth would be embarking on a tour of Africa in January, when Virginia burst into the room.

'I'm so sorry to have kept you waiting, my darling, but I just couldn't decide what to wear.'

He leapt up and kissed his fiancée on both cheeks, took a pace back, and once again thought how lucky he was that this beautiful woman had ever given him a second look.

'You look fabulous,' he said, admiring a yellow dress he'd never seen before, which emphasized her slim, graceful figure.

'A little risqué perhaps for the reading of a will?' suggested Virginia as she spun round in a circle.

'Certainly not,' said Giles. 'In fact, the moment you walk into the room, no one will be thinking of anything else.'

'I should hope not,' said Virginia as she checked her watch. 'Heavens, is it really that late? We'd better skip breakfast, Bunny, if we're going to be on time. Not that we don't already know the contents of your mother's will, but it must appear as if we don't.'

On the way down to Bristol, Virginia brought Giles up to date on the latest wedding arrangements. He was a little disappointed that she didn't ask how his speech from the front bench had been received the previous day, but then, William Hickey hadn't been in the press gallery. It wasn't until they were on the Great West Road that Virginia said something that demanded his full attention.

'The first thing we'll have to do once the will has been executed is look for a replacement for Marsden.'

'But he's been with the family for over thirty years,' said Giles. 'In fact, I can't remember when he wasn't there.'

'Which is part of the problem. But don't worry yourself, my darling, I think I may have found the perfect replacement.'

'But—'

'And if you feel that strongly about it, Bunny, Marsden can always go and work at the Manor House, and take care of my aunts.'

'But—'

'And while I'm on the subject of replacements,' continued Virginia, 'it's high time we had a serious talk about Jackie.'

'My personal secretary?'

'She's far too personal, in my opinion. I can't pretend that I approve of this modern habit of staff calling their bosses by their Christian names. No doubt it's all part of the Labour Party's absurd notion of equality. However, I felt it necessary to remind her that it's *Lady* Virginia.'

'I am sorry,' said Giles. 'She's usually so polite.'

'With you perhaps, but when I rang yesterday, she asked me to hold the line, something I'm not in the habit of doing.'

'I'll have a word with her about it.'

'Please don't bother,' said Virginia, which came as a relief to Giles. 'Because I shall not be contacting your office again while she remains on your staff.'

'Isn't that a little extreme? After all, she does a first-class job, and I'd find it almost impossible to replace her.'

Virginia leant over and kissed him on the cheek. 'I do hope,

Bunny, that I will be the only person you will find it almost impossible to replace.'

<o>

Mr Siddons entered the room, and was not surprised to find that everyone who had received the *To Whom It May Concern* letter was present. He sat down at his desk and peered at the hopeful faces.

In the front row sat Sir Giles Barrington and his fiancée, Lady Virginia Fenwick, who was even more striking in person than the photograph he'd seen of her in *Country Life* soon after the couple had announced their engagement. Mr Siddons was looking forward to making her acquaintance.

In the second row, seated directly behind them, were Mr Harry Clifton and his wife Emma, who was sitting next to her sister, Grace. It amused him to see that Miss Barrington was wearing blue stockings.

Mr and Mrs Holcombe sat in the third row, alongside the Reverend Mr Donaldson and a lady who was dressed in a matron's uniform. The back two rows were filled with staff who had served the Barrington family for many years, their selection of seats revealing their station.

Mr Siddons perched a pair of half-moon spectacles on the end of his nose and cleared his throat to indicate that proceedings were about to begin.

He looked over the top of his spectacles at the assembled gathering, before making his opening remarks. He didn't require any notes, as this was a responsibility he carried out on a regular basis.

'Ladies and gentlemen,' he began. 'My name is Desmond Siddons, and I have had the privilege of being the Barrington family's solicitor for the past twenty-three years, although it will be some time before I equal the record of my father, whose association with the family covered the careers of both Sir Walter and Sir Hugo Barrington. However, I digress.' Mr Siddons thought Lady Virginia looked as if she agreed with him.

'I am in possession,' he continued, 'of the last will and testament of Elizabeth May Barrington, which was executed by me at her request, and signed in the presence of two independent witnesses. Therefore this document,' he continued, holding it up for all to see, 'renders any previous will null and void.

'I shall not waste your time going over the pages of legal jargon that are demanded by the law, but rather I will concentrate on the several relevant bequests left by her ladyship. Should anyone wish to study the will in greater detail later, they are most welcome to do so.'

Mr Siddons looked down, turned the page and adjusted his glasses before continuing.

'Several charities close to the deceased's heart are named in the will. They include the parish church of St Andrew's, Dr Barnardo's homes, and the hospital that nursed Lady Barrington so compassionately through her final days. Each of these establishments will receive a bequest of five hundred pounds.'

Mr Siddons readjusted his spectacles once again.

'I shall now move on to those individuals who have served the Barrington household over the years. Every member of staff who was employed by Lady Barrington for more than five years will receive an additional year's salary, while the resident housekeeper and butler will also be granted a further five hundred pounds each.'

Marsden bowed his head and mouthed the words, thank you, m'lady.

'I now turn to Mrs Holcombe, formerly Mrs Arthur Clifton. To her is bequeathed the Victorian brooch that Lady Barrington wore on the day of her daughter's wedding, and that she hopes, and I quote her testament, will help Mrs Holcombe recall the many happy times they shared together.'

Maisie smiled, but could only wonder when she could possibly wear such a magnificent piece of jewellery.

Mr Siddons turned another page, and pushed his half-moon spectacles back up his nose before he continued.

'I leave to Jessica Clifton, née Piotrovska, my grandfather's favourite watercolour of the *Lock at Cleveland* by Turner. I hope it will inspire her, for I believe she possesses a remarkable gift that should be given every opportunity to blossom.'

Giles nodded, well remembering those words when his mother had explained why she had wanted Jessica to inherit the coveted Turner.

'And to my grandson, Sebastian Arthur Clifton,' Mr Siddons continued, 'I bequeath the sum of five thousand pounds, which he will receive when he comes of age, on March the ninth 1961.'

Giles nodded again. No surprise there, he thought.

'The remainder of my estate, including twenty-two per cent of Barrington Shipping, as well as the Manor House –' Mr Siddons couldn't resist a glance in the direction of Lady Virginia Fenwick, who was sitting on the edge of her seat – 'is to be left to my beloved . . . daughters Emma and Grace, to dispose of as they see fit, with the exception of my Siamese cat, Cleopatra, who I leave to Lady Virginia Fenwick, because they have so much in common. They are both beautiful, well-groomed, vain, cunning, manipulative predators, who assume that everyone else was put on earth to serve them, including my besotted son, who I can only pray will break from the spell she has cast on him before it is too late.'

It was clear to Mr Siddons from the looks of shock and the whispered chattering that broke out from all quarters of the room that no one had expected this, although he did observe that Mr Clifton remained remarkably calm. Calm was not a word that would have described Lady Virginia, who was whispering something in Giles's ear.

'That completes the reading of the will,' said Mr Siddons. 'If there are any questions, I will be happy to answer them.'

'Just one,' said Giles, before anyone else had a chance to speak. 'How long do I have to contest the will?'

'You can lodge an appeal against judgment in the High Court at any time during the next twenty-eight days, Sir Giles,' said Mr Siddons, having anticipated the question, and the questioner.

If there were any other questions, Sir Giles and Lady Virginia did not hear them, as they stormed out of the room without another word.

12

'I'LL DO ANYTHING, my darling,' he said, 'but please don't break off our engagement.'

'How can I be expected to face the world after your mother humiliated me in front of your family, your friends and even the servants?'

'I understand,' said Giles, 'of course I do, but Mother was clearly not in her right mind. She can't have realized what she was doing.'

'You said you'll do anything?' said Virginia, toying with her engagement ring.

'Anything, my darling.'

'The first thing you must do is sack your secretary. And her replacement must meet with my approval.'

'Consider it done,' said Giles meekly.

'And tomorrow, you will appoint a leading firm of lawyers to contest the will and, whatever the consequences, you'll fight tooth and nail to make sure we win.'

'I've already consulted Sir Cuthbert Makins KC.'

'Tooth and nail,' repeated Virginia.

'Tooth and nail,' said Giles. 'Anything else?'

'Yes. When the wedding invitations are sent out next week, I, and I alone, will approve the guest list.'

'But that could mean—'

'It will. Because I want everyone who was in that room to know what it feels like to be rejected.' Giles bowed his head.

'Ah, I see,' said Virginia, removing her engagement ring. 'So you didn't really mean you'd do *anything*.'

'Yes I did, my darling. I agree, you alone can decide who's invited to the wedding.'

'And finally,' said Virginia, 'you will instruct Mr Siddons to issue a court order removing every member of the Clifton family from Barrington Hall.'

'But where will they live?'

'I don't give a damn where they live,' said Virginia. 'The time has come for you to decide whether you want to spend the rest of your life with me, or with them.'

'I want to spend the rest of my life with you,' said Giles.

'Then that's settled, Bunny,' said Virginia, as she put the engagement ring back on, and began to undo the buttons on the front of her dress.

◄○►

Harry was reading *The Times*, and Emma the *Telegraph*, when the phone rang. The door opened and Denby entered the breakfast room.

'It's your publisher, Mr Collins, on the line, sir. He wondered if he might have a word with you.'

'I doubt if that's how he put it,' said Harry as he folded his newspaper.

Emma was so engrossed in the article she was reading that she didn't even look up when her husband left the room. She had come to the end of it by the time he returned.

'Let me guess,' she said.

'Billy's had calls from most of the national papers, as well as the BBC, asking if I want to make a statement.'

'What did you say?'

'No comment. I told him there was no need to add fuel to this particular fire.'

'I can't imagine that will satisfy Billy Collins,' said Emma. 'All he's interested in is selling books.'

'He didn't expect anything else, and he's not complaining.

He told me he'll be shipping a third reprint of the paperback into the bookshops early next week.'

'Would you like to hear how the *Telegraph* is reporting it?'

'Do I have to?' said Harry as he sat back down at the breakfast table.

Emma ignored the comment and began reading out loud.

'"The wedding took place yesterday of Sir Giles Barrington MC MP and The Lady Virginia Fenwick, the only daughter of the Ninth Earl of Fenwick. The bride wore a gown designed by Mr Norman—"'

'At least spare me that,' said Harry.

Emma skipped a couple of paragraphs. '"Four hundred guests attended the ceremony, which was held at the Church of St Margaret's, Westminster. The service was conducted by the Right Reverend George Hastings, Bishop of Ripon. Afterwards, a reception was held on the terrace of the House of Commons. Among the guests were Her Royal Highness Princess Margaret, The Earl Mountbatten of Burma, The Right Hon. Clement Attlee, Leader of the Opposition, and The Right Hon. Mr William Morrison, speaker of the House of Commons. The list of guests who attended the wedding makes interesting reading, but far more fascinating are the names of those who were absent, either because they did not receive an invitation, or because they did not wish to attend. Not one member of the Barrington family other than Sir Giles himself was on the guest list. The absence of his two sisters, Mrs Emma Clifton and Miss Grace Barrington, as well as his brother-in-law, Harry Clifton, the popular author, remains something of a mystery, especially as it was announced some weeks ago that he would be Sir Giles's best man."'

'So who was the best man?' asked Harry.

'Dr Algernon Deakins of Balliol College, Oxford.'

'Dear Deakins,' said Harry. 'An excellent choice. He certainly would have been on time, and there would have been no chance of him mislaying the ring. Is there anything else?'

'I'm afraid so. "What makes this even more of a mystery is

that six years ago, when the case of Barrington v. Clifton was before the House of Lords and a vote was taken to decide who should inherit the Barrington title and estates, Sir Giles and Mr Clifton seemed to be in accord when the Lord Chancellor gave judgment in favour of Sir Giles. The happy couple,"' continued Emma, '"will spend their honeymoon at Sir Giles's villa in Tuscany."

'That's a bit rich,' said Emma, looking up. 'The villa was left to Grace and me to dispose of as we saw fit.'

'Behave yourself, Emma,' said Harry. 'You saw fit to let Giles have the villa in exchange for us being allowed to move into the Manor House until the courts decide on the validity of the will. Is that it?'

'No, the really juicy bit is still to come. "However, it now looks as if a major rift has divided the family following the death of Sir Giles's mother, Lady Elizabeth Barrington. In her recently published will, she left the bulk of her estate to her two daughters, Emma and Grace, while bequeathing nothing to her only son. Sir Giles has issued proceedings to contest the will, and the case will be heard in the High Court next month." That's it. What about *The Times*?'

'Far more sober. Just the facts, no speculation. But Billy Collins tells me there's a photograph of Cleopatra on the front pages of the *Mail* and the *Express*, and the *Mirror*'s headline is "Battle of the Cats".'

'How can it have come to this?' said Emma. 'What I'll never understand is how Giles could have allowed that woman to stop his own family attending the wedding.'

'I can't understand it either,' said Harry, 'but then I never understood how the Prince of Wales could give up the throne for an American divorcee. I suspect your mother was right. Giles is simply besotted with the woman.'

'If my mother had wanted me to give you up,' said Emma, 'I would have defied her.' She gave him a warm smile. 'So I have some sympathy with my brother.'

◄○►

For the next fortnight, photographs of Sir Giles and Lady Barrington on their honeymoon in Tuscany appeared in most of the national papers.

Harry's fourth novel, *Mightier than the Sword*, was published on the day the Barringtons returned from Italy. The following morning the same photograph appeared on every front page except *The Times*.

When the happy couple stepped off the train at Waterloo, they had to pass a W.H. Smith bookshop on the way to their car. There was only one novel displayed in vast numbers in the window. A week later, *Mightier than the Sword* made it on to the bestseller list, and it remained there right up until the opening day of the trial.

All Harry had to say was that no one understood how to promote a book better than Billy Collins.

13

THE ONE THING Giles and Emma were able to agree on was that it would be wiser for the case to be heard in a closed court with a judge presiding, rather than risking the unpredictable whims of a jury and relentless hounding by the press. The Hon. Mr Justice Cameron was selected to preside over the case, and both counsel assured their clients that he was a man of probity, wisdom and common sense in equal proportions.

Although the press assembled in great numbers outside court No. 6, good morning and good night were the only comments they got from either party.

Giles was represented by Sir Cuthbert Makins KC, while Emma and Grace had selected Mr Simon Todd KC to put their case, although Grace made it clear that she would not be attending proceedings as she had far more important things to do.

'Like what?' asked Emma.

'Like teaching clever children, rather than listening to arguments from childish grown-ups. If I were given the choice, I'd just bang both your heads together,' was her final comment on the subject.

As the clock behind the judge's chair struck the first of ten chimes on the first day of the hearing, Mr Justice Cameron made his entrance. Everyone else in court followed the example of the two silks, rising and bowing to his lordship. Once he had returned the compliment, he took his seat in the high-backed leather chair in front of the royal coat of arms. He adjusted his wig, opened the thick red file in front of him and took a sip of water before addressing both parties.

'Ladies and gentlemen,' he began. 'It is my job to listen to the arguments presented by both leading counsel, assess the evidence of witnesses, and consider the points of law that are relevant to this case. I must begin by asking counsel for both the plaintiff and the defence if every effort has been made to come to an out-of-court settlement.'

Sir Cuthbert rose slowly from his place and tugged the lapels of his long black gown before addressing the court. 'I speak on behalf of both parties when I say that sadly, m'lud, that has not been possible.'

'Then let us proceed, Sir Cuthbert, with your opening statement.'

'If it so pleases your lordship, in this case I represent the plaintiff, Sir Giles Barrington. The case, m'lud, concerns the validity of a will, and whether the late Lady Barrington was of sufficiently sound mind to put her signature to a long and complex document, with far-reaching ramifications, only hours before she died. I submit, m'lud, that this frail and exhausted woman was in no position to make a considered judgement that would affect the lives of so many people. I shall also show that Lady Barrington had executed an earlier will, some twelve months prior to her death, when she was in rude health, and had more than enough time to consider her actions. And to that end, m'lud, I would like to call my first witness, Mr Michael Pym.'

A tall, elegantly dressed man with a head of silver hair entered the courtroom. Even before he'd taken the witness stand, he'd given the favourable impression Sir Cuthbert had planned. Once the witness had sworn the oath, Sir Cuthbert gave him a warm smile.

'Mr Pym, will you please state your name and occupation for the court record.'

'My name is Michael Pym, and I am the senior surgeon at Guy's Hospital in the City of London.'

'How long have you held that position?'

'Sixteen years.'

'So you are a man with a great deal of experience in your field. Indeed, one might say—'

'I accept that Mr Pym is an expert witness, Sir Cuthbert. Get on with it,' said the judge.

'Mr Pym,' said Sir Cuthbert, recovering quickly, 'would you please tell the court, with all your considerable experience, what a patient can expect to go through during the last week of his or her life when suffering from such a painful and debilitating disease as cancer?'

'It can vary, of course, but the vast majority of patients will spend long periods of time in a semi-conscious or unconscious state. In their waking moments they are often aware that their life is ebbing away, but apart from that they can lose all sense of reality.'

'Would you think it possible for a patient in this state of mind to make an important decision on a complex legal matter, such as the signing of a will?'

'No, I would not,' replied Pym. 'Whenever I require a medical consent form to be signed under such circumstances, I make sure it is done some time before the patient reaches that condition.'

'No more questions, m'lud,' said Sir Cuthbert, resuming his seat.

'Mr Pym,' said the judge, leaning forward, 'are you saying there are no exceptions to this rule?'

'The exception proves the rule, m'lud.'

'Quite so,' responded the judge. Turning to Mr Todd, he asked, 'Do you have any questions for this witness?'

'I most certainly do, m'lud,' said Mr Todd, rising from his place. 'Mr Pym, did you ever come across Lady Barrington, either socially or professionally?'

'No, but—'

'So you haven't had the chance to study her case history?'

'Of course not. She was not my patient, so that would be a breach of the Medical Council's code of conduct.'

'So you never met Lady Barrington, and you are not familiar with her case?'

'No, sir.'

'So it's quite possible, Mr Pym, that she could be the exception that proves the rule?'

'Possible, but highly improbable.'

'No further questions, m'lud.'

Sir Cuthbert smiled as Mr Todd sat down.

'Will you be calling any other expert witnesses Sir Cuthbert?' enquired the judge.

'No, m'lud, I feel I have made my point. However, in your bundle of evidence I have placed three written statements for your consideration from equally eminent members of the medical profession. If either you, m'lud, or Mr Todd feel they should appear before the court, they are all on hand and available to do so.'

'That's good of you, Sir Cuthbert. I have read all three statements, and they confirm Mr Pym's opinion. Mr Todd, do you wish to call any of these witnesses, or indeed all three of them?'

'That will not be necessary, m'lud,' said Todd. 'Unless of course any of them knew Lady Barrington personally, or were familiar with her case.'

The judge glanced at Sir Cuthbert, who shook his head. 'I have no further witnesses, m'lud.'

'Then you may call your first witness, Mr Todd,' said the judge.

'Thank you, m'lud. I call Mr Kenneth Langbourne.'

Mr Langbourne could not have been cut from more different cloth to Mr Pym. He was short, and a couple of buttons were missing from his waistcoat, which suggested either that he had recently put on some weight, or that he wasn't married. And either the few tufts of hair left on his head had a will of their own, or he didn't possess a comb.

'Would you please state your name and occupation.'

'My name is Kenneth Langbourne, and I am the senior surgeon at the Bristol Royal Infirmary.'

'How long have you held that position, Mr Langbourne?'

'For the past nine years.'

'And were you the surgeon in charge of Lady Barrington's case while she was at the Bristol Royal Infirmary?'

'Yes, I was. She was referred to me by Dr Raeburn, her family GP.'

'Am I right in saying that after carrying out several tests on Lady Barrington, you confirmed her family doctor's diagnosis of breast cancer, and informed her that she had only a few weeks to live?'

'Yes, it is one of a surgeon's more unenviable tasks to have to inform patients of a terminal prognosis. It's even harder when the patient in question is an old friend.'

'And can you tell his lordship how Lady Barrington reacted to this news?'

'Stoical is the word I would use to describe her. And once she'd accepted her fate, she displayed a determination that suggested she had something important to do, and hadn't a moment to lose.'

'But surely, Mr Langbourne, she must have been exhausted from the continual pain she was suffering, and drowsy as a result of her medication?'

'She certainly slept for long periods, but when she was awake, she was perfectly capable of reading *The Times*, and whenever visitors came to see her, it was often they who left exhausted.'

'How do you explain this, Mr Langbourne?'

'I can't. All I can tell you is that it's sometimes quite amazing how a human being will respond once they accept that their time is limited.'

'Based on your knowledge of the case, Mr Langbourne, do you consider that Lady Barrington would have been capable of understanding a complex legal document such as a will, and of putting her signature to it?'

'I can't see why not. During her time at the hospital she wrote several letters, and indeed she asked me to witness her signature on her will in the presence of her solicitor.'

'Is that a task you carry out regularly?'

'Only if I'm confident that the patient is fully aware of what they are signing. Otherwise I would refuse to do so.'

'But on this occasion, you were satisfied that Lady Barrington was fully aware of what she was doing?'

'Yes, I was.'

'No further questions, m'lud.'

'Sir Cuthbert, do you wish to question this witness?'

'I have only one question, m'lud,' said Sir Cuthbert. 'Mr Langbourne, how long did Lady Barrington live after you'd witnessed the signature on her will?'

'She died later that night.'

'Later that night,' repeated Sir Cuthbert. 'So, just a matter of hours?'

'Yes.'

'No more questions, m'lud.'

'Will you call your next witness, Mr Todd.'

'Yes, m'lud. I call Mr Desmond Siddons.'

Siddons entered the courtroom as if it was his front parlour, and delivered the oath like a seasoned professional.

'Would you please state your name and occupation?'

'My name is Desmond Siddons. I am the senior partner of Marshall, Baker and Siddons, and I have been the Barrington family's solicitor for the past twenty-three years.'

'Let me begin by asking you, Mr Siddons, if you were responsible for executing the earlier will, which Sir Giles contends was in fact Lady Barrington's final testament.'

'I was, sir.'

'And how long ago was that?'

'Just over a year before Lady Barrington's death.'

'And did Lady Barrington later get in touch to let you know that she wished to write a new will?'

'She did indeed, sir. Just a few days before she died.'

'And how did the latest will, the one that is the subject of this dispute, differ from the one executed by you just over a year before?'

'All the bequests to charities, her staff, her grandchildren and her friends remained unaltered. In fact there was only one significant change in the whole document.'

'And what was that, Mr Siddons?'

'That the bulk of the Harvey estate was no longer to be passed to her son, Sir Giles Barrington, but to her two daughters, Mrs Harold Clifton and Miss Grace Barrington.'

'Let me be absolutely clear about this,' said Mr Todd. 'With the exception of the one change, a significant change I concede, the earlier document remained intact?'

'That is correct.'

'What state of mind was Lady Barrington in when she asked you to make this one significant change to her will?'

'M'lud, I must object,' said Sir Cuthbert, leaping up from his place. 'How can Mr Siddons give a judgement on Lady Barrington's state of mind? He's a solicitor, not a psychiatrist.'

'I agree,' said the judge, 'but as Mr Siddons had known the lady for twenty-three years, I would be interested to hear his opinion.'

'She was very tired,' said Siddons, 'and she took more time than usual to express herself. However, she made it clear that she wished a new will to be prepared expeditiously.'

'Expeditiously – your word or hers?' asked the judge.

'Hers, m'lud. She often chastised me for writing a paragraph when a sentence would have done.'

'So you prepared the new will expeditiously?'

'I most certainly did, as I was aware that time was against us.'

'Were you present when the will was witnessed?'

'Yes. It was witnessed by Mr Langbourne and the matron on the wing, a Miss Rumbold.'

'And it remains your submission that Lady Barrington knew exactly what she was signing?'

'Most certainly,' said Siddons firmly. 'Otherwise I would not have been willing to go ahead with the procedure.'

'Quite so. No more questions, m'lud,' said Mr Todd.

'Your witness, Sir Cuthbert.'

'Thank you, m'lud. Mr Siddons, you told the court that you

were under considerable pressure to get the new will completed and signed, and for that reason you prepared it expeditiously, to use your own word.'

'Yes. I had been warned by Mr Langbourne that Lady Barrington didn't have long to live.'

'So, understandably, you did everything in your power to speed things up.'

'I didn't have much choice.'

'I don't doubt it, Mr Siddons. Can I ask how long it took you to execute the earlier will, the one that my client contends is Lady Barrington's authentic testament?'

Siddons hesitated for a moment before saying, 'Three, possibly four months.'

'With regular consultations with Lady Barrington, no doubt?'

'Yes, she was a stickler for detail.'

'I'm sure she was. But she wasn't given much time to consider the details of her later will. Five days to be precise.'

'Yes, but don't forget—'

'And on the final day, she only just managed to sign the will in the nick of time. Isn't that correct?'

'Yes, I suppose you could put it that way.'

Sir Cuthbert turned to the clerk of the court. 'Would you be kind enough to pass Mr Siddons Lady Barrington's two wills?'

Sir Cuthbert waited until the two documents had been handed to the witness, before he continued his cross-examination.

'Would you agree with me, Mr Siddons, that the signature on the earlier will is much bolder and more assured than that on the "nick of time" will? In fact, it's hard to believe they were signed by the same person.'

'Sir Cuthbert, are you suggesting that Lady Barrington didn't sign the second will?' asked the judge.

'Certainly not, m'lud, but I am suggesting she had no idea what she was signing.'

'Mr Siddons,' Sir Cuthbert continued, turning back to the

solicitor, who was now gripping the edge of the witness box with both hands, 'once you'd completed the new rushed will, did you take your client through it clause by clause?'

'No, I didn't. After all, there was only one major change from the earlier will.'

'If you didn't take Lady Barrington through the document clause by clause, Mr Siddons, we only have your word for that.'

'M'lud, that is an outrageous suggestion,' said Mr Todd, leaping to his feet. 'Mr Siddons has had a long and distinguished career in the legal profession, and does not deserve such a slur on his character.'

'I agree with you, Mr Todd,' said the judge. 'Sir Cuthbert, you will withdraw that statement.'

'I apologize, m'lud,' Sir Cuthbert said, offering a slight bow before turning back to the witness once again. 'Mr Siddons, in the earlier will, who was it that suggested that all thirty-six pages should be initialled with the letters EB?'

'I believe I did,' said Siddons, sounding a little flustered.

'But you did not insist on the same rigorous procedure for the second will, the expeditiously prepared document.'

'I didn't feel it was necessary. After all, there was, as I have said, only one significant change.'

'And on which page will we find this significant change, Mr Siddons?'

Siddons flicked through the will and smiled. 'Page twenty-nine, clause seven.'

'Ah yes, I have it in front of me,' said Sir Cuthbert. 'But I don't see the initials EB, either at the bottom of the page or next to the relevant clause. Perhaps Lady Barrington was too tired to manage two signatures on the same day?'

Siddons looked as if he wanted to protest, but said nothing.

'Let me ask you, Mr Siddons, on how many occasions in your long and distinguished career have you failed to advise a client to put their initials on every page of a will?'

Siddons didn't reply. Sir Cuthbert looked first at Mr Todd and then at the judge, before his eyes returned to the witness box. 'I'm still waiting, sir.'

Siddons stared desperately up at the bench, and blurted out, 'If you were to read the letter, m'lud, that Lady Barrington addressed to you, it might help you decide if she knew exactly what she was doing.'

'Letter?' said the judge, looking puzzled. 'I know nothing of a letter. It was certainly not among the court's bundle of papers. Are you aware of such a letter, Sir Cuthbert?'

'It's the first I've heard of it, m'lud. I'm as much in the dark as you are.'

'That's because,' Siddons spluttered, 'it was handed to me only this morning. I haven't even had time to alert Mr Todd to its existence.'

'What are you talking about, man?' said the judge.

Every eye was fixed on Siddons as he took an envelope from an inside pocket and held it aloft as if it were on fire. 'This is the envelope that was given to me this morning, m'lud.'

'By whom, Siddons?' demanded the judge.

'Mr Harry Clifton. He told me it had been given to him by Lady Barrington just hours before she died.'

'Have you opened the envelope, Mr Siddons?'

'No, I have not, sir. It is addressed to you, as the presiding judge.'

'I see,' said the judge. 'Mr Todd and Sir Cuthbert, would you be kind enough to join me in my chambers?'

◄○►

'This is a rum business, gentlemen,' said the judge as he placed the unopened envelope on his desk in front of the two barristers. 'Given the circumstances, I confess I don't know what the best course of action is.'

'Both of us,' said Mr Todd, 'could put forward a compelling argument that the letter should be treated as inadmissible evidence.'

'I agree,' said Sir Cuthbert, 'but frankly we're damned if we do, and we're damned if we don't. Because if you don't open the envelope now it's found its way into court, whichever side loses this case will certainly have grounds for an appeal.'

'I fear that may well be the case,' said the judge. 'If you both agree, perhaps it might be wise for you, Simon, to call Mr Clifton as a witness under oath, and see if he can throw some light on how he came into possession of this envelope in the first place. What do you think, Cuthbert?'

'I have no objection to that,' said Sir Cuthbert.

'Good. However, let me assure you,' continued the judge, 'that I will not open the envelope until I've heard Mr Clifton's evidence, and I will only do so then if you both approve. And should I do so, it will have to be in the presence of anyone who might be affected by the outcome of these proceedings.'

14

'CALL MR HARRY CLIFTON.'

Emma gripped Harry's hand before he rose from his place and walked calmly across to the witness box. Once he'd taken the oath, the judge leaned forward and said, 'Mr Clifton, I propose to ask you a few questions. When I have finished, if learned counsel wish to clarify any points, they will be free to do so. Can I confirm for the record that you are the husband of Emma Clifton, and the brother-in-law of Miss Grace Barrington, the two defendants in this case?'

'I am indeed, sir, and also the brother-in-law of Sir Giles Barrington, my oldest and closest friend.'

'Could you tell the court about your relationship with Lady Barrington?'

'I was twelve when I first met her at a tea party to celebrate Giles's birthday, so I knew her for almost twenty years.'

'That does not answer my question,' pressed the judge.

'I considered Elizabeth a dear and close friend, and I mourn her untimely death as deeply as anyone in this room. She was a truly remarkable woman, and if she had been born a generation later, the board of Barrington's shipping line wouldn't have had to look outside the family for a new chairman when her husband died.'

'Thank you,' said the judge. 'And now I would like to ask you about this envelope,' he said, holding it up for all to see, 'and how it came into your possession.'

'I went to see Elizabeth in hospital most evenings. My final visit took place on what turned out to be the last night of her life.'

'You were alone with her?'

'Yes, sir. Her daughter Grace had just left.'

'Please tell the court what happened.'

'Elizabeth told me that earlier in the day she'd had a visit from her solicitor, Mr Siddons, and had signed a new will.'

'We're talking about the evening of Thursday July twenty-sixth?'

'Yes, sir, just a few hours before Elizabeth died.'

'Could you tell the court what else happened during that visit?'

'She surprised me by taking a sealed envelope from under her pillow which she gave me for safe keeping.'

'Did she explain why she was giving it to you?'

'She only said that if Giles were to contest her new will, I was to hand the letter to the judge selected to preside over the case.'

'Did she give you any other instructions?'

'She said I was not to open the envelope or to let Giles or my wife know of its existence.'

'And if Sir Giles did not contest the will?'

'I was to destroy it, with the same instructions not to reveal it had ever existed.'

'So you have no idea what is in this envelope, Mr Clifton?' said the judge, holding it up.

'None whatsoever.'

'And we're expected to believe that,' said Virginia, loud enough for everyone to hear.

'Curiouser and curiouser,' said the judge, ignoring the interruption. 'I have no more questions for you, Mr Clifton. Mr Todd?'

'Thank you, m'lud,' said Mr Todd, rising from his place. 'You told his lordship, Mr Clifton, that Lady Barrington said she'd written a new will. Did she give you any reason why she had done so?'

'There's no doubt in my mind that Elizabeth loved her son,

but she told me she feared if he were to marry that dreadful woman Lady Virginia—'

'M'lud,' said Sir Cuthbert, leaping up from his place. 'This is hearsay, and clearly inadmissible.'

'I agree. It will be struck from the record.'

'But, m'lud,' intervened Mr Todd, 'the fact that Lady Barrington left her Siamese cat, Cleopatra, to Lady Virginia rather suggests—'

'You have made your point, Mr Todd,' said the judge. 'Sir Cuthbert, do you have any questions for this witness?'

'Only one, m'lud.' Looking directly at Harry, Sir Cuthbert asked, 'Were you a beneficiary of the earlier will?'

'No, sir, I was not.'

'I have no more questions for Mr Clifton, m'lud. But I would beg the court's indulgence and ask that before you decide whether or not the letter should be opened, I might be allowed to call one witness.'

'Who do you have in mind, Sir Cuthbert?' enquired the judge.

'The person who stands to lose the most should your judgment go against him, namely Sir Giles Barrington.'

'I have no objection, assuming Mr Todd is in agreement.'

'I welcome it,' said Todd, aware that nothing would be gained by objecting.

Giles made his way slowly to the witness box, and delivered the oath as if he was addressing the House of Commons. Sir Cuthbert greeted him with a warm smile.

'For the record, will you please state your name and occupation?'

'Sir Giles Barrington, Member of Parliament for Bristol Docklands.'

'And when did you last see your mother?' asked Sir Cuthbert.

The judge smiled.

'I visited her on the morning of the day she died.'

'Did she make any mention of the fact that she had changed her will?'

'None whatsoever.'

'So when you left her, you were under the impression that there was only one will, the one you had discussed with her in great detail over a year before?'

'Frankly, Sir Cuthbert, my mother's will was the last thing on my mind at that particular moment.'

'Quite so. But I do need to ask in what state of health you found your mother that morning.'

'She was very weak. Barely a word passed between us during the hour I spent with her.'

'So it must have come as a surprise to learn that shortly after you had left, she put her signature to a complex document some thirty-six pages in length.'

'I found it inconceivable,' said Giles, 'and still do.'

'Did you love your mother, Sir Giles?'

'I adored her. She was the family's rock. I only wish she was still with us, so this whole sorry business need never have arisen.'

'Thank you, Sir Giles. Please stay there, as Mr Todd may wish to question you.'

'I fear I might have to take the odd risk,' Todd whispered to Siddons before he stood to address the witness. 'Sir Giles, let me start by asking if you have any objection to his lordship opening the envelope that is addressed to him?'

'Of course he does!' said Virginia.

'I have no objection to the letter being opened,' said Giles, ignoring his wife. 'If it was written on the day of my mother's death, it will surely show that she was incapable of signing a document as important as a will. And if it was written before July the twenty-sixth, it is unlikely to be of any significance.'

'Does that mean that you accept Mr Clifton's account of what took place after you'd seen your mother for the last time?'

'No, it most certainly does not,' said Virginia.

'Madam, you will desist from these interjections,' said the judge, glaring down at her. 'If you offer any further opinions, other than from the witness box, I shall have no choice but to have you removed from the court. Do I make myself clear?'

Virginia bowed her head, which Mr Justice Cameron considered was about as much as he was going to get from that particular lady.

'Mr Todd, you may repeat your question.'

'There's no need for that, m'lud,' said Giles. 'If Harry says my mother handed him the letter that night, then that's what happened.'

'Thank you, Sir Giles. I have no further questions.'

The judge asked both counsel to rise. 'Following Sir Giles Barrington's evidence, if there are no objections, it is my intention to open the envelope.'

Both counsel nodded, aware that if they did object, it would only leave grounds for an appeal. In any case, neither believed there was a judge in the land who wouldn't dismiss any objection to the envelope being opened.

Mr Justice Cameron held up the envelope so that everyone in court could see it clearly. He slit it open and pulled out a single sheet of paper which he placed on the desk in front of him. He read it three times before he spoke.

'Mr Siddons,' he said finally.

The Barrington family solicitor rose nervously from his place.

'Can you tell me the date and the precise time that Lady Barrington died?'

Siddons shuffled through some papers before he found the document he was looking for. He looked up at the judge and said, 'I can confirm, sir, that the death certificate was signed at ten twenty-six p.m. on Thursday the twenty-sixth of July, 1951.'

'I am obliged, Mr Siddons. I shall now retire to my chambers to consider the significance of this piece of evidence. The court will adjourn for half an hour.'

◄o►

'It didn't look like a letter to me,' said Emma as their little group, heads down, gathered in a huddle. 'More like an official document. Did she sign anything else that day, Mr Siddons?'

Siddons shook his head. 'Not in my presence she didn't. Any ideas, Mr Todd?'

'It was very thin. It might have been a newspaper cutting, but at that distance I couldn't be sure.'

'Why ever did you allow the judge to open the letter, Giles?' Virginia hissed from the other side of the courtroom.

'Given the circumstances, Lady Virginia, your husband had little choice,' said Sir Cuthbert. 'Although I believe we had the case wrapped up until that last-minute intervention.'

'What can the judge be doing?' asked Emma, unable to mask how nervous she was.

Harry took his wife's hand. 'It won't be long now, darling.'

'If the judgment goes against us,' said Virginia, 'can we still claim that whatever was in the envelope is inadmissible?'

'I can't answer that question,' said Sir Cuthbert, 'until I've had a chance to study it. The contents might well prove that your husband was correct in suggesting that his mother was in no fit state to sign an important legal document during the final hours of her life, in which case it will be the other side who will have to decide whether or not to appeal.'

Both parties were still heads down, whispering in their respective corners, like boxers waiting for the bell to release them for the final round, when the door behind the judge's chair opened and the referee reappeared.

Everyone in court stood and bowed before Mr Justice Cameron resumed his place in the high-backed chair. He stared down at a dozen expectant faces.

'I have now had the opportunity to study the contents of the envelope.' Everyone's eyes remained fixed on him. 'I was fascinated to discover that Lady Barrington and I share a hobby, although I confess she was a far more accomplished exponent than I am, because on Thursday the twenty-sixth of July, she completed *The Times* crossword puzzle, leaving only one clue blank, which I have no doubt she did in order to prove her point. The reason I found it necessary to leave you was that I needed to visit the library in order to get hold of a copy of *The Times* for the following day, Friday July the twenty-seventh –

the day after Lady Barrington died. I wanted to check if she had made any mistakes in the previous day's crossword puzzle, which she hadn't, and to confirm the answer to the one clue she'd left blank. Having done so, I am in no doubt that Lady Barrington was not only capable of signing a will, but was well aware of the significance of its contents. I am therefore ready to pass judgment in this case.'

Sir Cuthbert was quickly on his feet. 'M'lud, I am curious to know, what was the missing clue that helped you reach your judgment?'

Mr Justice Cameron looked down at the crossword puzzle. 'Twelve across, six and six, *common pests I confused when in my right mind.*'

Sir Cuthbert bowed, and a smile crossed Harry's face.

'I therefore find in the case of Barrington versus Clifton and Barrington, in favour of Mrs Harold Clifton and Miss Grace Barrington.'

'We must appeal,' said Virginia, as Sir Cuthbert and Mr Todd bowed low.

'I shall not be appealing,' said Giles. 'Even my Latin is up to that.'

◄○►

'You were pathetic,' said Virginia as she stormed out of the courtroom.

'But Harry is my oldest friend,' Giles said, chasing after her.

'And I'm your wife, just in case you've forgotten.' Virginia pushed her way through the swing doors and hurried out on to the Strand.

'But what else could I have done, given the circumstances?' he asked once he'd caught up with her.

'You could have fought tooth and nail for what was rightly ours, as you promised you would,' she reminded him before hailing a cab.

'But isn't it possible that the judge was right when he said my mother knew exactly what she was doing?'

'If you believe that, Giles,' said Virginia, turning to face him, 'you obviously hold the same low opinion of me that she did.'

Giles was left speechless as a taxi drew up. Virginia opened the door, climbed in and wound down the window.

'I'm going to stay with my mother for a few days. If you haven't lodged an appeal by the time I get back, I suggest you seek advice from a solicitor who specializes in divorce.'

15

THERE WAS A firm rap on the front door. Giles checked his watch: 7.20 p.m. Who could it possibly be? He hadn't invited anyone for dinner, and he wasn't expected back at the House to hear the closing speeches until nine. A second rap, equally firm, and he remembered it was the housekeeper's night off. He placed yesterday's copy of Hansard on the side table, pushed himself up out of his chair and was heading towards the corridor when there was a third rap.

'Hold your horses,' Giles said. He pulled open the door to find the last person he would have expected standing on his doorstep in Smith Square.

'Grace?' he said, unable to mask his surprise.

'It's a relief to discover you still remember my name,' said his sister as she stepped inside.

Giles tried to think of an equally sharp rejoinder, but as he hadn't been in touch with his sister since the day of his mother's funeral, he had to accept that her barbed remark was justified. In truth, he hadn't been in contact with any of the family since Virginia had stormed out of the courtroom and left him standing on the pavement outside.

'What brings you to London, Grace?' he asked rather feebly, as he led his sister down the corridor and into the drawing room.

'You,' she replied. 'If Mohammed, etcetera.'

'Can I get you a drink?' he asked, still wondering what she could possibly want, unless . . .

'Thanks, a dry sherry would go down well, after that ghastly train journey.'

Giles walked across to the sideboard and poured her a sherry, and a half tumbler of whisky for himself, as he desperately searched for something to say. 'I've got a vote at ten,' he eventually managed, passing Grace her drink. His younger sister always made him feel like a naughty schoolboy who'd been caught smoking by the headmaster.

'That will be more than enough time for what I have to say.'

'Have you come to claim your birthright and throw me out of the house?'

'No, you chump, I've come to try and knock some common sense into that thick skull of yours.'

Giles collapsed into his chair and took a sip of whisky. 'I'm all ears.'

'It will be my thirtieth birthday next week, not that you would have noticed.'

'And you've come all this way just to tell me what present you want?' Giles said, trying to lighten the mood.

'Exactly that,' said Grace, taking him by surprise for a second time.

'And what did you have in mind?' Giles felt he was still on the back foot.

'I want you to come to my party.'

'But the House is in session, and since I've been promoted to the front bench, I'm expected—'

'Harry and Emma will be there,' said Grace, ignoring his excuses, 'so it will be just like old times.'

Giles took another gulp of whisky. 'It can never be like old times.'

'Of course it can, you fool, because you're the only person who's preventing it.'

'They want to see me?'

'Why wouldn't they?' said Grace. 'This stupid feud has gone on long enough, which is why I intend to bang all your heads together before it's too late.'

'Who else will be there?'

'Sebastian and Jessica, a few friends, mainly academics, but you don't have to talk to them, except perhaps your old friend Deakins. However,' she added, 'there's one person I won't be inviting. By the way, where is the bitch?'

Giles had thought there was nothing his sister could ever say that would shock him. How wrong he was.

'I've no idea,' he eventually managed. 'She hasn't been in contact with me for over a year. But if you believe the *Daily Express*, she's currently to be found in St Tropez on the arm of an Italian count.'

'I'm sure they'll make a delightful couple. More important, it gives you grounds for divorce.'

'I could never divorce Virginia, even if I wanted to. Don't forget what Mama went through. Not an experience I care to repeat.'

'Oh, I see,' said Grace. 'It's all right for Virginia to be gallivanting around the South of France with her Italian lover, but it's not all right for her husband to want a divorce?'

'You may mock,' said Giles, 'but that isn't the way a gentleman behaves.'

'Don't make me laugh. It was hardly the act of a gentleman to drag me and Emma through the courts over Mother's will.'

'That's below the belt,' said Giles as he took another large gulp of whisky. 'But I suppose it's no more than I deserved,' he added, 'and it's something I'll regret for the rest of my life. Will you ever forgive me?'

'I will if you come to my party, and apologize to your sister and your oldest friend for being such a chump.'

'I'm not sure I can face them.'

'You faced a battery of German soldiers with nothing more than a few hand grenades and a pistol to protect you.'

'And I'd do it again if I thought it would convince Emma and Harry to forgive me.'

Grace stood up, walked across the room and knelt down beside her brother. 'Of course they'll forgive you, you silly oaf.'

Giles bowed his head when his sister put her arms around him. 'You know only too well that Mother wouldn't have wanted us to be kept apart because of that woman.'

◄○►

As Giles drove past a signpost directing him to Cambridge, he thought it still wasn't too late to turn back, although he knew that if he did, he might never be given a second chance.

As he entered the university city, he could feel the collegiate atmosphere all around him. Young men and women in academic gowns of varying lengths were rushing in every direction. It brought back memories of his time at Oxford, cut short by Herr Hitler.

When Giles had found his way back to England five years later, having escaped from a prisoner-of-war camp, the principal of Brasenose had offered him the chance to return to his old college and complete his degree. But by then he was a 25-year-old battle-scarred veteran, and felt the moment had passed, as it had for so many young men of his generation, Harry included. In any case, the opportunity to fight another battle had arisen, and he couldn't resist the challenge of sparring for a place on the green benches of the House of Commons. No regrets, thought Giles. Well, there were always some regrets.

He drove down Grange Road, took a right and parked his car in Sidgwick Avenue. He walked under an archway declaring Newnham College, founded in 1871, before women could be awarded degrees, by a far-sighted visionary who believed that would happen in his lifetime. It didn't.

Giles stopped at the lodge and was about to ask directions to Miss Barrington's party when the porter said, 'Good evening, Sir Giles, you'll be wanting the Sidgwick Room.'

Recognized. No turning back.

'If you walk on down the corridor, it's at the top of the stairs, third door on the left. You can't miss it.'

Giles followed his directions, passing a dozen or so undergraduates dressed in long black skirts, white blouses and academic gowns. They didn't give him a second look, but then why should they? He was thirty-three, almost twice their age.

He climbed the stairs, and when he reached the top step he didn't need further directions because he could hear exuberant voices and laughter long before he reached the third door on the left. He took a deep breath and tried not to make an entrance.

Jessica was the first to spot him, and immediately ran across the room shouting, 'Uncle Giles, Uncle Giles, where have you been?' Where indeed, thought Giles, as he looked at the young girl he adored, not quite a swan, but no longer a cygnet. She leapt up and threw her arms around him. He looked over her shoulder to see Grace and Emma heading towards him. All three of them tried to hug him at once. Other guests looked on, wondering what all the fuss was about.

'I'm so sorry,' said Giles, after he'd shaken hands with Harry. 'I should never have put you through all that.'

'Don't dwell on it,' said Harry. 'And frankly, both of us have been through far worse.'

Giles was surprised how quickly he relaxed with his oldest friend. They were chatting about Peter May as if it were old times, when he first saw her. After that, he couldn't take his eyes off her.

'The best cover drive I've ever seen,' Harry said, placing his left foot firmly forward while trying to give a demonstration without a bat. He hadn't noticed how distracted Giles had become.

'Yes, I was at Headingley when he scored a century against the South Africans in his first Test.'

'I saw that innings as well,' said an elderly don who had joined them. 'A quite magnificent knock.'

Giles slipped away, and wove his way around the crowded room, only stopping to chat to Sebastian about how he was getting on at school. The young man seemed far more relaxed and confident than he ever remembered him being.

Giles was beginning to fear she might leave before he got the chance to meet her, and when Sebastian became distracted by a sausage roll, he moved on until he found himself standing by her side. She was chatting to an older woman and didn't seem to be aware of him. He stood there, tongue-tied, wondering why Englishmen found it so difficult to introduce themselves to women, particularly beautiful women. How right Betjeman was, and this wasn't even a desert island.

'I don't think Schwarzkopf's got the range for the part,' the other woman was saying.

'You may be right, but I'd still give up half my annual grant just to hear her sing.'

The older woman glanced at Giles and turned to speak to someone else, almost as if she knew. Giles introduced himself, hoping no one else would join them. They shook hands. Just touching her . . .

'Hello. I'm Giles Barrington.'

'You must be Grace's brother, the MP I keep reading about who has all those radical views. I'm Gwyneth,' she said, revealing her ancestry.

'Are you an undergraduate?'

'You flatter me,' she said, giving him a smile. 'No, I'm just completing my PhD. Your sister is my supervisor.'

'What's your thesis on?'

'The links between mathematics and philosophy in Ancient Greece.'

'I can't wait to read it.'

'I'll see that you get an early copy.'

'Who's the girl Giles is chatting to?' Emma asked her sister.

Grace turned and looked across the room. 'Gwyneth Hughes, one of my brighter PhD students. He'll certainly find her something of a contrast to Lady Virginia. She's the daughter of a Welsh miner, up from the valleys, as she likes to remind everyone, and she certainly knows the meaning of *compos mentis*.'

'She's very attractive,' Emma said. 'You don't think—'

'Good heavens, no, what would they have in common?'

Emma smiled to herself, before saying, 'Have you handed over your eleven per cent of the company to Giles?'

'Yes,' said Grace, 'along with my rights to Grandfather's home in Smith Square, as I agreed with Mama, once I was convinced the silly boy was finally free of Virginia.'

Emma didn't speak for some time. 'So you always knew the contents of Mama's new will?'

'And what was in the envelope,' said Grace casually, 'which was why I couldn't attend the trial.'

'How well Mother knew you.'

'How well she knew all three of us,' said Grace as she looked across the room at her brother.

16

'CAN YOU SET the whole thing up?' asked Giles.

'Yes, sir, just leave it to me.'

'I'd like to get it over with as quickly as possible.'

'Of course, sir.'

'Such a sordid business. I only wish there was a more civilized way of doing these things.'

'It's the law that needs changing, Sir Giles, and frankly that's more your department than mine.'

Giles knew the man was right, and undoubtedly the law would change in time, but Virginia had made it clear she couldn't wait. After months of not making any contact with him, she'd rung him out of the blue to tell him why she wanted a divorce. She didn't need to spell out what was expected of him.

'Thank you, Bunny, I knew you could be relied on,' she'd said before putting the phone down.

'When will I hear from you?' Giles asked.

'By the end of the week,' the man replied, before downing his half pint. He rose, gave a slight bow and limped away.

◄○►

Giles was wearing a large red carnation in his buttonhole so she couldn't miss him. He glanced at every female under the age of thirty who walked in his direction. None of them even gave him a glance, until a prim young woman came to a halt by his side.

'Mr Brown?' she asked.

'Yes,' Giles replied.

'My name is Miss Holt. I'm from the agency.'

Without another word, she linked her arm in his and led him along the platform like a guide dog until they reached a first-class carriage. Once they had taken their seats opposite each other, Giles wasn't altogether sure what he was meant to do next. As it was a Friday evening, every other seat was taken long before the train pulled out of the station. Miss Holt didn't say a word on the entire journey.

When the train pulled into Brighton, she was among the first to get off. Giles handed two tickets to the collector at the barrier and followed her towards the taxi rank. It was clear to Giles that Miss Holt had done this several times before. It was only when they were seated in the back of the taxi that she spoke again, and not to him.

'Grand Hotel.'

On their arrival at the hotel, Giles checked in, registering as Mr and Mrs Brown.

'Room thirty-one, sir,' said the receptionist. He looked as if he was about to wink, but only smiled and said, 'Have a good night, sir.'

A porter carried their cases up to the third floor. It wasn't until after he'd collected his tip and left that she spoke again.

'My name is Angela Holt,' she said, sitting upright on the end of the bed.

Giles remained standing, and looked at a woman he couldn't have been less likely to spend a dirty weekend in Brighton with. 'Can you guide me through the procedure?' he asked.

'Certainly, Sir Giles,' said Miss Holt, as if he'd asked her to take dictation. 'At eight o'clock, we'll go downstairs and have dinner. I've booked a table in the centre of the room, in the hope that someone might recognize you. After dinner, we'll return to the bedroom. I will remain fully dressed at all times, but you can get undressed in the bathroom, where you will put on your pyjamas and dressing gown. At ten o'clock, I will go and sleep on the bed and you will sleep on the couch. At two a.m., you will phone down to the front desk and order a bottle of vintage champagne, half a pint of Guinness and a round of ham sandwiches. When the night porter delivers your order, you will say that you asked for Marmite and tomato sandwiches, and tell him to bring the correct order immediately. When he returns, you will thank him and give him a five-pound note.'

'Why such a large tip?' asked Giles.

'Because if this should come to court, the night porter will undoubtedly be called to give evidence, and we need to be sure he won't have forgotten you.'

'I understand.'

'In the morning, we will have breakfast together, and when you check out you must pay the bill by cheque, so it can be easily traced. As we leave the hotel, you will embrace me and kiss me several times. You will then get into a taxi and wave goodbye.'

'Why several times?'

'Because we need to be sure that your wife's private detective gets an easily identifiable photograph of us together. Do you have any further questions, Sir Giles, before we go down to dinner?'

'Yes, Miss Holt. May I ask how often you do this?'

'You are my third gentleman this week, and the agency has already booked me for a couple of jobs for next week.'

'This is madness. Our divorce laws are frankly barbaric. The government ought to draft new legislation as soon as possible.'

'I hope not,' said Miss Holt, 'because if you were to do that, Sir Giles, I'd be out of a job.'

ALEX FISHER

1954–1955

17

'I QUITE SIMPLY want to destroy him,' she said. 'Nothing less will satisfy me.'

'I can assure you, Lady Virginia, I'll do anything I can to assist.'

'That's good to know, major, because if we're going to work together, we'll need to trust each other. No secrets. However, I still have to be convinced you're the right man for the job. Tell me why you think you're so well qualified?'

'I think you'll find I'm over-qualified, my lady,' said Fisher. 'Barrington and I go back a long way.'

'Then start at the beginning and take me through every detail, however insignificant it might seem.'

'It all began when the three of us were at St Bede's prep school, and Barrington made friends with the docker's son.'

'Harry Clifton,' said Virginia, spitting out the words.

'Barrington should have been expelled from St Bede's.'

'Why?' asked Virginia.

'He was caught stealing from the tuck shop, but he got away with it.'

'How did he manage that?'

'His father, Sir Hugo, another criminal, wrote out a cheque for a thousand pounds, which made it possible for the school to build a new cricket pavilion. So the headmaster turned a blind eye, which made it possible for Barrington to go to Oxford.'

'Did you also go up to Oxford?'

'No, I joined the army. But our paths crossed again in Tobruk while we were serving in the same regiment.'

'Which is where he made a name for himself, winning the Military Cross and later escaping from a prisoner-of-war camp?'

'It should have been my MC,' said Fisher, his eyes narrowing. 'I was his commanding officer at the time and responsible for leading an attack on an enemy battery. After I sent the Germans packing, the colonel put me up for an MC, but Corporal Bates, a friend of Barrington's, refused to endorse my citation, so I was downgraded to mentioned in dispatches, and Barrington ended up getting my MC.'

This wasn't Giles's version of what had taken place that day, but Virginia knew which one she wanted to believe. 'Have you come across him since?'

'No. I stayed in the army, but once I realized he'd scuppered my chance of getting any further promotion, I took early retirement.'

'So what do you do now, major?'

'I'm a stockbroker by profession, as well as being on the board of Bristol Grammar School. I'm also on the executive committee of the local Conservative Association. I joined the party so I could play a role in making sure Barrington doesn't win at the next election.'

'Well, I'm going to make sure you play a leading role,' said Virginia, 'because the one thing that man cares most about is holding on to his seat in the House of Commons. He's convinced that if Labour wins the next election, Attlee will offer him a place in the Cabinet.'

'Over my dead body.'

'I don't think we'll have to go that far. After all, if he were to lose his seat at the next election, there's not much chance they'll readopt him, and that would probably mean the end of his political career.'

'Amen to that,' said Fisher. 'But I have to point out that although he doesn't have a large majority, he's still very popular in the constituency.'

'I wonder how popular he'll be after I've sued him for adultery.'

'He's already prepared the ground for that, telling everyone he had to go through a charade in Brighton to protect your reputation. He's even campaigning to have the divorce laws changed.'

'But how would his constituents react if they discovered that for the past year he's been having an affair with a student in Cambridge?'

'Once your divorce has gone through, no one will give a damn.'

'But if it hasn't been settled and I let it be known that I'm trying desperately for a reconciliation . . .'

'That would change the situation completely,' said Fisher. 'And you can rely on me to make sure that news of your sad predicament reaches the right ears.'

'Good. Now, it would help our long-term aims considerably if you were to become chairman of the Bristol Docklands Conservative Association.'

'I'd like nothing more. The only problem is that I can't afford to spend that amount of time on politics, while I have to earn a living.' Fisher tried not to sound embarrassed.

'You won't have to worry about that once you've joined the board of the Barrington Shipping group.'

'There's not much hope of that ever happening. Barrington would veto the appointment the moment my name was proposed.'

'He can't veto anything as long as I own seven and a half per cent of the company's stock.'

'I'm not sure I understand.'

'Then allow me to explain, major. For the past six months, I've been purchasing Barrington's shares through a blind trust, and I now own seven and a half per cent of the company. If you check their bylaws, you'll find that allows me to appoint a member of the board, and I can't think of anyone better qualified to represent me, major.'

'How do I begin to thank you?'

'It's very simple. In the short term you will devote your time to becoming chairman of the local Conservative Association. Once you've achieved that, your sole purpose will be to make sure the voters of Bristol Docklands remove their Member of Parliament at the next election.'

'And in the long term?'

'I have an idea that may tickle your fancy. But we can't even consider that until you become chairman of the association.'

'Then I'd better get back to Bristol and start working on it immediately. But before I do, there's something I'd like to ask you.'

'Of course,' said Virginia, 'ask me anything. After all, we're partners now.'

'Why did you choose me for this job?'

'Oh, that's simple, major. Giles once told me you were the only man he's ever detested.'

◄○►

'Gentlemen,' said Bill Hawkins, the chairman of the Conservative Association as he tapped his gavel on the table, 'if I might call the meeting to order. Perhaps I could begin by asking our honorary secretary, Major Fisher, to read the minutes of the last meeting.'

'Thank you, Mr Chairman. At the last meeting, held on the fourteenth of June 1954, the committee instructed me to write to Central Office in London and request a list of candidates who might be considered to represent the party in this constituency at the next general election. The official candidates list arrived a few days later, and I circulated a copy to members so they could consider the applicants at this evening's meeting.

'It was agreed that the summer fête would be held at Castle Combe this year, by kind permission of the Hon. Mrs Hartley-Booth JP. There followed a discussion on the price of raffle tickets, and a vote was taken, after which it was agreed they should be sixpence each, and six for half a crown. The treasurer,

Mr Maynard, then reported that the association's bank account was in credit to the tune of forty-seven pounds and twelve shillings. He said he had written a follow-up letter to all those members who had not yet paid their annual subscription. There being no other business, the meeting was closed at twelve minutes past ten.'

'Thank you, major,' said the chairman. 'Now let us move on to item two, namely the list of candidates recommended by Central Office. You have all had several days to consider the names, so I will throw the meeting open for a general discussion before we shortlist those candidates you feel should be invited for an interview.'

Fisher had already shown the list of candidates to Lady Virginia, and they had agreed on the person they thought would best serve their long-term purpose. Fisher sat back and listened carefully as his fellow committee members expressed their opinions as to the merits and shortcomings of each candidate. It quickly became clear that his choice was not the front-runner, but at least no one was opposed to him.

'Do you wish to offer an opinion, major, before I call for a vote?' Hawkins asked.

'Thank you, chairman. I agree with those members who feel that Mr Simpson, having fought so gallantly at Ebbw Vale during the last election, deserves to be interviewed, but I believe we should also consider Mr Dunnett. After all, his wife is a local girl, which is a considerable advantage, especially when you consider Sir Giles Barrington's current marital status.'

Several 'Hear, hears' echoed around the table.

Forty minutes later, Gregory Dunnett was among those on the shortlist, together with Mr Simpson, the former candidate for Ebbw Vale, plus a local councillor, no hope, a bachelor over the age of forty, no hope, and the statutory woman, absolutely no hope. All Fisher needed to do now was find a good reason for them not to select Mr Simpson.

As the meeting was drawing to a close, the chairman called for any other business.

'I have something to report to the committee,' Fisher said,

screwing the top back on his pen, 'but I think it would be wise for it not to be recorded in the minutes.'

'I'm sure you're the best judge of that, major,' said the chairman, glancing around the table to confirm that everyone else present was in agreement.

'When I was staying at my club in London last week,' said Fisher, 'I picked up some disturbing information from a reliable source, concerning Sir Giles Barrington.' He now had the full attention of the entire committee. 'As all of you will be aware, Sir Giles is currently facing divorce proceedings following the unfortunate breakdown of his marriage. Most of us felt some sympathy for him when he decided to take "the Brighton route", especially after he let it be known, rather ungraciously in my opinion, that he did so to protect his wife's reputation. We're all grown men, and are all well aware that the divorce laws badly need reforming. However, I have since discovered that we have only heard half the story. Sir Giles, it seems, is conducting an affair with a young student at Cambridge University, despite the fact that his wife has been trying hard to bring about a reconciliation.'

'Good God, the man's a cad,' said Bill Hawkins. 'He should be made to resign.'

'I couldn't agree more, Mr Chairman. Indeed, he would have had no choice, if he'd been the Conservative candidate.'

Mumbled conversations broke out around the table.

'I do hope,' continued Fisher after the chairman had banged his gavel several times, 'that I can rely on the committee to make sure this information does not go beyond this room.'

'Of course, of course,' said the chairman. 'That goes without saying.'

Fisher leant back, confident that within hours the story would have reached several well-placed members of the local Labour Party, which would guarantee that at least half the constituency would have heard about it by the end of the week.

After the chairman closed the meeting and members began to make their way across the street to the local pub, Peter

Maynard, the treasurer, sidled up to Alex and asked if he could have a quiet word.

'Of course, old chap,' said Alex. 'How can I help?'

'As you know, the chairman has made it clear on several occasions that he intends to stand down before the next general election.'

'I had heard that.'

'One or two of us feel it's a job for a younger man, and I've been asked to sound you out and see if you would allow your name to be put forward.'

'How kind of you, Peter. If the majority of my colleagues felt I was the right person for the job, I would of course consider taking on this onerous task, but not, you understand, if another member of the committee felt he could make a better fist of it.'

◂◦▸

When the first cheque from Barrington Shipping Co. for his services as a board member was cleared, Alex closed his account at the Midland Bank, and moved across the road to Barclays. It already administered the Barrington company account, as well as acting for the Conservative Association. And unlike the Midland, the manager agreed to allow him an overdraft facility.

The following day, he travelled up to London and opened an account with Gieves & Hawkes, where he was measured up for three new suits, a dinner jacket and an overcoat, all black. After lunch at the Army & Navy he dropped into Hilditch & Key and selected half a dozen shirts, along with two pairs of pyjamas, a dressing gown and a selection of silk ties. After signing the bill, he went on to John Lobb and spent some time being fitted for two pairs of shoes, both brogues: one black, one brown.

'They should be ready in about three months, major,' he was told.

During the next four weeks, he took out every member of the committee for lunch or dinner, at Virginia's expense, by the end of which he was confident that most of them would back Gregory Dunnett as their second choice for party candidate at the upcoming election, and one or two of them had him as their preferred choice.

Over an after-dinner brandy with Peter Maynard, Fisher discovered that the party treasurer was experiencing some temporary financial difficulties. He travelled up to London the following day and, after a discreet word with Lady Virginia, those temporary financial difficulties were removed. One of the committee was now in his debt.

18

ALEX HAD BEEN on the board of Barrington Shipping for just a few months when he spotted an opportunity he thought might appeal to Virginia.

During that time, he had assiduously attended every board meeting, read every report, and always voted with the majority, so no suspicion was ever raised about what he was really up to.

Virginia hadn't been in any doubt that Giles would be suspicious when Alex was appointed to the board. She even wondered if he would try to find out who owned the 7½ per cent of the company's stock Fisher represented. If he did, all he would discover was that it was held by a blind trust. But Giles was neither blind nor dumb, so he wouldn't have needed to put two and two together to make 7½.

Although the chairman assured him that the major seemed a decent enough chap, rarely opened his mouth at board meetings and certainly wasn't causing any trouble, Giles was not convinced. He didn't believe Fisher was capable of changing his spots. But with an imminent election on the cards, at which the Tories were expected to increase their majority, as well as the mystery as to why Virginia still hadn't signed her decree nisi papers despite her having begged him to give her grounds for divorce, Fisher was the least of his problems.

◄○►

'Gentlemen,' said the chairman of Barrington Shipping, 'I don't think it would be an exaggeration to suggest that the proposal

I'm making today might well prove to be a turning point in the history of the company. This bold new venture proposed by Mr Compton, our managing director, has my full backing, and I will be inviting the board to support a plan that the company build its first new passenger liner since the war, in an attempt to keep pace with our great rivals, Cunard and P&O. I would like to believe that our founder, Joshua Barrington, would have applauded such an initiative.'

Alex listened intently. He had come to respect Sir William Travers, who had replaced Hugo Barrington – not that anyone ever referred to the past chairman – as a shrewd and intelligent operator, regarded by both the industry and the city as a safe pair of hands.

'The capital outlay will unquestionably stretch our reserves,' continued Sir William, 'but our bankers are willing to support us, as our figures show that even if we are able to sell only 40 per cent of the cabin space on the new vessel, we would recoup our investment within five years. I'll be happy to answer any of the board's questions.'

'Do you think the public might still have the fate of the *Titanic* fixed indelibly in their subconscious, making them wary of sailing on a new luxury liner?' asked Fisher.

'That's a fair point, major,' replied Sir William, 'but Cunard's recent decision to add another vessel to their fleet would rather suggest that a new generation of travellers have noticed that there hasn't been a major shipping accident involving a luxury liner since that tragic disaster in 1912.'

'How long would it take for us to build this ship?'

'If the board gives the go-ahead, we would put the contract out to tender immediately, and hope to appoint specialist marine architects by the end of the year, with a view to the vessel being launched in three years' time.'

Alex waited for another member of the board to ask a question he didn't want to ask himself.

'What is the estimated cost?'

'It's hard to give an exact figure,' admitted Sir William, 'but

I have allowed for three million pounds in our budget. However, I would consider that to be an overestimate.'

'Let's hope so,' said another board member. 'And we'll need to inform the shareholders what we have in mind.'

'I agree,' said Sir William. 'I will do so at our AGM next month, at which I shall also be pointing out that our profit forecasts are most encouraging, and I can see no reason why we shouldn't pay our shareholders the same dividend as last year. Even so, the board must face the possibility that some of our shareholders may be wary of this change in direction, not to mention such a large capital outlay. This might well cause a fall in our share price. However, once the City realizes we have the resources to cover any short-term difficulties, it should only be a matter of time before our shares fully recover. Any more questions?'

'Have we settled on a name for the new passenger division of the company, and for its first ship?' asked Fisher.

'We're thinking of calling the new division the Palace Line, and its first liner the *Buckingham*, signalling the company's commitment to a new Elizabethan era.'

On that, the board were in full agreement.

◄○►

'Explain it to me once again,' said Virginia.

'Sir William will announce at the AGM next Thursday that Barrington's is going to build a luxury liner to rival anything Cunard and P&O currently have on the high seas, with an estimated cost of three million pounds.'

'That sounds like a rather bold and imaginative step to me.'

'And risky to others, because most investors on the stock market are neither bold nor imaginative, and will be anxious about the construction costs rising and the difficulty of selling enough cabin space to cover the capital expenditure. But if they were to check the accounts carefully, they'd see that Barrington's has more than enough cash to cover any short-term losses.'

'Then why are you recommending that I sell my shares?'

'Because if you were to buy them back within three weeks of selling them, you'd make a killing.'

'That's the bit I don't understand,' said Virginia.

'Allow me to explain,' said Alex. 'When you buy a share, you don't have to settle your account for twenty-one days. Equally, when you sell a share, you don't get paid for three weeks. For that twenty-one-day period you can trade without having to pay out any money, and because we have inside knowledge, we can take advantage of that situation.'

'So what are you suggesting?'

'Barrington's AGM will open at ten next Thursday morning with the chairman's annual report. Within a few hours, I anticipate the share price will fall from its present level of just over four pounds to around three pounds and ten shillings. If you were to sell your seven and a half per cent holding as soon as the market opens at nine o'clock that day, it would cause the price to fall even further, possibly below three pounds. Then you wait until the price has bottomed out before moving back in and repurchasing any stock available at the lower price, until you've replaced your seven and a half per cent.'

'Won't the brokers become suspicious, and tell the board what we're up to?'

'They're not going to say a word as long as they get a commission when they sell the stock and another one when they buy it back. They can't lose either way.'

'But can we?'

'Only if the share price rises after the chairman's annual report, because you'd have to pay more to buy your shares back. But frankly, that's unlikely to happen once the company announces that it's putting three million pounds of its reserves at risk.'

'So what do I do next?'

'If you give me the authority to act on your behalf, I'll place the business through a broker I know in Hong Kong so it can't be traced back to either of us.'

'Giles will work out what we're up to. He's no fool.'

'Not if three weeks later the records show that the owner-ship of your seven and a half per cent of the company hasn't changed. In any case, he has far more pressing problems to occupy himself with at the moment.'

'Such as?'

'I'm told he's facing a vote of confidence from the local Labour Party executive committee, after they found out about his relationship with Miss Gwyneth Hughes. There's even a chance he won't be contesting the next election. That's assum-ing you still haven't signed those divorce papers.'

—◆—

'Can you assure me, Major Fisher, that this investigation has no connection with Sir Giles Barrington or Mrs Harry Clifton, because I've represented both of them in the past, and that would create an unacceptable conflict of interest.'

'My enquiries have nothing to do with the Barrington family,' said Fisher. 'It's simply that the local Conservative Association has shortlisted two candidates to be their represent-ative for Bristol Docklands. As secretary of the association, I want to be absolutely sure there's nothing in their backgrounds that might embarrass the party at some future date.'

'Are you looking for anything in particular, major?'

'With your contacts in the force, I need you to find out if either of their names appears in police records.'

'Does that include parking fines or other non-custodial offences?'

'Anything that the Labour Party could use to its advantage during an election campaign.'

'I get the picture,' said Mitchell. 'How much time do I have?'

'The selection process will take a couple of months, possibly three, but I'll need to know if you come up with anything long before then,' said Fisher, passing over a piece of paper with two names on it.

Mitchell glanced at the two names before placing the piece of paper in his pocket. He left without another word.

◄○►

Fisher phoned a private number in Hong Kong at nine o'clock on the morning of Barrington's Annual General Meeting. When he heard a familiar voice come on the line, he said, 'Benny, it's the major.'

'How are you, major? Long time, no hear.'

'There's a reason,' said Fisher, 'and I'll explain everything when you're next in London, but right now I need you to carry out a sell order for me.'

'My pen is poised,' said Benny.

'I want you to sell two hundred thousand shares in Barrington Shipping at spot price the moment the London Stock Exchange opens.'

Benny whistled. 'Consider it done,' he said.

'And once you've completed the order, I want you to buy back the same number of shares during the next twenty-one days, but not until you think they've bottomed out.'

'Understood. Just one question, major. Should Benny be placing a little flutter on this particular horse?'

'That's up to you, but don't get greedy, because there's going to be a lot more where this came from.'

The major put down the phone, walked out of his club on Pall Mall and took a taxi to the Savoy. He joined his fellow directors in the hotel's conference room just a few minutes before the chairman rose to deliver his annual address to the shareholders of the Barrington Shipping Company.

19

THE CONSTITUTIONAL HALL on Davis Street was packed. Several party members had to stand in the aisle or at the back of the room. One or two were even perched on windowsills in the hope of getting a better view of proceedings.

Both of the candidates on the shortlist, Neville Simpson and Gregory Dunnett, had delivered powerful speeches, but Fisher felt that at that moment Simpson had the edge over his preferred candidate. Simpson, a London barrister, was a few years older than Dunnett, had a fine war record and had already contested an election against Aneurin Bevan in Ebbw Vale, where he'd increased the Tory share of the vote. But Mitchell had been able to supply Fisher with enough information to embarrass the man.

Simpson and Dunnett were seated on either side of the chairman on the stage, while the committee were in the front row. The news that Sir Giles Barrington had survived a vote of no confidence at a closed meeting of the local Labour Party earlier in the week had pleased Fisher, although he didn't admit his reason to anyone, other than Virginia. He planned to humiliate Barrington publicly, in the glare of a general election campaign, rather than in a dimly lit Labour Party committee room. But his plan couldn't work unless Dunnett became the Tory candidate, and that was still in the balance.

The chairman rose from his seat and smiled benignly down on the assembled gathering. He gave his trademark cough before addressing the faithful.

'Before I call for questions, I should like you to know that this will be my last meeting as chairman. I feel the association should go into the general election with both a new candidate and a new chairman, preferably someone a lot younger than me.' He paused for a moment, to see if anyone would try to talk him out of it, but as no one did, he reluctantly continued.

'We now enter the final stage of the meeting before we select the man who will fight our cause at the next election. Members will have the opportunity to put their questions directly to the two prospective candidates.'

A tall man leapt up at the back of the hall and began to speak even before Bill Hawkins had called on anyone.

'Mr Chairman, can I ask both candidates, if they were to win the seat, would they live in the constituency?'

Simpson was the first to respond. 'I would certainly buy a house in the constituency,' he said, 'but I would expect to live in the House of Commons.'

This comment received laughter and a smattering of applause.

'I took the liberty of visiting an estate agent last week,' countered Dunnett, 'not in the anticipation, but in the hope, that you will select me.'

The applause suggested to Fisher that the gathering was fairly evenly divided.

The chairman pointed to a woman in the third row, who never failed to ask a question whenever the association met, so he decided to get her out of the way early.

'As one of you is a successful barrister, and the other an insurance broker, will you have enough time to devote to this key marginal seat in the run-up to the election?'

'If I am selected, I won't be returning to London tonight,' said Dunnett. 'I will devote every hour I'm awake to winning this seat and making sure we remove Giles Barrington once and for all.'

This time the applause was prolonged, and Fisher relaxed for the first time.

'It's not how many hours you spend,' said Simpson, 'but

how you spend them that matters. I've already fought a general election against a doughty opponent, so I know what to expect. It is important that you select someone who can learn quickly, and can use that knowledge to defeat Giles Barrington and win this seat for the Conservative Party.'

Fisher was beginning to feel that Dunnett might need a helping hand if Simpson was to be derailed. The chairman gestured to a well-known local businessman.

'Who do you consider would be the right person to succeed Winston Churchill as leader of our party?'

'I didn't realize there was a vacancy,' said Simpson, which was greeted by laughter and further applause, before he added in a more serious tone, 'We would be foolish to think of replacing the greatest prime minister of this century without a damn good reason for doing so.'

The applause was deafening, and it was some time before Dunnett could make himself heard.

'I believe Mr Churchill has made it clear that when the time comes, his preferred choice to succeed him would be Sir Anthony Eden, our distinguished and much admired foreign secretary. If that's good enough for Mr Churchill, it's good enough for me.'

The applause was not quite as deafening.

Over the next thirty minutes, as questions continued to come thick and fast, Fisher felt that Simpson was consolidating his position as favourite. However, Fisher was confident that the last three questions would assist his candidate, not least because he'd planted two of them, and had arranged with the chairman that he would ask the final question himself.

Bill Hawkins looked at his watch.

'I think there's just enough time left for three more questions.' He pointed to a man at the back, who had been constantly trying to catch his eye. Fisher smiled.

'Would the two candidates care to give their views on the proposed new divorce laws?'

There was an audible gasp, followed by an expectant hush, as few people in the room doubted that this question was aimed at Sir Giles Barrington rather than either of the two candidates on the stage.

'I intensely dislike our antiquated divorce laws, which clearly need reforming,' said the barrister. 'I only hope the subject doesn't dominate the election campaign in this constituency, because I would prefer to beat Barrington on merit, and not to have to rely on rumour and innuendo.'

Fisher didn't find it difficult to understand why Central Office considered Simpson to be a future cabinet minister, but he also knew that this wasn't the answer the local members wanted to hear.

Dunnett quickly gauged the reaction of the audience, and said, 'While I agree with much of what Mr Simpson has just said, I feel the voters of Bristol Docklands have the right to know the truth about Barrington's domestic arrangements before they go to the ballot box, and not after.'

The first round of applause was clearly in favour of Dunnett.

The chairman pointed to Peter Maynard, who was seated in the middle of the front row.

'We in this constituency are looking for more than a Member of Parliament,' said Maynard, reading from a prepared script. 'Rather, we are looking for a partnership, a team. Can both candidates assure us that we will regularly see their wives in the constituency supporting them during the run-up to the general election, because we never see Lady Barrington from one year to the next.'

The first questioner to receive a round of applause.

'My wife is already by my side,' said Dunnett, gesturing towards an attractive young woman seated in the second row, 'as she will be throughout the campaign. In fact if I become your Member of Parliament, you'll probably see a lot more of Connie than you will of me.'

Fisher smiled. He knew the question played to Dunnett's strengths and, just as important, to Simpson's weakness. Mind you, when he had sent out the letters inviting them to attend the meeting, he had addressed one envelope to Mr and Mrs Dunnett, and the other simply to N. Simpson Esq.

'My wife is a lecturer at the London School of Economics,' said Simpson, 'but she would be free to visit the constituency most weekends and during the university holidays.' Fisher could feel the votes slipping away. 'And I'm sure you'll agree there can be no greater calling than teaching the next generation.'

The applause that followed suggested that one or two people didn't altogether agree that the LSE was the best way of doing it.

'And finally,' said the chairman, 'I know that our secretary, Major Fisher, has a question for both candidates.'

'I read in the *Daily Mail* this morning,' said Fisher, 'so it's possibly not true' – both candidates laughed dutifully – 'that the London constituency of Fulham Central has also selected its shortlist, and will be interviewing prospective candidates on Monday. I wondered if either of you are on that shortlist and, if you are, would you be willing to withdraw from that contest before we vote tonight?'

'I did not apply for Fulham Central,' said Dunnett, 'as I have always wanted to represent a seat in the West Country, where my wife was born and bred, and where we hope to raise a family.'

Fisher nodded. Simpson had to wait for the applause to die down.

'I am on the shortlist for Fulham Central, Major Fisher,' he began, 'and I would consider it to be discourteous to withdraw my name at such short notice without good reason. However, if I were fortunate enough to be selected tonight, I couldn't have a better reason to withdraw.'

Good recovery, thought Fisher as he listened to the applause that followed. But was it good enough?

The chairman rose from his place. 'I am sure you will all join me in thanking both candidates not only for giving up their valuable time to be with us tonight, but for making such splendid contributions. I have no doubt that both will become Members of Parliament, but unfortunately we can only select one of them.' Yet more applause. 'And so now we come to the vote. Let me explain how I intend to proceed. If members will kindly make their way to the front of the hall, our association secretary Major Fisher will issue you with ballot papers. After you have placed a cross beside the name of the candidate of your choice, please drop your voting slip into the ballot box. Once the count has been completed and the secretary and I have checked the papers, which shouldn't take long, I will announce which candidate has been chosen to represent the Conservative Party in Bristol Docklands at the forthcoming general election.'

The members formed an orderly queue while Fisher handed out just over 300 ballot papers. After the last vote had been cast, the chairman asked a steward to remove the ballot box and take it to a private room behind the stage.

When the chairman and the secretary entered the room a few minutes later, they found the ballot box on a table in the centre, guarded by the steward. They sat down on two wooden chairs placed opposite each other. The steward unlocked the ballot box before leaving the room, closing the door behind him.

Once he heard the door close, the chairman stood up, opened the box and tipped the voting slips out on to the table. As he sat back down he asked Fisher, 'How do you want to proceed?'

'I suggest you count Simpson's votes while I count Dunnett's.'

The chairman nodded, and they began sifting through the votes. It quickly became clear to Fisher that Simpson was likely to win by twenty or thirty votes. He realized he'd have to be patient, and wait for the right moment. That moment came when the chairman placed the ballot box on the floor and bent down to check inside and make sure he hadn't missed any of the voting slips. It only took him a few seconds, but it gave Fisher enough time to reach into a pocket of his jacket and discreetly remove a handful of votes he'd marked in favour of Dunnett earlier that afternoon, an action he'd practised several times in front of a mirror. He skilfully slipped the votes on to his own pile, not sure if they'd be enough.

'So,' said Fisher, looking up, 'how many votes for Simpson?'

'One hundred and sixty-eight,' replied the chairman. 'And how many for Dunnett?'

'One hundred and seventy-three.'

The chairman looked surprised.

'As it was so close, chairman, perhaps it would be wise to double check so there can be no reprisals later.'

'Couldn't agree with you more,' said the chairman. 'Shall we change places?'

They did so and began to count a second time.

A few minutes later the chairman said, 'Spot on, Fisher. One hundred and seventy-three for Dunnett.'

'And I agree with your figure, chairman. A hundred and sixty-eight for Simpson.'

'You know, I wouldn't have thought there were that many people in the room.'

'There were an awful lot standing at the back,' said Fisher. 'And several sitting in the aisles.'

'That must explain it,' said the chairman. 'But I don't mind telling you on the QT, old boy, that I voted for Simpson.'

'So did I,' said Fisher. 'But that's democracy for you.'

The chairman laughed. 'Well, I suppose we'd better be getting back and tell them the result before the natives become restless.'

'Perhaps it might be wise, chairman, to simply announce the winner, and not reveal how close the vote was? After all, we must now all get behind the candidate the association has selected. Of course, I'll record the exact figures when I write up the minutes.'

'Good thinking, Fisher.'

◄o►

'I'm sorry to ring you at such a late hour on a Sunday night, Lady Virginia, but something has arisen, and if we're to take advantage of it, I'll need your authority to act immediately.'

'This had better be good,' said a sleepy voice.

'I've just heard that Sir William Travers, the chairman of Barrington's—'

'I know who William Travers is.'

'—died of a heart attack a couple of hours ago.'

'Is that good news or bad news?' asked a voice that was suddenly awake.

'Unquestionably good, because the share price is certain to fall the moment the press gets wind of it, which is why I called, because we've only got a few hours' start.'

'I presume you want to sell my shares again?'

'Yes, I do. I'm sure I don't have to remind you that you made a handsome profit on the last occasion, as well as damaging the company's reputation.'

'But if I do sell again, is there any chance the shares might go up?'

'Shares only go one way when the chairman of a public company dies, Lady Virginia, especially when it's a heart attack.'

'Then go ahead, sell.'

20

GILES HAD PROMISED his sister that he'd be on time for the meeting. He skidded to a halt on the gravel outside the main building and parked his Jaguar next to Emma's Morris Traveller. He was pleased to see she was already there because, although they both owned 11 per cent of the company, Emma took a far greater interest in Barrington Shipping's affairs than he did, even more since she'd embarked on her degree course at Stanford with that double Pulitzer Prize-winner, whose name he could never remember.

'You'd remember Cyrus Feldman's name well enough if he had a vote in your constituency,' Emma had mocked.

He hadn't attempted to deny the charge.

Giles smiled as he jumped out of his car and spotted a group of children coming out of Old Jack's Pullman carriage. Badly neglected in his father's day, it had recently been returned to its former glory and become a museum in memory of the great man. School parties paid regular visits to see Old Jack's VC and be given a history lesson on the Boer War. How long would it be, he wondered, before they were giving history lessons on the Second World War?

As he ran towards the building, he wondered why Emma had felt it was so important to meet the new chairman tonight, when the general election was almost upon them.

Giles didn't know a lot about Ross Buchanan, other than what he'd read about him in the *Financial Times*. After Fettes he'd studied economics at Edinburgh University and then joined P&O as a graduate trainee. He'd worked his way up from the ground floor to win a place on the board, before being appointed deputy chairman. He'd been tipped for chairman, but was denied the post when a member of the family decided they wanted the position.

When Buchanan accepted the Barrington board's invitation to succeed Sir William Travers, the company's shares rose five shillings on the announcement of his appointment, and within months they'd returned to the level they'd reached before Sir William's death.

Giles glanced at his watch, not just because he was a few minutes late, but because he had three more meetings that evening, including one with the dockers' union, who didn't appreciate being kept waiting. Despite his campaigning for a forty-eight-hour week and two weeks' guaranteed holiday on full pay for every union member, they remained suspicious of their Member of Parliament and his association with the shipping company that bore his name, even though this would be the first time he'd entered the building for over a year.

He noticed that the exterior had been given a lot more than a fresh lick of paint, and as he pushed through the door he stepped on to a thick blue and gold carpet that bore the new Palace Line crest. He stepped into a lift and pressed the button for the top floor, and for once it didn't feel as if it was being laboriously hauled up by reluctant galley slaves. As he stepped out, his first thought was of his grandfather, a revered chairman who had dragged the company into the twentieth century, before taking it public. But then his thoughts inevitably turned to his father, who had nearly brought the company to its knees in half the time. But his worst recollection, and one of the main reasons he avoided the building, was that this was where his father had been killed. The only good thing to come out of that dreadful incident was Jessica, the Berthe Morisot of the lower fourth.

Giles was the first Barrington not to become chairman of the board, but then he'd wanted to go into politics ever since he'd met Winston Churchill when he'd presented the prizes at Bristol Grammar School and Giles had been school captain. But it was his close friend Corporal Bates, killed while attempting to escape the Germans, who'd unwittingly turned him from blue to red.

He dashed into the chairman's office and gave his sister a huge hug before shaking hands with Ray Compton, who'd been the company's managing director for as long as he could remember.

The first thing that struck him as he shook hands with Ross Buchanan was how much younger he looked than his fifty-two years. But then he recalled the *Financial Times* pointing out that Buchanan didn't smoke or drink, played squash three times a week, turned the lights out at 10.30 p.m. and rose at 6 o'clock every morning. Not a regime that would suit a politician.

'It's a pleasure to meet you at last, Sir Giles,' said Buchanan.

'The dock workers call me Giles, so perhaps the management should as well.'

The laughter broke any slight tension that Giles's political antennae had picked up. He had assumed this was a casual get-together so he could finally meet Buchanan, but from the looks on their faces, something far more serious was on the agenda.

'This doesn't look good,' said Giles as he slumped into a seat next to Emma.

'I'm afraid it isn't,' said Buchanan, 'and I wouldn't have bothered you so close to the election if I hadn't thought you ought to be briefed immediately. I'll get straight to the point. You may have noticed that the company's share price fell quite dramatically following my predecessor's death.'

'Yes, I did,' said Giles. 'But I assumed there was nothing unusual in that.'

'In normal circumstances you'd be right, but what was unusual was how quickly the shares fell, and how far.'

'But they seem to have fully recovered since you took over.'

'They have,' said the chairman, 'but I don't think I was the sole reason for that. And I wondered if there could be another explanation for the inexplicable downturn in the company's share price after Sir William's death, especially after Ray brought to my attention that it wasn't the first time it had happened.'

'That's correct, chairman,' said Compton. 'The shares dropped just as suddenly when we announced our decision to go into the passenger liner business.'

'But if I remember correctly,' said Emma, 'they also returned to a new high.'

'They did indeed,' said Buchanan. 'But it took several months before they fully recovered, and it didn't do the company's reputation any good. While one can accept such an anomaly once, when it happens a second time, one starts to wonder if a pattern is emerging. I don't have the time to be continually looking over my shoulder, wondering when it might happen again.' Buchanan ran a hand through his thick, sandy hair. 'I'm running a public company, not a casino.'

'You're going to tell me that both these incidents took place after Alex Fisher joined the board.'

'You know Major Fisher?'

'That's far too involved a story to bore you with right now, Ross. That is, if I'm going to make the dock workers' meeting before midnight.'

'All the indications do seem to point in Fisher's direction,' said Buchanan. 'On both occasions a trade of two hundred thousand shares was executed, which happens to be almost exactly the seven and a half per cent of the company he represents. The first was just hours before the AGM at which we announced our change of policy, and the second immediately followed Sir William's untimely death.'

'It's too much of a coincidence,' said Emma.

'It gets worse,' said Buchanan. 'On each occasion, during the three-week window, after the share price had fallen so precipitously, the broker who sold them repurchased exactly the same amount, making his client a handsome profit.'

'And you think that client was Fisher?' asked Emma.

'No, it's too large a sum for him,' said Giles.

'I'm sure you're right,' said Buchanan. 'He must have been acting on behalf of someone else.'

'Lady Virginia Barrington would be my guess,' said Giles.

'That had crossed my mind,' admitted Buchanan, 'but I can prove that Fisher was behind it.'

'How?'

'I had the stock exchange records for both three-week periods checked,' said Compton, 'and both sales came out of Hong Kong, through a dealer called Benny Driscoll. It didn't take a lot of research to discover that not so long ago Driscoll left Dublin only a few hours ahead of the Garda, and he certainly won't be returning to the Emerald Isle in the near future.'

'It's thanks to your sister that we were able to get to the bottom of it,' said Buchanan. Giles looked at Emma in surprise. 'She recommended that we employ a Mr Derek Mitchell, who had assisted her in the past. Mr Mitchell flew to Hong Kong at our request, and once he located the one bar on the island that serves Guinness, it took him about a week and several emptied crates to find out the name of Benny Driscoll's biggest client.'

'So at last we can remove Fisher from the board,' said Giles.

'I wish it were that easy,' said Buchanan. 'He has the right to a place on the board, as long as he represents seven and a half per cent of the company's stock. And the only proof we have of his duplicity is a drunken stockbroker living in Hong Kong.'

'Does that mean there's nothing we can do?'

'Far from it,' said Buchanan. 'That's the reason I needed to see you and Mrs Clifton urgently. I believe the time has come to play Major Fisher at his own game.'

'Count me in.'

'I'd like to hear what you have in mind before I make a decision,' said Emma.

'Of course.' Buchanan opened a file in front of him. 'Between the two of you, you own twenty-two per cent of the company's stock. That makes you by far the largest shareholders, and I wouldn't consider going ahead with any plan without your blessing.'

'We have no doubt,' chipped in Ray Compton, 'that Lady Virginia's long-term aim is to cripple the company, making regular raids on our stock position until we lose all credibility.'

'And you think she'd do that simply to get back at me?' said Giles.

'As long as she's got someone on the inside, she knows exactly when to strike,' said Buchanan, avoiding Giles's question.

'But doesn't she risk losing a great deal of money using these tactics?' asked Emma.

'Virginia won't give a damn about that,' said Giles. 'If she could destroy the company and me along with it, she'd be more than satisfied, as my mother worked out long before I did.'

'What makes matters worse,' said the chairman, 'is that we estimate that her two previous raids on our stock have shown her a profit of over seventy thousand pounds. That's why we've got to move now, before she strikes again.'

'What do you have in mind?' asked Emma.

'Let us assume,' said Compton, 'that Fisher is just waiting for another piece of bad news so he can repeat the whole exercise again.'

'And if we were to supply him with it . . .' said Buchanan.

'But how does that help us?' said Emma.

'Because this time it would be our turn to be the insider traders,' said Compton.

'When Driscoll puts Lady Virginia's seven and a half per cent on the market, we'll buy it immediately, and the share price will go up, not down.'

'But that could cost us a fortune,' said Emma.

'Not if we feed Fisher the wrong information,' said Buchanan. 'With your blessing, I'm going to try to convince him that the company is facing a financial crisis that might threaten its very existence. I'll let him know we won't be declaring a profit this year due to the cost of building the *Buckingham*, which is already running twenty per cent over budget, so it won't be possible to offer our shareholders a dividend.'

'If you do that,' said Emma, 'you're assuming he'll advise Virginia to sell her stock, with the intention of buying it all back at a lower price during the three-week trading period.'

'Exactly. But if the share price were to rise during those three weeks,' continued Ray, 'Lady Virginia might be unwilling to buy her seven and a half per cent back, in which case Fisher would lose his place on the board, and we'd be rid of both of them.'

'How much are you going to need to make this happen?' asked Giles.

'I'm confident,' said Buchanan, 'if I had a war chest of half a million pounds, I could keep them at bay.'

'And the timing?'

'I'll deliver the bad news in confidence at the next board meeting, pointing out that the shareholders will have to be informed at the AGM.'

'When is the AGM?'

'That's where I need your advice, Sir Giles. Do you have any idea when the general election will be called?'

'The smart money's on May twenty-sixth, and that's certainly the date I'm planning on.'

'When will we know for certain?' asked Buchanan.

'There's usually about a month's warning before Parliament is prorogued.'

'Good, then I'll call the board meeting for –' he turned some pages in his diary – 'April eighteenth, and schedule the AGM for May fifth.'

'Why would you want to hold the AGM in the middle of an election campaign?' asked Emma.

'Because it's the one time I can guarantee that a constituency chairman will not be able to attend.'

'Chairman?' queried Giles, showing far more interest.

'You clearly haven't read the evening paper,' said Ray Compton, handing him a copy of the *Bristol Evening Post*.

Giles read the headline: *Former Tobruk hero becomes Bristol Docklands Conservative Chairman. Major Alex Fisher was unanimously voted . . .*

'What's that man up to?' he said.

'He assumes you're going to lose the election, and wants to be chairman when—'

'If that was true, he would have backed Neville Simpson and not Greg Dunnett to be the Conservative candidate, because Simpson would have proved a far more formidable opponent. He's up to something.'

'What would you like us to do, Mr Buchanan?' asked Emma, remembering why the chairman had asked to see her and Giles in the first place.

'I need your authority to buy every share that comes on to the market on May fifth, and to keep on buying for the following three weeks.'

'How much could we lose?'

'I'm afraid it might be as much as twenty to thirty thousand pounds. But at least this time we've chosen the date of the battle, and the battlefield, so you should break even at worst, and you might possibly make a bob or two.'

'If it means replacing Fisher on the board,' said Giles, 'as well as spiking Virginia's guns, thirty thousand pounds would be a cheap price to pay.'

'While we're on the subject of replacing Fisher as a board member . . .'

'I'm not available,' said Giles, 'even if I do lose my seat at the election.'

'I wasn't thinking of you, Sir Giles. I was rather hoping Mrs Clifton might agree to become a member of the board.'

◄o►

'The prime minister, Sir Anthony Eden, visited Buckingham Palace at four o'clock this afternoon, for an audience with Her Majesty The Queen. Sir Anthony asked Her Majesty's permission to dissolve Parliament in order that a General Election could be held on May 26th. Her Majesty graciously agreed to his request.'

'Just as you predicted,' said Virginia as she switched off the radio. 'When do you intend to tell the unfortunate Mr Dunnett what you have in mind for him?'

'Timing is everything,' said Fisher. 'I thought I'd wait until Sunday afternoon before I asked him to come and see me.'

'Why Sunday afternoon?'

'I don't want any other members of the committee to be around at the time.'

'Machiavelli would have been proud to have you as chairman of his committee,' said Virginia.

'Machiavelli didn't believe in committees.'

Virginia laughed. 'And when do you plan to ring our friend in Hong Kong?'

'I'll call Benny the night before the AGM. It's important that he places the sell order the moment Buchanan rises to address the meeting.'

Virginia took a Passing Cloud out of her cigarette case, sat back, and waited for the major to strike a match. She inhaled a couple of times before she said, 'Don't you think it's a coincidence, major, that everything is falling so neatly into place on the same day?'

21

'DUNNETT, IT'S GOOD of you to drop in at such short notice, especially on a Sunday afternoon.'

'My pleasure, Mr Chairman. I know you'll be pleased to hear how well our canvassing is going. The early returns suggest we should win the seat by over a thousand votes.'

'Let's hope you're right, Dunnett, for the party's sake, because I'm afraid my news is not so good. You'd better have a seat.'

The cheerful smile on the candidate's face was replaced with a quizzical look. 'What's the problem, Mr Chairman?' he asked as he sat down in the chair opposite Fisher.

'I think you know only too well what the problem is.'

Dunnett began biting his lower lip as he stared at the chairman.

'When you applied for this seat and supplied the committee with your CV,' continued Fisher, 'it appears you weren't entirely frank with us.' Fisher had only ever seen a man turn that white on the battlefield. 'You'll recall that you were asked to state what role you played during the war.' Fisher picked up Dunnett's CV from his desk and read out loud: 'Because of an injury sustained on the rugby field, I had no choice but to serve in the Royal Ambulance Corps.'

Dunnett slumped in his chair, like a marionette that had had its strings cut.

'I have recently discovered that this statement was at best misleading, and at worst duplicitous.' Dunnett closed his eyes.

'The truth is that you were a conscientious objector, and served six months in prison. It was only after being released that you joined the ambulance service.'

'But that was more than ten years ago,' said Dunnett desperately. 'There's no reason that anyone else should find out.'

'I wish that were the case, Dunnett, but sadly we've had a letter from someone who served in Parkhurst with you,' said Fisher, holding up an envelope that contained nothing more than a gas bill. 'If I were to go along with this deception, Dunnett, I would be condoning your dishonesty. And if the truth came out during the campaign or, even worse, when you were a Member of Parliament, I would have to admit to my colleagues that I already knew about it, and they would rightly call for my resignation.'

'But I can still win this election, if only you'll back me.'

'And Barrington would win by a landslide if the Labour Party got to hear of this. Don't forget that he not only won an MC, but escaped from a German prisoner-of-war camp.'

Dunnett bowed his head and began to weep.

'Pull yourself together, Dunnett, and behave like a gentleman. There's still an honourable way out.'

Dunnett looked up, and for a moment an expression of hope flickered across his face. Fisher pushed a blank sheet of the constituency's headed notepaper across to Dunnett, and took the top off his fountain pen.

'Why don't we work on this together?' he said as he handed the pen to him.

'Dear Mr Chairman,' dictated Fisher, as Dunnett reluctantly began to write. 'It is with great regret that I find it necessary to tender my resignation as the Conservative Party candidate at the forthcoming general election –' Fisher paused before adding – 'for health reasons.'

Dunnett looked up.

'Does your wife know you were a conscientious objector?'

Dunnett shook his head.

'Then let's keep it that way, shall we?' Fisher gave him an

understanding smile before continuing. 'I would like to say how sorry I am to have caused the committee this inconvenience so close to the election –' Fisher paused again, and watched as Dunnett's trembling hand stuttered across the page – 'and wish whoever is fortunate enough to take my place the best of luck. Yours sincerely . . .' He didn't speak again until Dunnett had written his signature at the bottom of the page.

Fisher picked up the letter and checked the text carefully. Satisfied, he slipped it into an envelope and pushed it back across the table.

'Just address it "The Chairman, private and personal".'

Dunnett obeyed, having accepted his fate.

'I'm so sorry, Dunnett,' said Fisher as he screwed the top back on his pen. 'I really do feel for you.' He placed the envelope in the top drawer of his desk, which he then locked. 'But chin up, old fellow.' He rose from his chair and took Dunnett by the elbow. 'I'm sure you'll realize I've always had your best interests at heart,' he added as he led him slowly to the door. 'It might be wise if you were to leave the constituency as quickly as possible. Wouldn't want some nosy journalist to get his hands on the story, would we?'

Dunnett looked horrified.

'And before you ask, Greg, you can rely on my discretion.'

'Thank you, Mr Chairman,' said Dunnett as the door closed.

Fisher returned to his office, picked up the phone on his desk and dialled a number that was written on the pad in front of him.

'Peter, it's Alex Fisher. Sorry to bother you on a Sunday afternoon, but a problem has arisen that I need to discuss with you urgently. I wonder if you're free to join me for dinner?'

◄○►

'Gentlemen, it is with considerable regret that I have to inform you that yesterday afternoon I had a visit from Gregory Dunnett, who sadly felt he had to tender his resignation as our parliamentary candidate, which is why I called this emergency meeting.'

Almost every member of the executive committee started talking at the same time. The word that kept being repeated was, why?

Fisher waited patiently for order to be restored before he answered that question. 'Dunnett confessed to me that he misled the committee when he suggested he had served with the Royal Ambulance Corps during the war, when in fact he had been a conscientious objector who served a six-month prison sentence. He got wind that one of his fellow inmates at Parkhurst had been approached by the press, which he felt left him with no option but to resign.'

The second outburst of opinions and questions was even more vociferous, but once again Fisher bided his time. He could afford to. He'd written the script and knew what was on the next page.

'I felt I was left with no choice but to accept his resignation on your behalf, and we agreed that he should leave the constituency as quickly as possible. I hope you won't feel I was too lenient on the young man.'

'How can we possibly find another candidate at such short notice?' asked Peter Maynard, bang on cue.

'That was also my first reaction,' said Fisher, 'so I immediately phoned Central Office to seek their guidance, but there were not many people at their desks on a Sunday afternoon. However, I did discover one thing when I spoke to their legal department, which you may feel is significant. Should we fail to adopt a candidate before May the twelfth, next Thursday, under electoral law we will be disqualified from taking any part in the election, which would guarantee Barrington a landslide victory, as his only opponent would be the Liberal candidate.'

The noise around the table reached fever pitch, but Fisher had never doubted it would. Once a semblance of order had returned, he continued. 'My next call was to Neville Simpson.'

A few hopeful smiles appeared among the committee members.

'But sadly he's been snapped up by Fulham Central, and has already signed his adoption papers. I then scoured the original list sent to us by Central Office, only to find that the better candidates have already secured a seat, and those who are still available would, frankly, be eaten alive by Barrington. So, I'm in your hands, gentlemen.'

Several hands shot up and Fisher selected Peter Maynard, as if he'd been the first person to catch his eye.

'This is a sad day for the party, Mr Chairman, but I don't feel anyone could have handled this delicate situation better than you have done.'

A general murmur of approval swept around the table.

'It's kind of you to say so, Peter. I simply did what I felt was best for the association.'

'And I can only speak for myself, Mr Chairman,' continued Maynard, 'when I say that, given the problem we find ourselves with, is it at all possible that you could be prevailed upon to step into the breach?'

'No, no,' said Fisher, waving a Cassius-like hand. 'I'm sure you'll be able to find someone far better qualified than me to represent you.'

'But no one knows the constituency, or for that matter our opponent, better than you, Mr Chairman.'

Fisher allowed several similar sentiments to be aired, before the party secretary said, 'I agree with Peter. We certainly can't afford to waste any more time. The longer we procrastinate, the happier Barrington will be.'

After Fisher felt confident that this opinion seemed to be accepted by the majority of the committee, he bowed his head, a sign for Maynard to stand up and say, 'I propose that Major Alex Fisher be invited to stand as the Conservative prospective parliamentary candidate for the Bristol Docklands division.'

Fisher raised an eye to see if anyone would second the proposal. The secretary obliged.

'Those in favour,' said Maynard. Several hands around the table shot up. Maynard waited until the last reluctant hand finally joined the majority, before saying, 'I declare the motion carried unanimously.' The announcement was followed by loud applause.

'I am quite overwhelmed, gentlemen,' said Fisher, 'and I accept the confidence you have shown in me with humility, because as you all know, I have always put the party first, and this is the last outcome I could have envisaged. However, you can be assured,' he continued, 'that I will do everything in my power to defeat Giles Barrington at the election, and return a Conservative to the House of Commons to represent Bristol Docklands' – a speech he had rehearsed several times, as he knew he wouldn't be able to refer to any notes.

The committee shot out of their seats and began applauding loudly. Fisher bowed his head and smiled. He would call Virginia as soon as he got home, and tell her that the small payment she'd authorized for Mitchell to discover if any of the candidates had something in their backgrounds that might embarrass the party had proved a more than worthwhile investment. Fisher now felt confident that he could humiliate Barrington, and this time it would be on the battlefield.

◄o►

'Benny, it's Major Fisher.'

'Always good to hear from you, major, especially as a little bird tells me that congratulations are in order.'

'Thank you,' said Fisher, 'but that's not why I'm phoning.'

'My pen is poised, major.'

'I want you to carry out the same transaction as before, but this time there's no reason why you shouldn't have a little flutter yourself.'

'You must be very sure of yourself, major,' said Benny. When he received no reply, he added, 'So that's a sell order for two hundred thousand Barrington's shares.'

'Confirmed,' said Fisher. 'But once again, the timing is vital.'

'Just tell me when you want to place the order, major.'

'On May the fifth, the day of Barrington's AGM. But it's important the transaction is settled before ten o'clock that morning.'

'Consider it done.' After a moment's pause, Benny added,

'So the whole transaction will be completed by the day of the election?'

'That's right.'

'What an ideal day for killing two birds with one stone.'

GILES BARRINGTON

1955

22

It was just after midnight when the phone rang. Giles knew there was only one person who'd dare to call him at that hour.

'Don't you ever go to bed, Griff?'

'Not when the Conservative candidate resigns halfway through an election campaign,' replied his agent.

'What are you talking about?' said Giles, suddenly wide awake.

'Greg Dunnett has resigned, stating health reasons. But there has to be a lot more to it than that, since Fisher has taken his place. Try to get some sleep, as I need you in the office by seven so we can decide how to play this. Frankly, as the Americans would say, it's a whole different ball game.'

But Giles didn't sleep. He'd thought for some time that Fisher was up to something, and now he knew what it was. He must have planned to be the candidate from the start. Dunnett was nothing more than a sacrificial lamb.

Giles had already accepted that as he was defending a majority of only 414, and the polls were predicting that the Tories would increase their number of seats, he had a real fight on his hands. And now he was up against someone he knew was willing to send men to their graves if he thought it would help him survive. Gregory Dunnett was his latest victim.

◄○►

Harry and Emma turned up at Barrington Hall the following morning. They found Giles having breakfast.

'No more lunches or dinners for the next three weeks,' said Giles as he buttered another piece of toast. 'Just wearing out shoe leather on hard pavements, and shaking hands with countless constituents. And make sure you two stay out of the way. I don't need anyone to be reminded that my sister and brother-in-law are staunch Tories.'

'We'll also be out there, working for a cause we believe in,' said Emma.

'That's all I need.'

'As soon as we heard Fisher was standing for the Conservatives, we decided to become fully paid-up members of the Labour Party,' said Harry. 'We even sent a donation to your fighting fund.'

Giles stopped eating.

'And for the next three weeks, we intend to work night and day for you, right up to the moment the polls close, if it will help ensure Fisher doesn't win.'

'But,' said Emma, 'there are one or two conditions before we agree to ditch our long-held principles and support you.'

'I knew there had to be a catch,' said Giles, pouring himself a large black coffee.

'You'll come and live with us in the Manor House for the rest of the campaign. Otherwise, with only Griff Haskins to take care of you, you'll end up eating fish and chips, drinking far too much beer, and sleeping on the floor of the constituency office.'

'You're probably right. But I warn you, I'll never be home before midnight.'

'That's fine. Just make sure you don't wake Jessica.'

'Agreed.' Giles stood up, a piece of toast in one hand, a newspaper in the other. 'See you this evening.'

'Don't leave the table until you've finished eating,' said Emma, sounding exactly like their mother.

Giles laughed. 'Mama never had to fight an election,' he reminded his sister.

'She'd have made a damn good MP,' said Harry.

'That's something we can all agree on,' said Giles as he dashed out of the room, still clutching the toast.

He had a quick word with Denby before running out of the house, where he found Harry and Emma sitting in the back of his Jaguar.

'What are you two doing?' he asked, as he climbed behind the wheel of his car and turned on the ignition.

'We're off to work,' said Emma. 'We need a lift if we're going to sign up as volunteers.'

'You do realize,' said Giles as he drove out on to the main road, 'it's an eighteen-hour day, and you're not paid.'

When they followed Giles into his constituency headquarters twenty minutes later, Emma and Harry were impressed by how many volunteers of all ages, shapes and sizes were bustling about in every direction. Giles hurried them through to his agent's office and introduced them to Griff Haskins.

'Two more volunteers,' he said.

'Some very strange people have been joining our cause since Alex Fisher became the Tory candidate. Welcome aboard, Mr and Mrs Clifton. Now, have either of you ever canvassed before?'

'No, never,' admitted Harry. 'Not even for the Tories.'

'Then follow me,' said Griff, leading them back into the main room. He stopped in front of a long trestle table laid out with rows of clipboards. 'Each one of these represents a street or road in the constituency,' he explained, handing each of them a clipboard and a set of red, green and blue pencils.

'It's your lucky day,' continued Griff. 'You've got the Woodbine estate, which is one of our strongholds. Let me explain the ground rules. When you knock on a door at this time of day, you're more likely to get the wife answering, because her husband will be at work. If a man opens the door, he's probably out of work, and therefore more likely to vote Labour. But whoever answers, all you have to say is, "Good morning, I'm here on behalf of Giles Barrington" – never Sir Giles – "the Labour Party candidate for the election on Thursday twenty-sixth May" – always emphasize the date – "and I hope you'll be supporting him." Now comes the bit where you have to use your nous. If they say, "I've been a Labour supporter all my life, you can rely on me," you mark their name with the red pencil. If they're elderly, you ask them if they'll need a car to take them to the polling station on the day. If they say yes, write "car" next to their name. If they say, "I've supported the Labour Party in the past, but I'm not sure this time," you mark them green, undecided, and the local councillor will call on them in the next few days. If they tell you they never discuss their politics, or that they'll have to think about it, or they haven't made up their mind, or any variation on those themes, they're Tories, so mark them with the blue pencil, and don't waste any more time on them. Have you understood so far?'

They both nodded.

'These canvassing returns are vital,' continued Griff, 'because on Election Day we'll revisit all the reds, to make sure they've voted. If they haven't, we knock them up again to remind them to go to the polling station. If you're in any doubt about someone's voting intentions, mark them green, for undecided, because the last thing we want to do is remind people to vote, or even worse, give them a lift to the polling station, if they're going to support the other side.'

A young volunteer ran up and handed Griff a piece of paper. 'What should I do about this one?' he asked.

Griff read the message and said, 'Tell him to bugger off. He's a well-known Tory who's just trying to waste your time. By the way,' he said turning back to Harry and Emma, 'if anyone keeps you on the doorstep for more than sixty seconds, saying they need to be convinced, or want to discuss Labour Party policy in greater detail or would like to know more about the candidate, they're also Tories trying to waste your time. Bid them good morning and move on. Good luck. Report back to me when you've completed a full canvass.'

◄○►

'Good morning, my name is Ross Buchanan, and I'm chairman of the Barrington Shipping Group. I would like to welcome you all to the company's Annual General Meeting. You will have found on your chairs a copy of the company's annual report. I would like to draw your attention to a few highlights. This year the annual profits have risen from £108,000 to £122,000, an improvement of twelve per cent. We have appointed architects to design our first luxury liner, and expect them to present their recommendations within the next six months.

'Let me assure all our shareholders that we will not go ahead with this project until we are convinced it is a viable proposition. With that in mind I am happy to announce that we will be increasing our shareholders' dividend this year to five per cent. I have no reason to believe that the company's growth will not be sustained, or even improved on, during the coming year.'

A round of applause allowed Buchanan to turn a page of his speech and check what he would be saying next. When he looked up, he noticed a couple of financial journalists scurrying out of the room to make sure they caught the first editions of their evening papers, aware that the chairman had already highlighted the main points, and would now take shareholders slowly through the details.

After Buchanan had come to the end of his speech, he and Ray Compton took questions for forty minutes. When the meeting finally came to a close, the chairman noted with some satisfaction that most of the chattering shareholders were leaving with smiles on their faces.

As Buchanan left the stage of the hotel's conference room, his secretary rushed up and said, 'You have an urgent call from Hong Kong, and the hotel operator is waiting to put it through to your room.'

◄○►

When Harry and Emma arrived back at Labour Party HQ, having completed their first canvass returns, they were exhausted.

'How did you get on?' asked Griff, checking their clipboards with a professional eye.

'Not bad,' said Harry. 'If the Woodbine estate is anything to go by, we're home and dry.'

'I wish,' said Griff. 'That estate should be rock-solid Labour, but tomorrow I'll let you loose on Arcadia Avenue, and then you'll really find out what we're up against. Before you go home, put your best reply of the day up on the notice board. The winner gets a box of Cadbury's Milk Tray.'

Emma grinned. 'One woman said to me, "My husband votes Tory, but I always support Sir Giles. Whatever you do, please don't let him know."'

Griff smiled. 'That's not uncommon,' he said. 'And, Emma, don't forget, your most important job is to make sure the candidate is fed and gets a good night's sleep.'

'And what about me?' said Harry, as Giles came bouncing into the room.

'I'm not interested in you,' Griff replied. 'It's not your name on the ballot paper.'

'How many meetings have I got this evening?' was Giles's first question.

'Three,' said Griff, without needing to refer to any notes. 'Hammond Street YMCA, seven o'clock, the Cannon Road snooker club at eight, and the Working Men's Club at nine. Make sure you're not late for any of them, and that you're safely tucked up in bed before midnight.'

'I wonder when Griff goes to bed,' said Emma after he had hurried off to deal with the latest crisis.

'He doesn't,' whispered Giles. 'He's a vampire.'

◄◦►

When Ross Buchanan walked into his hotel room, the phone was ringing. He strode across and grabbed the handset.

'Your call from Hong Kong is on the line, sir.'

'Good afternoon, Mr Buchanan,' said a Scottish voice down the crackling line. 'It's Sandy McBride. I thought I'd ring and let you know that it all happened just as you predicted, in fact almost to the minute.'

'And the name of the broker?'

'Benny Driscoll.'

'No surprises there,' said Buchanan. 'Fill me in on the details.'

'Within moments of the London Stock Exchange opening,

a sale order came up on the ticker tape for two hundred thousand Barrington shares. As per instructions, we immediately purchased all two hundred thousand.'

'At what price?'

'Four pounds and three shillings.'

'Have any more come on the market since?'

'Not many, and frankly, there have been more buy orders than sell following the excellent results you announced at your AGM.'

'What's the share price now?' Buchanan could hear the ticker tape clattering away in the background.

'Four pounds and six shillings,' said McBride. 'They seem to have settled around there.'

'Good,' said Buchanan. 'Don't buy any more unless they fall below four pounds three shillings.'

'Understood, sir.'

'That should keep the major awake at night for the next three weeks.'

'The major?' queried the broker, but Buchanan had already put the phone down.

◄○►

Arcadia Avenue was, as Griff had warned them, a Tory stronghold, but Harry and Emma didn't return to the constituency office empty-handed.

After Griff had checked their clipboards, he gave them a quizzical look.

'We stuck rigorously to your rules,' said Harry. 'If we were in any doubt, we marked them as green, undecided.'

'If you're right, this seat is going to be a lot closer than the polls are forecasting,' said Griff, as an out-of-breath Giles dashed in brandishing a copy of the *Bristol Evening Post*.

'Have you seen the front page, Griff?' he said, handing his agent the first edition of the paper.

Griff read the headline, passed it back to Giles and said, 'Ignore it. Say nothing, do nothing. That's my advice.'

Emma glanced over Giles's shoulder to see the headline.

Fisher challenges Barrington to debate. 'That sounds interesting,' she said.

'It would be interesting, but only if Giles was foolish enough to accept.'

'Why wouldn't he?' asked Harry. 'After all, he's a far better debater than Fisher, and he has a great deal more political experience.'

'That may well be the case,' said Griff, 'but you must never give your opponent a platform. While Giles is the sitting member, he can dictate the terms.'

'Yes, but have you read what the bastard went on to say?' said Giles.

'Why should I waste my time on Fisher,' said Griff, 'when it's not going to happen?'

Giles ignored the comment, and began reading the front page out loud. '"Barrington's got a lot of questions to answer if he still hopes to be the Member of Parliament for Docklands on May the twenty-sixth. Knowing him as I do, I'm confident the hero of Tobruk will not shirk the challenge. I will be at Colston Hall next Thursday, May the nineteenth, and will be happy to answer any questions put to me by members of the public. There will be three chairs on stage, and if Sir Giles doesn't show up, I'm sure the electors will be able to draw their own conclusions."'

'Three chairs?' queried Emma.

'Fisher knows the Liberals will turn up because they've got nothing to lose,' said Griff. 'But my advice remains the same. Ignore the bastard. There'll be another headline tomorrow, and by then,' he said, pointing to the newspaper, 'that will only be good for fish and chips.'

◄◦►

Ross Buchanan was sitting at his desk at Barrington's checking the latest report from Harland and Wolff when his secretary buzzed through.

'I've got Sandy McBride on the line from Hong Kong. Do you want to take the call?'

'Put him through.'

'Good morning, sir. I thought you'd like to know that Benny Driscoll has been phoning every few hours wanting to find out if we've got any Barrington's stock for sale. I've still got two hundred thousand on my books and, as the price continues to rise, I was calling to ask if you want me to release any of them?'

'Not until the three-week period is up, and a new account has been opened. Until then, we're buyers, not sellers.'

<o>

When Giles saw the headline in the *Evening Post* the following day, he knew he could no longer avoid a direct confrontation with Fisher. **Bishop of Bristol to chair election debate.** This time, Griff read the front page more carefully.

> The Bishop of Bristol, the Right Reverend Frederick Cockin, has agreed to act as moderator at an election debate to be held at Colston Hall next Thursday, May 19th at 7.30 p.m. Major Alex Fisher, the Conservative candidate, and Mr Reginald Ellsworthy, the Liberal candidate, have both agreed to take part. Sir Giles Barrington, the Labour candidate, has not yet responded to our invitation.

'I still think you should ignore it,' said Griff.

'But look at the picture on the front page,' said Giles, thrusting the paper back into his agent's hands.

Griff looked at the photograph, which showed an empty chair in the middle of the stage at Colston Hall with a spotlight beamed on to it, above a caption that read: *Will Sir Giles turn up?*

'Surely you see,' said Giles, 'if I don't turn up, they'll have a field day.'

'And if you do, they'll have a heyday.' Griff paused. 'But it's your choice, and if you're still determined to be there, we have to turn this situation to our advantage.'

'How do we do that?'

'You'll issue a press statement at seven o'clock tomorrow morning, so we get the headlines for a change.'

'Saying?'

'Saying that you're delighted to accept the challenge, because it will give you an opportunity to expose Tory policies for what they're worth, and at the same time let the people of Bristol decide who is the right man to represent them in Parliament.'

'What made you change your mind?' asked Giles.

'I've been looking at the latest canvass returns, and they suggest you're likely to lose by over a thousand votes, so you're no longer the favourite, you're now the challenger.'

'What else can go wrong?'

'Your wife could make an appearance, take a seat in the front row and ask the first question. Then your girlfriend turns up and slaps her in the face, in which case you needn't worry about the *Bristol Evening Post* because you'll be on the front page of every paper in the country.'

23

GILES TOOK HIS seat on the stage to loud applause. His speech to the packed hall could hardly have gone better, and speaking last had turned out to be an advantage.

The three candidates had all arrived half an hour early, and then waltzed around each other like schoolboys attending their first dance class. The bishop, acting as moderator, finally brought them together and explained how he intended to conduct the evening.

'I will invite each of you to make an opening speech, which mustn't last longer than eight minutes. After seven minutes, I will ring a bell.' He gave a demonstration. 'I'll ring it a second time after eight minutes, to show that your time is up. Once you've all delivered your speeches, I will open the meeting to questions from the floor.'

'How will the order be decided?' asked Fisher.

'By the drawing of straws.' The bishop then held out three straws in a clenched fist and invited each candidate to pick one.

Fisher drew the short straw.

'So you will be opening the batting, Major Fisher,' said the bishop. 'You will go second, Mr Ellsworthy, and, Sir Giles, you will go last.'

Giles smiled at Fisher and said, 'Bad luck, old chap.'

'No, I wanted to go first,' protested Fisher, causing even the bishop to raise an eyebrow.

When the bishop led the three men on to the stage at 7.25 p.m, it was the only time that night when everyone in the hall applauded. Giles took his seat and looked down at the packed audience. He estimated that over a thousand members of the public had turned up to watch the jousting.

Giles knew that each of the three parties had been issued with 200 tickets for their supporters, which left some 400 undecided votes to be played for; just about his majority at the last election.

At 7.30 p.m., the bishop opened proceedings. He introduced the three candidates, then invited Major Fisher to deliver his opening address.

Fisher made his way slowly to the front of the stage, placed his prepared speech on the lectern and tapped the microphone. He delivered his words nervously, keeping his head down, clearly fearful of losing his place.

When the bishop rang the bell to indicate that he had one minute left, Fisher began to speed up, which caused him to stumble over his words. Giles could have told him it was a golden rule that if you have been allocated eight minutes, you prepare a seven-minute speech. It's far better to end slightly early than to be stopped in the middle of your peroration. Despite this, when Fisher returned to his seat he was rewarded with prolonged applause from his supporters.

Giles was surprised when Reg Ellsworthy rose to present the Liberal case. He didn't have a prepared speech, or even a list of headings to remind him what subjects he should concentrate on. Instead, he chatted about local issues, and when the one-minute bell went, he stopped in the middle of a sentence and returned to his seat. Ellsworthy had achieved something Giles would have thought impossible; he'd made Fisher look good. Nevertheless, a fifth of those assembled still cheered their champion.

Giles rose to a warm reception from his two hundred supporters, although large sections of the crowd sat on their hands. Something he'd become familiar with whenever he addressed the government benches. He stood by the side of the lectern, only occasionally glancing at his notes.

He began by describing the Conservatives' failures in office, and outlining what the Labour Party's policies would be should it form the next government. He then touched on local issues, and even managed a dig about pavement politics at the expense of the Liberals, which brought laughter from the packed hall. By the time he'd come to the end of his speech, at least half the audience were applauding. If the meeting had ended then, there would have been only one winner.

'The candidates will now take questions from the floor,' announced the bishop, 'and I hope this will be done in a respectful and orderly manner.'

Thirty of Giles's supporters leapt up and threw their hands in the air, all of them with well-prepared questions calculated to assist their candidate and undermine the other two. The only problem was that sixty other equally determined hands also shot up at the same time.

The bishop was astute enough to have identified where the three different blocks of supporters were sitting, and skilfully selected non-partisan members of the general public who wanted to know such things as where the candidates stood on the introduction of parking meters in Bristol, which gave the Liberal candidate a chance to shine; the end of rationing, which they all approved of; and the proposed extension of the electrification of the railways, which didn't advance anyone's cause.

But Giles knew that eventually an arrow would be shot in his direction, and he would have to make sure it didn't hit the target. Finally he heard the bow twang.

'Could Sir Giles explain why he visited Cambridge more times during the last parliament than he did his own constituency?' asked a tall, thin, middle-aged man, whom Giles thought he recognized.

Giles sat still for a moment while he composed himself. He was just about to rise from his place when Fisher shot up, clearly not surprised by the question, while assuming everyone present knew exactly what the questioner was alluding to.

'Let me assure everyone in this hall,' he said, 'that I will be spending far more time in Bristol than in any other city, whatever the distractions.'

Giles looked down to see rows of blank faces. It seemed the audience had no idea what Fisher was talking about.

The Liberal candidate rose next. He clearly missed the point, because all he had to say was, 'Being an Oxford man, I never visit the other place unless I have to.'

A few people laughed.

Giles's two opponents had supplied him with the ammunition to fire back. He stood and turned to face Fisher.

'I feel bound to ask Major Fisher, if he intends to spend more time in Bristol than in any other city, does that mean that were he to win next Thursday, he won't be going up to London to take his seat in the House of Commons?'

Giles paused to wait for the laughter and applause to die down, before adding, 'I'm sure I don't have to remind the Conservative candidate of the words of Edmund Burke. "I was elected to represent the people of Bristol in Westminster, not the people of Westminster in Bristol." That's one Conservative I'm wholeheartedly in agreement with.' Giles sat down to sustained applause. Although he knew he hadn't really answered the question, he felt he'd got away with it.

'I think there's time for just one more question,' said the bishop, and pointed to a woman seated in the middle of the hall about halfway back, who he felt confident was neutral.

'Can each of the three candidates tell us where their wives are tonight?'

Fisher sat back and folded his arms, while Ellsworthy looked puzzled. Eventually, the bishop turned to Giles and said, 'I think it's your turn to go first.'

Giles stood and looked directly at the woman.

'My wife and I,' he began, 'are currently involved in divorce proceedings, which I hope will be settled in the near future.'

He sat down to an uncomfortable silence.

Ellsworthy jumped up and said, 'I have to admit that since

I've become the Liberal candidate I haven't managed to find anyone who's willing to go out with me, let alone marry me.'

This was greeted by peals of laughter and warm applause. Giles thought for a moment that Ellsworthy might have helped to lessen the tension.

Fisher slowly rose to his feet.

'My girlfriend,' he said, which took Giles by surprise, 'who has joined me here this evening and is sitting in the front row, will be by my side for the rest of the campaign. Jenny, why don't you stand up and take a bow.'

An attractive young woman rose, turned to face the audience, and gave them a wave. She was greeted with a round of applause.

'Where have I seen that woman before?' whispered Emma. But Harry was concentrating on Fisher, who hadn't returned to his seat and clearly had more to say.

'I thought it might also be of interest for you to know that this morning I received a letter from Lady Barrington.'

A silence descended on the hall that none of the candidates had achieved all evening. Giles was sitting on the edge of his seat as Fisher produced a letter from an inside jacket pocket. He slowly unfolded it and began to read.

'"Dear Major Fisher, I write to express my admiration for the gallant campaign you are waging on behalf of the Conservative Party. I wanted to let you know that if I were a citizen of Bristol, I would not hesitate to vote for you, as I believe you are by far the best candidate. I look forward to seeing you take your seat in the House of Commons. Yours sincerely, Virginia Barrington."'

Pandemonium broke out in the hall, and Giles realized that all he'd achieved in the past hour had evaporated in a single minute. Fisher folded up the letter, slipped it back into his pocket and returned to his place. The bishop tried valiantly to bring the meeting back to order, while Fisher's followers continued to cheer and cheer, leaving Giles's supporters to look on in despair.

Griff had been proved right. Never give your opponent a platform.

⊸◦⊸

'Have you managed to buy back any of those shares?'

'Not yet,' said Benny, 'Barrington's are still riding high on the back of the better than expected annual profits, and the expectation that the Tories will increase their majority at the election.'

'What's the share price standing at now?'

'Around four pounds seven shillings, and I can't see it dropping in the near future.'

'How much do we stand to lose?' asked Fisher.

'We? Not we,' said Benny, 'only you. Lady Virginia won't lose anything. She sold all her shares at a far higher price than she originally paid for them.'

'But if she doesn't buy them back, I'll lose my place on the board.'

'And if she did buy them back, she'd have to pay a hefty premium, and I imagine she wouldn't be happy about that.' Benny waited for a few seconds before adding, 'Try to look on the bright side, major. By this time next week, you'll be a Member of Parliament.'

⊸◦⊸

The following day, the two local papers didn't make good reading for the sitting member. Hardly a mention of Giles's speech, just a large photograph of Virginia on the front page, looking her most radiant, with a copy of her letter to Fisher printed underneath.

'Don't turn the page,' said Griff.

Giles immediately turned the page to find the latest poll, predicting that the Tories would increase their majority by twenty-three seats. Bristol Docklands was eighth on the list of Labour marginals most likely to fall to the Conservatives.

'There's not a lot a sitting member can do when the national tide turns against his party,' said Griff, once Giles had finished reading the article. 'I reckon a damn good member is worth an extra thousand votes, and a poor opposing candidate can lose a thousand, but frankly, I'm not even sure an extra couple of thousand will be enough. But that won't stop us fighting for every last vote until nine o'clock on Thursday night. So make sure you never let your guard down. I want you out on the streets shaking hands with anything that moves. Except Alex Fisher. If you come across that man, you have my permission to throttle him.'

◄○►

'Have you managed to buy back any Barrington's shares?'

'I'm afraid not, major. They never once fell below four pounds and three shillings.'

'Then I've lost my place on the board.'

'I think you'll find that was always part of Barrington's plan,' said Benny.

'What do you mean?'

'It was Sandy McBride who picked up your shares the moment they came on the market, and he's been the main buyer for the past twenty-one days. Everyone knows he's Barrington's broker.'

'The bastard.'

'They obviously saw you coming, major. But it's not all bad news, because Lady Virginia made a profit of over seventy thousand pounds on her original investment, so I reckon she owes you one.'

◄○►

Giles couldn't have worked any harder during the final week of the campaign, even if at times he felt like Sisyphus pushing his boulder up a hill.

When he turned up at campaign headquarters on the eve of the poll, it was the first time he'd seen Griff looking depressed.

'Ten thousand of these were dropped into letterboxes right across the constituency last night, just in case anybody might have missed it.'

Giles looked at a reproduction of the front page of the *Bristol Evening Post* with Virginia's photograph above her letter to Fisher. Underneath it were the words: *If you want to be represented in Parliament by an honest and decent man, vote Fisher.*

'That man's a piece of shit,' said Griff. 'And he's been dumped right on top of us from a great height,' he added as one of the first volunteers strolled in carrying the morning papers.

Giles slumped back in his chair and closed his eyes. But a moment later he could have sworn he heard Griff laughing. He was laughing. He opened his eyes and Griff passed him a copy of the *Daily Mail*. 'It's going to be close, my boy, but at least we're back in the race.'

Giles didn't immediately recognize the pretty girl on the front page, who had just been chosen to star in *The Benny Hill Show*. Jenny had told the showbiz correspondent about the job she'd been doing before she got her big break.

'I was paid ten pounds a day to escort a Tory candidate around his constituency, and tell everyone I was his girlfriend.'

Giles didn't think it was a very good photograph of Fisher.

◄○►

Fisher swore out loud when he saw the front page of the *Daily Mail*.

He drained his third cup of black coffee and got up to leave for campaign headquarters, just as he heard the morning post landing on the mat. Any letters would have to wait until tonight, and he would have ignored them if he hadn't spotted one with the Barrington's company crest on it. He bent down, picked it up and returned to the kitchen. He tore it open and extracted two cheques, one made out to him, for £1,000, his quarterly payment as a director of Barrington's, the second for £7,341, Lady Virginia's annual dividend, also made out to 'Major Alexander Fisher' so that no one would know it was her 7½ per cent stockholding that made it possible for him to be on the board. No longer.

When he got back this evening, he would make out a

cheque for the same amount and send it on to Lady Virginia. Wondering if it was too early to phone her, he checked his watch. It was a few minutes past eight, and he was meant to be standing outside Temple Meads meeting voters as they came out of the station on their way to work. Surely she would be awake by now. He picked up the phone and dialled a Kensington number.

It rang several times before a sleepy voice came on the line. He nearly put the phone down.

'Who is this?' Virginia demanded.

'It's Alex Fisher. I thought I'd call to let you know I've sold all your Barrington's stock, and you've made a profit of over seventy thousand.' He waited for a thank you, but nothing was forthcoming. 'I wondered if you had any plans to buy back your shares?' he asked. 'After all, you've made a handsome return since I've been on the board.'

'And so have you, major, as I'm sure I don't have to remind you. But my plans for the future have changed somewhat, and they no longer include Barrington's.'

'But if you don't buy back your seven and a half per cent, I'll forfeit my place on the board.'

'I won't be losing a lot of sleep over that, major.'

'But I wondered, given the circumstances . . .'

'What circumstances?'

'Whether you might consider a small bonus would be appropriate,' he said, looking down at the cheque for £7,341.

'How small?'

'I thought, perhaps five thousand pounds?'

'I'll give it some thought.' The line went quiet and Alex even wondered if he'd been cut off. Finally, Virginia said, 'I've given it some thought, major, and decided against it.'

'Then perhaps a loan . . .' he said, trying not to sound desperate.

'Didn't your nanny tell you, neither a borrower nor a lender be? No, of course she didn't, because you didn't have a nanny.'

Virginia turned around and rapped loudly three times on the wooden bedstead.

'Ah, the maid has just arrived with my breakfast, major, so I have to say goodbye. And when I say goodbye, I mean goodbye.'

Fisher heard the phone click. He stared at the cheque for £7,341, made out to him, and remembered Benny's words: *She owes you one.*

24

GILES WAS UP at five on the morning of the election, and not just because he couldn't sleep.

As he went downstairs Denby opened the door to the breakfast room and said, 'Good morning, Sir Giles,' as if there was a general election every day.

Giles entered the dining room, picked up a bowl from the sideboard and filled it with cornflakes and fruit. He was going over his schedule for the day when the door opened and in walked Sebastian, dressed in a smart blue blazer and grey flannels.

'Seb. When did you get back?'

'Late last night, Uncle Giles. Most schools have been given the day off because they're being used as polling stations, so I asked if I could come home and help you.'

'What would you like to do?' asked Giles as Denby placed a plate of eggs and bacon in front of him.

'Anything I can to help you win.'

'If that's what you want to do, listen carefully. On Election Day, the party has eight committee rooms spread across the constituency. They're all manned by volunteers, some of whom have experience of a dozen elections. They'll have up-to-date canvass returns for the district they're in charge of. Every street, road, avenue and cul-de-sac will be marked to show where our supporters live. We'll also have a volunteer sitting outside each polling station, checking off the names of people who've cast their vote. Our biggest problem is getting that list

197

of names back to the committee room, so we can keep track of our supporters who haven't voted yet, and make sure we get them to the polls before they close at nine o'clock tonight. A general rule,' continued Giles, 'is that more of our people vote between eight and ten a.m., soon after the polls open, while at ten o'clock the Tories will begin to turn out, and keep going until four in the afternoon. But after that, when voters are coming home from work, that's our most vital time, because if they don't vote on the way home, it's almost impossible to get them back out,' he added as Emma and Harry came into the room.

'What's Griff got you two doing today?' asked Giles.

'I'm manning a committee room,' said Emma.

'I'm knocking up red voters,' said Harry. 'And if they need a lift, I'll be driving them to the polling station.'

'Don't forget,' said Giles, 'for some of them, the last time they had a ride in a car was probably at the last election, unless there's been a wedding or a funeral in their family in the past four years. Which committee room has Griff allocated you to?' he asked Emma.

'I'm to assist Miss Parish on the Woodbine estate.'

'You should be flattered,' said Giles. 'Miss Parish is a legend. Grown men fear for their lives if they forget to vote. By the way, Seb has volunteered to be one of your runners. I've already explained what his duties will be.'

Emma smiled at her son.

'I'm off,' said Giles, leaping up from his place, but not before placing two rashers of bacon between two slices of brown bread.

Emma accepted that only Elizabeth could have told him off, and probably not even her on Election Day.

'I'll be visiting every committee room at some point during the day,' he said on the move, 'so I'll catch up with you later.'

Denby was waiting for him outside the front door.

'I'm sorry to trouble you, sir, but I hope it won't be inconvenient if the staff at the hall were to take half an hour off between four and four thirty this afternoon.'

'Any particular reason?'

'To vote, sir.'

Giles looked embarrassed. 'How many votes?' he whispered.

'Six for you, sir, and one undecided.' Giles raised an eyebrow. 'The new gardener, sir, has ideas above his station. Thinks he's a Tory.'

'Then let's hope I don't lose by one vote,' said Giles as he ran out of the front door.

Jessica was standing in the driveway holding the car door open for him, as she did every morning. 'Can I come with you, Uncle Giles?' she asked.

'Not this time. But I promise you'll be by my side at the next election. I'll tell everyone you're my girlfriend, and then I'll win by a landslide.'

'Isn't there anything I can do to help?'

'No . . . yes. Do you know the new gardener?'

'Albert? Yes, he's very nice.'

'He's thinking of voting Conservative. See if you can convert him by four o'clock this afternoon.'

'I will, I will,' said Jessica as Giles climbed in behind the wheel.

◄○►

Giles parked outside the entrance to the docks just before 7 a.m. He shook hands with every man before they clocked on for the morning shift, and with everyone coming off the night shift. He was surprised how many of them wanted to talk to him.

'I won't let you down this time, guv.'

'You can count on me.'

'I'm on my way to the polls right now.'

When Dave Coleman, the night foreman, clocked off, Giles took him to one side and asked if he knew the reason for the men's fervour.

'A lot of them think it's high time you sorted out your marital problems,' said Coleman, who was known for his bluntness, 'but they detest Major stuck-up Fisher so much, they certainly wouldn't want him representing our grievances in Parliament. At a personal level,' he added, 'I would have respected Fisher more if he'd had the courage to show his face on the docks. There are a handful of Tories in the union, but he hasn't even bothered to find out who they are.'

Giles was heartened by the response he received when he visited the W.D. & H.O. Wills cigarette factory, and again when he went on to meet the workers at the Bristol Aeroplane Company. But he knew that on the day of a general election, every candidate is convinced he is going to win, even the Liberals.

Giles turned up at the first committee room a few minutes after ten. The local chairman told him that 22 per cent of their known supporters had already voted, which was in line with the 1951 election, when Giles had won by 414 votes.

'What about the Tories?' Giles asked.

'Sixteen per cent.'

'How does that compare with 'fifty-one?'

'They're up one per cent,' admitted the committee room chairman.

By the time Giles had reached the eighth committee room, it was just after 4 p.m. Miss Parish was standing by the door waiting for him, a plate of cheese and tomato sandwiches in one hand, a large glass of milk in the other. Miss Parish was one of the few people on the Woodbine estate who owned a fridge.

'How's it going?' Giles asked.

'Thank heavens it rained between ten and four, but now the sun's come out. I'm beginning to believe that God might be a socialist. But we've still got a lot of work to do if we're going to make up the lost ground in the last five hours.'

'You've never called an election wrong, Iris. What are you predicting?'

'The truth?'

'The truth.'

'Too close to call.'

'Then let's get back to work.' Giles began to move around the room, thanking every one of the helpers.

'Your family have come up trumps,' said Miss Parish, 'remembering they're Tories.'

'Emma can turn her hand to anything.'

'She's good,' said Miss Parish, as Giles watched his sister transferring the figures just in from a polling station to the canvass sheet. 'But it's young Sebastian who's the superstar. If we had ten of him, we'd never lose.'

Giles smiled. 'So where is the young man at the moment?'

'Either on his way to a polling station, or on his way back. He doesn't believe in standing still.'

—◦—

Sebastian was actually standing still, waiting for a teller to hand over the latest list of names so he could get them back to Miss Parish, who continued to fuel him on Tizer and Fry's milk chocolate, despite the occasional disapproving look from his mother.

'The trouble is,' the teller was saying to a friend who'd just voted, 'the Millers over there at number twenty-one, all six of them, can't even be bothered to cross the road, despite the fact that they never stop complaining about this Tory government. So if we lose by half a dozen votes, we'll know who to blame.'

'Why don't you get Miss Parish on to them?' said the friend.

'She's got enough on her plate without having to come down here. I'd do it myself, but I can't leave my post.'

Sebastian turned and found himself walking across the road. He came to a halt outside number 21, but it was some time before he plucked up enough courage to knock. He nearly ran away when he saw the size of the man who opened the door.

'What do you want, nipper?' the man bellowed.

'I represent Major Fisher, the Conservative candidate,' said Sebastian, in his best public school accent, 'and he was rather hoping that you'd be able to support him today, as the polls are showing it's likely to be a close-run thing.'

'Bugger off before I give you a clip round the ear,' said Mr Miller, and slammed the door in his face.

Sebastian ran back across the road and, as he collected the latest figures from the teller, he saw the door of number 21 open, and Mr Miller reappeared, leading five members of his family across the road. Sebastian added the Millers to his canvass return before running back to the committee room.

◄○►

Giles was back at the docks by six o'clock, to meet the day shift coming off and the night shift clocking on.

'Have you been standing there all day, guv?' quipped one of them.

'Feels like it,' said Giles, as he shook another hand.

One or two turned back when they saw him standing there and quickly headed for the nearby polling station, while those coming out all seemed to be going in one direction, and it wasn't to the nearest pub.

At 6.30 p.m., after all the dockers had either clocked on or gone home, Giles did what he'd done for the past two elections and jumped aboard the first double-decker bus heading back into the city.

Once on board, he climbed on to the top deck and shook hands with several surprised passengers. When he'd covered the lower deck, he jumped off at the next stop and got on another bus going in the opposite direction. He went on jumping on and off buses for the next two and a half hours, continuing to shake hands until one minute past nine.

Giles got off the last bus and sat alone at the stop. There was nothing more he could do to win this election.

◄○►

Giles heard a single chime echo in the distance and glanced at his watch: 9.30 p.m.; time to make a move. He decided he couldn't face another bus, and began to walk slowly towards the city centre, hoping the evening air might clear his head before the count.

By now the local constabulary would have begun to collect the ballot boxes from all over the constituency before delivering them to City Hall; a process that would take more than an hour to complete. Once they had all been delivered, checked and double checked, Mr Wainwright, the town clerk, would give the order for the seals to be broken so the count could begin. If the result was announced before 1 o'clock that morning, it would be a miracle.

Sam Wainwright was not a man destined to break speed records on land or sea. 'Slowly, but surely' would be the words etched on his gravestone. Giles had dealt with the town clerk on local matters for the past decade and still didn't know which party he supported. He suspected he just didn't vote. What Giles did know was that this would be Wainwright's last election, as he would be retiring at the end of the year. In Giles's opinion, the city would be very lucky to find a worthy successor. Someone might succeed Wainwright, but no man could replace him, as Thomas Jefferson had said when he followed Benjamin Franklin into the post of American ambassador to France.

One or two passers-by waved as Giles continued on his way to City Hall, while others simply ignored him. He began to think about his life, and what he might do if he were no longer the MP for Bristol Docklands. He would be thirty-five in a couple of weeks. True, no great age, but since returning to Bristol just after the war ended he'd only ever done one job, and frankly he wasn't qualified to do much else; the perennial problem for any Member of Parliament who doesn't have a safe seat.

His thoughts turned to Virginia, who could have made his life so much easier simply by signing a piece of paper some six months ago. He now realized that had never been part of her plan. She had always intended to wait until after the election in order to cause him the maximum possible embarrassment. He was now certain she had been responsible for putting Fisher on the board of Barrington's, and he even wondered if it was she who'd sown the seed in Fisher's mind that he could defeat Giles and replace him as Member of Parliament.

She was probably sitting at home in London right now waiting for the election results to come in, although in truth she was only interested in one seat. Was she preparing for another raid on the company's shares as part of her long-term plan to bring the Barrington family to its knees? Giles was confident that in Ross Buchanan and Emma, she had met her match.

It was Grace who had finally brought him to his senses about Virginia, and having done so, she never mentioned the subject again. He also had her to thank for introducing him to Gwyneth. She had been keen to come to Bristol and help him retain his seat, but she had been the first to acknowledge that if she'd been seen canvassing with him on the high street, the only person who would have gained from it would be Fisher.

Giles had rung Gwyneth in Cambridge every morning before going into the office, but not when he returned at night, despite her telling him to wake her, because he rarely arrived home before midnight. If he lost tonight, he would drive up to Cambridge in the morning and unburden his troubles on her. If he won, he would join her in the afternoon and share his triumph with her. Whatever the outcome, he wasn't going to lose her.

'Good luck, Sir Giles,' said a passing voice that brought him back to the real world. 'I'm sure you'll make it.' Giles returned his confident smile, but he wasn't sure.

He could now see the massive bulk of City Hall looming in front of him. The two golden unicorns perched high on the roof at each end of the building grew larger with every step he took.

The volunteers who'd been chosen to assist with the count would already be in place. This was considered a great responsibility, and was usually undertaken by local councillors or senior party officials. Miss Parish would be in charge of the six Labour scrutineers, as she had been for the past four elections, and he knew she had invited Harry and Emma to join her select team.

'I would have asked Sebastian as well,' she had told Giles, 'but he's not old enough.'

'He'll be disappointed,' Giles had replied.

'Yes, he was. But I got him a pass, so he can watch everything that's going on from the balcony.'

'Thank you.'

'Don't thank me,' said Miss Parish. 'I only wish I'd had him for the whole campaign.'

Giles took a deep breath as he climbed the steps of City Hall. Whatever the outcome, he mustn't forget to thank the many people who had supported him, whose only reward would be victory. He recalled Old Jack's words after he'd scored a century at Lord's: anyone can be a good winner. The sign of a great man is how you handle defeat.

25

GRIFF HASKINS WAS striding back and forth in the lobby of City Hall when he spotted Giles walking towards him. The two shook hands as if they hadn't seen each other for weeks.

'If I win,' said Giles, 'you—'

'Don't get sentimental on me,' said Griff. 'We've still got a job to do.'

They made their way through the swing doors into the main auditorium to find that the thousand seats that usually filled the room had been replaced by two dozen trestle tables in rows, with wooden chairs on either side of them.

Sam Wainwright, hands on hips, feet apart, stood in the middle of the stage. He blew a whistle to announce that the game had begun. Scissors appeared, seals were cut, ballot boxes were thrown open and turned upside down to allow thousands of little slips of paper, each one bearing three names, to spill out on to the tables in front of the counters.

Their first job was to sort the ballot papers into three piles before the counting could begin. One side of the table concentrated on Fisher, while the other worked on Barrington. The search for Ellsworthy's votes took a little longer.

Giles and Griff paced nervously around the room, trying to work out from the piles of ballot papers if one side or the other had an obvious lead. After one complete circuit, it was clear to both of them that neither had. Giles appeared to be comfortably ahead if you looked at the pile of slips from the boxes collected from the Woodbine estate, but Fisher was a clear winner if you checked the ballot boxes from the Arcadia Avenue wards. Another circuit of the hall, and they were none the wiser. The only thing they could predict with any certainty was that the Liberals would end up in third place.

Giles looked up when he heard a burst of applause coming from the other side of the hall. Fisher had just entered the room with his agent and a few key supporters. Giles recognized some of them from the evening of the debate. He couldn't help noticing that Fisher had changed into a fresh shirt and was wearing a smart double-breasted suit, already looking every inch a Member of Parliament. After chatting to one or two of the counters, he also began to move around the room, making quite sure he didn't bump into Barrington.

Giles and Griff, along with Miss Parish, Harry and Emma, continued to walk slowly up and down the aisles, watching carefully as piles of ballot papers were stacked in tens, and then, once they totalled a hundred, were bound by thick red, blue or yellow bands, so they could be identified quickly. Finally they were lined up in five-hundreds, like soldiers on parade.

The scrutineers took a row each, checking that the tens were not nines or elevens, and, even more important, that the hundreds weren't hundred-and-tens or nineties. If they thought a mistake had been made, they could ask for a pile to be re-counted in the presence of Mr Wainwright or one of his deputies. Not something to be done lightly, Miss Parish warned her team.

After two hours of counting, Griff shrugged his shoulders in answer to Giles's whispered question as to how he thought things were going. By this time in 1951, he'd been able to tell Giles he'd won, even if it was only by a few hundred votes. Not tonight.

Once the counters had their neat, well-ordered piles of five-hundreds in place, they raised a hand to let the town clerk know that they'd completed the task and were ready to confirm their results. Finally, when the last hand was raised, Mr Wainwright once again blew a sharp blast on his whistle and said, 'Now double check every pile one more time.' He then added,

'Would the candidates and their agents please join me on stage.'

Giles and Griff were the first to climb the steps, with Fisher and Ellsworthy only a stride behind. On a table in the centre of the stage, where everyone could observe exactly what was taking place, was a small pile of ballot papers. No more than a dozen of them, Giles estimated.

'Gentlemen,' announced the town clerk, 'these are the spoilt ballot papers. Electoral law decrees that I, and I alone, must decide if any of them should be included in the final count. However, you have the right to disagree with any of my judgements.'

Wainwright stood over the pile of votes, adjusted his glasses and studied the top slip. It had a cross in Fisher's box, but also scribbled across it were the words 'God Save the Queen'.

'That's obviously a vote for me,' said Fisher, before Wainwright could give his opinion.

The town clerk looked at Giles, and then at Ellsworthy, and they both nodded, so the ballot paper was placed to his right. On the next slip a tick, not a cross, had been placed in Fisher's box.

'They clearly intended to vote for me,' said Fisher firmly. Once again, Giles and Ellsworthy nodded.

The town clerk placed the vote on Fisher's pile, which caused the Conservative candidate to smile, until he saw that the next three ballot papers had ticks in Barrington's box.

On the next paper, the names of all three candidates had been crossed out and replaced by *Vote for Desperate Dan*. They all agreed it was spoilt. The next had a tick by Ellsworthy's name, and it was accepted as a vote for the Liberal candidate. The eighth declared *Abolish hanging*, and joined the spoilt pile without comment. The ninth had a tick in Barrington's box, and Fisher had no choice but to allow it, giving Giles a 4–2 lead with only two papers left to consider. The next had a tick in Barrington's box, with the word *NEVER* written next to Fisher's name.

'That must be a spoilt ballot,' said Fisher.

'In which case,' said the town clerk, 'I will have to treat "God Save the Queen" in the same way.'

'That's logical,' said Ellsworthy. 'Better take them both out.'

'I agree with Major Fisher,' said Giles, realizing it would increase his lead from 4–2 to 4–1. Fisher looked as if he wanted to protest, but said nothing.

They all looked at the last ballot paper. Wainwright smiled.

'Not in my lifetime, I suspect,' he said, placing a paper with the words *Independence for Scotland* scrawled across it on the spoilt pile.

Wainwright then checked each ballot paper again, before saying, 'That's four votes for Barrington, one for Fisher and one for Ellsworthy.' He wrote down the numbers in his note book and said, 'Thank you, gentlemen.'

'Let's hope that's not the only vote you win tonight,' Griff mumbled to Giles as they left the stage and joined Miss Parish and her scrutineers.

The town clerk returned to the front of the stage and once again blew his whistle. His team of deputies immediately began walking up and down the aisles writing down the final numbers from each counter, before taking them on to the stage and handing them to the town clerk.

Mr Wainwright studied each figure carefully before entering the numbers into a large adding machine, his only concession to the modern world. Once he'd pressed the add button for the last time, he wrote down the final figures against the three names, considered them for a moment, then invited the candidates to join him on the stage once again. He then told them the result and agreed to Giles's request.

Miss Parish frowned when she saw Fisher giving his supporters a thumbs-up sign, and realized they had lost. She glanced up towards the gallery to see Sebastian waving energetically at her. She waved back, but looked down again when Mr Wainwright tapped the microphone, creating a hush of expectation in the hall.

'I, the returning officer for the constituency of Bristol Docklands, declare the total number of votes cast for each candidate to be as follows:

Sir Giles Barrington	18,714
Mr Reginald Ellsworthy	3,472
Major Alexander Fisher	18,908.'

A huge cheer and prolonged clapping rose from the Fisher camp. Wainwright waited for order to be restored before he added, 'The sitting member has asked for a re-count, and I have granted his request. Will every teller please re-check their piles most carefully, and make sure no mistakes have been made.'

The counters began to check, and re-check, every ten, then every hundred, and finally every five hundred, before raising their hands to signal that they had completed the task a second time.

Giles looked up to the heavens in silent prayer, only to see Sebastian waving frantically, but then something Griff said distracted him.

'You ought to be thinking about your speech,' said Griff. 'You must thank the town clerk, his workers, your workers, and above all, if Fisher wins, you must appear magnanimous. After all, there'll always be another election.'

Giles wasn't so sure there would be another election for him. He was about to say so, when Miss Parish hurried across to join them.

'I'm sorry to interrupt,' she said, 'but Sebastian seems to be trying to catch your attention.'

Giles and Griff looked up at the balcony where Sebastian was leaning well over the rail, almost begging one of them to join him.

'Why don't you go up and see what his problem is,' said Griff, 'while Giles and I prepare for the new order.'

Miss Parish climbed the stairs to the balcony to be met by Sebastian waiting on the top step. He grabbed her by the arm, pulled her towards the railing and pointed down into the body of the hall. 'You see that man sitting on the end of the third row wearing a green shirt?'

Miss Parish looked in the direction he was indicating. 'Yes. What about him?'

'He's been cheating.'

'What makes you say that?' asked Miss Parish, trying to sound calm.

'He reported five hundred votes for Fisher to one of the deputy town clerks.'

'Yes, that's right,' said Miss Parish. 'He's got five piles of one hundred in front of him.'

'I know,' said Sebastian, 'but one of those piles has a Fisher ballot paper on top, and the ninety nine underneath are for Uncle Giles.'

'Are you certain of that?' asked Miss Parish. 'Because if Griff asks Mr Wainwright to check those votes personally, and you turn out to be wrong . . .'

'I'm certain,' said Sebastian defiantly.

Miss Parish still didn't look sure, but she got as near to running as she had for some years. Once she arrived back on the floor, she hurried up to Giles, who was trying to look confident as he chatted to Emma and Griff. She told them what Sebastian was claiming, only to be greeted by expressions of disbelief. All four of them looked up to the balcony, to see Sebastian pointing frantically at the man in the green shirt.

'I find what Sebastian is suggesting quite easy to believe,' said Emma.

'Why?' asked Griff. 'Did you actually see that man put a Fisher ballot paper on top of one of our piles?'

'No, but I did see him at the debate last Thursday. He was the one who asked why Giles had visited Cambridge more times than Bristol during the last parliament.'

Giles looked at the man closely, as more and more hands began to shoot up around the room to indicate that the recount was nearly complete.

'I think you're right,' he said.

Griff left them without another word and quickly made his

way back up on to the stage, where he asked the town clerk if he could have a private word.

Once he had heard what the agent was claiming, Mr Wainwright looked up at Sebastian, and then transferred his gaze to the counter who was seated at the end of the third row of tables.

'That's a very serious allegation to be making on the word of a child,' he said, his eyes returning to Sebastian.

'He's not a child,' said Griff. 'He's a young man. And in any case, this is an official request for you to make an inspection.'

'Then on your head be it,' said Wainwright, after looking once again at the counter concerned. Without another word, he summoned two of his deputies and announced without explanation, 'Follow me.'

The three men walked down the steps to the floor and headed straight for the table at the end of the third row, with Giles and Griff only a pace behind. The town clerk looked down at the man in the green shirt, and said, 'I wonder if you would allow me to take your place, sir, as Sir Giles's agent has asked me to check your numbers personally.'

The man got up slowly, and stood to one side as Wainwright sat down in his chair and studied the five piles of Fisher votes on the table in front of him.

He picked up the first stack, removed the blue elastic band and studied the top ballot paper. He needed only a cursory inspection to confirm that all one hundred votes had been correctly allocated to Fisher. The second pile yielded the same result, as did the third, by which time only Sebastian, looking down from the balcony, still appeared confident.

When Wainwright removed the top ballot paper from the fourth stack, he was greeted with a cross next to the name of Barrington. He checked the rest of the pile slowly and carefully, to find that all ninety-nine of them had voted for Barrington. Finally he checked the fifth pile, which were all Fisher's.

No one had noticed that the Conservative candidate had joined the little group surrounding the end table.

'Is there a problem?' asked Fisher.

'Nothing I can't handle,' said the town clerk, turning to one of his deputies and saying, 'Ask the police to escort this gentleman from the premises.'

He then had a word with his secretary, before returning to the stage and resuming his place behind the adding machine. Once again, he took his time entering each figure that was presented by his deputies. After he'd pressed the add button for the last time, he entered the new numbers against each candidate's name, and when he was finally satisfied, he asked them all to come back on stage. This time, after he had informed them of the revised figures, Giles did not ask for a re-count.

Wainwright returned to the microphone to announce the result of the second count to an audience who, until then, had been surviving on Chinese whispers.

'. . . declare the total number of votes cast for each candidate to be as follows:

Sir Giles Barrington	18,813
Mr Reginald Ellsworthy	3,472
Major Alexander Fisher	18,809.'

This time it was the Labour supporters who erupted, holding up proceedings for several minutes before Wainwright was able to announce that Major Fisher had requested a re-count.

'Will all the counters please check their numbers carefully for a third time, and immediately inform one of my deputies if there are any changes you wish to report.'

When the town clerk returned to the desk, his secretary handed him the reference book he had requested. He turned several pages of *Macaulay's Election Law* until he came to an entry he'd marked earlier that afternoon. While Wainwright was confirming his understanding of the returning officer's duties, Fisher's scrutiny team were charging up and down the aisles demanding to be shown the second ballot paper of every Barrington stack.

Despite this, forty minutes later Wainwright was able to

announce that there were no changes from the result of the second count. Fisher immediately demanded another re-count.

'I am not willing to grant that request,' said Wainwright. 'The numbers have been consistent on three separate occasions,' he added, quoting Macaulay's exact words.

'But that is blatantly not the case,' barked Fisher. 'They've only been consistent twice. You will recall that I won the first count quite comfortably.'

'They have been consistent three times,' repeated Wainwright, 'remembering the unfortunate mistake your colleague made on the first count.'

'My colleague?' said Fisher. 'That is a disgraceful slur on my character. I've never seen the man before in my life. If you don't withdraw that statement and allow a re-count, I'll have no choice but to consult my lawyers in the morning.'

'That would be most unfortunate,' said Wainwright, 'because I wouldn't want to see Councillor Peter Maynard in the witness box, trying to explain how he'd never come across the chairman of his local party's association, who also happens to be its prospective parliamentary candidate.'

Fisher turned scarlet and marched off the stage.

Mr Wainwright rose from his place, walked slowly towards the front of the stage and tapped the microphone for the last time. He cleared his throat and announced, 'I, the returning officer for the constituency of Bristol Docklands, declare the total number of votes cast for each candidate to be as follows:

Sir Giles Barrington	18,813
Mr Reginald Ellsworthy	3,472
Major Alexander Fisher	18,809.

'I therefore declare Sir Giles Barrington to be the duly elected Member of Parliament for the constituency of Bristol Docklands.'

The Member of Parliament for Bristol Docklands looked up to the balcony and bowed low to Sebastian Clifton.

SEBASTIAN CLIFTON

1955–1957

26

'RAISE YOUR GLASSES to the man who won us the election!' yelled Griff, who was teetering precariously on a table in the middle of the room, a glass of champagne in one hand, a cigarette in the other.

'To Sebastian!' everyone shouted, to laughter and applause.

'Have you ever drunk champagne before?' asked Griff after he had stepped unsteadily down to join Sebastian.

'Only once,' admitted Sebastian, 'when my friend Bruno celebrated his fifteenth birthday, and his father took the two of us out to supper at a local pub. So I suppose this is my second glass.'

'Take my advice,' said Griff, 'don't get used to it. It's the nectar of the rich. We working-class lads,' he said, putting an arm around him, 'can only expect to have a couple of glasses a year, and then at someone else's expense.'

'But I intend to be rich.'

'Why am I not surprised?' said Griff, filling his glass again. 'In that case you'll have to become a champagne socialist, and heaven knows we've got enough of them in our party.'

'I'm not in your party,' said Sebastian firmly. 'I'm a Tory in every other seat, apart from the one Uncle Giles is standing in.'

'Then you'll have to come and live in Bristol,' said Griff as the newly re-elected member strolled across to join them.

'Not much chance of that,' said Giles. 'His parents tell me they have high hopes of him winning a scholarship to Cambridge.'

'Well, if it's to be Cambridge rather than Bristol, you'll prob-ably end up seeing more of your uncle than we do.'

'You've had too much to drink, Griff,' said Giles, patting his agent on the back.

'Not as much as I would have had if we'd lost,' said Griff, downing his glass. 'And try not to forget the bloody Tories have increased their majority in the House.'

'We ought to be getting home, Seb, if you're going to be in any shape for school tomorrow. Heaven knows how many rules you've broken in the last couple of hours.'

'Can I say goodnight to Miss Parish before I go?'

'Yes, of course. Why don't you do that while I go and pay the drinks bill. The drinks are on me, now the election is over.'

Sebastian wove his way through groups of volunteers, some swaying like branches in the wind, while others, heads down on the nearest table, had passed out, or were simply incapable of movement. He spotted Miss Parish seated in an alcove on the far side of the room with two empty bottles of champagne for company. When he finally reached her, he wasn't altogether sure she recognized him.

'Miss Parish, I just wanted to thank you for allowing me to be in your team. I've learnt so much from you. I only wish you were one of my teachers at the Abbey.'

'That is indeed a compliment, Sebastian,' said Miss Parish. 'But I fear I was born in the wrong century. It will be a long time before women are offered the chance to teach at an independent boys' school.' She hauled herself up and gave him a huge hug. 'Good luck, Sebastian,' she said. 'I hope you get that scholarship to Cambridge.'

'What did Miss Parish mean, she was born in the wrong century?' asked Sebastian as Giles drove them back to the Manor House.

'Simply that women of her generation weren't given the opportunity to pursue a proper career,' said Giles. 'She would have made a great teacher, and hundreds of children would have benefited from her wisdom and common sense. The truth is, we lost two generations of men in world wars, and two generations of women who weren't given the chance to take their places.'

'Fine words, Uncle Giles, but what are you going to do about it?'

Giles laughed. 'I could have done a damned sight more if we'd won the election, because tomorrow I would probably have been in the Cabinet. Now I'll have to be satisfied with another stint on the Opposition front bench.'

'Is my mother going to suffer from the same problem?' asked Sebastian. 'Because she'd make a damned good MP.'

'No, although I can't see her wanting to enter the House. I'm afraid she doesn't suffer fools gladly, and that's part of the job description. But I have a feeling she'll end up surprising us all.'

Giles brought the car to a halt outside the Manor House, switched off the engine and placed a finger to his lips. 'Shh. I promised your mother I wouldn't wake Jessica.'

The two of them tiptoed across the gravel and Giles opened the front door tentatively, hoping it wouldn't creak. They were about halfway across the hall when Giles saw her, curled up in a chair by the last embers of a dying fire, fast asleep. He lifted her gently and carried her up the stairs in his arms. Sebastian ran ahead, opened her bedroom door and pulled back the blanket as Giles lowered her on to the bed. He was about to close the door behind him when he heard a voice say, 'Did we win, Uncle Giles?'

'Yes we did, Jessica,' Giles whispered. 'By four votes.'

'One of them was mine,' said Jessica after a lengthy yawn, 'because I got Albert to vote for you.'

'Then that's worth two votes,' said Sebastian. But before he could explain why, Jessica had fallen asleep again.

◄o►

By the time Giles put in an appearance at breakfast the following morning, it might have been better described as brunch.

'Good morning, good morning, good morning,' Giles said as

he walked around the table. He took a plate from the sideboard, lifted the lids of three silver salvers and selected large portions of scrambled eggs, bacon and baked beans, as if he was still a schoolboy. He sat down between Sebastian and Jessica.

'Mummy says you ought to have a glass of fresh orange juice and some cornflakes with milk before you visit the hotplate,' said Jessica.

'And she's right,' said Giles, 'but it's not going to stop me sitting next to my favourite girlfriend.'

'I'm not your favourite girlfriend,' said Jessica, which silenced him more effectively than any Tory minister had ever managed. 'Mummy told me that Gwyneth is your favourite girlfriend. Politicians!' she added, mimicking Emma, who burst out laughing.

Giles tried to move on to safer ground, turning to Sebastian and asking, 'Will you be playing for the first eleven this year?'

'Not if we want to win any matches,' he replied. 'No, I'll have to spend most of my time making sure I pass eight O levels if I'm to have any chance of joining the remove next year.'

'That would please your aunt Grace.'

'Not to mention his mother,' said Emma, not looking up from her paper.

'What will be your chosen subject if you make it to the remove?' asked Giles, still trying to dig himself out of a hole.

'Modern languages, with maths as my back-up.'

'Well, if you do win a scholarship to Cambridge, you'll have outdone both your father and I.'

'Your father and me,' corrected Emma.

'But not my mama or Aunt Grace,' Sebastian reminded him.

'True,' admitted Giles, who decided to keep quiet and concentrate on his morning post, which Marsden had brought across from Barrington Hall. He slit open a long white envelope and extracted a single sheet of paper that he'd been expecting for the past six months. He read the document a second time, before leaping joyfully in the air. Everyone stopped eating and stared at him, until Harry eventually asked, 'Has the Queen asked you to form a government?'

'No, it's far better news than that,' said Giles. 'Virginia has finally signed her divorce papers. I'm a free man at last!'

'It would appear that she's signed them in the nick of time,' said Emma, looking up from the *Daily Express*.

'What do you mean?' asked Giles.

'There's a photograph of her in the William Hickey column this morning, and she looks to me about seven months pregnant.'

'Does it say who the father is?'

'No, but the Duke of Arezzo is the man with his arm around her in the photo.' Emma passed the paper to her brother. 'And apparently he wants everyone to know that he's the happiest man in the world.'

'The second happiest,' said Giles.

'Does that mean I'll never have to speak to Lady Virginia again?' asked Jessica.

'Yes it does,' said Giles.

'Yippee,' said Jessica.

Giles slit open another envelope and extracted a cheque. As he studied it he raised his coffee cup to his grandfather, Sir Walter Barrington, coupled with the name of Ross Buchanan.

Emma nodded as he held it up to show her, and mouthed the words, 'I got one too.'

A few moments later, the door opened and Denby entered the room.

'I'm sorry to disturb you, Sir Giles, but Dr Hughes is on the line.'

'I was just about to call her,' said Giles, picking up his morning post and heading for the door.

'Why don't you take it in my study,' said Harry, 'then you won't be disturbed.'

'Thank you,' said Giles, almost running out of the room.

'And we'd better be on our way, Seb,' said Harry, 'if you still hope to be back in time for prep tonight.'

Sebastian allowed his mother to give him a perfunctory kiss

before going upstairs to collect his suitcase. When he came back down a few moments later, Denby was holding the front door open for him.

'Goodbye, Master Sebastian,' he said. 'We'll look forward to seeing you again in the summer holidays.'

'Thank you, Denby,' Sebastian said as he ran out on to the drive, where he found Jessica standing by the passenger door of the car. He gave her a big hug before climbing into the front seat next to his father.

'Make sure you pass all eight O levels,' Jessica said, 'so I can tell my friends how clever my big brother is.'

27

THE HEADMASTER WOULD have been the first to admit that the boy who had taken a couple of days off to assist his uncle at the general election was not the same young man who returned to Beechcroft Abbey a few days later.

Sebastian's housemaster, Mr Richards, described it as his 'St Paul on the road to Bristol' epiphany, because when Clifton came back to begin swotting for his end-of-term exams, he was no longer satisfied with simply coasting and relying on the natural gift for languages and maths that had always got him over the finishing line in the past. For the first time in his life he began to work just as hard as his less gifted chums, Bruno Martinez and Vic Kaufman.

When the results of their O levels were posted on the school notice board, no one was surprised that all three of them would be starting the new academic year in the sixth form, although several people, not including his aunt Grace, were amazed when Sebastian was invited to join the select group who were chosen to sit for a prize scholarship to Cambridge.

◄o►

Sebastian's housemaster agreed that Clifton, Kaufman and Martinez could share a study during their final year, and although Sebastian seemed to be working just as hard as his two friends, Mr Richards told the headmaster it still worried him that the boy might at some time revert to his old ways. Those misgivings might have proved unfounded if four separate incidents hadn't taken place during Sebastian's last year at Beechcroft Abbey that would shape his future.

The first occurred early in the new term, when Bruno invited Sebastian and Vic to join him and his father for supper at the Beechcroft Arms to celebrate defeating the examiners. Sebastian happily accepted, and was looking forward to a further introduction to the joys of champagne when the celebration was called off at the last moment. Bruno explained that something had arisen that caused his father to change his plans.

'More likely he changed his mind,' said Vic after Bruno had left for choir practice.

'What are you getting at?' asked Sebastian, looking up from his prep.

'I think you'll find that when Mr Martinez discovered I was Jewish, and Bruno wouldn't agree to celebrate without me, he called the whole thing off.'

'I could quite understand him calling the whole thing off because you're a wet and a weed, Kaufman, but who gives a damn that you're Jewish?'

'Far more people than you realize,' said Vic. 'Don't you remember when Bruno invited you to his fifteenth birthday party? He explained at the time that he was only allowed to take one guest, and it would be my turn next. We Jews don't forget these things.'

'I still can't believe Mr Martinez would cancel the dinner for no other reason than that you're Jewish.'

'Of course you can't, Seb, but that's only because your parents are civilized. They don't judge people on which cot they were born in, and they've passed that lack of prejudice on to you, without you being aware of it. But sadly you don't represent the majority, even in this school.'

Sebastian wanted to protest, but his friend had more to say on the subject.

'I know some people think we Jews are paranoid about the Holocaust – and who could blame us after the revelations that keep coming out about what really took place in those German concentration camps? But believe me, Seb, I can smell an anti-Semite at thirty paces, and it will only be a matter of time before your sister has to face up to the same problem.'

Sebastian burst out laughing. 'Jessica's not Jewish. A little bohemian perhaps, but not Jewish.'

'I can assure you, Seb, although I've only met her once, she's Jewish.'

It took a lot to render Sebastian speechless, but Vic had managed it.

The second incident happened during the summer holiday, when Sebastian joined his father in his study to go through his end-of-year report. Sebastian was glancing at the large selection of family photographs on Harry's desk when one in particular caught his attention: a picture of his mother linked arm in arm with his father and Uncle Giles on the lawn of the Manor House. Mama must have been about twelve, perhaps thirteen at the time, and was dressed in her Red Maids' school uniform. For a moment Sebastian thought it was Jessica, they looked so alike. Surely it was nothing more than a trick of the light. But then he recalled their visit to Dr Barnardo's, and how quickly his parents had given way when he insisted that Jessica was the only girl he would consider for a sister.

'Overall, very satisfactory,' said his father after he'd turned the last page of Sebastian's report. 'I'm sorry you're dropping Latin, but I'm sure the headmaster will have had his reasons for that. And I agree with Dr Banks-Williams that, if you continue to work hard, you've got a good chance of winning a scholarship to Cambridge.' Harry smiled. 'Banks-Williams is not a man given to hyperbole, but he told me on speech day that he's making arrangements for you to visit his old college some time next term, as he hopes you'll follow in his footsteps at Peterhouse, where of course he was himself the prize scholar.'

Sebastian was still staring at the photograph.

'Did you hear what I just said?' asked his father.

'Papa,' said Seb quietly, 'don't you think the time has come to tell me the truth about Jessica?' He transferred his gaze from the photograph to his father.

Harry pushed the report to one side, hesitated for a moment, then sat back and told Sebastian everything. He started with how Sebastian's grandfather had died at the hands of Olga Piotrovska, then moved on to the little girl who had been discovered in a basket in his office, and how Emma had tracked her down to a Barnardo's home in Bridgwater. When he came to the end, Sebastian only had one question.

'And when will you tell her the truth?'

'I ask myself that same question every day.'

'But why have you waited so long, Papa?'

'Because I don't want her to have to go through what you told me your friend Vic Kaufman experiences every day.'

'Jessica will go through far worse if she stumbles across the truth herself,' said Sebastian.

Harry was shocked by his next question.

'Do you want me to tell her?'

Harry stared in disbelief at his 17-year-old son. When does a child become an adult, he wondered. 'No,' he finally said. 'Your mother and I must take that responsibility. But we'll have to find the right moment.'

'There won't be a right moment,' said Seb.

Harry tried to recall the last time he heard those words.

The third incident arose when Sebastian fell in love for the first time. Not with a woman, but a city. It was love at first sight, because he'd never come across anything so beautiful, demanding, desirable and tempting all at the same time. By the time he turned his back on her to go back to Beechcroft, he was even more determined to see his name printed in gold leaf on the school's honours board.

Once Sebastian had returned from Cambridge, he began to work hours he hadn't realized existed, and even the headmaster was beginning to believe that the unlikely might prove possible. But then Sebastian met his second love, which caused the final incident.

He had been aware of Ruby's existence for some time, but it wasn't until his final term at Beechcroft that he really noticed her. He might not have done so even then if she hadn't touched his hand while he was standing at the serving plate waiting for a bowl of porridge. Sebastian assumed it was an accident, and wouldn't have given it a second thought if it hadn't happened again the next day.

He was queuing for a second helping of porridge, despite the fact that Ruby had already given him more than anyone else the first time round. As he turned to go back to his table, Ruby pressed a slip of paper into his hand. He didn't read it until he was alone in his study after breakfast.

See you in Skool Lane at five?

Sebastian was well aware that School Lane was out of bounds, and if a boy was caught there he would get six of the best from his housemaster. But he thought it was worth the risk.

When the bell rang to announce the end of the final lesson, Seb slipped out of the classroom and took a long, circuitous route around the playing fields before climbing over a wooden fence and stumbling down a steep bank into School Lane. He was fifteen minutes late, but Ruby appeared from behind a tree and headed straight for him. Sebastian thought she looked quite different, and not just because she wasn't wearing an apron and had changed into a white blouse and a black pleated skirt. She had also let her hair down, and it was the first time he had seen her wearing lipstick.

They didn't find a lot to talk about, but after that first encounter they met twice, sometimes three times a week, but never for more than half an hour, as they both had to be back in time for supper at six o'clock.

Seb had kissed Ruby several times during their second get-together before she introduced him to the sensation of what happened when their lips parted and their tongues touched. However, he didn't progress much beyond groping and trying to discover different parts of her body as they hid behind a tree. But with only a fortnight to go before the end of term, she allowed him to undo the buttons of her blouse and place a hand on her breast. A week later he located the clip on the back of her bra, and decided that once the exams were over, he was going to graduate in two subjects.

And that's when it all went wrong.

28

'RUSTICATED?'

'You have left me with no choice, Clifton.'

'But there are only four days to go before the end of term, sir.'

'And heaven knows what you'd get up to during that time if I didn't rusticate you,' countered the headmaster.

'But what have I done to deserve such a harsh punishment, sir?'

'I think you know only too well what you've done, Clifton, but if you wish me to spell out how many school rules you've broken in the last few days, I will happily do so.'

Sebastian had to stop himself from grinning as he recalled his latest escapade.

Dr Banks-Williams lowered his head and studied some notes he'd jotted down before summoning the boy to his study. It was some time before he spoke again.

'As there is less than a week to go before the end of term, Clifton, and as you have completed your final exams, I might have turned a blind eye to you being caught smoking in the old pavilion, even ignored the empty beer bottle found under your bed, but your latest indiscretion cannot be dismissed that easily.'

'My latest indiscretion?' repeated Sebastian, enjoying the headmaster's embarrassment.

'Being found in your study with a serving maid after lights out.'

Sebastian wanted to ask if it would have been all right if she hadn't been a serving maid, and he'd left the lights on. However, he realized that such levity might land him in even deeper trouble, and that if he hadn't won an open scholarship to Cambridge, the first the school had achieved for over a generation, he might well have been expelled, and not just rusticated. But he was already considering how he could turn his rustication from a disgrace into a badge of honour. After Ruby had made it clear that, for a small remuneration, she was willing to pass on her favours, Sebastian had happily accepted her terms, and she'd agreed to climb through the window of his study after lights out that evening. Although it had been the first time Sebastian had seen a naked woman, it quickly became clear to him that Ruby had climbed through that window before. The headmaster interrupted his thoughts.

'I need to ask you something, man to man,' he said, sounding even more pompous than usual. 'Your response may well influence my decision as to whether I advise the admissions tutor at Cambridge to withdraw your scholarship, which would be a great sadness for us all at Beechcroft. However, my paramount responsibility is to uphold the school's reputation.'

Sebastian clenched his fists, and tried to remain calm. Being rusticated was one thing, but losing his place at Cambridge would be quite another. He stood there, waiting for the headmaster to continue.

'Take your time before you answer my next question, Clifton, because it may well determine your future. Did Kaufman or Martinez play any part in your –' the headmaster hesitated, clearly searching for the right word, but finally settled on repeating – 'indiscretions?'

Sebastian suppressed a smile. The idea of Victor Kaufman uttering the word 'knickers', let alone trying to remove said article of clothing from Ruby, would have caused incredulity and mirth, even among the lower fifth.

'I can assure you, headmaster,' said Sebastian, 'that Victor has never, to my knowledge, smoked a cigarette or taken a sip of beer. And as for women, he's embarrassed when he has to undress in front of Matron.'

The headmaster smiled. Clearly Clifton had given the answer he'd wanted to hear, and it had the added advantage of being the truth.

'And Martinez?'

Sebastian had to think on his feet if was going to save his closest friend. He and Bruno had been inseparable since Sebastian had come to his aid during a dormitory pillow fight in his first term, when the new boy's only crime was being 'Johnny Foreigner' and, even worse, hailing from a country that didn't play cricket, a pastime Sebastian loathed – which only made their bond stronger. Sebastian knew that Bruno indulged in the occasional cigarette, and he had once joined him at a local pub for a beer, but only after their exams. He also knew that Bruno wouldn't be averse to what Ruby had to offer. What he couldn't be sure of was how much the headmaster already knew. Added to that was the fact that Bruno had also been offered a place at Cambridge in September and, although he'd only met his friend's father a couple of times, he wouldn't want to be the one held responsible for his son not going up to Cambridge.

'And Martinez?' the headmaster repeated a little more firmly.

'Bruno, as I'm sure you know, headmaster, is a devout Roman Catholic, and he has told me on several occasions that the first woman he sleeps with will be his wife.' That much was true, even if he hadn't expressed that view quite so vociferously lately.

The headmaster nodded thoughtfully, and Sebastian wondered for a moment if he'd got away with it, until Dr Banks-Williams added, 'And what about the smoking and drinking?'

'He did once try a cigarette during the holidays,' admitted Sebastian, 'but it made him sick, and to my knowledge he hasn't indulged since.' Well, not since last night, he was tempted to add. The headmaster looked unconvinced. 'And I did see him drink a glass of champagne on one occasion, but only after he'd been offered a place at Cambridge. And he was with his father at the time.'

What Sebastian didn't admit was that after Mr Martinez had driven them back to school in his red Rolls-Royce that evening, Sebastian had smuggled the bottle into his study, where they'd finished it off after lights out. But Sebastian had read too many of his father's detective novels not to know that guilty people often condemn themselves by saying one sentence too many.

'I am obliged, Clifton, for your frankness in this matter. It can't have been easy for you to be questioned about a friend. Nobody likes a sneak.'

This was followed by another long pause, but Sebastian didn't break it.

'Clearly there is no reason for me to trouble Kaufman,' the headmaster eventually managed, 'although I will need to have a word with Martinez, just to ensure he doesn't break any school rules during his last few days at Beechcroft.'

Sebastian smiled, as a bead of sweat trickled down his nose.

'Nevertheless, I have written to your father, explaining why you will be returning home a few days early. But because of your candour and evident remorse, I shall not be informing the admissions tutor at Cambridge that you have been rusticated.'

'I'm most grateful, sir,' said Sebastian, sounding genuinely relieved.

'You will now return to your study, pack your belongings and prepare to leave immediately. Your housemaster has been forewarned, and will sort out your travel arrangements to Bristol.'

'Thank you, sir,' said Sebastian, his head bowed, for fear the headmaster might see the smirk on his face.

'Do not attempt to contact either Kaufman or Martinez before you leave the school premises. And one other thing, Clifton, school rules will still apply to you until the last day of term. Should you break even one of them, I will not hesitate to reconsider my position concerning your place at Cambridge. Is that understood?'

'Absolutely,' said Sebastian.

'Let us hope you have learnt something from this experience, Clifton, something that will benefit you in the future.'

'Let's hope so,' said Sebastian, as the headmaster rose from behind his desk and handed him a letter.

'Please give this to your father as soon as you get home.'

'I most certainly will,' said Sebastian, placing the letter in an inside pocket of his jacket.

The headmaster thrust out his hand and Sebastian shook it, but without a great deal of enthusiasm.

'Good luck, Clifton,' the headmaster said unconvincingly.

'Thank you, sir,' Sebastian replied, before closing the door quietly behind him.

◆

The headmaster sat back down, well satisfied with how the meeting had gone. He was relieved, though not surprised, that Kaufman had not been involved in such a distasteful incident, especially as his father, Saul Kaufman, was a school governor, as well as chairman of Kaufman's Bank, one of the most respected financial institutions in the City of London.

And he certainly didn't want to fall out with Martinez's father, who had recently hinted that he would be giving a donation of £10,000 to the school library appeal if his son was offered a place at Cambridge. He wasn't altogether sure how Don Pedro Martinez had made his fortune, but any fees or extras were always paid by return of post.

Clifton, on the other hand, had been a problem from the moment he had walked through the school gates. The headmaster had tried to be understanding, in view of all that the boy's mother and father had been through, but there was a limit to how much the school could be expected to tolerate. In fact, if Clifton hadn't been likely to win that open scholarship to Cambridge, Dr Banks-Williams wouldn't have hesitated to expel him some time ago. He was glad to have finally seen the back of him, and only hoped he wouldn't join the Old Boys.

'Old Boys,' he said out loud, jogging his memory. He was due to address their annual dinner in London that evening,

233

when he would present his end-of-term report; his last, after fifteen years as headmaster. He didn't much care for the Welshman who had been chosen to succeed him; the sort of chap who didn't tie his bow tie, and probably would have let Clifton off with a warning.

His secretary had typed up his speech and left a copy on his desk for him to go over in case he wanted to make some late changes. He would have liked to read it one more time, but having to deal with Clifton had made that impossible. Any last-minute emendations would have to be added by hand during the train journey up to London.

He checked his watch, placed the speech in his briefcase and headed upstairs to his private quarters. He was pleased to find that his wife had already packed his dinner jacket and trousers, a starched white shirt, a bow tie, a change of socks and a wash bag. He'd made it clear to the chairman of the Old Boys that he didn't approve when they'd voted to stop wearing white tie and tails for the annual dinner.

His wife drove him to the station, and they arrived only minutes before the express to Paddington was due. He purchased a first-class return ticket and hurried across the bridge to the far platform, where an engine was just coming to a halt before disgorging its passengers. He stepped on to the platform and checked his watch again. Four minutes to spare. He nodded to the guard, who was exchanging a red flag for a green one.

'All aboard,' the guard shouted, as the headmaster headed for the first-class section at the front of the train.

He climbed into the carriage and sank back into a corner seat, only to be greeted by a cloud of smoke. A disgusting habit. He agreed with *The Times*' correspondent who had recently suggested that the Great Western Railway should designate far more no-smoking carriages for first-class passengers.

The headmaster took the speech out of his briefcase and placed it on his lap. He looked up as the smoke cleared, and saw him sitting on the other side of the carriage.

29

SEBASTIAN STUBBED OUT his cigarette, leapt up, grabbed his suitcase from the rack above him and left the carriage without a word. He was painfully aware that although the headmaster said nothing, his eyes never left him.

He humped his suitcase through several carriages to the far end of the train, where he squeezed himself into an over-crowded third-class carriage. As he stared out of the window, he tried to think if there was any way out of his present predicament.

Perhaps he should return to first class and explain to the headmaster that he was going to spend a few days in London with his uncle, Sir Giles Barrington, MP? But why would he do that, when he'd been instructed to return to Bristol and hand Dr Banks-Williams's letter to his father? The truth was that his parents were in Los Angeles attending a ceremony at which his mother was to be awarded her business degree, summa cum laude, and they wouldn't be arriving back in England before the end of the week.

Then why didn't you tell me that in the first place, he could hear the headmaster saying, and then your housemaster could have issued you with the correct ticket? Because he had intended to return to Bristol on the last day of term, so when they turned up on Saturday, they would be none the wiser. He might even have got away with it, if he hadn't been in a first-class carriage, smoking. After all, he'd been warned what the consequences would be if he broke another school rule before the end of term. End of term. He'd broken three school rules within an hour of leaving the premises. But then, he never thought he'd see the headmaster again in his life.

He wanted to say, I'm an Old Boy now and I can do as I please, but he knew that wouldn't work. And if he did decide to return to first class, there was a risk that the headmaster would discover he only had a third-class ticket; a wheeze he always tried on whenever he travelled to and from school at the beginning and end of term.

He would occupy the corner seat of a first-class carriage, making sure he had a clear view of the corridor. The moment the ticket collector entered the far end of the carriage, Sebastian would nip out and disappear into the nearest lavatory, not locking the door but leaving the vacant sign in place. Once the ticket collector had moved on to the next carriage, he would slip back into the first-class compartment for the rest of the journey. And as it was a non-stop service, the wheeze never failed. Well, it had nearly failed once, when a vigilant conductor had doubled back and caught him in the wrong carriage. He'd immediately burst into tears and apologized, explaining that his mother and father always travelled first class, and he didn't even realize there was a third class. He had got away with it, but then he'd only been eleven at the time. Now he was seventeen, and it wouldn't only be the ticket collector who didn't believe him.

He dismissed any chance of a reprieve and, accepting that he wouldn't be going up to Cambridge in September, Sebastian began to consider what he should do once the train pulled into Paddington.

◄o►

The headmaster didn't even glance at his speech as the train sped through the countryside towards the capital.

Should he go and look for the boy and demand an explanation? He knew Clifton's housemaster had supplied him with a third-class single to Bristol, so what was he doing in a first-class carriage bound for London? Had he somehow got on the wrong train? No, that boy always knew in which direction he was going. He just hadn't expected to be caught. In any case, he'd been smoking, despite having been explicitly told that school rules would apply until the last day of term. The boy hadn't even waited an hour to defy him. There were no mitigating circumstances. Clifton had left him with no choice.

He would announce at assembly tomorrow morning that Clifton had been expelled. He would then phone the admissions tutor at Peterhouse, and then the boy's father, to explain why his son would no longer be going up to Cambridge that Michaelmas. After all, Dr Banks-Williams had to consider the good name of the school, which he had nurtured assiduously for the past fifteen years.

He turned several pages of his speech before he came across the relevant passage. He read the words he'd written about Clifton's achievement, hesitated for a moment, and then drew a line through them.

◄○►

Sebastian was considering whether he should be the first or the last off the train when it pulled into Paddington. It didn't matter much, as long as he avoided bumping into the headmaster.

He decided to be first, and perched on the edge of his seat for the last twenty minutes of the journey. He checked his pockets to find he had one pound twelve shillings and sixpence, far more than usual, but then his housemaster had reimbursed all his unspent pocket money.

He had originally planned to spend a few days in London before returning to Bristol on the last day of term, when he had absolutely no intention of handing the headmaster's letter to his father. He removed the envelope from his pocket. It was addressed to H.A. Clifton Esq.: Private. Sebastian glanced around the carriage to check that no one was looking at him before he ripped it open. He read the headmaster's words slowly, and then reread them. The letter was measured, fair and, to his surprise, made no mention of Ruby. If only he'd taken the train to Bristol, gone home and handed the letter to his father after he returned from America, things might have been so different. Damn it. What was the headmaster doing on the train in the first place?

Sebastian returned the letter to his pocket and tried to concentrate on what he would do in London, because he certainly wouldn't be returning to Bristol until this had all blown over, and that might not be for some time. But how long could he hope to survive on one pound twelve shillings and sixpence? He was about to find out.

He was standing by the carriage door long before the train pulled into Paddington, and had opened it even before it had come to a halt. He leapt out, ran towards the barrier as fast as his heavy suitcase would allow and handed his ticket to the collector before disappearing into the crowd.

Sebastian had only visited London once before, and on that occasion he'd been with his parents, and there had been a car waiting to pick them up and whisk them off to his uncle's town house in Smith Square. Uncle Giles had taken him to the Tower of London to see the Crown Jewels, and then on to Madame Tussaud's to admire the waxworks of Edmund Hillary, Betty Grable and Don Bradman before having tea and a sticky bun at the Regent Palace Hotel. The following day he'd given them a tour of the House of Commons, and they'd seen Winston Churchill glowering from the front bench. Sebastian had been surprised to find how small he was.

When it was time for him to go home, Sebastian had told his uncle that he couldn't wait to come back to London. Now he had, there was no car to pick him up, and the last person he could risk visiting was his uncle. He had no idea where he would spend the night.

As he made his way through the crowd, someone bumped into him, nearly knocking him over. He turned to see a young man hurrying away – he hadn't even bothered to apologize.

Sebastian walked out of the station and into a street crammed with Victorian terraced houses, several of which displayed bed-and-breakfast signs in their windows. He selected the one with the brightest polished door knocker and the neatest window boxes. A comely woman wearing a floral nylon housecoat answered his knock, and gave her potential guest a welcoming smile. If she was surprised to find a young man in school uniform standing on her doorstep, she didn't show it.

'Come in,' she said. 'Are you looking for accommodation, sir?'

'Yes,' said Sebastian, surprised to be called 'sir'. 'I need a room for the night, and wondered how much you charge?'

'Four shillings a night, including breakfast, or a pound for a week.'

'I only need a room for one night,' said Sebastian, having realized he would have to search for cheaper accommodation in the morning if he intended to stay in London for any length of time.

'Of course,' she said as she picked up his suitcase and headed down the corridor.

Sebastian had never seen a woman carrying a suitcase before, but she was halfway up the stairs before he could do anything about it.

'My name's Mrs Tibbet,' she said, 'but my regulars call me Tibby.' When she reached the first-floor landing, she added, 'I'll be putting you in number seven. It's at the back of the house, so you're less likely to be woken by the morning traffic.'

Sebastian had no idea what she was talking about, as he'd never been woken by traffic in his life.

Mrs Tibbet unlocked the door to room seven and stood aside to allow her guest to enter. The room was smaller than his study at Beechcroft, but, like its owner, it was neat and tidy. There was a single bed, with clean sheets, and a washbasin in the corner.

'You'll find the bathroom at the end of the corridor,' Mrs Tibbet said before he could ask.

'I've changed my mind, Mrs Tibbet,' he said, 'I'll take it for a week.'

She took a key out of her housecoat but before she handed it over she said, 'Then that will be one pound, in advance.'

'Yes, of course,' said Sebastian. He reached into his trouser pocket, only to find it was empty. He tried another pocket, and then another, but there was no sign of his money. He finally fell to his knees, opened his suitcase, and began frantically searching among his clothes.

Mrs Tibbet placed her hands on her hips, her smile no longer on display. Sebastian rummaged in vain among his clothes until he finally gave up, collapsed on to the bed and prayed that Tibby would be more sympathetic than the headmaster.

◄○►

The headmaster checked into his room at the Reform Club and had a quick bath before changing into his dinner jacket. He checked his bow tie in the mirror above the washbasin, then returned downstairs to join his host.

Nick Judd, the chairman of the Old Boys, was waiting at the bottom of the stairs, and led his guest of honour into the reception room, where they joined other members of the committee at the bar.

'What will you have to drink, headmaster?' asked the chairman.

'Just a dry sherry, please.'

Judd's next words disconcerted him. 'Allow me to be the first to congratulate you,' he said after he'd ordered the drinks, 'on the school being awarded the top scholarship to Peterhouse. A worthy accolade to crown your final year.'

The headmaster said nothing, but realized that the three lines he had crossed out of his speech would have to be reinstated. The news of Clifton's expulsion needn't come out until later. After all, the boy had won the scholarship, and that wouldn't change until he had spoken to the admissions tutor at Cambridge in the morning.

Unfortunately, the chairman wasn't the only person to refer to Clifton's achievement, and by the time the headmaster rose to deliver his annual report, he saw no reason to let the assembled gathering know what he had planned to do the following day. He was surprised that the announcement of the top scholarship received such prolonged applause.

The speech was well received, and when Dr Banks-Williams sat down, so many Old Boys came up to the top table to wish him a happy retirement that he nearly missed the last train back to Beechcroft. No sooner had he settled down in his first-class compartment than his thoughts returned to Sebastian Clifton. He began to write down a few words for his address to morning assembly: 'standards', 'decency', 'honour', 'discipline' and 'respect' came to mind, and by the time the train pulled into Beechcroft, he had completed the first draft.

When he handed in his ticket, he was relieved to see his wife sitting in the car waiting for him, despite the late hour

'How did you get on?' she asked, even before he'd pulled the car door closed.

'I think I can say my speech was well received, given the circumstances.'

'The circumstances?'

By the time they had reached the headmaster's house, he had told his wife all about the unfortunate encounter with Clifton that had taken place on the train to London.

'And what do you intend to do about it?' she asked as he unlocked the front door.

'He's left me with no choice. I shall announce at morning assembly that Clifton has been expelled, and therefore sadly will not be taking up his place at Cambridge in September.'

'Isn't that a little draconian?' suggested Mrs Banks-Williams. 'After all, he may well have had a good reason for being on the London train.'

'Then why did he leave the carriage the moment he saw me?'

'He probably didn't want to spend the whole journey with you, my dear. After all, you can be quite intimidating.'

'But don't forget, I also caught him smoking,' he said, ignoring her comment.

'Why shouldn't he? He was off the premises, and no longer *in statu pupillari*.'

'I made it quite clear that school rules would apply to him until the end of term, otherwise he would have to face the consequences.'

'Would you care for a nightcap, my dear?'

'No, thank you. I must try and get a good night's sleep. Tomorrow isn't going to be easy.'

'For you, or for Clifton?' she enquired before turning the light out.

—◦—

Sebastian sat on the end of the bed and told Mrs Tibbet everything that had taken place that day. He left nothing out, even showing her the letter the headmaster had written.

'Don't you think it might be wise to go home? After all, your parents will be worried to death if you're not there when they get back. And in any case, you can't be certain the head-master is going to expel you.'

'Believe me, Mrs Tibbet, Hilly-Billy will have made up his mind, and he'll announce his decision at assembly tomorrow.'

'You should still go home.'

'I can't, after letting them down. The one thing they've always wanted was for me to go to Cambridge. They'll never forgive me.'

'I wouldn't be so sure of that,' said Mrs Tibbet. 'My father always used to say, if you've got a problem, sleep on it before you make a decision you might later regret. Things always look rosier in the morning.'

'But I haven't even got anywhere to sleep.'

'Don't be silly,' Mrs Tibbet said, placing an arm around his shoulder. 'You can spend the night here. But not on an empty stomach, so once you've unpacked, come down and join me in the kitchen.'

30

'I'VE GOT A PROBLEM with table three,' said the waitress as she barged through the door and into the kitchen.

'What sort of problem, Janice?' asked Mrs Tibbet calmly, cracking two eggs and dropping them into a large frying pan.

'I can't understand a word they're saying.'

'Ah, yes, Mr and Mrs Ferrer. I think they're French. All you need to know is un, deux and oeuf.' Janice didn't look convinced. 'Just speak slowly,' said Mrs Tibbet, 'and don't raise your voice. It's not their fault they can't speak English.'

'Would you like me to have a word with them?' asked Sebastian as he put down his knife and fork.

'Can you speak French?' asked Mrs Tibbet, placing the pan back on the Aga.

'Yes I can.'

'Then be my guest.'

Sebastian rose from the kitchen table and accompanied Janice back to the dining room. All nine tables were occupied, and Janice walked across to a middle-aged couple who were seated in the far corner of the room.

'Bonjour, monsieur,' said Sebastian. 'Comment puis-je vous aider?'

The startled guest gave Sebastian a puzzled look. 'Somos español.'

'Buenas dias, señor. Cómo puedo ayudarle?' said Sebastian. Janice waited while Mr and Mrs Ferrer had finished speaking

243

to him. 'Volveré en uno momento,' said Sebastian, and returned to the kitchen.

'So what do our French friends want?' asked Mrs Tibbet, as she cracked two more eggs.

'They're Spanish, not French,' said Sebastian, 'and they'd like some lightly toasted brown bread, a couple of three-minute boiled eggs and two cups of black coffee.'

'Anything else?'

'Yes, directions to the Spanish Embassy.'

'Janice, you serve their coffee and toast while I take care of the eggs.'

'And what can I do?' asked Sebastian.

'There's a telephone directory on the hall table. Look up the Spanish Embassy, then find a map and show them how to get there.'

'By the way,' Sebastian said, placing a sixpence on the table, 'they gave me this.'

Mrs Tibbet smiled. 'Your first tip.'

'The first money I've ever earned,' said Sebastian, pushing the coin across the table. 'So now I only owe you three and six.' He left the kitchen without another word and picked up the telephone directory from the hall table. He looked up the Spanish Embassy and, after finding it on a map, he told Mr and Mrs Ferrer how to get to Chesham Place. A few moments later he returned to the kitchen with another sixpence.

'Keep this up,' said Mrs Tibbet, 'and I'll have to make you a partner.'

Sebastian took off his jacket, rolled up his sleeves and made his way across to the sink.

'Now what do you think you're doing?'

'I'm going to do the washing-up,' he replied, as he turned on the hot tap. 'Isn't that what customers in films do, when they can't pay their bill?'

'I'll bet that's another first for you,' said Mrs Tibbet, as she placed two rashers of bacon next to two fried eggs. 'Table one, Janice, Mr and Mrs Ramsbottom from Yorkshire. I can't understand a word they say either. So tell me, Sebastian,' she said as

Janice walked out of the kitchen, 'can you speak any other languages?'

'German, Italian, French and Hebrew.'

'Hebrew? Are you Jewish?'

'No, but one of my pals at school was, and he taught it to me during chemistry lessons.'

Mrs Tibbet laughed. 'I think you should get yourself off to Cambridge as quickly as possible, because you're just not qualified to be a dishwasher.'

'I won't be going to Cambridge, Mrs Tibbet,' Sebastian reminded her, 'and I've got no one to blame but myself. However, I do plan to visit Eaton Square and try to find out where my friend Bruno Martinez lives. He should be back from school by Friday afternoon.'

'Good idea,' said Mrs Tibbet. 'He's sure to know if you've been expelled or just . . . what was the other word?'

'Rusticated,' said Sebastian, as Janice came bustling back into the kitchen carrying two empty plates; the most sincere praise a cook can ever receive. She handed them to Sebastian before picking up two more boiled eggs.

'Table five,' Mrs Tibbet reminded her.

'And table nine want more cornflakes,' said Janice.

'Then pick up a fresh packet from the pantry, you dozy numskull.'

Sebastian didn't finish the washing-up until just after ten. 'What next?' he asked.

'Janice hoovers the dining room and then lays up for tomorrow's breakfast, while I clean the kitchen. Check out is at twelve, and once the guests have left, we change the sheets, make up the beds and water the window boxes.'

'So what would you like me to do?' said Sebastian, rolling his sleeves back down.

'Take a bus to Eaton Square and find out if your friend is expected back on Friday.' Sebastian put on his jacket. 'But not before you've made your bed and checked that your room is tidy.'

He laughed. 'You're beginning to sound like my mother.'

'I'll take that as a compliment. Be sure you're back before one o'clock, because I'm expecting some Germans, and you just might be useful.' Sebastian headed for the door. 'You'll need these,' she added, handing back the two sixpenny pieces. 'That is, unless you intend to walk to Eaton Square and back.'

'Thank you, Mrs Tibbet.'

'Tibby. As you're clearly going to be a regular.'

Sebastian pocketed the money and kissed her on both cheeks, which silenced Mrs Tibbet for the first time.

He left the kitchen before she could recover, bounded up the stairs, made his bed and tidied his room before returning to the hall, where he checked the map. He was surprised to find that Eaton Square was spelt differently from the school that had turned down his uncle Giles for some misdemeanour none of the family ever talked about.

Before he left, Janice told him to catch a No. 36 bus, get off at Sloane Square and walk from there.

The first thing Sebastian noticed when he closed the guest house door behind him was how many people were rushing about in every direction, at quite a different pace from Bristolians. He joined a queue at the bus stop and watched several red double-deckers arrive and depart before one displaying No. 36 turned up. He climbed on board, walked up to the top deck and took a seat at the front as he wanted to have a good view of everything that was going on below.

'Where to, young man?' asked the bus conductor.

'Sloane Square,' said Sebastian. 'And please could you let me know when we get there?'

'That'll be tuppence.'

Sebastian became engrossed by all the sights as he travelled past Marble Arch, down Park Lane and around Hyde Park Corner, but tried to concentrate on what he would do once he arrived. All he knew was that Bruno lived in Eaton Square, but he didn't know the number. He just hoped it was a small square.

'Sloane Square!' shouted the conductor as the bus came to a halt outside W.H. Smith.

Sebastian quickly made his way down the steps. Once he was on the pavement, he looked around for a landmark. His eyes settled on the Royal Court theatre, where Joan Plowright was performing in *The Chairs*. He checked his map, walked past the theatre and took a right, estimating that Eaton Square was only a couple of hundred yards away.

Once he'd reached it, he slowed down in the hope of spotting Don Pedro's red Rolls-Royce, but there was no sign of the car. He realized that unless he got lucky it could take hours for him to find out where Bruno lived.

As he walked along the pavement, he noticed that about half the houses had been converted into flats, and displayed a list of the occupants' names by their doorbells. The other half were houses and gave no indication of who lived there, having only a brass knocker or a bell marked 'Tradesmen'. Sebastian felt sure Bruno's father wasn't the kind of man who would share a front door with someone else.

He stood on the top step of No. 1 and pressed the tradesmen's bell. Moments later a butler appeared, wearing a long black coat and white tie, which reminded him of Marsden at Barrington Hall.

'I'm looking for a Mr Martinez,' Sebastian said politely.

'No gentleman of that name resides here,' said the butler, and he closed the door before Sebastian had a chance to ask if he had any idea where Mr Martinez did live.

During the next hour, Sebastian experienced everything from 'He doesn't live here' to the door being slammed in his face. It was towards the end of the second hour, by which time he'd reached the far side of the square, that in response to his oft-repeated question, a maid asked, 'Is he a foreign gentleman who drives a red Rolls-Royce?'

'Yes, that's him,' said Sebastian with a feeling of relief.

'I think you'll find he lives at number forty-four, two doors down,' said the maid, pointing to her right.

'Thank you very much,' said Sebastian. He walked briskly on to No. 44, climbed the steps, took a deep breath and banged twice with the brass knocker.

It was some time before the door was opened and Sebastian was greeted by a heavily built man, who must have been well over six feet tall and looked more like a boxer than a butler.

'What do you want?' he asked in an accent Sebastian didn't recognize.

'I wondered if this is where Bruno Martinez lives?'

'Who wants to know?'

'My name is Sebastian Clifton.'

The man's tone suddenly changed. 'Yes, I've heard him talk about you, but he's not here.'

'Do you know when he's expected to return?'

'I think I heard Mr Martinez saying he'd be home on Friday afternoon.'

Sebastian decided not to ask any more questions, and simply said, 'Thank you.' The giant gave a curt nod, and slammed the door. Or was he just closing it?

Sebastian began running towards Sloane Square as he was determined to be back in time to help Mrs Tibbet with her German guests. He took the first bus heading in the direction of Paddington. Once he was back at No. 37 Praed Street, he joined Mrs Tibbet and Janice in the kitchen.

'Did you have any luck, Seb?' she asked even before he'd had the chance to sit down.

'I managed to find out where Bruno lives,' said Sebastian triumphantly, 'and—'

'Number forty-four Eaton Square,' said Mrs Tibbet as she placed a plate of sausages and mash in front of him.

'How do you know that?'

'There's a Martinez listed in the phone directory, but you'd already gone by the time I thought of that. Did you discover when he's coming home?'

'Yes, some time on Friday afternoon.'

'Then I'm stuck with you for another couple of days.' Sebastian looked embarrassed until she added, 'Which could work out quite well, because the Germans are staying until Friday afternoon, so you—' A firm rap on the door interrupted her thoughts. 'If I'm not mistaken, that will be Mr Kroll and his friends. Come with me, Seb, and let's find out if you can understand a word they're saying.'

Sebastian reluctantly left his sausage and mash, and followed Mrs Tibbet. He'd caught up with her by the time she opened the front door.

◄○►

He only managed to catch a few moments' sleep during the next forty-eight hours, between lugging suitcases up and down the stairs, hailing taxis, serving drinks and, most important, translating a myriad questions, from 'Where is the London Palladium?' to 'Do you know any good German restaurants?', most of which Mrs Tibbet was able to answer without having to refer to a map or guidebook. On the Thursday evening, their last night, Sebastian blushed when he was asked a question to which he didn't know the answer. Mrs Tibbet came to his rescue.

'Tell them they'll find all the girls they need at the Windmill Theatre in Soho.'

The Germans bowed low.

When they left on the Friday afternoon, Herr Kroll gave Sebastian a pound and shook him warmly by the hand. Sebastian handed the money to Mrs Tibbet, but she refused it, saying, 'It's yours. You've more than earned it.'

'But I still haven't paid for my board and lodging. And if I don't, my grandmother, who used to be the manageress of the Grand Hotel in Bristol, would never let me hear the end of it.'

Mrs Tibbet took him in her arms. 'Good luck, Seb,' she said. When she finally let him go, she stood back and added, 'Take your trousers off.'

Sebastian looked even more embarrassed than when Herr Kroll had asked him where he could find a strip joint.

'I need to iron those, if you're not going to look as if you've just come from work.'

31

'I'M NOT SURE if he's in,' said a man Sebastian could never forget. 'But I'll check.'

'Seb!' a voice echoed down the marble corridor. 'It's so good to see you, old chap,' Bruno added as he shook hands with his friend. 'I was afraid I might never see you again, if the rumours were true.'

'What rumours?'

'Karl, please ask Elena to serve tea in the drawing room.'

Bruno led Sebastian into the house. At Beechcroft, Sebastian had always taken the lead, with Bruno his willing lieutenant. Now the roles were reversed as the guest followed his host down a corridor and into the drawing room. Sebastian had always thought he had been brought up in a degree of comfort, even luxury, but what greeted him when he entered the drawing room would have taken minor royalty by surprise. The paintings, the furniture, even the carpets wouldn't have looked out of place in a museum.

'What rumours?' repeated Sebastian nervously, as he took a seat on the edge of the sofa.

'I'll come to that in a moment,' said Bruno. 'But first, tell me why you left so suddenly? One minute you were sitting with Vic and me in the study, and the next you'd disappeared.'

'Didn't the headmaster say anything at morning assembly the next day?'

'Not a word, which only added to the mystery. Everyone had a theory of course, but as both the housemaster and Banks-

Williams were silent as the grave, no one knew what was fact and what was fiction. I asked Matron, that fount of all knowledge, but she clammed up whenever your name was mentioned. Most unlike her. Vic feared the worst, but then his glass is always half empty. He was convinced you'd been expelled and that was the last we'd hear of you, but I told him we'd all meet up again at Cambridge.'

'I'm afraid not,' said Sebastian. 'Vic was right.' He then told his friend everything that had happened since his interview with the headmaster earlier in the week, leaving Bruno in no doubt how devastated he was to have lost his place at Cambridge.

When he came to the end of his story, Bruno said, 'So that's why Hilly-Billy called me to his study after assembly on Wednesday morning.'

'What punishment did you get?'

'Six of the best, my prefect status removed, plus a warning that any further indiscretions and I'd be rusticated.'

'I might have got away with just being rusticated,' said Sebastian, 'if Hilly-Billy hadn't caught me smoking on the train to London.'

'Why go to London when you had a ticket for Bristol?'

'I was going to hang around here until Friday, and then go home on the last day of term. Ma and Pa aren't due back from the States until tomorrow, so I figured they'd be none the wiser. If I hadn't bumped into Hilly-Billy on the train, I would have got away with it.'

'But if you take the train to Bristol today, they still won't be any the wiser.'

'No chance,' said Sebastian. 'Don't forget what Hilly-Billy said. "School rules will still apply to you until the last day of term," he mimicked, clinging on to the lapels of his jacket. "Should you break even one of them, I will not hesitate to reconsider my position concerning your place at Cambridge. Is that understood?" Within an hour of being booted out of his office, I'd broken three rules, right under his nose!'

A maid entered the room carrying a large silver tray

weighed down with food that neither of them had ever experienced at Beechcroft.

Bruno buttered a hot muffin. 'As soon as we've had tea, why don't you go back to the guest house and pick up your things. You can stay here tonight, and we'll try and work out what you should do next.'

'But how will your pa feel about that?'

'On the way here from school, I told him I wouldn't be going up to Cambridge in September if it hadn't been for you taking the blame. He said I was lucky to have such a friend, and he'd like the chance to thank you personally.'

'If Banks-Williams had seen you first, Bruno, you would have done exactly the same thing.'

'That's not the point, Seb. He saw you first, so I got away with a thrashing and Vic escaped scot free, and only just in time, because Vic had been hoping to get to know Ruby more intimately.'

'Ruby,' repeated Sebastian. 'Did you find out what happened to her?'

'She disappeared on the same day as you. Cook told me we wouldn't be seeing her again.'

'And you *still* think I have a chance of going to Cambridge?'

Both boys fell silent.

'Elena,' said Bruno when the maid returned, carrying a large fruitcake, 'my friend will be returning to Paddington to pick up his things. Would you ask the chauffeur to drive him, and have a guest room prepared by the time he gets back?'

'I'm afraid the chauffeur has just left to pick up your father from the office. I'm not expecting them back before dinner.'

'Then you'll have to take a taxi,' said Bruno. 'But not until you've sampled cook's fruitcake.'

'I've barely enough money for a bus, let alone a taxi,' whispered Sebastian.

'I'll book you one and put it on my father's account,' said Bruno as he picked up the cake knife.

◄○►

'That's wonderful news,' said Mrs Tibbet, once Sebastian had told her everything that had happened that afternoon. 'But I still think you should phone your parents and let them know where you are. After all, you still can't be certain you've lost your place at Cambridge.'

'Ruby's been sacked, my housemaster refuses to discuss the subject, even Matron, who is never short of an opinion, wouldn't say a word. I can promise you, Mrs Tibbet, I won't be going up to Cambridge. In any case, my parents aren't back from America until tomorrow, so I couldn't get in touch with them even if I wanted to.'

Mrs Tibbet kept her counsel. 'Well, if you're leaving,' she said, 'you'd better go and pack your things because I could use the room. I've already had to turn away three customers.'

'I'll be as quick as I can.' Sebastian left the kitchen and ran back up the stairs to his room. Once he'd packed and tidied up, he returned to find Mrs Tibbet and Janice standing in the hall waiting for him.

'It's been a memorable week, quite memorable,' said Mrs Tibbet as she opened the front door, 'and one Janice and me are unlikely to forget.'

'When I write my memoirs, Tibby, you'll get a whole chapter,' Sebastian said as they walked out on to the pavement together.

'You'll have forgotten us both long before then,' she said wistfully.

'Not a hope. This will become my second home, you'll see.' Sebastian planted a kiss on Janice's cheek, before giving Tibby a long hug. 'You're not going to get rid of me quite that easily,' he added as he climbed back into the waiting taxi.

Mrs Tibbet and Janice waved as the cab began its journey back to Eaton Square. Tibby had wanted to tell him one more time, for heaven's sake ring your mother the minute she gets back from America, but she knew it would be pointless.

'Janice, go and change the sheets in number seven,' she said as the taxi turned right at the end of the road and disappeared out of sight. Mrs Tibbet quickly returned to the house. If Seb wouldn't get in touch with his mother, she would.

◄o►

That evening, Bruno's father took the boys to the Ritz for dinner; more champagne, and Sebastian's first experience of oysters. Don Pedro, as he insisted Sebastian call him, thanked him again and again for shouldering the blame and making it possible for Bruno still to go to Cambridge. 'So British,' he kept repeating.

Bruno sat silently picking at his food, rarely joining in the conversation. All his confidence of the afternoon seemed to have evaporated in the presence of his father. But the biggest surprise of the evening came when Don Pedro revealed that Bruno had two older brothers, Diego and Luis, something he'd never mentioned before, and they'd certainly never visited him at Beechcroft Abbey. Sebastian wanted to ask why, but as his friend kept his head bowed, he decided he'd wait until they were alone.

'They work alongside me in the family business,' said Don Pedro.

'And what is the family business?' asked Sebastian innocently.

'Import and export,' said Don Pedro without going into detail.

Don Pedro offered his young guest his first Cuban cigar, and asked what he planned to do now he wouldn't be going to Cambridge. Sebastian admitted between coughs, 'I suppose I'll have to look for a job.'

'Would you like to earn yourself a hundred pounds cash? There's something you could do for me in Buenos Aires, and you'd be back in England by the end of the month.'

'Thank you, sir, that's most generous. But what would I be expected to do for such a large sum of money?'

'Come to Buenos Aires with me next Monday, stay for a few days as my guest, then take a package back to Southampton on the *Queen Mary*.'

'But why me? Surely one of your staff could carry out such a simple task?'

'Because the package contains a family heirloom,' said Don Pedro without missing a beat, 'and I need someone who speaks both Spanish and English, and can be trusted. The way you conducted yourself when Bruno was in trouble convinces me that you're the right man –' and looking at Bruno, he added, 'and perhaps this is my way of saying thank you.'

'That's kind of you, sir,' said Sebastian, not able to believe his luck.

'Let me give you ten pounds in advance,' Don Pedro said, taking a wallet out of his pocket. 'You'll get the other ninety on the day you sail back to England.' He removed two five-pound notes from his wallet and pushed them across the table. It was more money than Sebastian had been given in his life. 'Why don't you and Bruno enjoy yourselves this weekend? After all, you've earned it.'

Bruno said nothing.

◄○►

As soon as the last guest had been served, Mrs Tibbet instructed Janice to hoover the dining room and lay up for tomorrow's breakfast, but not until she'd finished the washing-up, as if she'd never given the order before. Then Mrs Tibbet disappeared upstairs. Janice assumed she was going to her office to prepare the morning shopping list, but instead she just sat at her desk staring at the phone. She poured herself a glass of whisky, something she rarely did before her last guest had gone to bed, took a gulp and picked up the receiver.

'Directory enquiries,' she said, and waited until another voice came on the line.

'What name?' asked the voice.

'Mr Harry Clifton,' she replied.

'And which city?'

'Bristol.'

'And the address?'

'I don't have it, but he's a famous author,' said Mrs Tibbet,

255

trying to sound as if she knew him. She waited for some time and began to wonder if she'd been cut off, until the voice said, 'That subscriber's number is ex-directory, madam, so I'm afraid I'm unable to put you through.'

'But this is an emergency.'

'I'm sorry, madam, but I couldn't put you through if you were the Queen of England.'

Mrs Tibbet put down the phone. She sat for some time wondering if there was any other way of getting in touch with Mrs Clifton. Then she thought of Janice, and returned to the kitchen.

'Where do you buy those paperbacks you've always got your head in?' she asked Janice.

'At the station, on my way in to work,' Janice replied as she continued with the washing-up. Mrs Tibbet cleaned the Aga while she thought about Janice's reply. Once she'd completed the job to her satisfaction, she took off her apron, folded it neatly, picked up her shopping basket and announced, 'I'm off to the shops.'

After leaving the guest house, she didn't turn right as she did every other morning, when she would head for the butcher in search of the finest slices of Danish bacon, the greengrocer for the freshest fruit, and the baker for the warmest loaves as they were taken from the oven, and even then she would only buy them if the price was sensible. But not today. Today she turned left and walked towards Paddington Station.

She kept a firm grip on her purse, as she'd been told once too often by disillusioned guests that they'd been robbed within moments of setting foot in London – Sebastian being the latest example. The boy was so mature for his age, and yet still so naïve.

Mrs Tibbet felt unusually nervous as she crossed the road and joined the bustling crowd of commuters making their way into the station. Perhaps it was because she'd never been inside a bookshop before. She hadn't had much time to read since her husband and baby son had been killed fifteen years ago in a bombing raid on the East End. If the child had lived, he would have been about the same age as Sebastian.

Without a roof to cover her head, Tibby had migrated west, like a bird that needs to find new feeding grounds. She took a job at the Safe Haven guest house as a general dogsbody. Three years later she became the waitress, and when the owner died, she didn't so much inherit the guest house as take it on, since the bank was looking for someone, anyone, to pay the mortgage.

She nearly went under, but in 1951 she was rescued by the Festival of Britain, which attracted a million extra visitors to London, making it possible for the guest house to show a profit for the first time. That profit had increased every year, if only by a small margin, and now the mortgage had been paid off and the business was hers. She relied on her regulars to get her through the winter, as she had learned early on that those who rely solely on passing trade soon have to close their doors.

Mrs Tibbet snapped out of her daydream and looked around the station until her eyes settled on a W.H. Smith sign. She watched as seasoned travellers dashed in and out. Most only bought a morning paper for a halfpenny, but others at the back of the shop were browsing among the bookshelves.

She ventured in but then stood helplessly in the middle of the shop, getting in the customers' way. When she spotted a woman at the back stacking books on to the shelves from a wooden trolley, she walked over to her, but didn't interrupt her work.

The assistant looked up. 'Can I help you, madam?' she asked politely.

'Have you heard of an author called Harry Clifton?'

'Oh yes,' the assistant replied. 'He's one of our most popular authors. Was there a particular title you were looking for?' Mrs Tibbet shook her head. 'Then let's go and see what we have in stock.' The assistant walked to the other side of the shop, with Mrs Tibbet following in her wake, stopping when she reached a section labelled CRIME. The William Warwick Mysteries were stacked in a neat row, with several gaps confirming how popular the author was. 'And of course,' continued the assistant, 'there are the prison diaries, and a biography by Lord Preston, called *The Hereditary Principle*, which is about the fascinating Clifton-Barrington inheritance case. Perhaps you remember it? It dominated the headlines for weeks.'

'Which of Mr Clifton's novels would you recommend?'

'Whenever I'm asked that question about any author,' replied the assistant, 'I always suggest, start with the first.' She took a copy of *William Warwick and the Case of the Blind Witness* from the shelf.

'Will the other one, the hereditary one, tell me more about the Clifton family?'

'Yes, and you'll find it as gripping as any novel,' the assistant said as she walked over to the biography section. 'That will be three shillings, madam,' she said, handing her both books.

When Mrs Tibbet returned to the guest house just before lunch, Janice was surprised to see that her shopping basket was empty, and even more surprised when she locked herself into the office, only coming out when a knock on the front door announced a prospective customer.

It took her two days and two nights to read *The Hereditary Principle* by Reg Preston, by which time Mrs Tibbet realized she was going to have to visit another place she had never entered before, and it would be far more nerve-racking than a bookshop.

◄○►

Sebastian came down to breakfast early on Monday morning, as he wanted to have a word with Bruno's father before he left for work.

'Good morning, sir,' he said as he took a seat at the breakfast table.

'Good morning, Sebastian,' said Don Pedro, putting down his newspaper. 'So, have you made up your mind if you're going to come to Buenos Aires with me?'

'Yes, I have, sir. I'd love to come, if I haven't left it too late.'

'That won't be a problem,' said Don Pedro. 'Just be sure you're ready by the time I return.'

'What time will we be leaving, sir?'

'Around five o'clock.'

'I'll be ready and waiting,' said Sebastian as Bruno came into the room.

'You will be pleased to hear that Sebastian will be travelling to Buenos Aires with me,' said Don Pedro as his son sat down. 'He'll be back in London by the end of the month. Make sure you take care of him when he returns.'

Bruno was about to comment when Elena came in and placed a rack of toast in the centre of the table.

'What would you like for breakfast, sir?' she asked Bruno.

'Two boiled eggs, please.'

'Me too,' said Sebastian.

'I must go,' said Don Pedro, as he rose from his place at the head of the table. 'I have an appointment in Bond Street.' He turned to Sebastian and added, 'Be sure you're packed and ready to leave by five o'clock. We can't afford to miss the tide.'

'I can't wait, sir,' said Sebastian, sounding genuinely excited.

'Have a good day, Papa,' said Bruno as his father left the room. He didn't speak again until he heard the front door close, when he looked across the table and said to his friend, 'Are you certain you're making the right decision?'

◄○►

Mrs Tibbet couldn't stop shaking. She wasn't convinced she could go through with it. When the guests sat down for breakfast that morning, they were served with hard-boiled eggs, burnt toast and lukewarm tea, and it was Janice who ended up taking the blame. It didn't help that Mrs Tibbet hadn't done any shopping for the past two days, so the bread was stale, the fruit was over-ripe and they'd run out of bacon. Janice was relieved when the last disgruntled guest filed out of the breakfast room. One even refused to pay the bill.

She went down to the kitchen to see if Mrs Tibbet was

feeling poorly, but there was no sign of her. Janice wondered where she could possibly be.

Mrs Tibbet was in fact on a No. 148 bus heading down Whitehall. She still didn't know if she could go through with it. Even if he did agree to see her, what would she say to him? After all, what business was it of hers? She became so preoccupied that the bus had crossed Westminster Bridge before she got off. She took her time walking back across the Thames, and not because, like the tourists, she was admiring the views up and down the river.

She changed her mind several times before she reached Parliament Square, where her pace became slower and slower until she finally came to a halt outside the entrance to the House of Commons, when, like Lot's wife, she turned to salt.

The senior doorkeeper, used to dealing with people who were overawed by their first visit to the Palace of Westminster, smiled at the frozen statue and asked, 'May I help, madam?'

'Is this where I come to see an MP?'

'Do you have an appointment?'

'No, I don't,' said Mrs Tibbet, hoping she would be turned away.

'Don't worry, not many people do. You'll just have to hope he's in the House, and free to see you. If you'd like to join the queue, one of my colleagues will assist you.'

Mrs Tibbet walked up the steps, past Westminster Hall, and joined a long, silent queue. By the time she reached the front over an hour later, she remembered she hadn't told Janice where she was going.

She was escorted into the Central Lobby, where an official ushered her across to the reception desk.

'Good afternoon, madam,' said the duty clerk. 'Which Member were you hoping to see?'

'Sir Giles Barrington.'

'Are you a constituent of his, madam?'

Another chance to escape, was her first thought. 'No. I need to speak to him concerning a personal matter.'

'I understand,' said the clerk, as if nothing would surprise him. 'If you'll give me your name, I'll fill in a visitor's card.'

'Mrs Florence Tibbet.'

'And your address?'

'Thirty-seven Praed Street, Paddington.'

'And what is it you wish to discuss with Sir Giles?'

'It's about his nephew, Sebastian Clifton.'

The clerk completed the card and handed it to a badge messenger.

'How long will I have to wait?' she asked.

'Members usually respond fairly quickly if they're in the House. But perhaps you'd like to have a seat while you're waiting,' he said, pointing to the green benches that circled the walls of Central Lobby.

The badge messenger marched down the long corridor to the Lower House. When he entered the members' lobby he handed the card to one of his colleagues, who in turn took it into the chamber. The house was packed with members who had come to hear Peter Thorneycroft, the Chancellor of the Exchequer, announce that petrol rationing would be lifted following the end of the Suez Crisis.

The messenger spotted Sir Giles Barrington seated in his usual place and handed the card to a member at the end of the third row, from where it began its slow progress along the packed bench, each member checking the name and then passing it down the line, until it finally reached Sir Giles.

The Member for Bristol Docklands stuffed the card in a pocket as he leapt to his feet the moment the foreign secretary had dealt with the previous question, in the hope of catching the speaker's eye.

'Sir Giles Barrington,' called the speaker.

'Can the foreign secretary tell the House how the president's announcement will affect British industry, in particular those of our citizens who work in the defence field?'

Mr Selwyn Lloyd once again rose to his feet and, clutching the dispatch box, said, 'I can tell the honourable and gallant gentleman that I am in constant touch with our ambassador in Washington, and he assures me . . .'

By the time Mr Lloyd had answered the final question some forty minutes later, Giles had quite forgotten about his visitor's card.

It was about an hour later, when he was sitting in the tea-room with some colleagues, that he pulled out his wallet and the card fell to the floor. He picked it up and glanced at the name, but couldn't place a Mrs Tibbet. He turned it over and read the message, shot out of his seat, bolted out of the tearoom and didn't stop running until he had reached Central Lobby, praying that she hadn't given up on him. When he stopped at the duty clerk's desk, he asked him to page a Mrs Tibbet.

'I'm sorry, Sir Giles, but the lady left a few moments ago. Said she had to get back to work.'

'Damn,' said Giles, as he turned the card over and checked the address.

32

'PRAED STREET, PADDINGTON,' said Giles as he climbed into a taxi outside the members' entrance. 'And I'm already late,' he added, 'so step on it.'

'Wouldn't want me to break the speed limit, would you, guv,' said the cabbie as he drove out of the main gates and nosed his way into Parliament Square.

Yes I would, Giles wanted to say, but he held his tongue. Once he learned Mrs Tibbet had left the Commons, he had rung his brother-in-law to tell him about the stranger's cryptic message. Harry's first reaction was to want to jump on the next train to London, but Giles advised him against it, in case it turned out to be a false alarm. In any case, Giles told him, it was just possible that Sebastian was on his way back to Bristol.

Giles sat on the edge of his seat, willing every traffic light to turn green, and urging the driver to change lanes whenever he saw a chance to grab a few yards. He couldn't stop thinking about what Harry and Emma must have been through during the past two days. Had they told Jessica? If so, she'd be sitting on the top step at the Manor House waiting anxiously for Sebastian to return.

As the taxi pulled up outside No. 37, the cabbie couldn't help wondering why a Member of Parliament could possibly be visiting a guest house in Paddington. But it was none of his business, especially as the gentleman gave him such a large tip.

Giles leapt out of the taxi, ran to the door and hammered several times on the knocker. A few moments later, the door was opened by a young woman who said, 'I'm sorry, sir, but the last room has been taken.'

'I'm not looking for a room,' Giles told her. 'I was hoping to see –' he glanced once again at the visitor's card – 'a Mrs Tibbet.'

'Who shall I say wants to see her?'

'Sir Giles Barrington.'

'If you'll just wait there, sir, I'll let her know,' she said before closing the door.

Giles stood on the pavement, wondering if Sebastian had been just a hundred yards from Paddington Station the whole time. He only had to wait a couple of minutes before the door was flung open again.

'I'm so sorry, Sir Giles,' said Mrs Tibbet, sounding flustered. 'Janice had no idea who you are. Please come through to the parlour.'

Once Giles had settled into a comfortable high-backed chair, Mrs Tibbet offered him a cup of tea.

'No, thank you,' he said. 'I'm anxious to find out if you have any news about Seb. His parents are worried out of their minds.'

'Of course they are, poor things,' said Mrs Tibbet. 'I did tell him several times that he should get in touch with his mother, but—'

'But?' interrupted Giles.

'It's a long story, Sir Giles, but I'll be as quick as I can.'

Ten minutes later, Mrs Tibbet was telling him that the last time she'd seen Sebastian was when he left in a taxi to return to Eaton Square, and she hadn't heard from him since.

'So as far as you know, he's staying with his friend Bruno Martinez at forty-four Eaton Square?'

'That's right, Sir Giles. But I did—'

'I am greatly in your debt,' said Giles, rising from his seat and taking out his wallet.

'You owe me nothing, sir,' said Mrs Tibbet, waving a hand. 'Everything I did was for Sebastian, not for you. But if I may be allowed to give you one piece of advice . . .'

'Yes, of course,' said Giles, sitting back down.

'Sebastian is anxious that his parents will be angry with him because he's thrown away the chance of going to Cambridge, and—'

'But he hasn't lost his place at Cambridge,' interrupted Giles.

'That's the best news I've heard all week. You'd better find him quickly and let him know that, because he won't want to go home while he thinks his parents are still angry with him.'

'My next stop will be number forty-four Eaton Square,' said Giles as he rose a second time.

'Before you go,' said Mrs Tibbet, still not budging, 'you should know that he took the blame for his friend, which is why Bruno Martinez didn't suffer the same punishment. So perhaps he deserves a pat on the back rather than a telling off.'

'You're wasted, Mrs Tibbet – you should have joined the diplomatic corps.'

'And you're an old flatterer, Sir Giles, like most members of parliament. Not that I've ever come across one before,' she admitted. 'But don't let me hold you up any longer.'

'Thank you again. Once I've caught up with Sebastian and sorted things out,' said Giles as he rose a third time, 'perhaps you'll come back to the Commons and join us both for tea?'

'That's most considerate of you, Sir Giles. But I can't afford to take two days off in one week.'

'Then it will have to be next week,' said Giles as she opened the front door and they walked out on to the pavement. 'I'll send a car to pick you up.'

'That's kind of you,' said Mrs Tibbet, 'but—'

'No buts. Sebastian got lucky, very lucky, when he stopped at number thirty-seven.'

◄○►

When the phone rang Don Pedro walked across the room, but he didn't pick it up until he'd checked his study door was closed.

'Your international call from Buenos Aires is on the line, sir.'

He heard a click, before a voice said, 'It's Diego.'

'Listen carefully. Everything has fallen into place, including our Trojan horse.'

'Does that mean Sotheby's have agreed to—?'

'The sculpture will be included in their sale at the end of this month.'

'So all we need now is a courier.'

'I think I have the ideal person. A school friend of Bruno's who needs a job and speaks fluent Spanish. Better still, his uncle is a Member of Parliament and one of his grandfathers was a lord, so he's what the English consider blue blood, which can only smooth the way.'

'Does he know why you picked him?'

'No. That's best kept secret,' said Don Pedro, 'which will allow us to remain at arm's length for the whole exercise.'

'When does he arrive in Buenos Aires?'

'He'll be joining me on the ship this evening, and he will be safely back in England long before anyone works out what we were up to.'

'Do you think he's old enough to carry out such an important job?'

'The boy's older than his years and, as important, he's a bit of a risk-taker.'

'Sounds ideal. And have you put Bruno in the picture?'

'No. The less he knows, the better.'

'Agreed,' said Diego. 'Is there anything else you want me to do before you arrive?'

'Just make sure the cargo is ready for loading and is booked on to the *Queen Mary* for its return journey.'

'And the bank notes?'

Don Pedro's thoughts were interrupted by a gentle knock on the door. He turned to see Sebastian entering the room.

'I hope I'm not interrupting you, sir.'

'No, no,' said Don Pedro, replacing the receiver and smiling at the young man who had become the last piece in the jigsaw.

◄○►

Giles thought about stopping at the nearest phone box so he could ring Harry and let him know that he'd tracked Sebastian down and was on the way to collect him, but he wanted to see the boy face to face before he made that call.

The Park Lane traffic was bumper to bumper, and the cabbie showed no interest in slipping into gaps, let alone running amber lights. He took a deep breath. What difference would a few minutes make, he thought as they circled Hyde Park Corner.

The taxi finally drew up outside No. 44 Eaton Square, and Giles paid the exact sum on the meter before walking up the steps and knocking on the door. A giant of a man answered, and smiled at Giles almost as if he'd been expecting him.

'May I help you, sir?'

'I'm looking for my nephew, Sebastian Clifton, who I understand is staying here with his friend Bruno Martinez.'

'He was staying here, sir,' said the butler politely. 'But they left for London Airport about twenty minutes ago.'

'Do you know which flight they're on?' he asked.

'I have no idea, Sir Giles.'

'Or where they're going?'

'I didn't ask.'

'Thank you,' said Giles, who after years as an opening batsman recognized stonewalling when he faced it. He turned to look for another taxi as the door closed behind him. He spotted an illuminated yellow sign and hailed the cab, which immediately performed a U-turn to pick him up.

'London Airport,' he said, before climbing quickly into the back. 'And I'll give you double what's on the clock if you get me there in forty minutes.' They pulled away just as the door of No. 44 opened and a young man came running down the steps, waving at him frantically.

'Stop!' Giles shouted. The taxi screeched to a halt.

'Make your mind up, guv.'

Giles pulled down the window as the young man ran towards him.

'My name is Bruno Martinez,' he said. 'They haven't gone

to the airport. They're on their way to Southampton to join the SS *South America*.'

'What's her departure time?' asked Giles

'They're sailing on the last tide around nine o'clock this evening.'

'Thank you,' said Giles. 'I'll let Sebastian know—'

'No, please don't, sir,' said Bruno. 'And whatever you do, don't tell my father I've spoken to you.'

Neither of them noticed that someone was staring out of the window of No. 44.

◄○►

Sebastian enjoyed sitting in the back of a Rolls-Royce, but was surprised when they came to a halt in Battersea.

'Ever flown in a helicopter before?' asked Don Pedro.

'No, sir. I've never been on a plane before.'

'It will take two hours off our journey. If you're going to work for me, you'll quickly learn that time is money.'

The helicopter soared into the sky, banked to the right and headed south towards Southampton. Sebastian looked down on the early evening traffic as it continued its snail-like pace out of London.

◄○►

'I can't do Southampton in forty minutes, guv,' said the cabbie.

'Fair enough,' said Giles, 'but if you can get me to the dockside before the SS *South America* sails, I'll still double your fare.'

The taxi driver shot off like a thoroughbred out of the stalls, and did his best to overcome the rush-hour traffic, taking back doubles, going down side streets Giles hadn't realized existed, moving across into the oncoming lane before swerving back to run lights that had already turned red. But it still took over an hour before he emerged on to Winchester Road, only to find that long stretches of roadworks restricted them to a single lane and the speed of its slowest driver. Giles looked out of the window and didn't see that much road work in progress.

268

He kept checking his watch, but the second hand was the only thing that kept a steady pace, and the chances of them making it to the docks before nine were looking more and more unlikely by the minute. He prayed that the ship would be held up for just a few minutes, although he knew the captain couldn't afford to miss the tide.

Giles sat back and thought about Bruno's words. Whatever you do, don't tell my father I've spoken to you. Sebastian couldn't have asked more of a friend. He looked at his watch again: 7.30 p.m. How could the butler have made such a simple mistake when he said they were on their way to London Airport? 7.45 p.m. It clearly wasn't a mistake, because the man had addressed him as 'Sir Giles', although he had no way of knowing that he was about to turn up on his doorstep. Unless . . . 8 p.m. And when he said *they* left for London Airport', who was the other person he was referring to? Bruno's father? 8.15 p.m. Giles hadn't been able to come up with a satisfactory answer to any of these questions by the time the taxi swung off the Winchester Road and headed for the docks. 8.30 p.m. Giles set aside all his misgivings and began to think about what needed to be done if they arrived at the dockside before the ship had raised its anchor. 8.45 p.m.

'Faster!' he demanded, although he suspected the driver already had his foot flat to the floor. At last he spotted the great liner, and as it grew larger and larger by the minute, he began to believe that they just might make it. But then he heard a sound he had been dreading: three loud, prolonged blasts of a fog horn.

'Time and tide wait for no man,' said the driver. An observation Giles could have lived without at that particular moment.

The taxi came to a halt by the side of the *South America*, but the passenger ramp had already been raised and the mooring ropes released to allow the vast ship to ease its way slowly away from the dockside and out into the open sea.

Giles felt helpless as he watched two tugs guide the ship out into the estuary, like ants leading an elephant to safer ground.

'The harbourmaster's office!' he shouted, without any idea

where that might be. The driver had to stop twice to ask for directions before he pulled up outside the only office building that still had all its lights on.

Giles jumped out of the taxi and charged into the harbour-master's office without knocking. Inside, he came face to face with three startled men.

'Who are you?' demanded a man dressed in a port authority uniform, displaying more gold braid than his fellow officers.

'Sir Giles Barrington. My nephew is on board that ship,' he said, pointing out of the window. 'Is there any way of getting him off?'

'I wouldn't have thought so, sir, unless the captain is willing to stop the ship and allow him to be lowered on to one of our pilot boats, which I'd have thought was most unlikely. But I'll give it a try. What's the passenger's name?'

'Sebastian Clifton. He's still a minor, and I have his parents' authority to get him off that ship.'

The harbourmaster picked up a microphone and began twiddling some knobs on a control panel as he tried to get the captain on the line.

'I don't want to get your hopes up,' he said, 'but the captain and I did serve together in the Royal Navy, so . . .'

'This is the captain of the SS *South America*,' said a very English voice.

'It's Bob Walters, skipper. We've got a problem, and I'd be grateful for any assistance you can give,' the harbourmaster said before passing on Sir Giles's request.

'In normal circumstances I'd be happy to oblige, Bob,' said the captain, 'but the owner's on the bridge, so I'll have to ask his permission.'

'Thank you,' said Giles and the harbourmaster in unison, before the line went dead.

'Are there any circumstances in which you have the author-ity to over-rule a captain?' asked Giles as they waited.

'Only while his ship's in the estuary. Once it's passed the northern lighthouse, it's deemed to be in the Channel and beyond my jurisdiction.'

'But you can give a captain an order while his ship's still in the estuary?'

'Yes, sir, but remember, it's a foreign vessel, and we don't want a diplomatic incident, so I wouldn't be willing to over-rule the captain unless I was convinced a criminal act was taking place.'

'What's taking them so long?' asked Giles as the minutes passed. Suddenly a voice crackled over the intercom.

'Sorry, Bob. The owner's unwilling to grant your request as we're approaching the harbour wall and will soon be in the Channel.'

Giles grabbed the microphone from the harbourmaster. 'This is Sir Giles Barrington. Please put the owner on the line. I want to speak to him personally.'

'I'm sorry, Sir Giles,' said the captain, 'but Mr Martinez has left the bridge and gone to his cabin, and he left strict instructions that he's not to be disturbed.'

HARRY CLIFTON

1957

33

HARRY HAD ASSUMED that nothing could surpass the pride he felt when he heard Sebastian had been awarded a scholarship to Cambridge. He was wrong. He felt just as proud as he watched his wife climbing the steps and on to the platform to receive her business degree, summa cum laude, from Wallace Sterling, the president of Stanford University.

Harry knew better than anyone the sacrifices Emma had made to meet the impossibly high standards Professor Feldman set himself and his students, and he had expected even more from Emma, as he had made clear over the years.

As she left the stage to warm applause, her navy hood in place, like all the students before her, she hurled her mortar board joyfully into the air, the sign that her undergraduate days were behind her. She could only wonder what her dear mother would have made of such behaviour from a 36-year-old English lady, and in public.

Harry's gaze moved from his wife to the distinguished professor of business studies, who was seated on the stage only a couple of places away from the university president. Cyrus Feldman made no attempt to hide his feelings when it came to his star pupil. He was the first on his feet to applaud Emma, and the last to sit down. Harry often marvelled at how his wife could subtly make powerful men, from Pulitzer Prize-winners to company chairmen, bend to her will, just as her mother had done before her.

How proud Elizabeth would have been of her daughter

today, but no prouder than his own mother, because Maisie had experienced every bit as painful a journey before she could place the letters BA after her name.

Harry and Emma had dined with Professor Feldman and his long-suffering wife Ellen the previous evening. Feldman hadn't been able to take his eyes off Emma, and had even suggested that she should return to Stanford and, under his personal supervision, complete a thesis for a PhD.

'What about my poor husband?' Emma had said, linking her arm through Harry's.

'He'll just have to learn to live without you for a couple of years,' said Feldman, making no attempt to disguise what he had in mind. Many a red-blooded Englishman hearing such a proposition made to his wife might have punched Feldman on the nose, and a less tolerant wife than Mrs Feldman might well have been forgiven for initiating divorce proceedings as her three predecessors had done. Harry just smiled, while Mrs Feldman pretended not to notice.

Harry had agreed with Emma's suggestion that they should fly to England straight after the ceremony, as she wanted to be back at the Manor House before Sebastian returned from Beechcroft. Their son was no longer a schoolboy, she mused, and only three months away from being an undergraduate.

Once the degree ceremony was over, Emma strolled around the lawn, enjoying the celebratory atmosphere and making the acquaintance of her fellow graduates, who, like her, had spent countless lonely hours of study while residing on distant shores, and were now meeting for the first time. Spouses were introduced, family photographs shown off and addresses exchanged.

By six o'clock, when the waiters began to fold up the chairs, collect the drained champagne bottles and stack the last of the empty plates, Harry suggested that perhaps they should make their way back to their hotel.

Emma didn't stop chatting all the way back to the Fairmont, while she was packing, during the taxi ride to the airport, and as they waited for their flight in the first-class lounge. No sooner had she climbed aboard the aircraft, found her place and fastened her seat belt, than she closed her eyes and immediately fell into a deep sleep.

⦿

'You're sounding positively middle-aged,' said Emma as they started out on the long drive back from London Airport to the Manor House.

'I am middle-aged,' said Harry. 'I'm thirty-seven, and what's worse, young women have started calling me sir.'

'Well, I don't feel middle-aged,' said Emma, looking down at the map. 'Take a right at the traffic lights and you'll be on the Great Bath Road.'

'That's because life has just begun for you.'

'What do you mean?'

'Exactly that. You've just been awarded your degree, and appointed to the board of Barrington's, both of which have opened up a whole new life for you. Let's face it, twenty years ago neither opportunity would have been possible.'

'They've only been possible in my case because Cyrus Feldman and Ross Buchanan are enlightened men when it comes to treating women as equals. And don't forget that Giles and I own twenty-two per cent of the company between us, and Giles has never shown the slightest interest in sitting on the board.'

'That may well be the case, but if you're seen to do the job well, it might help convince other chairmen to follow Ross's example.'

'Don't kid yourself. It will still be decades before competent women are given the chance to replace incompetent men.'

'Well, let's at least pray it will be different for Jessica. I'm hoping that by the time she leaves school, her sole purpose in life won't be to learn how to cook and to find someone suitable to marry.'

'Do you think those were my sole purpose in life?'

'If they were, you failed on both counts,' said Harry. 'And don't forget you chose me when you were eleven.'

'Ten,' said Emma. 'But it still took you another seven years to work it out.'

'Anyway,' said Harry, 'we shouldn't assume that just because we both won places at Oxford, and Grace is a don at Cambridge, that's a path Jessica will want to tread.'

'And why should she, when she's so gifted? I know she admires what Seb has achieved, but her role models are Barbara Hepworth and someone called Mary Cassatt, which is why I've been considering what alternatives are open to her.' Emma looked back down at the map. 'Turn right in about half a mile. It should be signposted Reading.'

'What have you two been plotting behind my back?' asked Harry.

'If Jessica is good enough, and her art teacher assures me she is, the school want her to apply for a place at the Royal College of Art, or the Slade School of Fine Art.'

'Didn't Miss Fielding go to the Slade?'

'Yes, and she regularly reminds me that Jessica is a far better artist at the age of fifteen than she was in her diploma year.'

'That must be a bit galling.'

'Typical man's reaction. Actually, Miss Fielding is only interested in seeing Jessica fulfil her potential. She wants her to be the first girl from Red Maids' to win a place at the Royal College.'

'That would be quite a double,' said Harry, 'as Seb's the first boy from Beechcroft Abbey to win the top scholarship to Cambridge.'

'The first since 1922,' Emma corrected him. 'Turn left at the next roundabout.'

'They must love you on the board of Barrington's,' said Harry as he carried out her instruction. 'By the way, just in case you've forgotten, my latest book is coming out next week.'

'Are they sending you anywhere interesting to promote it?'

'I'm speaking at a *Yorkshire Post* literary lunch on Friday, and I'm told they've sold so many tickets they've had to move it from a local hotel to the York racecourse.'

Emma leant over to give him a kiss on the cheek. 'Congratulations, my darling!'

'Nothing to do with me, I'm afraid, because I'm not the only speaker.'

'Tell me the name of your rival so I can have him killed.'

'*Her* name is Agatha Christie.'

'So is William Warwick at last proving a challenger to Hercule Poirot?'

'Not yet, I'm afraid. But then, Miss Christie has written forty-nine novels, while I've only just completed my fifth.'

'Perhaps you'll catch her up by the time you've written forty-nine.'

'I should be so lucky. So while I'm gallivanting around the country trying to get on to the bestseller list, what will you be up to?'

'I told Ross I'd drop into the office and see him on Monday. I'm trying to convince him not to go ahead with the building of the *Buckingham*.'

'But why?'

'Now is not the time to risk investing that kind of money on a luxury liner while passengers are rapidly switching their allegiance to aeroplanes.'

'I see your point, though I'd much rather sail to New York than fly.'

'That's because you're middle-aged,' said Emma, patting him on the thigh. 'I also promised Giles I'd pop over to Barrington Hall and make sure Marsden has everything ready for him and Gwyneth when they come down for the weekend.'

'Marsden will be more than ready for them.'

'He'll be sixty next year, and I know he's thinking about retiring.'

'He won't be easy to replace,' said Harry as they passed the first signpost for Bristol.

'Gwyneth doesn't want to replace him. She says it's high time Giles was dragged into the second half of the twentieth century.'

'What does she have in mind?'

'She thinks there might be a Labour government after the

next election, and as Giles would almost certainly be a minister, she intends to prepare him for the task, which doesn't include being mollycoddled by servants. In future the only servants she wants assisting him will be civil.'

'Giles got lucky when he met Gwyneth.'

'Hasn't the time come for him to propose to the poor girl?'

'Yes it has, but he's still bruised from his experience with Virginia, and I don't think he's quite ready to make another commitment.'

'Then he'd better get on with it, because women as good as Gwyneth don't come around that often,' said Emma, turning her attention back to the map.

Harry accelerated past a lorry. 'I still can't get used to the idea of Seb no longer being a schoolboy.'

'Have you got anything planned for his first weekend back home?'

'I thought I'd take him to see Gloucestershire play Blackheath at the County Ground tomorrow.'

Emma laughed. 'That will be character building, to be made to watch a team that loses more often than it wins.'

'And perhaps we could all go to the Old Vic one evening next week,' he added, ignoring her comment.

'What's on?'

'*Hamlet*.'

'Who's playing the prince?'

'A young actor called Peter O'Toole, who Seb says is the in thing, whatever that means.'

'It will be wonderful to have Seb back for the summer. Perhaps we should throw a party for him before he goes to Cambridge. Give him a chance to meet some girls.'

'He'll have more than enough time for girls. I think it's a crying shame that the government's ending National Service. Seb would make a fine officer, and it would be the making of him to take responsibility for other men.'

'You're not middle-aged,' said Emma as they turned into the drive, 'you're positively prehistoric.'

Harry laughed as he brought the car to a halt outside the

Manor House, and was delighted to see Jessica sitting on the top step, waiting for them.

'Where's Seb?' was Emma's first question as she climbed out of the car and gave Jessica a hug.

'He didn't come back from school yesterday. Perhaps he went straight to Barrington Hall and spent the night with Uncle Giles.'

'I thought Giles was in London,' said Harry. 'I'll give him a call and find out if they can both join us for dinner.'

Harry climbed the steps and went into the house. He picked up the phone in the hall and dialled a local number.

'We're back,' he announced when he heard Giles's voice on the line.

'Welcome home, Harry. Did you have a good time in the States?'

'Couldn't have been better. Emma stole the show, of course. I think Feldman wants her to be his fifth wife.'

'Well, it would have some definite advantages,' said Giles. 'It's never a long-term commitment when that man's involved, and being California, there'll be a pretty healthy divorce settlement at the end.'

Harry laughed. 'By the way, is Seb with you?'

'No, he's not. In fact, I haven't seen him for some time. But I'm sure he can't be far away. Why don't you ring the school and find out if he's still there? Call me back when you find out where he is, because I've got some news for you.'

'Will do,' said Harry. He put the phone down and looked up the headmaster's number in his telephone book.

'Don't worry, darling, he's no longer a schoolboy, as you keep reminding me,' he said when he saw the anxious look on Emma's face. 'I'm sure there'll be a simple explanation.' He dialled Beechcroft 117, and while he waited for someone to answer, he took his wife in his arms.

'Dr Banks-Williams speaking.'

'Headmaster, it's Harry Clifton. I'm sorry to bother you after the school has broken up, but I wondered if you had any idea where my son Sebastian might be.'

'I've no idea, Mr Clifton. I haven't seen him since he was rusticated earlier in the week.'

'Rusticated?'

'I'm afraid so, Mr Clifton. I fear I was left with little choice.'

'But what did he do to deserve that?'

'Several minor offences, including smoking.'

'And any major offences?'

'He was caught drinking in his study with a serving maid.'

'And that was considered worthy of rustication?'

'I might have turned a blind eye, as it was the last week of term, but unfortunately neither of them had any clothes on.'

Harry stifled a laugh, and was only glad that Emma couldn't hear the other side of the conversation.

'When he reported to me the following day, I told him that after some deliberation, and having consulted his housemaster, I was left with no choice but to rusticate him. I then gave him a letter which I asked him to pass on to you. It's clear that he has not done so.'

'But where can he be?' asked Harry, becoming anxious for the first time.

'I've no idea. All I can tell you is that his housemaster supplied him with a third-class single ticket to Temple Meads, and I assumed that would be the last I would see of him. However, I had to travel up to London that afternoon to attend an Old Boys' reunion dinner, and to my surprise I found him travelling on the same train.'

'Did you ask him why he was going to London?'

'I would have done so,' said the headmaster dryly, 'if he hadn't left the carriage the moment he saw me.'

'Why would he do that?'

'Possibly because he was smoking, and I'd previously warned him that if he broke any more school rules during term time he would be expelled. And he knew only too well that would mean me calling the admissions tutor at Cambridge and recommending that his prize scholarship be withdrawn.'

'And did you?'

'No, I did not. You have my wife to thank for that. If I'd

had my way, he would have been expelled and forfeited his place at Cambridge.'

'For smoking, when he wasn't even on the school premises?'

'That was not his only offence. He was also occupying a first-class carriage when he didn't have the money for a first-class ticket, and earlier he'd lied to his housemaster about going straight back to Bristol. That, on top of his other offences, would have been quite enough to convince me that he was unworthy of a place at my old university. I've no doubt I will live to regret my leniency.'

'And that was the last you saw of him?' said Harry, trying to remain calm.

'Yes, and it's the last I want to see of him,' said the headmaster, before putting the phone down.

Harry reported the other end of the conversation to Emma, only leaving out the incident with the serving maid.

'But where could he be now?' asked Emma anxiously.

'The first thing I'm going to do is ring Giles back and let him know what's happened, before we decide what to do next.' Harry picked up the phone again, and took some time repeating the headmaster's conversation almost verbatim.

Giles was silent for a few moments. 'It's not hard to work out what must have been going through Seb's mind after Banks-Williams found him on the train.'

'Well I'm damned if I can work it out,' said Harry.

'Put yourself in his shoes,' said Giles. 'He thinks that because the headmaster's caught him smoking while travelling up to London without permission, he must have been expelled, and lost his place at Cambridge. I suspect you'll find he's afraid of returning home and having to face you and Emma.'

'Well, that's no longer the problem, but we still have to find him and let him know. If I drive up to London straight away, can I stay at Smith Square?'

'Of course you can, but that doesn't make any sense, Harry. You should stay at the Manor House with Emma. I'll go up to London and then we'll have both ends covered.'

'But you and Gwyneth are meant to be spending a weekend together, in case you'd forgotten.'

'And Seb's still my nephew, Harry, in case you've forgotten.'

'Thank you,' said Harry.

'I'll ring you as soon as I get to London.'

'You said you had some news?'

'It's not important. Well, not as important as finding Seb.'

◄o►

Giles drove up to London that evening, and when he arrived in Smith Square his housekeeper confirmed that Sebastian hadn't been in touch.

Once Giles had passed that news on to Harry, his next call was to the assistant commissioner at Scotland Yard. He couldn't have been more sympathetic, but he pointed out that a dozen children were reported missing in London every day, and most of them were a lot younger than Sebastian. In a city with a population of eight million, it was like looking for a needle in a haystack. But he said he would put out an alert to every police district in the Met area.

Harry and Emma sat up late into the night calling Sebastian's grandmother Maisie, his aunt Grace, Deakins, Ross Buchanan, Griff Haskins, and even Miss Parish, as they tried to find out if Sebastian had been in touch with any of them. Harry spoke to Giles several times the following day, but he had nothing new to report. A needle in a haystack, he repeated.

'How's Emma bearing up?'

'Not well. She fears the worst as each hour passes.'

'And Jessica?'

'Inconsolable.'

'I'll call you the moment I hear anything.'

◄o►

The following afternoon, Giles rang Harry from the House of Commons to tell him he was on his way to Paddington to visit a woman who'd asked to see him because she had news about Sebastian.

284

Harry and Emma sat by the phone, expecting Giles to ring back within the hour, but he didn't call again until just after nine o'clock that evening.

'Tell me he's fit and well,' said Emma after she'd grabbed the phone out of Harry's hand.

'He's fit and well,' said Giles, 'but I'm afraid that's the only good news. He's on his way to Buenos Aires.'

'What are you talking about?' said Emma. 'Why would Seb want to go to Buenos Aires?'

'I've no idea. All I can tell you is that he's on board the SS *South America* with someone called Pedro Martinez, the father of one of his school friends.'

'Bruno,' said Emma. 'Is he on board as well?'

'No, he can't be, because I saw him at his house in Eaton Square.'

'We'll drive up to London immediately,' said Emma. 'Then we can visit Bruno first thing in the morning.'

'I don't think that would be wise in the circumstances,' said Giles.

'Why not?' demanded Emma.

'For several reasons, not least because I've just had a call from Sir Alan Redmayne, the cabinet secretary. He's asked if the three of us would join him in Downing Street at ten o'clock tomorrow. I can't believe it's a coincidence.'

34

'GOOD DAY, SIR ALAN,' said Giles as the three of them were shown into the cabinet secretary's office. 'May I introduce my sister, Emma, and my brother-in-law, Harry Clifton?'

Sir Alan Redmayne shook hands with Harry and Emma before introducing Mr Hugh Spencer.

'Mr Spencer is an assistant secretary at the Treasury,' he explained. 'The reason for his presence will become clear.'

They all sat down around a circular table in the centre of the room.

'I realize this meeting was called to discuss a most serious matter,' said Sir Alan, 'but before I begin, I would like to say, Mr Clifton, that I am an avid follower of William Warwick. Your latest book is on my wife's side of the bed, so unfortunately I won't be allowed to read it until she's turned the last page.'

'That's very kind of you, sir.'

'Let me begin by explaining why we needed to see you at such short notice,' said Sir Alan, his tone of voice changing. 'I would like to reassure you, Mr and Mrs Clifton, that we are just as concerned about your son's welfare as you are, even if our interests may differ from yours. The government's interest,' he continued, 'centres around a man called Don Pedro Martinez, who has fingers in so many pies that we now have a filing cabinet exclusively devoted to him. Mr Martinez is an Argentinian citizen with a residence in Eaton Square, a country house at Shillingford, three cruise liners, a string of polo ponies stabled at the Guards Polo Club in Windsor Great Park, and a box at Ascot. He always comes to London during the season, and has a wide circle of friends and associates who believe him to be a wealthy cattle baron. And why shouldn't they? He owns three hundred thousand acres of pampas in Argentina, with around five hundred thousand head of cattle grazing on it. Although this yields him a handsome profit, in fact it's nothing more than a front to shield his more nefarious activities.'

'And what are they?' asked Giles.

'To put it bluntly, Sir Giles, he's an international crook. He makes Moriarty look like a choir boy. Allow me to tell you a little more of what we know about Mr Martinez, and then I'll be happy to answer any questions you might have. Our paths first crossed in 1935, when I was a special assistant attached to the War Office. I discovered he was doing business with Germany. He had forged a close relationship with Heinrich Himmler, the head of the SS, and we know he met Hitler on at least three occasions. During the war he made a vast fortune supplying the Germans with whatever raw materials they were short of, although he was still living in Eaton Square.'

'Why didn't you arrest him?' asked Giles.

'It suited our purposes not to,' said Sir Alan. 'We were keen to find out who his contacts in Britain were, and what they were up to. Once the war was over, Martinez returned to Argentina and continued trading as a cattle farmer. In fact, he never once went back to Berlin after the Allies had entered the city. He continued to visit this country regularly. He even sent all three of his sons to English public schools, and his daughter is currently at Roedean.'

'Forgive me for interrupting,' said Emma, 'but how does Sebastian fit into all of this?'

'He didn't, Mrs Clifton, until last week, when he turned up unannounced at forty-four Eaton Square, and his friend Bruno invited him to stay.'

'I've met Bruno a couple of times,' said Harry, 'and I thought he was a charming young man.'

'I'm sure he is,' said Sir Alan. 'Which only adds to Martinez's image as a decent family man who loves England. However, your son unwittingly became involved in an operation our law-enforcement agencies have been working on for several years when he met Don Pedro Martinez for the second time.'

'The second time?' queried Giles.

'On June eighteenth 1954,' said Sir Alan, referring to his notes, 'Martinez invited Sebastian to join him at the Beechcroft Arms public house to celebrate Bruno's fifteenth birthday.'

'You keep that close an eye on Martinez?' said Giles.

'We most certainly do.' The cabinet secretary extracted a brown envelope from the papers in front of him, took out two five-pound notes and placed them on the table. 'And Mr Martinez gave your son these two bank notes on Friday evening.'

'But that's more money than Sebastian has ever had in his life,' said Emma. 'We only give him half a crown pocket money each week.'

'I expect Martinez realized that such a sum would be more than enough to turn the young man's head. He then trumped it by inviting Sebastian to accompany him to Buenos Aires at a time when he knew the boy was at his most vulnerable.'

'How did you come into possession of the two random five-pound notes Martinez gave to my son?' asked Harry.

'They're not random,' said the man from the Treasury, speaking for the first time. 'We've collected over ten thousand of them in the past eight years, as a result of information supplied by what I believe the police call a reliable source.'

'What reliable source?' demanded Giles.

'Have you ever heard of an SS officer called Major Bernhard Krüger?' asked Spencer.

The silence that followed suggested that none of them had.

'Major Krüger is a resourceful and intelligent man, who was a police inspector in Berlin before he joined the SS. In fact, he'd ended up in charge of the anti-counterfeit squad. After Britain declared war on Germany, he convinced Himmler that it would be possible for the Nazis to destabilize the British economy by flooding England with perfect copies of the five-pound note, but only if he was allowed to select the finest printers, copper engravers and retouchers from Sachsenhausen concentration camp, where he was the commandant. However, his biggest coup was to recruit the master forger Salomon Smolianoff, whom he had arrested and sent to prison on no fewer than three occasions when he was with the Berlin police. Once Smolianoff was on board, Krüger's team were able to forge around twenty-seven million five-pound notes, with a face value of a hundred and thirty-five million pounds.'

Harry had the grace to gasp.

'Some time in 1945, when the Allies were advancing on Berlin, Hitler gave the order that the presses were to be destroyed, and we have every reason to believe they were. However, a few weeks before Germany surrendered, Krüger was arrested trying to cross the German-Swiss border with a suitcase full of the forged notes. He spent two years in prison in the British sector of Berlin.

'We might have lost interest in him if the Bank of England hadn't set alarm bells ringing by informing us that the notes found in Krüger's possession were in fact genuine. The governor of the bank at the time claimed that no one on earth was capable of counterfeiting a British five-pound note, and nothing could convince him otherwise. We questioned Krüger about how many of these notes were in circulation, but before he would give us that information, he skilfully negotiated terms for his release, using Don Pedro Martinez as his bargaining chip.'

Mr Spencer paused to take a sip of water, but no one interrupted him.

'An agreement was struck to release Krüger after he'd served only three years of his seven-year sentence, but not until he'd informed us that, towards the end of the war, Martinez had made a deal with Himmler to smuggle twenty million pounds' worth of forged five-pound notes out of Germany and somehow get them to Argentina, where he was to await further orders. That wouldn't have proved difficult for a man who'd smuggled everything from a Sherman tank to a Russian sub-marine into Germany.

'In return for another year off his sentence, Krüger informed us that Himmler, along with a handful of carefully selected members of the top Nazi leadership, including possibly even Hitler himself, were hoping to escape their fate by somehow getting to Buenos Aires, where they would then live out their days at the Bank of England's expense.

'However, when it became clear that Himmler and his cronies would not be showing up in Argentina,' continued Spencer, 'Martinez found himself in possession of twenty million pounds in forged notes that he needed to dispose of. Not an easy task. To begin with, I dismissed Krüger's story as pure fantasy, invented to save his own skin, but then, as the years passed, and more and more bogus five-pound notes appeared on the market whenever Martinez was in London or his son Luis was working the tables in Monte Carlo, I realized we had a real problem. This was proved yet again when Sebastian spent one of his two five-pound notes on a Savile Row suit and the assistant didn't suggest that they were not genuine.'

'As recently as two years ago,' chipped in Sir Alan, 'I expressed my frustration with the Bank of England's stance to Mr Churchill. With the simplicity of genius, he gave orders that a new five-pound note should be put into circulation as quickly as possible. Of course, bringing such a note into circulation could not be done overnight, and when the Bank of England finally announced its plans to issue a new five-pound note, they gave Martinez notice that he was running out of time in which to dispose of his vast fake fortune.'

'And then those mountebanks at the Bank of England,' came back Mr Spencer with some feeling, 'announced that any old five-pound notes presented to the Bank before December thirty-first, 1957, would be exchanged for new ones. So all Martinez had to do was smuggle his forged notes into Britain, when the Bank of England would happily convert them into legal tender. We estimate that over the past ten years, Martinez has been able to dispose of somewhere between five and ten million pounds, but that leaves him with another eight, perhaps nine million still secreted in Argentina. Once we realized there was nothing we could do to alter the Bank of England's stance, we had a clause inserted into last year's budget, with the sole purpose of making Martinez's task more difficult. Last April, it became illegal for anyone to bring more than one thousand pounds in cash into the United Kingdom. And he's recently discovered, to his cost, that neither he nor his associates can cross any border in Europe without customs taking their luggage apart.'

'But that still doesn't explain what Sebastian is doing in Buenos Aires,' said Harry.

'We have reason to believe, Mr Clifton, that your son has been sucked into Martinez's net,' said Spencer. 'We think he is going to be used by Don Pedro to smuggle the last eight or nine million pounds into England. But we don't know how or where.'

'Then Sebastian must be in great danger?' said Emma, staring directly at the cabinet secretary.

'Yes and no,' said Sir Alan. 'As long as he doesn't know the real reason Martinez wanted him to go to Argentina, not a hair on his head will be harmed. But if he were to stumble on the truth while he's in Buenos Aires, and by all accounts he's bright and resourceful, we wouldn't hesitate to move him into the safety of our embassy compound at a moment's notice.'

'Why don't you just do that as soon as he steps off the ship?' asked Emma. 'Our son is worth considerably more to us than ten million pounds of anybody's money,' she added, looking to Harry for support.

'Because that would alert Martinez to the fact that we know what he's up to,' said Spencer.

'But there must be a risk that Seb could be sacrificed, like a pawn on a chessboard you have no control over.'

'That won't happen as long as he remains oblivious to what's going on. We're convinced that without your son's help, Martinez can't hope to move that amount of money. Sebastian is our one chance of finding out how he intends to go about it.'

'He's seventeen,' Emma said helplessly.

'Not a lot younger than your husband was when he was arrested for murder, or Sir Giles when he won his MC.'

'Those were completely different circumstances,' insisted Emma.

'Same enemy,' said Sir Alan.

'We know Seb would want to help in any way he could,' said Harry, taking his wife's hand, 'but that's not the point. The risks are far too great.'

'You're right, of course,' said the cabinet secretary, 'and if you tell us you want him taken into custody the moment he disembarks from the ship, I'll give the order immediately. But,' he said before Emma could agree, 'we have come up with a plan. However, it cannot succeed without your cooperation.'

He waited for further protests, but his three guests remained silent.

'The *South America* doesn't arrive in Buenos Aires for another five days,' continued Sir Alan. 'If our plan is to succeed, we need to get a message to our ambassador before it docks.'

'Why don't you just phone him?' asked Giles.

'I wish it was that easy. The international switchboard in Buenos Aires is manned by twelve women, every one of whom is in the pay of Martinez. The same thing applies to telegraphs. Their job is to pick up any information that might be of interest to him, information about politicians, bankers, businessmen, even police operations, so he can then use it to his advantage and make himself even more money. Just the mention of his name on a phone line would set alarm bells ringing, and his son Diego would be informed within minutes. In fact, there have been times when we've been able to take advantage of the situation and feed Martinez with false information, but that's too risky on this occasion.'

'Sir Alan,' said the assistant treasury secretary, 'why don't you tell Mr and Mrs Clifton what we have in mind, and let them make the decision.'

35

He walked into London Airport and headed straight for the *Crew Only* sign.

'Good morning, Captain May,' said the duty officer after he'd checked his passport. 'Where are you flying today, sir?'

'Buenos Aires.'

'Have a good flight.'

Once his bags had been checked, he passed through customs and headed straight for gate No. 11. Don't stop, don't look round, don't draw attention to yourself, were the instructions given by the anonymous man who was more used to dealing with spies than authors.

The last forty-eight hours had been non-stop, after Emma had finally agreed, albeit reluctantly, that he could assist them with Operation Run Out. Since then his feet, to quote his old master sergeant, hadn't touched the ground.

The fitting of a BOAC captain's uniform had taken up one of those hours, the photograph for the fake passport another; the briefing on his new background, including a divorced wife and two children, three hours; a lesson on the duties of a modern BOAC captain, three hours; a tourist's guide to Buenos Aires, one hour; and over dinner with Sir Alan at his club, he still had dozens more questions that needed to be answered.

Just before he left the Athenaeum to spend a sleepless night at Giles's house in Smith Square, Sir Alan had handed him a thick file, a briefcase and a key.

'Read everything in this file during your journey to Buenos

Aires, then hand it to the ambassador, who will destroy it. You're booked into the Milonga Hotel. Our ambassador, Mr Philip Matthews, is expecting to see you at the embassy at ten on Saturday morning. You will also hand him this letter from Mr Selwyn Lloyd, the foreign secretary, which will explain why you're in Argentina.'

Once he'd reached the gate, he walked straight up to the attendant at the desk.

'Good morning, captain,' she said, even before he'd opened his passport. 'I hope you have a pleasant flight.'

He walked out on to the tarmac, climbed the steps to the aircraft and entered an empty first-class cabin.

'Good morning, Captain May,' said an attractive young woman. 'My name is Annabel Carrick. I'm the senior stewardess.'

The uniform, and the discipline, made it feel like being back in the army, even if he was up against a different enemy this time, or was it, as Sir Alan had suggested, the same one?

'May I show you to your seat?'

'Thank you, Miss Carrick,' he said as she led him to the rear of the first-class cabin. Two empty seats, but he knew only one of them would be occupied. Sir Alan didn't leave that sort of thing to chance.

'The first leg of the flight should take about seven hours,' said the stewardess. 'Can I get you a drink before we take off, captain?'

'Just a glass of water, thank you.' He took off his peaked cap and put it on the seat beside him, then placed the briefcase on the floor under his seat. He had been told not to open it until the plane had taken off, and to be certain no one could see what he was reading. Not that the file mentioned Martinez by name from the first page to the last, referring to him only as 'the subject'.

A few moments later, the first passengers began to make their way on to the plane, and for the next twenty minutes they located their seats, placed their bags in the overhead lockers, shed their coats, and some of them their jackets, settled themselves down, enjoyed a glass of champagne, clicked on their seat belts, selected a newspaper or magazine, and waited for the words, 'This is your captain speaking.'

Harry smiled at the thought of the captain being taken ill during the flight and Miss Carrick running back to ask him for his assistance. How would she react when he told her that he'd served in the British merchant navy and the US army, but never the air force?

The plane taxied on to the runway, but Harry didn't unlock his briefcase until they were in the air and the captain had turned off the seat-belt sign. He pulled out a thick file, opened it and began to study its contents, as if he was preparing for an exam.

It read like an Ian Fleming novel; the only difference was that he was cast in the role of Commander Bond. As Harry turned the pages, Martinez's life unfolded in front of him. When he took a break for dinner, he couldn't help thinking that Emma was right, they should never have allowed Sebastian to go on being involved with this man. It was far too big a risk.

However, he'd agreed with her that if at any time he felt their son's life was in danger, he would return to London on the next plane with Sebastian sitting beside him. He glanced out of the window. Instead of flying south, he and William Warwick were meant to be on their way up north that morning to begin a book tour. He'd been looking forward to meeting Agatha Christie at the *Yorkshire Post* literary lunch. Instead, he was heading to South America, hoping to avoid Don Pedro Martinez.

He closed the file, returned it to the briefcase, slid it under the seat and drifted into a light sleep, but 'the subject' never left him. By the age of fourteen, Martinez had left school and begun life as an apprentice in a butcher's shop. He was fired a few months later (reason unknown), and the only skill he took with him was how to dismember a carcase. Within days of becoming unemployed, the subject had drifted into petty crime, including theft, mugging, and raiding slot machines, which ended with him being arrested and sent to prison for six months.

While he was locked up, he shared a cell with Juan Delgado, a minor criminal who'd spent more years behind bars than on the outside. After Martinez had served his sentence, he joined Juan's gang and quickly became one of his most trusted lieutenants. When Juan was arrested yet again and returned to jail, Martinez was left in charge of his dwindling empire. He was seventeen at the time, the same age as Sebastian, and he looked set for a life of crime. But destiny took an unexpected turn when he fell in love with Consuela Torres, a telephone operator who worked on the international exchange. However, Consuela's father, a local politician who was planning to run for mayor of Buenos Aires, made it clear to his daughter that he didn't want a petty criminal as a son-in-law.

Consuela ignored her father's advice, married Pedro Martinez, and gave birth to four children, in the correct South American order, three boys followed by a girl. Martinez finally gained his father-in-law's respect when he raised the necessary cash to fund his victorious election campaign for mayor.

Once the mayor had taken up residence in city hall, there were no municipal contracts that didn't pass through Martinez's hands, always with an added 25 per cent 'service charge'. However, it wasn't long before the subject became bored with both Consuela and local politics, and began to expand his interests when he worked out that a European war meant there would be endless opportunities for those who could claim neutrality.

Although Martinez was naturally inclined to support the British, it was the Germans who offered him the opportunity to turn his small fortune into a large one.

The Nazi regime needed friends who could deliver, and although the subject was only twenty-two when he first turned up in Berlin with an empty order book, he left a couple of months later with demands for everything from Italian pipelines to a Greek oil tanker. Whenever he attempted to close a deal, the subject would make it known that he was a close friend of Reichsführer Heinrich Himmler, the head of the SS, and had met Herr Hitler himself on several occasions.

For the next ten years, the subject slept in aeroplanes and on ships, trains, buses and once even a horse and cart, as he travelled around the world, ticking off a long list of German requirements.

His meetings with Himmler became more frequent. Towards the end of the war, when an Allied victory looked inevitable and the Reichsmark collapsed, the SS leader began paying the subject in cash; crisp English five-pound notes, hot off the Sachsenhausen press. The subject would then cross the border and bank the money in Geneva, where it was converted into Swiss francs.

Long before the war had ended, Don Pedro had amassed a fortune. But it was not until the Allies were within striking distance of the German capital that Himmler offered him the opportunity of a lifetime. The two men shook hands on the deal, and the subject left Germany with twenty million pounds in forged five-pound notes, his own U-boat, and a young lieutenant from Himmler's personal staff. He never set foot in the fatherland again.

On his arrival back in Buenos Aires, the subject purchased an ailing bank for fifty million pesos, hid his twenty million pounds in the vaults, and waited for the surviving members of the Nazi hierarchy to turn up in Buenos Aires and cash in their retirement policy.

◄o►

The ambassador stared down at the ticker tape machine as it clattered away in the far corner of his office.

A message was being sent direct from London. But as with all Foreign Office directives, he would need to read between the lines, because everyone knew that the Argentinian secret service would be getting the message at the same time, in an office just a hundred yards up the road.

Peter May, the captain of the England cricket team, will be opening the batting on the first day of the Lord's Test match this Saturday at ten o'clock. I have two tickets for the match, and I hope Captain May will be able to join you.

The ambassador smiled. He was well aware, as was any English schoolboy, that Test matches always began at 11.30 a.m on a Thursday, and that Peter May didn't open the batting. But then, Britain had never been at war with a nation that played cricket.

◄○►

'Have we met before, old chap?'

Harry quickly closed the file and looked up at a middle-aged man who clearly lived on 'expenses' lunches. He was clinging to the headrest of the empty seat next to him with one hand, while holding a glass of red wine in the other.

'I don't think so,' said Harry.

'I could have sworn we had,' the man said, peering down at him. 'Perhaps I've mistaken you for someone else.'

Harry heaved a sigh of relief when the man shrugged and walked unsteadily back towards his seat at the front of the cabin. He was just about to open the file again and continue his background study of Martinez, when the man turned round and made his way slowly back towards him.

'Are you famous?'

Harry laughed. 'That's most unlikely. As you can see, I'm a BOAC pilot, and have been for the past twelve years.'

'You don't come from Bristol then?'

'No,' said Harry, sticking to his new persona. 'I was born in Epsom, and I now live in Ewell.'

'It will come to me in a moment who you remind me of.' Once again the man set off back to his seat.

Harry reopened the file, but like Dick Whittington the man turned a third time, before he had a chance to read even another line. This time he picked up Harry's captain's hat and collapsed into the seat beside him. 'You don't write books, by any chance?'

'No,' said Harry even more firmly, as Miss Carrick appeared carrying a tray of cocktails. He raised his eyebrows and gave her what he hoped was a 'please rescue me' look.

'You remind me of an author who comes from Bristol, but I'm damned if I can remember his name. Are you sure you're not from Bristol?' He took a closer look, before releasing a cloud of cigarette smoke in Harry's face.

Harry saw Miss Carrick opening the door of the cockpit.

'It must be an interesting life, being a pilot—'

'This is your captain speaking. We are about to experience some turbulence, so would all passengers please return to their seats and fasten their seat belts.'

Miss Carrick reappeared in the cabin and walked straight to the back of the first-class section.

'I'm sorry to bother you, sir, but the captain has requested that all passengers—'

'Yes, I heard him,' said the man, hauling himself up, but not before he'd blown another cloud of smoke in Harry's direction. 'It'll come to me, who you remind me of,' he said, before making his way slowly back to his seat.

36

DURING THE SECOND leg of the journey to Buenos Aires, Harry completed the file on Don Pedro Martinez.

After the war, the subject bided his time in Argentina, sitting on a mountain of cash. Himmler had committed suicide before coming to trial at Nuremberg, while six of the henchmen on his list were sentenced to death. Eighteen more were sent to prison, including Major Bernhard Krüger. No one came knocking at Don Pedro's door claiming their life insurance.

Harry turned the page to find that the next section of the file was devoted to the subject's family. He rested for some time before he continued.

Martinez had four children. His first born, Diego, was expelled from Harrow after tying a new boy to a boiling-hot radiator. He returned to his native land, without an O level to his name, where he joined his father and, three years later, graduated with honours in crime. Although Diego wore pin-striped, double-breasted suits tailored in Savile Row, he would have spent most of his time in a prison uniform if his father hadn't had countless judges, police officers and politicians on his payroll.

His second son, Luis, immatured from boy to playboy during one summer vacation on the Riviera. He now spent most of his waking hours at the roulette tables in Monte Carlo, gambling with his father's five-pound notes in an attempt to earn them back in a different currency.

Whenever Luis had a good run, a flood of Monegasque

Francs would find their way into Don Pedro's account in Geneva. But it still annoyed Martinez that the casino was making a better return than he was.

The third child, Bruno, was not a chip off the old block, as he displayed far more of his mother's qualities than his father's shortcomings, although Martinez was happy to remind his London friends that he had a son who would be going up to Cambridge in September.

Little was known about the fourth child, Maria-Theresa, who was still at Roedean, and always spent the holidays with her mother.

Harry stopped reading when Miss Carrick set up a dinner table for him, but even during the meal, the damn man lingered in his mind.

During the years after the war, Martinez set about building up his bank's resources. The Family Farmers Friendly Bank operated accounts for those clients who possessed land but not money. Martinez's methods were crude but effective. He would loan farmers any amount of money they required, at exorbitant interest rates, as long as the loans were covered by the value of the farmers' land.

If customers were unable to make their quarterly payment, they received a foreclosure notice, giving them ninety days to clear the entire debt. If they failed to do so, and almost all of them did, the deeds for the land were confiscated by the bank, and added to the vast acreage Martinez had already accumulated. Anyone who complained received a visit from Diego, who reshaped their face; so much cheaper and more effective than employing lawyers.

The only thing that might have undermined the avuncular cattle baron image Martinez had worked so hard to cultivate in London was the fact that his wife Consuela finally came to the conclusion that her father had been right all along, and sued for divorce. As the proceedings took place in Buenos Aires, Martinez told anyone in London who asked, that Consuela had sadly died of cancer, thus turning any possible social stigma into sympathy.

After Consuela's father failed to be re-elected as mayor – Martinez had backed the opposition candidate – she ended up living in a village a few miles outside Buenos Aires. She received a monthly allowance, which didn't allow her many shopping trips in the capital, and no possibility of travelling abroad. And sadly for Consuela, only one of her sons showed any interest in keeping in touch with her, and he now lived in England.

Only one person who was not a member of the Martinez family warranted his own page in Harry's file: Karl Ramirez, whom Martinez employed as a butler/handyman. Although Ramirez had an Argentinian passport, he bore a striking resemblance to one Karl Otto Lunsdorf, a member of the 1936 German Olympic wrestling team who later became a lieutenant in the SS, specializing in interrogation. Ramirez's paperwork was as impressive as Martinez's five-pound notes, and almost certainly came from the same source.

Miss Carrick cleared away the dinner tray and offered Captain May brandy and a cigar, which he politely declined, after thanking her for the turbulence. She smiled.

'Turned out not to be quite as bad as the captain had originally thought,' she said, masking a grin. 'He asked me to let you know that, if you're staying at the Milonga, you'd be most welcome to join us on the BOAC bus, which would allow you to avoid Mr Bolton' – Harry raised an eyebrow – 'the man from Bristol, who's absolutely convinced he's met you somewhere before.'

Harry couldn't help noticing that Miss Carrick had glanced at his left hand more than once, on which a pale band of skin clearly indicated that a wedding ring had been removed. Captain Peter May had been divorced from his wife Angela for just over two years. They had two children: Jim, aged ten, who was hoping to go to Epsom College, and Sally, aged eight, who had her own pony. He even had a photograph of them to prove it. Harry had handed his ring to Emma for safe keeping just before he departed. Something else she didn't approve of.

◄○►

'London has asked me to make an appointment to see a Captain Peter May at ten o'clock tomorrow morning,' said the ambassador.

His secretary made a note in the diary. 'Will you require any background notes on Captain May?'

'No, because I haven't a clue who he is, or why the Foreign Office wants me to see him. Just be sure to bring him straight to my office the moment he arrives.'

◄○►

Harry waited until the last passenger had disembarked before he joined the crew. After he'd been checked through customs, he walked out of the airport to find a minibus waiting at the kerb.

The driver placed his suitcase in the baggage hold as Harry climbed on board to be greeted by a smiling Miss Carrick.

'May I join you?' he asked.

'Yes, of course,' she replied, moving over to make room for him.

'My name's Peter,' he said as they shook hands.

'Annabel. What brings you to Argentina?' she asked as the bus made its way into the city.

'My brother Dick works out here. We haven't seen each other for far too many years, so I thought I ought to make the effort as it's his fortieth birthday.'

'Your older brother?' said Annabel with a grin. 'What does he do?'

'He's a mechanical engineer. He's been working on the Paraná Dam project for the past five years.'

'Never heard of it.'

'No reason you should have. It's in the middle of nowhere.'

'Well he's going to get a bit of a culture shock when he comes to Buenos Aires, because it's one of the most cosmopolitan cities on earth, and certainly my favourite stopover.'

'How long will you be here this time?' said Harry, wanting to change the subject before he ran out of details about his recently adopted family.

'Forty-eight hours. Do you know Buenos Aires, Peter? If you don't, you're in for a real treat.'

'No, this is my first time,' said Harry, word perfect so far. Don't lose your concentration, Sir Alan had warned him, because that's when you'll slip up.

'So what route do you usually fly?'

'I'm on the transatlantic hop – New York, Boston and Washington.' The anonymous man from the Foreign Office had settled on that route because it took in three cities Harry had visited on his book tour.

'That sounds like fun. But make sure you sample the night life while you're here. The Argentinians make the Yanks look conservative.'

'Anywhere in particular I should take my brother?'

'The Lizard has the best tango dancers, but I'm told the Majestic has the finest cuisine, not that I've ever experienced it. The crew usually end up at the Matador Club on Independence Avenue. So if you and your brother find you've got time on your hands, you'd be welcome to join us.'

'Thank you,' said Harry as the bus drew up outside the hotel. 'I might just take you up on that.'

He carried Annabel's case into the hotel.

'This place is cheap and cheerful,' she said as they checked in, 'so if you want a bath but don't want to wait for the water to heat up, it's best to have it last thing at night, or first thing in the morning,' she added as they stepped into the one lift.

When they reached the fourth floor, Harry left Annabel and stepped out into a badly lit corridor before making his way to room 469. After he'd let himself in, he discovered the room wasn't a great improvement on the corridor. A large double bed that sank in the middle, a tap that dripped brown water, a towel rail that offered one face cloth, and a notice informing him that the bathroom was at the end of the corridor. He recalled Sir Alan's note, *We've booked you into a hotel Martinez and his cronies would never consider visiting.* He'd already realized why. This place needed his mother to be appointed as the manager, and preferably yesterday.

He took off his peaked cap and sat down on the end of the bed. He wanted to call Emma and tell her how much he missed her, but Sir Alan couldn't have been clearer: no phone calls, no night clubs, no sightseeing, no shopping; don't even leave the hotel until it's time to visit the ambassador. He put his feet up on the bed and lowered his head on to the pillow. He thought about Sebastian, Emma, Sir Alan, Martinez, the Matador Club . . . Captain May fell asleep.

37

WHEN HARRY WOKE, the first thing he did was to turn on the light by his bed and check his watch: 2.26 a.m. He cursed when he realized he hadn't undressed.

He almost fell off the bed, walked across to the window and stared out at a city that from the noise of the traffic and the sparkling lights was clearly still wide awake. He closed the curtains, got undressed and climbed back into bed, hoping he would drop off again quickly. But he was robbed of sleep by thoughts of Martinez, Seb, Sir Alan, Emma, Giles and even Jessica, and the harder he tried to relax and dismiss them from his mind, the more they demanded his attention.

At 4.30 a.m., he gave up and decided he would have a bath. That's when he fell asleep. When he woke, he jumped out of bed and pulled back the curtains to see the first rays of sunlight bathing the city. He checked the time. It was 7.10 a.m. He felt grubby, and smiled at the thought of a long, hot bath.

He went in search of a dressing gown, but the hotel could only manage a thin bath towel and a sliver of soap. He stepped into the corridor and headed for the bathroom. A sign saying *Occupado* was hanging on the door handle, and he could hear someone splashing around inside. Harry decided to wait, so no one would take his place in the queue. When the door eventually opened after about twenty minutes, Harry came face to face with the one man he'd hoped never to see again.

'Good morning, captain,' he said, blocking his path.

'Good morning, Mr Bolton,' Harry replied, trying to edge past him.

'No rush, old fellow,' he said. 'It will take a quarter of an hour for the tub to empty, and then another fifteen minutes to fill it up again.' Harry hoped that if he said nothing, Bolton would take the hint and move on. He didn't. 'Your exact double,' said the persistent intruder, 'writes detective novels. The weird thing is that I can remember the name of the detective, William Warwick, but I'm damned if I can recall the name of the author. It's on the tip of my tongue.'

When Harry heard the last few drops of water gurgling down the drain, Bolton reluctantly moved aside, allowing him to enter the bathroom.

'It's on the tip of my tongue,' Bolton repeated as he walked off down the corridor.

Harry closed the door and locked it, but no sooner had he turned on the tap than there was a knock on the door.

'How long are you going to be?'

By the time there was enough water for him to step into the bath, he could hear two people holding a conversation on the other side of the door. Or was it three?

The bar of soap only just lasted long enough to reach his feet, and by the time he had dried between his toes, the towel was soaking. He opened the bathroom door to find a queue of disgruntled guests, and tried not to think what time it would be before the last of them went down to breakfast. Miss Carrick was right, he should have taken a bath when he woke in the middle of the night.

Once he was back in his room, Harry shaved and dressed quickly, realizing that he hadn't eaten anything since he'd stepped off the plane. He locked his room, took the lift down to the ground floor and strolled across the lobby to the breakfast room. As he entered, the first person he spotted was Mr Bolton, sitting on his own, spreading marmalade on a piece of toast. Harry turned and fled. He thought about room service, but not for long.

His appointment with the ambassador wasn't until ten

o'clock, and he knew from his notes that it would take only ten to fifteen minutes to reach the embassy on foot. He would have gone for a walk and looked for a café but for one of Sir Alan's repeated instructions: no unnecessary exposure. Nevertheless, he decided to leave a little early and walk slowly. He was relieved to find that Mr Bolton wasn't lurking in the corridor, the lift or the lobby, and he managed to make it out of the hotel without a further encounter.

Three blocks to the right, then two more to the left, and he would find himself in Plaza de Mayo, the tourist guidebook assured him. Ten minutes later, it was proved right. Union Jacks were being raised on flagpoles around the square, and Harry could only wonder why.

He crossed the road, not easy in a city that prided itself on having no traffic lights, and continued down Constitutional Avenue, stopping for a moment to admire a statue of someone called Estrada. His instructions told him that if he kept walking, in 200 yards he'd come to a set of wrought-iron gates emblazoned with the royal coat of arms.

Harry found himself standing outside the embassy at 9.33. Once around the block: 9.43. Once again, even slower: 9.56. Finally, he walked through the gates, across a pebbled courtyard and up a dozen steps, where a large double door was opened for him by a guard whose medals indicated that they had served in the same theatre of war. Lieutenant Harry Clifton of the Texas Rangers would have liked to stop and chat to him, but not today. As he was walking towards the reception desk a young woman stepped forward and asked, 'Are you Captain May?'

'Yes, I am.'

'My name is Becky Shaw. I'm the ambassador's private secretary, and he's asked me to take you straight through to his office.'

'Thank you,' said Harry. She led him down a red carpeted corridor, at the end of which she stopped, knocked gently on an imposing double door and entered without waiting for a response. Any fears Harry might have had of the ambassador not expecting him were proving unfounded.

He entered a large elegant room to find the ambassador sitting behind his desk in front of a vast semi-circle of windows. His Excellency, a small, square-jawed man who exuded energy, stood up and walked briskly over to Harry.

'How nice to meet you, Captain May,' he said, shaking him firmly by the hand. 'Would you care for a coffee, and perhaps some ginger biscuits?'

'Ginger biscuits,' repeated Harry. 'Yes please.'

The ambassador nodded, and his secretary quickly left the room, closing the door behind her.

'Now, I must be frank with you, old chap,' said the ambassador as he guided Harry towards a pair of comfortable chairs that looked out on to the embassy's manicured lawn that boasted several beds of roses. They could have been in the Home Counties. 'I have absolutely no idea what this meeting is about, except that if the cabinet secretary wants me to see you urgently, it has to be important. He's not a man given to wasting anyone's time.'

Harry removed an envelope from his jacket pocket and handed it to the ambassador, along with the thick file he had been entrusted with.

'I don't get many of these,' said His Excellency, looking at the crest on the back of the envelope.

The door opened and Becky returned with a tray of coffee and biscuits, which she placed on the table between them. The ambassador opened the foreign secretary's letter and read it slowly, but didn't say anything until Becky had left the room.

'I thought there was nothing new I could learn about Don Pedro Martinez, but it seems you're about to prove me wrong. Why don't you start at the beginning, Captain May?'

'My name is Harry Clifton,' he began, and two cups of coffee and six biscuits later, he had explained why he was staying at the Hotel Milonga and why he'd been unable to telephone his son and let him know that he should return to England immediately.

The ambassador's response took Harry by surprise. 'Do you know, Mr Clifton, if the foreign secretary had instructed me to assassinate Martinez, I would have carried out the order with considerable pleasure. I cannot begin to imagine how many lives that man has ruined.'

'And I fear my son may be next in line.'

'Not if I have anything to do with it. Now, as I see it, our first priority is to ensure your son's safety. Our second, and I suspect Sir Alan thinks it's equally important, is to discover how Martinez intends to smuggle such a large sum of money through customs. It's clear that Sir Alan believes' – he glanced at the letter – 'that your son might be the one person who can find out how he plans to go about that. Is that a fair assessment?'

'Yes, sir, but he won't be able to achieve that unless I can speak to him without Martinez being aware of it.'

'Understood.' The ambassador leant back, closed his eyes and placed his fingertips together as if he was deep in prayer. 'The trick,' he said, his eyes remaining closed, 'will be to offer Martinez something money cannot buy.'

He jumped up, marched across to the window and stared out on to the lawn, where several members of his staff were busying themselves preparing for a garden party.

'You said that Martinez and your son aren't due to arrive in Buenos Aires until tomorrow?'

'Their SS *South America* docks at around six tomorrow morning, sir.'

'And you're no doubt aware of the imminent arrival of Princess Margaret, on an official visit?'

'So that's why there were so many Union Jacks in Plaza de Mayo.'

The ambassador smiled. 'HRH will only be with us for forty-eight hours. The highlight of her trip will be a garden party held in her honour here at the embassy on Monday afternoon, to which the great and the good of Buenos Aires have been invited. Martinez was not included, for obvious reasons, despite making it abundantly clear to me on more than one occasion how much he would like to be. But if my plan is to succeed, we're going to have to move, and move quickly.'

The ambassador swung round and pressed a button under his desk. Moments later Miss Shaw reappeared, pad and pencil in hand.

'I want you to send an invitation to Don Pedro Martinez for the royal garden party on Monday.' If his secretary was surprised, she didn't show it. 'And I also want to send him a letter at the same time.'

He closed his eyes, clearly composing the letter in his mind.

'Dear Don Pedro, I have great pleasure, no, *particular* pleasure, in enclosing an invitation to the embassy's garden party, at which we will be particularly, no, no, I've already used "particular", especially honoured by the presence of Her Royal Highness The Princess Margaret New paragraph. As you will see, the invitation is for you and a guest. Far be it from me to advise you, but if there are any English men on your staff who might be able to attend, I think Her Royal Highness would consider that appropriate. I look forward to seeing you, yours etc. Did that sound pompous enough?'

'Yes,' said Miss Shaw with a nod. Harry kept his mouth shut.

'And, Miss Shaw, I'll sign it as soon as you've typed it, then I want you to arrange to have it and the invitation delivered to his office immediately, so it's on his desk before he arrives back tomorrow morning.'

'What date should I put on it, sir?'

'Good thinking,' said the ambassador as he glanced at the calendar on his desk. 'What date did your son leave England, Captain May?'

'Monday June the tenth, sir.'

The ambassador looked at the calendar once again. 'Date it the seventh. We can always blame its late arrival on the postal service. Everyone else does.' He didn't speak again until his secretary had left the room.

'Now, Mr Clifton,' he said, returning to his seat. 'Let me tell you what I have in mind.'

◄○►

Harry didn't actually witness Sebastian, accompanied by Martinez, coming down the gangway of the SS *South America* the following morning, but the ambassador's secretary did. She later delivered a note to Harry's hotel, confirming that they had arrived and asking him to report to the embassy's side entrance off Dr Luis Agote at two o'clock the following afternoon, a full hour before the first guests were due to turn up for the garden party.

Harry sat on the end of the bed, wondering if the ambassador would prove right when he'd said that Martinez would rise to the bait quicker than a salmon on the Tweed. The only time he'd ever fished, the salmon had ignored him.

◄o►

'When did this invitation arrive?' shouted Martinez, holding the gilt-edged card high in the air.

'It was hand-delivered yesterday morning by a member of the ambassador's personal staff,' said his secretary.

'Not like the British to send out an invitation that late,' said Martinez suspiciously.

'The ambassador's personal secretary rang to apologize. She told me they hadn't received replies to a number of the invitations that had been sent out by post, and assumed they'd gone astray. In fact she said if you get another one in the mail, please ignore it.'

'Damned postal service,' said Martinez. He passed the invitation to his son, and began to read the ambassador's letter.

'As you can see from the card,' said Martinez, 'I can take a guest. Would you like to join me?'

'You must be joking,' said Diego. 'I'd rather fall to my knees during high mass at the cathedral than be seen bowing and scraping at an English garden party.'

'Then perhaps I'll take young Sebastian with me. After all, he is the grandson of a lord, so there's no harm in giving the impression that I'm well connected with the British aristocracy.'

'Where is the boy now?'

'I've booked him into the Royal Hotel for a couple of days.'

'What reason did you give for bringing him out here in the first place?'

'I told him he could have a few days' holiday in Buenos Aires before returning to England with a consignment I need delivered to Sotheby's, for which he would be well paid.'

'Are you going to tell him what's in the crate?'

'Certainly not. The less he knows the better.'

'Perhaps I ought to go with him, just to make sure there aren't any slip-ups.'

'No, that would defeat the whole purpose of the exercise. The boy will return to England on the *Queen Mary*, while we fly to London a few days later. That will allow him to slip through the net while British customs concentrate their fire-power on us. And we'll still be in London well in time for the auction.'

'Do you still want me to bid on your behalf?'

'Yes. I can't risk involving anyone outside the family.'

'But isn't it possible that someone will recognize me?'

'Not if you're bidding by phone.'

38

'IF YOU'LL BE kind enough to stand here, Mr President,' said the ambassador. 'Her Royal Highness will come to you first. I'm sure you'll have a lot to talk about.'

'My English not good,' said the president.

'Not to worry, Mr President, HRH is used to coping with that problem.'

The ambassador took a pace to his right. 'Good afternoon, Prime Minister. You will be the second person to be presented to the princess, once she's finished her conversation with the president.'

'Could you remind me of the correct way to address Her Majesty?'

'Of course, sir,' said the ambassador, not correcting his faux pas. 'Her Royal Highness will say "Good afternoon, Prime Minister", and before you shake hands, you should bow.' The ambassador gave a slight nod to demonstrate. Several people standing nearby began to practise the movement, just in case. 'Having bowed, you will then say, "Good afternoon, Your Royal Highness." She will open the conversation with a subject of her choice, to which you can respond appropriately. It is not considered courteous for you to ask her any questions, and you should address her as ma'am, which rhymes with jam, not harm. When she leaves you to move on to the mayor, you bow once again, and say, "Goodbye, Your Royal Highness."'

The prime minister looked perplexed.

'HRH should be with us in a few minutes,' said the

ambassador, before moving on to the Mayor of Buenos Aires. He gave him the same instructions, before adding, 'Yours will be the last official presentation.'

The ambassador couldn't miss Martinez, who had placed himself a couple of feet behind the mayor. He could see that the young man standing by his side was Harry Clifton's son. Martinez headed straight for the ambassador, leaving Sebastian in his wake.

'Will I get to meet Her Majesty?' he asked.

'I was hoping to present you to Her Royal Highness. So if you'd be kind enough to stay exactly where you are, Mr Martinez, I'll bring her across as soon as she's finished talking to the mayor. But I'm afraid that does not include your guest. The princess is not accustomed to having to speak to two people at once, so perhaps the young gentleman would be kind enough to stand back a little.'

'Of course he will,' said Martinez, without consulting Sebastian.

'Now, I'd better get going, or this show will never get off the ground.' The ambassador made his way across the crowded lawn, avoiding stepping on the red carpet, as he walked back into his office.

The guest of honour was seated in a corner of the room, smoking a cigarette and chatting to the ambassador's wife. A long, elegant ivory cigarette holder dangled from her white gloved hand.

The ambassador bowed. 'We're ready, ma'am, whenever you are.'

'Then let's get on with it, shall we?' said the princess, taking one last puff before stubbing out her cigarette in the nearest ashtray.

The ambassador accompanied her out on to the balcony, where they paused for a moment. The bandmaster of the Scots Guards raised his baton, and the band began to play the unfamiliar sound of the guest's national anthem. Everyone fell silent, and most of the men copied the ambassador and stood rigidly to attention.

When the last chord had been played, Her Royal Highness proceeded slowly down the red carpet and on to the lawn, where the ambassador first introduced her to President Pedro Aramburu.

'Mr President, how nice to see you again,' the princess ventured. 'Thank you for a most fascinating morning. I did so enjoy seeing the assembly in session, and having lunch with you and your cabinet.'

'We were honoured to have you as our guest, ma'am,' he said, delivering the one sentence he had rehearsed.

'And I have to agree with you, Mr President, when you said that your beef is the equal of anything we can produce in the Highlands of Scotland.'

They both laughed, although the president wasn't sure why.

The ambassador glanced over the president's shoulder, checking that the prime minister, the mayor and Mr Martinez were all planted in their correct positions. He noticed that Martinez couldn't take his eyes off the princess. He gave Becky a nod, and she immediately stepped forward, took her place behind Sebastian, and whispered, 'Mr Clifton?'

He swung round. 'Yes?' he said, surprised anyone knew his name.

'I'm the ambassador's private secretary. He has asked if you would be kind enough to come with me.'

'Shall I let Don Pedro know?'

'No,' said Becky firmly. 'This will only take a few minutes.'

Sebastian looked uncertain, but followed her as she weaved her way through the chattering crowd of morning suits and cocktail dresses, and entered the embassy by a side door that was being held open for her. The ambassador smiled, pleased that the first part of the operation had gone so smoothly.

'I will indeed pass on your best wishes to Her Majesty,' said the princess, before the ambassador guided her across to the prime minister. Although he tried to concentrate on every word the princess was saying in case anything needed to be followed up, he allowed himself the occasional glance in the direction of his study window, in the hope of spotting Becky coming back out on to the terrace, which would be the sign that the meeting between father and son had taken place.

When he felt that the princess had had quite enough of the prime minister, he moved her on to the mayor.

'How nice to meet you,' said the princess. 'Only last week, the Lord Mayor of London was telling me how much he'd enjoyed visiting your city.'

'Thank you, ma'am,' the mayor replied. 'I am looking forward to returning the compliment some time next year.'

The ambassador glanced in the direction of his study, but there was still no sign of Becky.

The princess didn't last long with the mayor, and discreetly made it clear that she wanted to move on. The ambassador reluctantly fell in with her wishes.

'And may I be allowed, ma'am, to present one of the city's leading bankers, Don Pedro Martinez, who I am sure you will be interested to know spends the season at his home in London every year.'

'This is indeed a great honour, Your Majesty,' said Martinez, bowing low, before the princess had a chance to speak.

'Where is your home in London?' enquired the princess.

'Eaton Square, Your Majesty.'

'How very nice. I have a lot of friends who live in that part of town.'

'If that's the case, Your Majesty, perhaps you'd like to join me for dinner one night. Do bring along anyone you like.'

The ambassador couldn't wait to hear the princess's reply.

'What an interesting idea,' she managed, before rapidly moving on.

Martinez bowed low once again. The ambassador hurried after his royal guest. He was relieved when she stopped to chat to his wife, but the only sentence he caught was, 'What a frightful little man, how did he ever get invited?'

Once again, the ambassador glanced towards his study, and breathed a sigh of relief when he saw Becky walk out on to the terrace and give him a firm nod. He tried to concentrate on what the princess was saying to his wife.

'Marjorie, I'm desperate for a cigarette. Do you think I could escape for a few minutes?'

'Yes, of course, ma'am. Shall we go back into the embassy?'

As they walked away, the ambassador turned to check on Martinez. The besotted man hadn't moved an inch. His eyes were still firmly fixed on the princess, and he didn't seem to notice Sebastian quietly returning to his place just a few feet behind him.

Once the princess had disappeared out of sight, Martinez turned and beckoned Sebastian to join him.

'I was the fourth person to meet the princess,' were his opening words. 'Only the president, the prime minister and the mayor were presented before me.'

'What a great honour, sir,' said Sebastian, as if he'd witnessed the whole encounter. 'You must be very proud.'

'Humbled,' said Martinez. 'This has been one of the great days of my life. Do you know,' he added, 'I think Her Majesty agreed to have dinner with me when I'm next in London.'

'I feel guilty,' said Sebastian.

'Guilty?'

'Yes, sir. It should be Bruno who's standing here to share in your triumph, not me.'

'You can tell Bruno all about it once you're back in London.'

Sebastian watched the ambassador and his secretary walk back into the embassy, and wondered if his father was still there.

'I've only got as long as it takes the princess to smoke a cigarette,' said the ambassador as he burst into his study, 'but I couldn't wait to find out how the meeting with your son went.'

'He was shocked to begin with, of course,' said Harry as he slipped his BOAC jacket back on. 'But when I told him he hadn't been expelled, and they were still expecting him at Cambridge in September, he relaxed a little. I suggested that he fly back to England with me, but he said he'd promised to take a package to Southampton on the *Queen Mary*, and that as Martinez had been so kind to him, it was the least he could do.'

'Southampton,' repeated the ambassador. 'Did he tell you what was in the package?'

'No, and I didn't press him, in case he stumbled on the real reason I'd travelled all this way.'

'Wise decision.'

'I also thought about going back on the *Queen Mary* with him, but I realized that if I did Martinez would soon work out why I was here.'

'I agree,' said the ambassador. 'So how did you leave it?'

'I promised I'd be there to meet him when the *Queen Mary* docks at Southampton.'

'How do you think Martinez will react if Sebastian tells him you're in Buenos Aires?'

'I suggested it might be wise not to mention it, as he'd be certain to want Seb to fly back to London with me, so he agreed to say nothing.'

'So now all I've got to do is find out what's in that package, while you get back to London before someone recognizes you.'

'I can't begin to thank you for all you've done, sir,' said Harry. 'I'm painfully aware that I'm a distraction you could have done without at the moment.'

'Don't give it a second thought, Harry. I haven't enjoyed myself so much in years. However, it might be wise for you to slip away before—'

The door opened, and the princess walked in. The ambassador bowed, as Her Royal Highness stared at the man dressed in a BOAC captain's uniform.

'May I present Captain Peter May, ma'am,' said the ambassador, not missing a beat.

Harry bowed.

The princess took the cigarette holder out of her mouth. 'Captain May, how nice to meet you.' Giving Harry a closer look, she added, 'Have we met before?'

'No, ma'am,' Harry replied. 'I have a feeling I would remember it if we had.'

'Very droll, Captain May.' She gave him a warm smile

before stubbing out her cigarette. 'Well, ambassador, ring the bell. I have a feeling it's time for the second round.'

As Mr Matthews accompanied the princess out on to the lawn, Becky took Harry in the opposite direction. He followed her down the back stairs, through the kitchen and out of the tradesmen's entrance at the side of the building.

'I hope you have a pleasant flight home, Captain May.'

Harry made his way slowly back to the hotel, with several thoughts colliding in his mind. How he wanted to phone Emma to let her know that he'd seen Sebastian, and that he was safe and would be returning to England in a few days' time.

After he'd arrived back at the hotel, he packed his few belongings, took his case down to the concierge's desk and asked if there were any flights to London that evening.

'I'm afraid it's too late to get you on this afternoon's BOAC flight,' he replied. 'But I could book you on to the Pan Am flight to New York that leaves at midnight, and from there you could—'

'Harry!'

Harry swung round.

'Harry Clifton! I knew it was you. Don't you remember? We met when you addressed the Bristol Rotary Club last year?'

'You're mistaken, Mr Bolton,' Harry said. 'My name is Peter May,' he added as Annabel walked past them carrying a suitcase. He strolled across to join her, as if they'd arranged to meet.

'Let me help you,' he said, taking her case and walking out of the hotel with her.

'Thank you,' said Annabel, looking a little surprised.

'My pleasure.' Harry handed their suitcases to the driver and followed her on to the bus.

'I didn't realize you were flying back with us, Peter.'

Neither did I, Harry wanted to tell her. 'My brother had to get back. Some problem with the dam. But we had a great party last night, thanks to you.'

'Where did you end up?'

'I took him to the Majestic Hotel. You were right, the food is sensational.'

'Tell me more. I've always wanted to have a meal there.'

During the drive to the airport, Harry had to invent a fortieth birthday present (an Ingersoll watch), and a three-course meal – smoked salmon, steak, of course, and lemon tart. He wasn't impressed by his culinary imagination, and was grateful Annabel didn't ask about the wines. He hadn't got to bed, he told her, until three in the morning.

'I wish I'd taken your advice on the bath as well,' said Harry, 'and had one before I went to bed.'

'I took one at 4 a.m. You'd have been welcome to join me,' she said, as the bus came to a halt outside the airport.

Harry stuck close to the crew as they made their way through customs and on to the plane. He returned to the back corner seat, wondering if he'd made the right decision or if he should have stayed put. But then he recalled Sir Alan's words, so oft repeated. If your cover is blown, get out, and get out quickly. He felt sure he was doing the right thing – that loudmouth would be running around town telling everyone, 'I've just seen Harry Clifton posing as a BOAC pilot.'

Once the other passengers had settled in their seats, the aircraft taxied out on to the runway. Harry closed his eyes. The briefcase was empty, the files destroyed. He fastened his seat belt and looked forward to a long, uninterrupted sleep.

'This is your captain speaking. I have turned off the seat-belt signs, so you are now free to move around the aircraft.'

Harry closed his eyes again. He was just dozing off when he heard someone slump into the seat next to him.

'I've worked it out,' he said, as Harry opened one eye. 'You were in Buenos Aires to do research for your next book. Am I right, or am I right?'

SEBASTIAN CLIFTON

1957

39

Don Pedro was among the last to leave the garden party, and not until he was finally convinced that the princess would not be returning.

Sebastian joined him in the back of the Rolls. 'This has been one of the great days of my life,' Don Pedro repeated. Sebastian remained silent, because he couldn't think of anything new to say on the subject. Don Pedro was clearly drunk, if not on wine, then on the thought of mixing with royalty. Sebastian was surprised that such a successful man could be so easily flattered. Suddenly, Martinez changed tack.

'I want you to know, my boy, that if you ever need a job, there will always be one for you in Buenos Aires. The choice is yours. You could be a cowboy or a banker. Come to think of it, there's not a great deal of difference,' he said, laughing at his own joke.

'That's kind of you, sir,' said Sebastian. Although he wanted to tell him that he would be joining Bruno at Cambridge after all, he thought better of it, because he would have to explain how he'd found out. But he was already beginning to wonder why his father had come halfway round the world just to tell him ... Don Pedro interrupted his thoughts by taking a wad of five-pound notes from his pocket, peeling off ninety pounds and handing it to Sebastian.

'I always believe in paying in advance.'

'But I haven't done the job yet, sir.'

'I know you'll keep your side of the bargain.' The words

only made Sebastian feel more guilty about his little secret, and if the car hadn't come to a halt outside Martinez's office, he might have ignored his father's advice.

'Take Mr Clifton back to his hotel,' Don Pedro instructed his driver. Turning to Sebastian he said, 'A car will pick you up on Wednesday afternoon and take you to the dock. Make sure you enjoy your last couple of days in Buenos Aires, because this city has a lot to offer a young man.'

◄o►

Harry was not a man who had ever felt it necessary to resort to foul language, even in his books. His churchgoing mother simply wouldn't have approved. However, after an hour of listening to an endless monologue on Ted Bolton's life, from his daughter's responsibilities as a senior-sixer in the Girl Guides, in which she'd won badges for needlework and cookery, to his wife's role as membership secretary of the Bristol Mothers' Union, to the guest speakers he had booked for the Rotary Club this autumn, not to mention his views on Marilyn Monroe, Nikita Khrushchev, Hugh Gaitskell and Tony Hancock, he finally snapped.

He opened his eyes and sat up straight. 'Mr Bolton, why don't you bugger off?'

To Harry's surprise and relief, Bolton got up and returned to his seat without another word. Harry fell asleep within moments.

◄o►

Sebastian decided to take Don Pedro's advice and make the most of his last two days in the city, before the time came to board the *Queen Mary* and return home.

After breakfast the following morning, he exchanged four of his five-pound notes for three hundred pesos and left the hotel to go in search of the Spanish arcade, where he hoped to find a present for his mother and sister. He chose a brooch set in rhodochrosite for his mother, in a pale pink shade that the salesman told him could not be found anywhere else in the world. The price came as a bit of a shock, but then Sebastian remembered what he'd put his mother through during the past two weeks.

As he strolled along the promenade on his way back to the hotel, a drawing in a gallery window caught his eye and made him think of Jessica. He stepped inside to take a closer look. The dealer assured him that the young artist had a future, so not only was it a fine still-life, but it would be a shrewd investment. And, yes, he would accept English money. Sebastian only hoped that Jessica would feel the same way about Fernando Botero's *Bowl of Oranges* as he did.

The only thing he bought for himself was a magnificent leather belt with a rancher's buckle. It wasn't cheap, but he couldn't resist it.

He stopped to have lunch in a street café, and ate too much Argentinian roast beef while he read an out-of-date copy of *The Times*. Double yellow lines were to be introduced in all major British city centres. He couldn't believe his uncle Giles would have voted for that.

After lunch, with the help of his guidebook, he found the only cinema showing English-language films in Buenos Aires. He sat alone in the back row watching *A Place in the Sun*, fell in love with Elizabeth Taylor, and wondered how you got to meet a girl like that.

On his way back to the hotel, he dropped into a second-hand bookshop that boasted a shelf of English novels. He smiled when he saw his father's first book had been reduced to three pesos, and left after he'd purchased a much-thumbed copy of *Officers and Gentlemen*.

In the evening, Sebastian had dinner in the hotel restaurant and, with the help of his guidebook, selected several places of interest he still hoped to visit if he had time: the Catedral Metropolitana, the Museo Nacional de Bellas Artes, La Casa Rosada, and the Jardín Botánico Carlos Thays in the old Palermo neighbourhood. Don Pedro was right – the city had a lot to offer.

He signed the bill, and decided to return to his room and continue reading Evelyn Waugh. He would have done just that if he hadn't noticed her sitting on a stool at the bar. She gave him a coquettish smile, which stopped him in his tracks. The second smile acted like a magnet, and moments later he was standing by her side. She looked about the same age as Ruby, but much more alluring.

'Would you like to buy me a drink?' she asked.

Sebastian nodded as he climbed on to the stool next to her. She turned to the barman and ordered two glasses of champagne.

'My name is Gabriella.'

'Sebastian,' he said, offering his hand. She shook it. He'd had no idea a woman's touch could have that effect on him.

'Where do you come from?'

'England,' he replied.

'I'm going to visit England one day. The Tower of London and Buckingham Palace,' she said, as the barman poured them two glasses of champagne. 'Cheers. Isn't that what the English say?'

Sebastian raised his glass and said, 'Cheers.' He found it difficult not to stare at her slim, graceful legs. He wanted to touch them.

'Are you staying at the hotel?' she asked, placing a hand on his thigh.

Sebastian was glad the lights in the bar were so muted she wasn't able to see the colour of his cheeks. 'Yes, I am.'

'And are you alone?' she said, not removing her hand.

'Yes,' he managed.

'Would you like me to come up to your room, Sebastian?'

He couldn't believe his luck. He'd found Ruby in Buenos Aires, and the headmaster was 7,000 miles away. He didn't need to reply, because she had already slipped off the stool, taken him by the hand and was leading him out of the bar.

They headed towards a bank of lifts on the far side of the lobby.

'What's your room number, Sebastian?'

'One one seven zero,' he said, as they stepped into the lift.

When they reached his room on the eleventh floor, Sebastian fumbled with his key as he tried to open the door. She began to kiss him even before they'd stepped inside, and went on kissing him as she deftly removed his jacket and unbuckled his belt, only stopping when his trousers fell to the floor.

When he opened his eyes, he found her blouse and skirt had joined them. He wanted to just stand there and admire her body, but once again she took him by the hand, this time guiding him towards the bed. He pulled off his shirt and tie, desperate to touch every part of her at once. She fell back on the bed and pulled him on top of her. Moments later he let out a loud sigh.

He lay still for a few seconds before she slipped out from under him, gathered up her clothes and disappeared into the bathroom. He pulled the sheet over his naked body and impatiently waited for her to return. He was looking forward to spending the rest of the night with this goddess, and wondered how many times he could make love before the morning. But when the bathroom door opened, Gabriella stepped out, fully dressed, and looked as if she was about to leave.

'Was that your first time?' she asked.

'Of course not.'

'I thought so,' she said. 'But it's still three hundred pesos.'

Sebastian sat bolt upright, not sure what she meant.

'You don't think it was your good looks and English charm that persuaded me to come up to your room?'

'No, of course not,' said Sebastian. He got off the bed, picked up his jacket from the floor and took out his wallet. He stared at the remaining five-pound notes.

'Twenty pounds,' she said, obviously having come across this problem before.

He took out four five-pound notes and handed them to her.

She took the money and disappeared even more quickly than he had come.

◄o►

When the plane finally touched down at London Airport, Harry took advantage of his uniform and joined the crew as they strolled unhindered through customs. He declined Annabel's offer to accompany her on the bus into London, and instead joined the long queue for a taxi.

Forty minutes later, the cab came to a halt outside Giles's house in Smith Square. Looking forward to a long bath, an English meal and a good night's sleep, Harry banged on the brass knocker, hoping Giles would be at home.

A few moments later, the door swung open, and when Giles saw him he burst out laughing, stood to attention and saluted.

'Welcome home, captain.'

⊷◦►

When Sebastian woke the next morning, the first thing he did was to check his wallet. He only had ten pounds left, and he'd hoped to start life at Cambridge having saved eighty. As he looked at his clothes strewn across the floor, even his new leather belt had lost its allure. This morning he would only be able to visit places with no entrance charge.

Uncle Giles had been right when he'd told him there are defining moments in one's life when you learn a lot about yourself, and you deposit that knowledge in the experience account, so you can draw on it at some later date.

Once Sebastian had packed his few belongings and gathered up his presents, his thoughts turned to England, and starting life as an undergraduate. He couldn't wait. When he stepped out of the lift on the ground floor, he was surprised to see Don Pedro's chauffeur, peaked cap under his arm, standing in the lobby. He put the cap back on the moment he saw Sebastian, and said, 'Boss wants to see you.'

Sebastian climbed into the back of the Rolls-Royce, glad to have an opportunity to thank Don Pedro for all he'd done, although he wasn't going to admit that he was down to his last ten pounds. On arrival at Martinez House, he was shown straight through to Don Pedro's office.

'Sebastian, I am sorry to drag you in like this, but a small problem has arisen.'

Sebastian's heart sank as he feared he wasn't going to be allowed to escape. 'A problem?'

'I had a call from my friend Mr Matthews at the British Embassy this morning. He pointed out that you'd entered the country without a passport. I told him you'd travelled on my ship, and that while you were in Buenos Aires you were my guest, but, as he explained, that won't help you get back into Britain.'

'Does that mean I'll miss the ship?' Sebastian couldn't hide his dismay.

'Certainly not,' said Martinez. 'My driver will take you to the embassy on the way to the port, and the ambassador has promised there will be a passport for you at reception.'

'Thank you,' said Sebastian.

'Of course, it helps that the ambassador is a personal friend,' said Martinez with a smile. He then handed him a thick envelope and said, 'Be sure you hand this in to customs when you land at Southampton.'

'Is this the package I'm meant to take back to England?' asked Sebastian.

'No, no,' said Martinez, laughing. 'These are just the export documents to verify what's in the crate. All you have to do is present them to customs, and then Sotheby's will take over.'

Sebastian had never heard of Sotheby's, and made a mental note of the name.

'And Bruno rang last night to say he's looking forward to seeing you once you're back in London, and hopes you'll stay with him at Eaton Square. After all, it must be a better alternative than a guest house in Paddington.'

Sebastian thought about Tibby, and would have liked to tell Don Pedro that the Safe Haven guest house was the equal of the Majestic Hotel in Buenos Aires. 'Thank you, sir,' was all he said.

'Bon voyage, and just make sure that Sotheby's picks up my package. Once you get to London, let Karl know you've delivered it and remind him that I'll be back on the Monday.'

He stepped out from behind his desk, gripped Sebastian by

the shoulders and kissed him on both cheeks. 'I look upon you as my fourth son.'

Don Pedro's first son was standing by the window in his office on the floor below when Sebastian left the building carrying a thick envelope worth eight million pounds. He watched as Sebastian climbed into the back of the Rolls, but didn't move until he'd seen the driver ease away from the kerbside to join the morning traffic.

Diego ran up the stairs and joined his father.

'Is the statue safely on board?' Don Pedro asked once the door had been closed.

'I watched it being lowered into the hold earlier this morning. But I'm still not convinced.'

'About what?'

'There's eight million pounds of your money hidden in that statue, and not one of our team on board to keep an eye on it. You've left a boy, barely out of school, responsible for the entire operation.'

'Which is exactly why no one will take any interest in the statue, or him,' said Don Pedro. 'The paperwork is in the name of Sebastian Clifton, and all he has to do is present the manifest to customs, sign the release form, and then Sotheby's will take over, with no suggestion that we are in any way involved.'

'Let's hope you're right.'

'When we arrive at London Airport that Monday,' said Don Pedro, 'my bet is that there will be at least a dozen customs officers crawling all over our luggage. All they'll discover is the brand of aftershave I prefer, by which time the statue will be safely at Sotheby's awaiting the opening bid.'

―◦―

When Sebastian walked into the embassy to pick up his passport, he was surprised to find Becky standing by the reception desk. 'Good morning,' she said. 'The ambassador is looking forward to meeting you,' and without another word, she turned and walked down the corridor towards Mr Matthews's office.

Sebastian followed her for a second time, wondering if his

father was on the other side of that door and would be coming back to England with him. He hoped so. Becky gave a gentle tap, opened the door and stood to one side.

The ambassador was staring out of the window when Sebastian entered the room. The moment he heard the door open, he turned, marched across and shook Sebastian warmly by the hand.

'I'm glad to meet you at last,' he said. 'I wanted to give you this in person,' he added, picking up a passport from his desk.

'Thank you, sir,' said Sebastian.

'Can I also just check that you won't be taking more than a thousand pounds into Britain? Wouldn't want you to break the law,'

'I'm down to my last ten pounds,' Seb admitted.

'If that's all you've got to declare, you should sail through customs.'

'Except that I'm delivering a sculpture on behalf of Don Pedro Martinez that's to be collected by Sotheby's. I don't know anything about it, except that according to the manifest it's called *The Thinker*, and it weighs two tons.'

'Mustn't keep you,' said the ambassador as he accompanied him to the door. 'By the way, Sebastian, what's your middle name?'

'Arthur, sir,' he said as he stepped back into the corridor. 'I was named after my grandfather.'

'Have a pleasant voyage, my boy,' were Mr Matthews's last words before he closed the door. He returned to his desk and wrote three names on his pad.

40

'I RECEIVED THIS communiqué yesterday morning from Philip Matthews, our ambassador in Argentina,' said the cabinet secretary, handing out copies to everyone seated around the table. 'Please read it carefully.'

After Sir Alan had received the sixteen-page communiqué from Buenos Aires on his ticker tape machine, he'd spent the rest of the morning checking each paragraph carefully. He knew that what he was looking for would be secreted among the reams of trivia about what Princess Margaret had been up to on her official visit to the city.

He was puzzled about why the ambassador had invited Martinez to the royal garden party, and even more surprised to discover that he had been presented to Her Royal Highness. He assumed that Matthews must have had a good reason for flouting protocol in this way, and hoped there wasn't a photograph filed away in some newspaper cuttings library to remind everyone of the occasion at some time in the future.

It was just before midday when Sir Alan came across the paragraph he'd been searching for. He asked his secretary to cancel his lunch appointment.

Her Royal Highness was gracious enough to bring me up to date on the result of the first Test match at Lord's, wrote the ambassador. *What a splendid effort by Captain Peter May, and such a pity that he was run out unnecessarily at the last minute.*

Sir Alan looked up and smiled at Harry Clifton, who was also engrossed in the communiqué.

I was delighted to learn that Arthur Barrington will be returning for the second Test in Southampton on Sunday 23rd June, because with a test average of just over 8, it could make all the difference for England.

Sir Alan had underlined the words Arthur, Sunday, Southampton, and the number 8, before he continued reading.

However, I was puzzled when HRH told me that Tate would be a welcome edition at No. 5, but she assured me that no less a figure than John Rothenstein, the director of cricket, had told her, which had me thinking.

The cabinet secretary underlined Tate, No. 5, edition and Rothenstein, before he continued reading.

I shall be returning to London in Auguste, well in time to see the last Test at Millbank, so let us hope by then we've won the series of nine. And, by the way, that particular pitch will need a two-ton roller.

This time Sir Alan had underlined Auguste, Millbank, nine and two-ton. He was beginning to wish he'd taken a greater interest in cricket when he was at Shrewsbury, but then he'd been a wet bob, not a dry bob. However, as Sir Giles, who was sitting at the end of the table, had been awarded an Oxford cricket blue, he was confident that the intricacies of leather upon willow were about to be explained to him.

Sir Alan was pleased to see that everyone appeared to have finished reading the communiqué, although Mrs Clifton was still making notes.

'I think I've worked out most of what our man in Buenos Aires is trying to tell us, but there are still one or two niceties that are eluding me. For example, I'll need some help on Arthur Barrington, because even I know the great Test batsman is called Ken.'

'Sebastian's middle name is Arthur,' said Harry. 'So I think we can assume that he will be arriving in Southampton on Sunday June the twenty-third, because Test matches are never played on a Sunday, and there isn't a Test ground at Southampton.'

The cabinet secretary nodded.

'And eight must be how many million pounds the ambassador thinks is involved,' suggested Giles from the far end of the table, 'because Ken Barrington's Test average is over fifty.'

'Very good,' said Sir Alan, making a note. 'But I'm unable to explain why Matthews misspelt addition as edition, and August as Auguste.'

'And Tate,' said Giles. 'Because Maurice Tate used to bat for England at number nine, certainly not number five.'

'That also had me stumped,' said Sir Alan, amused by his own little play on words. 'But can anyone explain the two misspellings?'

'I think I can,' said Emma. 'My daughter Jessica is an artist, and I remember her telling me that many sculptors cast nine editions of their work, which are then stamped and numbered. And the spelling of Auguste hints at the identity of the artist.'

'I'm still none the wiser,' said Sir Alan, and from the expressions around the table, it was clear that he was not alone.

'It has to be Renoir or Rodin,' said Emma. 'And as it wouldn't be possible to conceal eight million pounds in an oil painting, I suspect you'll find it's been hidden in a two-ton sculpture by Auguste Rodin.'

'And is he hinting that Sir John Rothenstein, the director of the Tate Gallery on Millbank, will be able to tell me which sculpture?'

'He's already told us,' said Emma triumphantly. 'It's one of the words you failed to underline, Sir Alan.' Emma was unable to resist a smirk. 'My late mother would have spotted it long before I did, even on her death bed.'

Both Harry and Giles smiled.

'And what word did I fail to underline, Mrs Clifton?'

No sooner had Emma answered the question, than the cabinet secretary picked up the phone by his side and said, 'Call John Rothenstein at the Tate, and make an appointment for me to see him this evening after the gallery has closed.'

Sir Alan put the phone down and smiled at Emma. 'I've always been an advocate of employing more women in the Civil Service.'

'I do hope, Sir Alan, that you'll underline *more* and *women*,' said Emma.

◄○►

Sebastian stood on the upper deck of the *Queen Mary* and leaned over the railings as Buenos Aires receded in the distance until it looked like no more than a traced outline on an architect's drawing board.

So much had happened in the short time since he'd been rusticated from Beechcroft, although he was still puzzled why his father had travelled all that way just to let him know he hadn't lost his place at Cambridge. Wouldn't it have been a lot easier just to phone the ambassador, who clearly knew Don Pedro? And why had the ambassador personally given him his passport, when Becky could have handed it to him at the reception desk? And even stranger, why had the ambassador wanted to know his middle name? He still didn't have any answers to these questions by the time Buenos Aires had disappeared from sight. Perhaps his father would supply them.

He turned his thoughts to the future. His first responsibility, for which he had already been handsomely recompensed, was to ensure that Don Pedro's sculpture passed smoothly through customs, and he didn't intend to leave the dockside until Sotheby's had picked it up.

But until then, he decided to relax and enjoy the voyage. He intended to read the last few pages of *Officers and Gentlemen*, and hoped he might find the first volume in the ship's library.

Now that he was on the way home, he felt he should give some thought to what he could achieve in his first year at Cambridge that would impress his mother. That was the least he could do after all the trouble he'd caused.

◄○►

'*The Thinker*,' said Sir John Rothenstein, the director of the Tate Gallery, 'is considered by most critics to be one of Rodin's most iconic works. It was originally designed to be part of *The*

Gates of Hell, and was at first entitled *The Poet*, as the artist wished to pay homage to his hero, Dante. And such became the artist's association with the piece that the maestro is buried under a cast of this bronze at Meudon.'

Sir Alan continued to circle the great statue. 'Correct me if I'm wrong, Sir John, but is this the fifth of the nine editions that were originally cast?'

'That is correct, Sir Alan. The most sought after works by Rodin are those that were cast in his lifetime by Alexis Rudier at his foundry in Paris. Since Rodin's death, unfortunately in my opinion, the French government has allowed limited editions to be reproduced by another foundry, but these are not considered by serious collectors to have the same authenticity as the lifetime casts.'

'Is it known where all the nine original casts are now?'

'Oh yes,' said the director. 'Apart from this one, there are three in Paris – at the Louvre, the Musée Rodin, and the one at Meudon. There is also one at the Metropolitan Museum in New York, and another in the Hermitage in Leningrad, leaving three in hands of private collectors.'

'Is it known who owns those three?'

'One is in Baron de Rothschild's collection, and another is owned by Paul Mellon. The whereabouts of the third has long been shrouded in mystery. All we know for certain is that it's a lifetime cast and was sold to a private collector by the Marlborough Gallery some ten years ago. However, that shroud might finally be lifted next week.'

'I'm not sure I'm following you, Sir John.'

'A 1902 cast of *The Thinker* is coming under the hammer at Sotheby's on Monday evening.'

'And who owns that one?' asked Sir Alan innocently.

'I've no idea,' admitted Rothenstein. 'In the Sotheby's catalogue, it's simply listed as the property of a gentleman.'

The cabinet secretary smiled at the thought, but satisfied himself with, 'And what does that mean?'

'That the seller wishes to remain anonymous. It often turns out to be an aristocrat who doesn't want to admit that he's fallen on hard times and is having to part with one of the family's heirlooms.'

'How much would you expect the piece to fetch?'

'It's difficult to estimate, because a Rodin of this importance hasn't come on the market for several years. But I would be surprised if it went for less than a hundred thousand pounds.'

'Would a layman be able to tell the difference between this one,' Sir Alan said, admiring the bronze in front of him, 'and the one that's coming up for sale at Sotheby's?'

'There is no difference,' said the director, 'other than the cast number. Otherwise they are identical in every way.'

The cabinet secretary circled *The Thinker* several more times before he tapped the massive mound the man was sitting on. He was now in no doubt where Martinez had secreted the eight million pounds. He took a pace back and looked more closely at the bronze cast's wooden base. 'Would all nine casts have been fixed on the same kind of base?'

'Not exactly the same, but similar, I suspect. Every gallery or collector will have their own opinion on how it should be displayed. We chose a simple oak base that we felt would be harmonious with its surroundings.'

'And how is the base attached to the statue?'

'For a bronze of this size, there would usually be four small steel lips moulded on to the inside of the bottom of the statue. Each will have had a hole drilled in it, through which a bolt and a bevelled rod can be lowered. Then all you have to do is drill four holes through the base, and attach it to the bottom of the statue with what are called butterfly screws. Any decent carpenter could do the job.'

'So if you wanted to remove the base, all you would have to do is unscrew the butterfly bolts and it would become detached from the statue?'

'Yes, I suppose so,' said Sir John. 'But why would anyone want to do that?'

'Why indeed,' said the cabinet secretary, allowing himself the suggestion of a smile. He now knew not only where Martinez had hidden the money, but how he intended to smuggle it into Britain. And, far more important, how he planned to be reunited with his £8 million in counterfeit five-pound notes without anyone becoming aware of what he was up to.

'Clever man,' he said as he gave the hollow bronze one final tap.

'A genius,' said the director.

'Well, I wouldn't go that far,' said Sir Alan. But to be fair, they were talking about two different people.

41

THE DRIVER OF the white Bedford van drew up outside Green Park tube station on Piccadilly. He left his engine running and flashed his headlights twice.

Three men, who were never late, emerged from the underground carrying the tools of their trade and walked quickly to the back of the van, which they knew would be unlocked. Between them, they placed a small brazier, a petrol can, a bag of tools, a ladder, a thick coil of rope and a box of Swan Vesta matches in the back before joining their commanding officer.

If anyone had given them a second look, and no one did at six o'clock on a Sunday morning, they would have assumed that they were just tradesmen and, indeed, that is what they had been before they joined the SAS. Corporal Crann had been a carpenter, Sergeant Roberts a foundry worker and Captain Hartley a structural engineer.

'Good morning, gentlemen,' Colonel Scott-Hopkins said as the three of them climbed into the van.

'Good morning, colonel,' they replied in unison as their commanding officer pushed the gear lever into first, and the Bedford van set out on the journey to Southampton.

◄o►

Sebastian had already been on deck for a couple of hours before the *Queen Mary* lowered its passenger ramp. He was among the first to disembark, and quickly made his way across to the customs office. He presented the cargo manifest to a young officer, who inspected it briefly before giving Sebastian a closer look.

'Please wait there,' he said, and disappeared into a back office. A few moments later, an older man appeared, with three silver stripes on the cuffs of his uniform. He asked to see Sebastian's passport, and once he'd checked the photograph, he immediately signed the clearance order.

'My colleague will accompany you, Mr Clifton, to where the crate will be unloaded.'

Sebastian and the young officer walked out of the customs shed to see a crane lowering its hoist into the *Queen Mary*'s hold. Twenty minutes later, the first piece to appear was a massive wooden crate Sebastian had never seen before. It was lowered slowly on to the dockside, coming to rest at loading bay six.

A group of dockers removed the hoist and chains from around the crate, so the crane could swing back and gather up its next piece of cargo, while the crate was transferred by a waiting forklift truck into shed No. 40. The whole process had taken forty-three minutes. The young officer asked Sebastian to return to the office, as there was some paperwork to be completed.

◄o►

The police car turned on its siren, overtook the Sotheby's van on the road from London to Southampton and indicated to the driver that he should pull into the nearest layby.

Once the van had come to a halt, two officers stepped out of the police car. The first approached the front of the van, while his colleague made his way to the rear. The second officer took a Swiss army knife from his pocket, opened it and thrust the blade firmly into the back left-hand tyre. Once he heard a hissing sound, he returned to the police car.

The van driver wound down his window and gave the officer a quizzical look. 'I don't think I was breaking the speed limit, officer.'

'No you were not, sir. But I thought you should know you have a puncture in your left-hand rear tyre.'

The driver got out, walked to the back of the van and stared in disbelief at the flat tyre.

'You know officer, I never felt a thing.'

'It's always the same with slow punctures,' said the officer, as a white Bedford van drove past them. He saluted, said, 'Happy to have been of assistance, sir,' then joined his colleague in the patrol car and drove off.

If the Sotheby's driver had asked to see the policeman's warrant card, he would have discovered that he was attached to the Metropolitan Police in Rochester Row, and was therefore miles outside his jurisdiction. But then, as Sir Alan had discovered, not many officers who'd served under him in the SAS were currently working for the Hampshire police force, and were also available at short notice on a Sunday morning.

—◦—

Don Pedro and Diego were driven to Ministro Pistarini international airport. Their six large suitcases went through customs without being checked, and they later boarded a BOAC aircraft bound for London.

'I always prefer to travel on a British carrier,' Don Pedro told the purser as they were shown to their seats in first class.

The Boeing Stratocruiser took off at 5.43 p.m., just a few minutes behind schedule.

—◦—

The driver of the white Bedford van swung on to the dockside and headed straight for shed No. 40 at the far end of the docks. No one in the van was at all surprised that Colonel Scott-Hopkins knew exactly where he was going. After all, he'd carried out a recce forty-eight hours before. The colonel was a details man; never left anything to chance.

When the van came to a halt, he handed a key to Captain Hartley. His second-in-command got out and unlocked the shed's double doors. The colonel drove the van into the vast building. In front of them, in the middle of the floor, stood a massive wooden crate.

While the engineer locked the door, the other three went to the back of the van and removed their equipment.

The carpenter placed the ladder up against the crate, climbed up and began to remove the nails that kept the lid in place with a claw hammer. While he went about his work, the colonel walked to the far end of the shed and climbed into the cab of a small crane that had been left there overnight, then drove it across to the crate.

The engineer removed the heavy coil of rope from the back of the van, then made a noose at one end before throwing it over his shoulder. He stood back and waited to perform the hangman's duties. It took the carpenter eight minutes to remove all the nails from the thick lid on the top of the packing case, and when he'd completed the task he climbed back down the ladder and placed the lid on the floor. The engineer took his place on the ladder, the coil of rope still hanging over his left shoulder. When he reached the top step, he bent down, lowered himself into the box and passed the thick rope securely under each arm of *The Thinker*. He would have preferred to use a chain, but the colonel had stressed that the sculpture was in no circumstances to be damaged.

Once the engineer was certain that the rope was secure, he tied a double reef knot and held the noose up to indicate that he was ready. The colonel lowered the crane's steel chain until the hook on its end was inches from the top of the open crate. The engineer grabbed the hook, placed the noose over it and gave a thumbs-up.

The colonel took up the slack before he began to raise the statue inch by inch out of the crate. First, the inclined head appeared, its chin resting on the back of a hand, followed by the torso and then the muscular legs, and finally the large bronze mound on which *The Thinker* sat, contemplating. The last thing to appear was the wooden base to which the bronze statue was fixed. Once it had cleared the top of the crate, the colonel slowly lowered it until it was suspended a couple of feet above the ground.

The foundry worker lay on his back, slid under the statue

and studied the four butterfly screws. He then took a pair of pliers from his tool bag.

'Hold the damn thing still,' he said.

The engineer grabbed *The Thinker*'s knees and the carpenter held on to his backside in an attempt to keep the statue steady. The foundry worker had to strain every sinew in his body before he felt the first screw that held the wooden base in place give just half an inch, and then another half, until it came finally loose. He repeated the exercise three more times, and then suddenly, without warning, the wooden base fell on top of him.

But that wasn't what grabbed the attention of his three colleagues, because a split second later, millions of pounds in pristine five-pound notes came pouring out of the statue and buried him.

'Does that mean I can collect my war pension at last?' asked the carpenter as he stared in disbelief at the mountain of cash.

The colonel allowed himself a wry smile as the foundry worker emerged, grumbling, from under the mountain of money.

'Afraid not, Crann. My orders couldn't have been clearer,' he said as he climbed out of the crane. 'Every last one of those notes is to be destroyed.' If an SAS officer had ever been tempted to disobey an order, surely it was then.

The engineer unscrewed the cap on the petrol can and reluctantly splattered a few drops over the coals in the brazier. He struck a match, and stood back as the flames danced into the air. The colonel took the lead and threw the first £50,000 on to the brazier. Moments later, the other three reluctantly joined him, hurling thousands upon thousands into the insatiable flames.

Once the last bank note had been burnt to a cinder, the four men remained silent for some time as they stared at the pile of ashes and tried not to think about what they had just done.

The carpenter broke the silence. 'That's brought a totally new meaning to the phrase "money to burn".'

They all laughed except the colonel, who said sharply, 'Let's get on with it.'

The foundry worker lay back down on the floor and slid under the statue. Like a weightlifter, he picked up the wooden base and held it in the air, while the engineer and the carpenter guided the little steel rods back through the four holes in the bottom of the statue.

'Hold firm!' shouted the foundry worker, as the engineer and carpenter clung on to the sides of the base while he replaced the four butterfly screws, first with his fingers, then with the pliers, until they were all firmly back in place. Once he was satisfied they couldn't be any tighter, he slid out from under the statue and gave the colonel another thumbs-up.

The colonel pushed the up lever in his cab and slowly raised *The Thinker* high into the air, until it hovered a few inches above the open packing case. The engineer climbed the ladder as the colonel began gently lowering the statue, while Captain Hartley guided it safely back into the crate. Once the rope had been removed from under *The Thinker*'s arms, the carpenter replaced the engineer on the top step and nailed the heavy lid back in place.

'Right, gentlemen, let's start clearing up while the corporal is going about his work, then we won't waste time later.'

The three of them set about dousing the fire, sweeping the floor and returning everything that had already served its purpose to the back of the van.

The ladder, the hammer and three spare nails were the last things to end up in the back of the van. The colonel drove the crane back to the exact position in which he'd found it, while the carpenter and the foundry worker climbed into the van. The engineer unlocked the door of the shed and stood aside to allow the colonel to drive out. He kept the engine running while his second-in-command locked the door and then joined him in the front.

The colonel drove slowly along the dock until he reached the customs shed. He stepped out of the van, walked into the office and handed over the shed key to the officer with three silver stripes on his arm.

'Thank you, Gareth,' said the colonel. 'I know Sir Alan will be most grateful, and will no doubt thank you personally when we all meet up at our annual dinner in October.' The customs officer saluted as Colonel Scott-Hopkins walked out of his office, climbed back behind the wheel of the white Bedford van, switched on the ignition and set off on the journey back to London.

◄o►

The Sotheby's van with its newly fitted tyre arrived at the dockside about forty minutes later than scheduled.

When the driver brought the van to a halt outside shed No. 40, he was surprised to see a dozen customs officials surrounding the package he had come to pick up.

He turned to his mate and said, 'Something's up, Bert.'

As they stepped out of the van, a forklift truck picked up the massive crate and, with the assistance of several customs officials, far too many in Bert's opinion, manoeuvred it into the back of the van. A handover that would normally take a couple of hours was completed in twenty minutes, including the paperwork.

'What can possibly be in that crate?' said Bert as they drove away.

'Search me,' said the driver. 'But don't complain, because now we'll be back in time to hear *Henry Hall's Guest Night* on the Home Service.'

Sebastian was also surprised by the speed and efficiency with which the whole operation had been carried out. He could only assume that either the statue must be extremely valuable, or that Don Pedro wielded as much influence in Southampton as he did in Buenos Aires.

After Sebastian had thanked the officer with the three silver stripes, he made his way back to the terminal, where he joined the few remaining passengers waiting at passport control. A first stamp in his first passport made him smile, but that smile turned to tears when he walked into the arrivals hall to be greeted by his parents. He told them how desperately sorry he was, and within moments it was as if he'd never been away. No recriminations and no lectures, which only made him feel more guilty.

On the journey back to Bristol, he had so much to tell them: Tibby, Janice, Bruno, Mr Martinez, Princess Margaret, the ambassador and the customs officer all made their entrances and exits, although he decided not to mention Gabriella – he'd save her for Bruno.

As they drove through the gates of the Manor House, the first thing Sebastian saw was Jessica running towards them.

'I never thought I'd miss you,' he said as he stepped out of the car and threw his arms around her.

◄○►

The Sotheby's van turned into Bond Street just after seven. The driver was not surprised to see half a dozen porters hanging around on the pavement. Although they were all on overtime, they would still be keen to get home.

Mr Dickens, the head of the Impressionist Department, supervised transferring the crate from the roadside to the storeroom in the auction house. He waited patiently for the wooden slats to be stripped and the shavings swept away, so he could check that the number in the catalogue matched the number on the sculpture. He bent down to see '6' etched into the bronze below the signature of Auguste Rodin. He smiled, and placed a tick on the manifest.

'Many thanks, chaps,' he said. 'You can all go home now. I'll deal with the paperwork in the morning.'

As Mr Dickens was the last to leave the building that night, he locked up before walking off in the direction of Green Park station. He didn't notice a man standing in the entrance of an antique shop on the opposite side of the street.

Once Mr Dickens was out of sight, the man emerged from the shadows and walked to the nearest telephone box on Curzon Street. He had four pennies ready, but then he never left anything to chance. He dialled a number he knew by heart. When he heard a voice on the other end of the line, he pressed button A, and said, 'An empty thinker is spending the night in Bond Street, sir.'

'Thank you, colonel,' said Sir Alan, 'and there's another matter I need you to handle. I'll be in touch.' The line went dead.

‐◄o►‐

After BOAC flight number 714 from Buenos Aires touched down at London Airport the following morning, Don Pedro wasn't at all surprised that every one of his and Diego's suitcases was opened, checked and double checked by several over-zealous customs officials. When they had finally placed a chalk cross on the side of the last case, Martinez sensed a little frisson of disappointment among the customs officers, as he and his son walked out of the airport.

Once they were seated in the back of the Rolls-Royce and on their way to Eaton Square, Don Pedro turned to Diego and said, 'All you have to remember about the British is that they lack imagination.'

42

ALTHOUGH THE FIRST lot would not come under the hammer until seven that evening, the auction house was packed long before the appointed hour, as it always was on the opening night of a major Impressionist sale.

The three hundred seats were filled with gentlemen wearing dinner jackets, while many of the ladies were adorned in long gowns. They might have been attending an opening night at the opera, and indeed this promised to be as dramatic as anything on offer at Covent Garden. And although there was a script, it was always the audience who had the best lines.

The invited guests fell into several different categories. The serious bidders, who often turned up late because they had reserved seats, and might not be interested in the first few lots, which, like minor characters in a Shakespeare play, are simply there to warm up the audience. The dealers and the gallery owners, who preferred to stand at the back with their colleagues and share among themselves any scraps that fell from the rich man's table, when a lot failed to reach its reserve price and had to be withdrawn. And then there were those who treated it as a social occasion. They had no interest in bidding, but enjoyed the spectacle of the super-rich taking up arms against each other.

And last, the more deadly of the species, with sub-categories of their own. The wives, who came to watch how much their husbands would spend on objects that they had no interest in, preferring to spend their money in other establishments in the same street. Then there were the girlfriends, who remained silent, because they were hoping to become wives. And finally, the simply beautiful, who had no other purpose in life than to remove the wives and girlfriends from the battlefield.

But, as with everything in life, there were exceptions to the rule. One such was Sir Alan Redmayne, who would be there to represent his country. He would be bidding for lot 29, but hadn't yet decided how high he would go.

Sir Alan was not unfamiliar with the West End auction houses and their strange traditions. Over the years he had built up a small collection of eighteenth-century English water-colours, and he had also, on occasion, bid on behalf of the government, for a painting or sculpture his masters felt should not be allowed to leave the country. However, this was the first time in his career that he would be bidding for a major work in the hope of being outbid by someone from overseas.

The Times had predicted that morning that Rodin's *The Thinker* could sell for £100,000 – a record for any piece by the French master. However, what *The Times* couldn't know was that Sir Alan intended to take the bidding above £100,000, because not until then could he be certain that the only bidder left on the floor would be Don Pedro Martinez, who believed the statue's true value to be over eight million pounds.

Giles had asked the cabinet secretary the one question he'd been trying to avoid answering: 'If you were to end up outbidding Martinez, what would you do with the sculpture?'

'It will be given a home in the National Gallery of Scotland,' he had replied, 'as part of the government's arts acquisition policy. You will be able to write about it in your memoirs, but not until after I'm dead.'

'And if you should prove to be right?'

'Then it will warrant a whole chapter in *my* memoirs.'

When Sir Alan entered the auction house, he slipped into a seat in the back left-hand corner of the sale room. He had phoned Mr Wilson earlier to let him know he would be bidding on lot 29, and sitting in his usual place.

By the time Mr Wilson climbed the five steps to the

rostrum, most of the major players had taken their seats. Standing on both sides of the auctioneer was a row of Sotheby's employees. Most of them would be bidding for clients who were unable to attend in person, or who couldn't trust them-selves not to be carried away by the occasion and end up bidding far more than they had intended. On the left-hand side of the room stood a long table on a raised platform. Seated behind it were some of the auction house's most experienced senior staff. On the table in front of them was a row of white telephones that would only be whispered into when the lot their client was interested in came up for sale.

From his seat at the back of the room, Sir Alan could see that almost every place was taken. However, there were still three empty chairs in the third row that must have been reserved for a major client. He wondered who would be seated on either side of Don Pedro Martinez. He flicked through the pages of his catalogue until he came to Rodin's *The Thinker*, lot 29. There would be more than enough time for Martinez to make an entrance.

At 7 p.m. precisely, Mr Wilson gazed down at his clients and, like the Pope, smiled benignly. He tapped the microphone and said, 'Good evening, ladies and gentlemen, and welcome to Sotheby's Impressionist sale. Lot number one,' he announced, glancing to his left to make sure the porter had placed the correct picture on the easel, 'is a delightful Degas pastel, show-ing two ballerinas in rehearsal at the Trocadero. I'll open the bidding at five thousand pounds. Six thousand. Seven thousand. Eight thousand . . .'

Sir Alan watched with interest as almost all of the early lots exceeded their estimates, proving, as *The Times* had suggested that morning, that there was a new breed of collectors who had made their fortunes since the war, and wished to show they had arrived by investing in art.

It was during the twelfth lot that Don Pedro Martinez entered the room, accompanied by two young men. Sir Alan recognized Martinez's youngest son, Bruno, and assumed the other must be Sebastian Clifton. The presence of Sebastian convinced him that Martinez must be confident that the money was still inside the statue.

The dealers and gallery owners began to discuss among themselves if Martinez was likely to be more interested in lot 28, *A Corner of the Garden at St Paul's Hospital at St Rémy* by Van Gogh, or lot 29, Rodin's *The Thinker*.

Sir Alan had always considered himself to be a calm and collected man under pressure, but at that moment he felt his heart rate rising beat by beat as each new lot was placed on the easel. When the bidding opened at £80,000 for *A Corner of the Garden at St Paul's Hospital at St Rémy*, and the hammer finally came down at £140,000, a record for a Van Gogh, he took out his handkerchief and dabbed his forehead.

He turned the page of his catalogue to look at the masterpiece he admired, but for which, ironically, he still hoped to end up as the under-bidder.

'Lot number twenty-nine, Auguste Rodin's *The Thinker*,' said Mr Wilson. 'If you look in your catalogue you will see that this is a lifetime cast by Alexis Rudier. The work is on display at the entrance to the sale room,' the auctioneer added. Several heads turned to admire the massive bronze sculpture. 'Considerable interest has been shown in this piece, so I shall open the bidding at forty thousand pounds. Thank you, sir,' said the auctioneer, pointing to a gentleman sitting directly in front of him on the centre aisle. Several more heads turned, this time in the hope of identifying who the bidder might be.

Sir Alan responded with a slight, almost imperceptible nod.

'Fifty thousand,' declared the auctioneer, his attention returning to the man seated on the aisle, who raised his hand again. 'I have sixty thousand.' With no more than a glance in Sir Alan's direction, Mr Wilson received the same slight nod, turned back to the man on the centre aisle and suggested £80,000, but was greeted with a frown of disappointment, followed by a firm shake of the head.

'I have seventy thousand pounds,' he said, looking back at Sir Alan, who felt a creeping doubt entering his mind. But then Mr Wilson looked to his left and said, 'Eighty thousand. I have a bid on the telephone at eighty thousand.' He immediately switched his attention back to Sir Alan. 'Ninety thousand?' he purred.

Sir Alan nodded.

Wilson looked back towards the phone, where a hand was raised a few seconds later. 'One hundred thousand. One hundred and ten thousand?' he asked, looking once again at Sir Alan and giving him his best Cheshire cat smile.

Could he risk it? For the first time in his life, the cabinet secretary took a gamble. He nodded.

'I have one hundred and ten thousand pounds,' said Wilson, looking directly at the Sotheby's employee who was holding the phone to his ear and awaiting his instructions.

Martinez turned around to see if he could identify who was bidding against him.

The whispered phone conversation continued for some time. Sir Alan became more nervous with each passing second. He tried not to consider the possibility that Martinez had double-crossed him and had somehow managed to smuggle £8 million into the country while the SAS had set fire to counterfeits of counterfeits. What felt like an hour to him turned out to be less than twenty seconds. And then without warning, the man on the phone raised his hand.

'I have a bid of one hundred and twenty thousand on the phone,' said Wilson, trying not to sound triumphant. He switched his attention back to Sir Alan, who didn't move a muscle. 'I have a bid of one hundred and twenty thousand on the telephone,' he repeated. 'I am letting the piece go at a hundred and twenty thousand, this is your last chance,' he said, looking directly at Sir Alan, but the cabinet secretary had reverted to his more natural role of mandarin, displaying no expression.

'Sold, for one hundred and twenty thousand pounds,' said Wilson, bringing the hammer down with a thud as he transferred his smile to the bidder on the telephone.

Sir Alan breathed a sigh of relief, and was particularly pleased to see the self-satisfied grin on Martinez's face that convinced him that the Argentinian believed he'd repurchased his own statue, containing £8 million pounds, for a mere £120,000. And tomorrow, no doubt, he intended to exchange old lamps for new.

A couple of lots later, Martinez rose from his place in the third row and barged along the line of people without the slightest concern that they might still be following the auction. Once he'd reached the aisle, he marched back down, a look of satisfaction on his face, and disappeared out of the room. The two young men who followed in his wake had the grace to look embarrassed.

Sir Alan waited for half a dozen more lots to find new owners before he slipped out. When he stepped on to Bond Street, it was such a pleasant evening that he decided to walk to his club in Pall Mall and treat himself to half a dozen oysters and a glass of champagne. He would have given a month's salary to see Martinez's face when he discovered that his victory had turned out to be hollow.

43

THE FOLLOWING MORNING, the anonymous telephone bidder made three phone calls before he left 44 Eaton Square a few minutes after ten o'clock. He hailed a taxi and asked the driver to take him to 19 St James's Street. When they drew up outside the Midland Bank, he instructed the cabbie to wait.

He wasn't surprised that the bank manager was available to see him. After all, he couldn't have too many customers who had never seen red. The manager invited him into his office, and once the customer was seated he asked, 'Who would you like the banker's draft made out to?'

'Sotheby's.'

The manager wrote out the draft, signed it, placed it in an envelope, then passed it to young Mr Martinez, as the banker thought of him. Diego placed the envelope in an inside pocket and left without another word.

'Sotheby's,' was again the only word he uttered as he pulled the taxi door closed and sank into the back seat.

When the taxi came to a halt outside the Bond Street entrance of the auction house, Diego once again instructed the driver to wait. He got out of the cab, pushed his way through the front door and headed straight for the settlement desk.

'How can I help you, sir?' asked the young man standing behind the counter.

'I purchased lot number twenty-nine in last night's sale,' said Diego, 'and I'd like to settle my bill.' The young man leafed through the catalogue.

'Ah yes, Rodin's *The Thinker*.' Diego wondered how many items got the 'Ah yes' treatment. 'That will be one hundred and twenty thousand pounds, sir.'

'Of course,' said Diego. He took the envelope out of his pocket, extracted the banker's draft – an instrument that ensured the buyer could never be traced – and placed it on the counter.

'Shall we deliver the piece, sir, or would you prefer to pick it up?'

'I will collect it in one hour's time.'

'I'm not sure that will be possible,' said the young man. 'You see, sir, the day after a major sale we're always run off our feet.'

Diego took out his wallet and placed a five-pound note on the counter, probably more than the young man earned in a week.

'Make those feet run in my direction,' he said. 'And if the package is waiting for me when I return in an hour, there'll be two more where this one came from.'

The young man slipped the note into a back pocket to confirm the deal had been closed.

Diego returned to the waiting taxi and this time gave the driver an address in Victoria. When he pulled up outside the building, Diego got out of the cab and parted with another of his father's five-pound notes. He waited for the change, and placed two real pound notes in his wallet and gave the cabbie sixpence. He walked into the building and went straight up to the only available sales assistant.

'May I help you?' asked a young woman dressed in a brown and yellow uniform.

'My name is Martinez,' he said. 'I called earlier this morning and booked a large heavy-duty truck.'

Once Diego had filled in the obligatory form he parted with another five-pound note, and placed three more legal notes in his wallet.

'Thank you, sir. You'll find the truck in the back yard. It's parked in bay number seventy-one.' She handed him a key.

Diego strolled into the yard and, after identifying the truck, he unlocked the back door and checked inside. It was perfect for the job. He climbed behind the wheel, switched on the ignition and set off on the return journey to Sotheby's. Twenty minutes later, he parked outside the rear entrance on George Street.

As he climbed out of the van, the rear door of the auction house swung open and a large packing case with several red *SOLD* stickers plastered all over it was wheeled out on to the pavement, accompanied by six men in long green coats who, from their solid build, looked as if they might have been professional pugilists before they came to work for Sotheby's.

Diego opened the back door of the truck, and twelve hands lifted the crate off the trolley as if it contained a feather duster and slid it into the back of the vehicle. Diego locked the door and handed the young man from the settlement desk two more five-pound notes.

Once he was back behind the wheel, he checked his watch: 11.41. No reason he shouldn't make it to Shillingford in a couple of hours, although he knew his father would be pacing up and down the driveway long before then.

◄o►

When Sebastian spotted the light blue crest of Cambridge University among the morning mail, he grabbed the envelope and opened it immediately. The first thing he always did with any letter was to check the signature at the bottom of the page. Dr Brian Padgett, a name he was unfamiliar with.

> *Dear Mr Clifton,*

That was still taking him a little time to get used to.

> *Many congratulations on being awarded the College's Modern Languages scholarship. As I am sure you know, Michaelmas Term begins on September 16th, but I am hoping we can meet before then in order to discuss one or two matters, including your reading list before term begins.*

I would also like to guide you through the syllabus for your freshman year.

Perhaps you could drop me a line or, better still, give me a ring.

Yours sincerely,

Dr Brian Padgett

Senior Tutor

After he'd read it a second time, he decided to phone Bruno and find out if he'd received a similar letter, in which case they could travel up to Cambridge together.

—◦—

Diego wasn't at all surprised to see his father come running out of the front door the moment he drove through the entrance gates. But what did surprise him was to see his brother Luis and every member of the Shillingford Hall staff following a few paces behind. Karl was bringing up the rear clutching a leather bag.

'Have you got the statue?' asked his father, even before Diego had stepped out of the truck.

'Yes,' replied Diego, who shook hands with his brother before walking around to the back of the truck. He unlocked the door to reveal the massive crate with over a dozen red *SOLD* stickers. Don Pedro smiled and patted the crate as if it was one of his pet dogs, then stepped aside to allow everyone else to do the heavy work.

Diego supervised the team, who began to push and pull the vast packing case out of the truck inch by inch until it was about to topple over. Karl and Luis quickly grabbed two of the corners while Diego and the chef clung on to the other end, and the chauffeur and the gardener held on firmly to the middle.

The six unlikely porters staggered around to the back of the house and dumped the crate in the middle of the lawn. The gardener didn't look pleased.

'Do you want it upright?' asked Diego, once they'd caught their breath.

'No,' said Don Pedro, 'leave it on its side, then it will be easier to remove the base.'

Karl took a claw hammer out of his tool bag and set about loosening the deeply embedded nails that held the wooden slats in place. At the same time, the chef, the gardener and the chauffeur began to rip off the wooden panels from the sides with their hands.

Once the last piece of wood had been removed, they all stood back and stared at *The Thinker* as he lay unceremoniously on his backside. Don Pedro's eyes never left the wooden base. He bent down and looked more closely, but couldn't detect anything that might suggest it had been tampered with. He glanced up at Karl and nodded.

His trusted bodyguard bent down and studied the four butterfly screws. He took a pair of pliers out of the tool bag and began to unscrew one of them. It moved grudgingly at first, then a little more easily, until finally it swivelled off its bevelled rod and fell on the grass. He repeated the exercise three more times until all four screws had been removed. He then paused, but only for a moment before he grabbed hold of both sides of the wooden base and, with all the strength he could muster, pulled it off the statue and dropped it on the grass. With a smile of satisfaction, he stood aside to allow his master the pleasure of being the first to look inside.

Martinez fell to his knees and stared into the gaping hole, while Diego and the rest of the team awaited his next command. There was a long silence before Don Pedro suddenly let out a piercing scream that would have woken those resting peacefully in the nearby parish graveyard. The six men, displaying different degrees of fear, stared down at him, not sure what had caused the outburst, until he shouted at the top of his voice, 'Where's my money?'

Diego had never seen his father so angry. He quickly knelt down by his side, thrust his hands into the statue and flailed about in search of the missing millions, but all he managed to retrieve was a rogue five-pound note that had got stuck to the inside of the bronze.

'Where the hell's the money?' said Diego.

'Someone must have stolen it,' said Luis.

'That's stating the fucking obvious!' bellowed Don Pedro.

No one else considered offering an opinion while he continued to stare into the hollow base, still unwilling to accept that all he had to show after a year of preparing for this moment was a single counterfeit five-pound note. Several minutes passed before he rose unsteadily to his feet, and when he finally spoke he appeared remarkably calm.

'I don't know who is responsible for this,' he said, pointing at the statue, 'but if it's the last thing I do, I will track them down, and leave my calling card.'

Without another word, Don Pedro turned his back on the statue and marched towards the house. Only Diego, Luis and Karl dared to follow him. He walked through the front door, across the hall, into the drawing room, and stopped in front of a full-length portrait of Tissot's mistress. He lifted Mrs Kathleen Newton off the wall and propped her up against the windowsill. He then began to swivel a dial several times, first to the left and then to the right, until he heard a click, when he heaved open the heavy door of the safe. Martinez stared for a moment at the piles of neatly stacked five-pound notes that members of his family and trusted staff had smuggled into England over the past ten years, before removing three large bundles of notes and handing one to Diego, another to Luis and the third to Karl. He looked fixedly at the three of them. 'No one rests until we've found out who was responsible for stealing my money. Each one of you must play your part, and you will only be rewarded by results.'

He turned to Karl. 'I want you to find out who informed Giles Barrington that his nephew was on the way to Southampton and not London airport.'

Karl nodded, as Martinez swung round to face Luis. 'You will go down to Bristol this evening and find out who Barrington's enemies are. Members of Parliament always have enemies, and don't forget that many of them will be on his own side. And while you're down there, try to pick up any information you can about the family's shipping company. Are they facing any financial difficulties? Do they have any trouble with the unions? Are there any policy disagreements among the board members? Are the shareholders voicing any misgivings? Dig deep, Luis. Remember, you may not come across any water until you've reached several feet below the surface.'

'Diego,' he said, switching his attention to his eldest son, 'go back to Sotheby's and find out who was the under-bidder for lot twenty-nine, because they must have known that my money was no longer in the statue, otherwise they couldn't have risked raising the stakes so high.'

Don Pedro paused for a moment before he began jabbing a forefinger at Diego's chest. 'But your most important task will be to build a team that will allow me to destroy whoever is responsible for this theft. Start by instructing the sharpest lawyers available, because they'll know who the bent coppers are as well as the criminals that never get caught, and they won't ask too many questions as long as the money is right. Once all these questions have been answered and everything is in place, I'll be ready to do to them what they've done to us.'

44

'A HUNDRED AND twenty thousand pounds,' said Harry. 'A phone bidder, but *The Times* doesn't seem to know who the buyer was.'

'Only one person could have paid that much for the piece,' said Emma. 'And by now, Mr Martinez will realize he didn't get what he bargained for.' Harry looked up from the newspaper to see his wife trembling. 'And if there's one thing we know about that man, he'll want to know who was responsible for stealing his money.'

'But he has no reason to believe Seb was involved. I was only in Buenos Aires for a few hours, and no one other than the ambassador even knew my name.'

'Except for Mr . . . what was his name?'

'Bolton. But he came back on the same plane as me.'

'If I was Martinez,' said Emma, her voice breaking, 'the first person I'd assume was involved is Seb.'

'But why, especially when he wasn't?'

'Because he was the last person to see the statue before it was handed over to Sotheby's.'

'That's not proof.'

'Believe me, it will be proof enough for Martinez. I think we have no choice but to warn Seb that—'

The door opened and Jessica burst into the room.

'Mama, you'll never guess where Seb's going tomorrow.'

◄○►

'Luis, brief me on what you found out when you were in Bristol.'

'I've spent most of my time turning over stones to see if anything would crawl out.'

'And did it?'

'Yes, I discovered that although Barrington is well respected and popular in his constituency, he's made several enemies along the way, including his ex-wife, and—'

'What's her problem?'

'Feels Barrington let her down badly over his mother's will, and she also objects to being replaced by a Welsh coalminer's daughter.'

'Then perhaps you should try to contact her?'

'I have already tried, but it's not that simple. The English upper classes always expect someone they know to make the introduction. But while I was in Bristol, I came across a man who claims he knows her well.'

'What's his name?'

'Major Alex Fisher.'

'And what's his connection with Barrington?'

'He was the Conservative candidate at the last election when Barrington defeated him by four votes. Fisher claims Barrington cheated him out of the seat, and I got the feeling he'd do almost anything to get even.'

'Then we must assist him in his cause,' said Don Pedro.

'I also discovered that since losing the election Fisher's been running up debts all over Bristol, and he's desperately searching for a lifeline.'

'Then I'll have to throw him one, won't I?' said Don Pedro. 'What can you tell me about Barrington's girlfriend?'

'Dr Gwyneth Hughes. She teaches maths at St Paul's girls' school in London. The local Labour Party has been expecting an announcement about their future together ever since his divorce went through, but, to quote a committee member who has met her, she couldn't be described as a "dolly bird".'

'Forget her,' said Don Pedro. 'She won't be any use to us unless she gets ditched. Concentrate on his ex-wife and, if the major can arrange a meeting, find out if she's interested in money or revenge. Almost every ex-wife wants one or the other and, in most cases, both.' He smiled at Luis before adding, 'Well done, my boy.' Turning to Diego, he asked, 'What have you got for me?'

'I haven't finished yet,' said Luis, sounding a little aggrieved. 'I also came across someone else who knows more about the Barrington family than they do themselves.'

'And who's that?'

'A private detective called Derek Mitchell. He's worked for both the Barringtons and the Cliftons in the past, but I have a feeling that, if the money was right, I could persuade him to—'

'Don't go anywhere near him,' said Don Pedro firmly. 'If he's willing to double-cross his former employers, what makes you think he wouldn't do the same to us when it suits him? But that doesn't mean you shouldn't keep a close eye on the man.'

Luis nodded, although he looked disappointed.

'Diego?'

'A BOAC pilot called Peter May stayed at the Hotel Milonga for two nights at exactly the same time Sebastian Clifton was in Buenos Aires.'

'So what?'

'The same man was seen coming out of the back door of the British Embassy on the day of the garden party.'

'That could just be a coincidence.'

'And the concierge at the Milonga overheard someone who seemed to know the man address him as Harry Clifton, which just happens to be the name of Sebastian's father.'

'Less of a coincidence.'

'And once his cover had been blown, the man took the next plane back to London.'

'No longer a coincidence.'

'What's more, Mr Clifton left without paying his hotel bill, which was later picked up by the British Embassy, proving not only that father and son were in Buenos Aires at the same time, but that they must have been working together.'

'Then why didn't they stay at the same hotel?' asked Luis.

'Because they didn't want to be seen together, would be my bet,' said Don Pedro. He paused before adding, 'Well done, Diego. And was this Harry Clifton also the under-bidder for my statue?'

'I don't think so. When I asked the chairman of Sotheby's who it was, he claimed he had no idea. And although I hinted, Mr Wilson is clearly not a man who can be tempted by a backhander, and I suspect if he was in any way threatened, his next call would be to Scotland Yard.' Don Pedro frowned. 'But I may have identified Wilson's one weakness,' continued Diego. 'When I hinted that you were considering putting *The Thinker* back up for sale, he let slip that the British government might be interested in buying it.'

Don Pedro exploded, and delivered a tirade of expletives that would have shocked a prison warden. It was some time before he calmed down again, and when he finally did, he said almost in a whisper, 'So now we know who stole my money. And by now, they'll have destroyed the notes or handed them over to the Bank of England. Either way,' he spat out, 'we'll never see a penny of that money again.'

'But even the British government couldn't have carried out such an operation without the cooperation of the Clifton and Barrington family,' suggested Diego, 'so our target hasn't moved.'

'Agreed. How's your team shaping up?' he asked, quickly changing the subject.

'I've put a small group together who don't like the idea of paying tax.' The other three laughed for the first time that morning. 'For the moment, I'm keeping them on a retainer, ready to move whenever you give the order.'

'Do they have any clue who they'll be working for?'

'No. They think I'm a foreigner with far too much money, and frankly they don't ask too many questions as long as they're paid on time and in cash.'

'Good enough.' Don Pedro turned to Karl. 'Have you been able to identify who told Barrington that his nephew was on the way to Southampton and not London?'

'I can't prove it,' said Karl, 'but I'm sorry to report the only name in the frame is Bruno's.'

'That boy has always been too honest for his own good. I blame his mother. We must make sure we never discuss what I have in mind while he's around.'

'But none of us are quite sure what it is you do have in mind,' said Diego.

Don Pedro smiled. 'Never forget that if you want to bring an empire to its knees you start by killing the first in line to the throne.'

45

THE FRONT DOORBELL rang at one minute to ten, and Karl answered it.

'Good morning, sir,' he said. 'How may I help you?'

'I have an appointment with Mr Martinez at ten o'clock.'

Karl gave a slight bow and stood aside to allow the visitor to enter. He then led him across the hall, tapped on the study door and said, 'Your guest has arrived, sir.'

Martinez rose from behind his desk and thrust out a hand. 'Good morning. I've been looking forward to meeting you.'

As Karl closed the study door and made his way to the kitchen, he passed Bruno, who was chatting on the phone.

'. . . my father's given me a couple of tickets for the men's semi-final at Wimbledon tomorrow, and he suggested I invite you.'

'That's very decent of him,' said Seb, 'but I've got an appointment to see my tutor in Cambridge on Friday, so I don't think I'll be able to make it.'

'Don't be so feeble,' said Bruno. 'There's nothing to stop you coming up to London tomorrow morning. The match doesn't start until two, so as long as you can get here by eleven, you'll have more than enough time.'

'But I still have to be in Cambridge by midday the following day.'

'Then you can stay here overnight, and Karl can drive you to Liverpool Street first thing Friday morning.'

'Who's playing?'

'Fraser versus Cooper, promises to be a sizzler. And if you're really good, I'll drive you to Wimbledon in my snazzy new car.'

'You've got a car?' said Sebastian in disbelief.

'An orange MGA, drophead coupé. Dad gave it to me for my eighteenth.'

'You jammy bastard,' said Sebastian. 'My pa gave me the complete works of Proust for mine.'

Bruno laughed. 'And if you behave yourself, on the way I might even tell you about my latest girlfriend.'

'Your latest?' mocked Sebastian. 'You've got to have had at least one before you can have a "latest".'

'Do I detect a twinge of envy?'

'I'll let you know after I've met her.'

'You're not going to get the chance, because I won't be seeing her again until Friday, and by then you'll be on the train to Cambridge. See you around eleven tomorrow.'

Bruno put the phone down and was on his way to his room when the study door opened and his father appeared, an arm around the shoulder of a military-looking gentleman. Bruno wouldn't have considered eavesdropping on his father's conversation, if he hadn't heard the name Barrington.

'We'll have you back on the board in no time,' his father was saying as he accompanied his guest to the front door.

'That's a moment I will savour.'

'However, I want you to know, major, that I'm not interested in the occasional raid on Barrington's simply to embarrass the family. My long-term plan is to take over the company and install you as chairman. How does that sound?'

'If it brings down Giles Barrington at the same time, nothing would please me more.'

'Not just Barrington,' said Martinez. 'It's my intention to destroy every member of that family, one by one.'

'Even better,' said the major.

'So the first thing you must do is start buying Barrington shares as and when they come on the market. The moment you have seven and a half per cent, I'll put you back on the board as my representative.'

'Thank you, sir.'

'Don't call me sir. I'm Pedro to my friends.'

'And I'm Alex.'

'Just remember, Alex, from now on you and I are partners and have only one purpose.'

'Couldn't be better, Pedro,' said the major as the two men shook hands. When he walked away, Don Pedro could have sworn he heard him whistling.

When Don Pedro stepped back into the house, he found Karl waiting for him in the hall.

'We need to have a word, sir.'

'Let's go to my office.'

Neither man spoke again until the door was closed. Karl then repeated the conversation he'd overheard between Bruno and his friend.

'I knew he'd find those Wimbledon tickets irresistible.' He picked up the phone on his desk. 'Get me Diego,' he barked. 'And now let's see if we can tempt the boy with something even more irresistible,' he said as he waited for his son to come on the line.

'What can I do for you, Father?'

'Young Clifton has risen to the bait and will be coming up to London tomorrow and going to Wimbledon. If Bruno can persuade him to take up my other offer, can you have everything in place by Friday?'

◄○►

Sebastian had to borrow his mother's alarm clock to make sure he was up in time to catch the 7.23 to Paddington. Emma was waiting for him in the hall and offered to drive him to Temple Meads.

'Are you expecting to see Mr Martinez when you're in London?'

'Almost certainly,' said Sebastian, 'as it was his suggestion I join Bruno at Wimbledon. Why do you ask?'

'No particular reason.'

Sebastian wanted to ask why Mama seemed to be so

concerned about Mr Martinez, but suspected that if he did he'd only get the same response. No particular reason.

'Will you have time to see Aunt Grace while you're in Cambridge?' his mother asked, rather too obviously changing the subject.

'She's invited me to tea at Newnham on Saturday afternoon.'

'Don't forget to give her my love,' Emma said as they drew up outside the station.

On the train, Sebastian sat in a corner of the carriage, trying to work out why his parents seemed to be so concerned about a man they'd never met. He decided to ask Bruno if he was aware of any problem. After all, Bruno had never sounded convinced about him going to Buenos Aires.

By the time the train pulled into Paddington, Sebastian was no nearer to solving the mystery. He handed in his ticket to the collector at the barrier, walked out of the station and across the road, not stopping until he reached No. 37. He knocked on the door.

'Oh my goodness,' said Mrs Tibbet when she saw who it was standing on the doorstep. She threw her arms around him. 'I never thought I'd see you again, Seb.'

'Does this establishment do breakfast for impecunious university freshmen?'

'If that means you're going to Cambridge after all, then I'll see what I can rustle up.' Sebastian followed her inside. 'And close the door behind you,' she added. 'Anybody would think you were born in a barn.'

Sebastian nipped back and shut the front door, before heading down the stairs to join Tibby in the kitchen. When Janice saw him, she said, 'Look what the cat dragged in,' and gave him a second hug followed by the best breakfast he'd had since he'd last sat in that kitchen.

'So what have you been up to since we last saw you?' asked Mrs Tibbet.

'I've been to Argentina and met Princess Margaret.'

'Where's Argentina?' asked Janice.

'It's a long way away,' said Mrs Tibbet.

'And I'll be going up to Cambridge in September,' he added between mouthfuls. 'Thanks to you, Tibby.'

'I hope you didn't mind me getting in touch with your uncle. And what made matters worse, he ended up having to come to me in Paddington.'

'Thank God you did,' said Sebastian. 'Otherwise I might still be in Argentina.'

'And what brings you to London this time?' asked Janice.

'Missed you both so much I had to come back,' said Seb. 'And where else would I get a decent breakfast?'

'Pull the other one, it's got bells on,' said Mrs Tibbet as she forked a third sausage on to his plate.

'Well, there was one other reason,' admitted Sebastian. 'Bruno's invited me to Wimbledon this afternoon for the men's semi-final, Fraser versus Cooper.'

'I'm in love with Ashley Cooper,' said Janice, dropping her dishcloth.

'You'd fall in love with anyone who reached the semis,' chided Mrs Tibbet.

'That's not fair! I've never been in love with Neale Fraser.'

Sebastian laughed, and didn't stop laughing for the next hour, which was why he didn't turn up at Eaton Square until nearly half past eleven. When Bruno opened the door, Seb said, 'Mea culpa, but in my defence, I was held up by two of my girlfriends.'

⊷◦⊷

'Take me through it one more time,' said Martinez, 'and don't leave out any details.'

'A team of three experienced drivers have carried out several practice runs during the past week,' said Diego. 'They'll be doing a final time check later this afternoon.'

'What can go wrong?'

'If Clifton doesn't take up your offer, the whole exercise will have to be called off.'

'If I know that boy, he won't be able to resist it. Just be sure I don't bump into him before he leaves for Cambridge in the morning. Because I can't guarantee I wouldn't throttle him.'

'I've done my best to make sure your paths don't cross. You're having dinner at the Savoy this evening with Major Fisher, and tomorrow you have an appointment in the city first thing in the morning, when you'll be briefed by a company lawyer on your legal rights once you've acquired seven and a half per cent of Barrington's.'

'And in the afternoon?'

'We're both going to Wimbledon. Not to watch the women's final, but to give you ten thousand alibis.'

'And where will Bruno be?'

'Taking his girlfriend to the cinema. The film starts at two fifteen and ends around five, so he won't hear the sad news about his friend until he gets back in the evening.'

◄○►

When Sebastian climbed into bed that night, he couldn't get to sleep. Like a silent film, he reran everything that had taken place during the day frame by frame: breakfast with Tibby and Janice; a trip to Wimbledon in the MG, before watching a nail-biting semi-final with the fourth set finally going to Cooper, 8–6. The day ended with a visit to Madame JoJo's on Brewer Street, where he was surrounded by a dozen Gabriellas. Something else he wouldn't be telling his mother.

And then, to top it all, on the way home Bruno asked him if he'd like to drive the MG to Cambridge the next day rather than go by train.

'But won't your father object?'

'It was his idea.'

◄○►

When Sebastian came down to breakfast the following morning, he was disappointed to find that Don Pedro had already left for a meeting in the City, as he wanted to thank him for all his kindness. He would write to him as soon as he got back to Bristol.

'What an amazing time we had yesterday,' said Sebastian as he filled a bowl with cornflakes and took a seat next to Bruno.

'To hell with yesterday,' said Bruno, 'I'm far more worried about today.'

'What's the problem?'

'Do I tell Sally how I feel about her, or do I just assume she already knows?' Bruno blurted out.

'That bad?'

'It's all right for you. You're so much more experienced in these matters than I am.'

'True,' said Sebastian.

'Stop smirking, or I won't let you borrow the MG.'

Sebastian tried to look serious. Bruno leant across the table and asked, 'What do you think I should wear?'

'You should be casual, but smart. A cravat rather than a tie,' suggested Sebastian as the phone in the hall began ringing. 'And don't forget that Sally will also be worrying about what she should wear,' he added as Karl entered the room.

'There's a Miss Thornton on the line for you, Mr Bruno.'

Sebastian burst out laughing as Bruno slipped meekly out of the room. He was spreading some marmalade on a second piece of toast when his friend returned a few minutes later and greeted him with the words, 'Damn, damn, damn.'

'What's the matter?'

'Sally can't make it. Says she's got a cold and is running a temperature.'

'In the middle of the summer?' said Sebastian. 'Sounds to me as if she's looking for an excuse to call it all off.'

'Wrong again. She said she'll be fine by tomorrow, and can't wait to see me.'

'Then why not come to Cambridge with me, because I'm not fussed about what you wear?'

Bruno grinned. 'You're a poor substitute for Sally, but the truth is I've got nothing better to do.'

46

'DAMN, DAMN, DAMN' caused Karl to come up from the kitchen and try to find out what the problem was. He arrived just in time to see the two boys disappearing out of the front door. He ran across the hall and out on to the pavement, but could only watch as the orange MG pulled away from the kerb, with Sebastian behind the wheel.

'Mr Bruno!' shouted Karl at the top of his voice, but neither head turned, because Sebastian had switched on the radio so they could listen to the latest news from Wimbledon. Karl ran out into the middle of the road and waved his arms frantically, but the MG didn't slow down. He sprinted after the car as it approached a green traffic light at the end of the road.

'Turn red!' he screamed, and it did, but not before Sebastian had swung left and begun to accelerate away towards Hyde Park Corner. Karl had to accept that they'd escaped. Was there a possibility that Bruno had asked to be dropped off somewhere, before Clifton drove on to Cambridge? After all, wasn't he meant to be taking his girlfriend to the cinema that afternoon? It was not a risk Karl could afford to take.

He turned back and ran towards the house, trying to remember where Mr Martinez was meant to be that day. He knew he would be spending the afternoon watching the women's final at Wimbledon, but wait, Karl recalled he had an earlier appointment in the City, so it was possible he might still be at the office. A man who didn't believe in God prayed that he hadn't already left for Wimbledon.

He charged through the open door, grabbed the phone in the hall and dialled the office number. A few moments later Don Pedro's secretary came on the line.

'I need to speak to the boss, urgently, urgently,' he repeated.

'But Mr Martinez and Diego left for Wimbledon a few minutes ago.'

◄o►

'Seb, I need to discuss something with you that's been worrying me for some time.'

'Why I think it's unlikely that Sally will turn up tomorrow?'

'No, it's far more serious than that,' said Bruno. Although Sebastian detected a change of tone in his friend's voice, he couldn't turn to look at him more closely, while he attempted to negotiate Hyde Park Corner for the first time.

'It's nothing I can put my finger on, but since you've been in London, I've had a feeling my father's been avoiding you.'

'But that doesn't make any sense. After all, it was he who suggested I join you at Wimbledon,' Sebastian reminded him as they headed up Park Lane.

'I know, and it was also Pa's idea that you borrow my MG today. I just wondered if anything had happened when you were in Buenos Aires that might have annoyed him.'

'Not that I'm aware of,' said Sebastian as he spotted a signpost for the A1 and moved across to the outside lane.

'And I still can't work out why your father travelled halfway round the world to see you, when all he had to do was pick up a phone.'

'I meant to ask him the same question, but he was preoccupied, preparing for his latest book tour to America. When I raised the subject with my mother, she acted dumb. And I can tell you one thing about Mama, she ain't dumb.'

'And another thing I don't understand is why you remained in Buenos Aires when you could have flown back to England with your pa.'

'Because I promised your father that I'd deliver a large crate to Southampton, and I didn't want to let him down after all the trouble he'd gone to.'

'That must have been the statue I saw lying on the lawn at Shillingford. But that only adds to the mystery. Why would my father ask you to bring a statue back from Argentina, put it up for auction and then buy it himself?'

'I've no idea. I signed the release forms as he asked me to, and once Sotheby's had picked up the crate, I travelled down to Bristol with my parents. Why the third degree? I only did exactly what your father asked me to do.'

'Because yesterday a man came to visit Papa at the house, and I overheard him mention the name Barrington.'

Sebastian came to a halt at the next traffic light. 'Do you have any idea who the man was?'

'No, I've never seen him before, but I did hear my father call him "major".'

◄○►

'This is a public announcement,' said a voice over the loud-speaker. The crowd fell silent, even though Miss Gibson was about to serve for the first set. 'Would Mr Martinez please report to the secretary's office immediately?'

Don Pedro didn't react at once, and then he rose slowly from his place, and said, 'Something must have gone wrong.' Without another word, he began to barge his way past the seated spectators towards the nearest exit, with Diego only a pace behind. Once Don Pedro had reached the gangway, he asked a programme seller where the secretary's office was.

'It's that large building with the green roof, sir,' said the young corporal, pointing to his right. 'You can't miss it.'

Don Pedro walked quickly down the steps and out of Centre Court, but Diego had overtaken him long before he reached the exit. Diego quickened his pace and headed towards the large building that dominated the skyline. He occasionally glanced back to make sure his father wasn't too far behind.

When he spotted a uniformed official standing by a set of double doors, he slowed down and shouted, 'Where's the secretary's office?'

'Third door on the left, sir.'

Diego didn't slow down again until he saw the words *Club Secretary* printed on a door.

When he opened it, he came face to face with a man wearing a smart purple and green jacket.

'My name is Martinez. You just called for me on the tannoy.'

'Yes, sir. A Mr Karl Ramirez phoned and asked if you would ring him at home immediately. He stressed that it couldn't be more important.'

Diego grabbed the phone on the secretary's desk and was dialling his home number when his father came charging through the door, his cheeks flushed.

'What's the emergency?' he demanded between breaths.

'I don't know yet. I only have instructions to ring Karl at home.'

Don Pedro seized the phone when he heard the words, 'Is that you, Mr Martinez?'

'Yes, it is,' he said, and listened carefully to what Karl had to say.

'What's happened?' said Diego, trying to remain calm, although his father had turned ashen white and was clinging to the edge of the secretary's desk.

'Bruno's in the car.'

◄○►

'I'm going to have it out with my father when I get back this evening,' said Bruno. 'After all, what can you possibly have done to annoy him, if you only carried out his instructions?'

'I've no idea,' said Sebastian as he took the first exit off the roundabout on to the A1 and merged with the traffic travelling up the dual carriageway. He pressed his foot down on the accelerator and enjoyed the sensation of the wind blowing through his hair.

'It could be that I'm overreacting,' said Bruno, 'but I'd prefer to get this mystery sorted out.'

'If the major is someone called Fisher,' said Sebastian, 'then I can tell you, even you won't be able to sort it out.'

'I don't understand. Who the hell is Fisher?'

'He was the Conservative candidate who stood against my uncle at the last election. Don't you remember? I told you all about him.'

'Was he the chap who tried to cheat your uncle out of the election by fixing the vote?'

'That's him, and he also tried to destabilize Barrington Shipping by buying and selling the company's shares whenever they were under any pressure. And it might not have helped that when the chairman finally got rid of him, my mother took his place on the board.'

'But why would my father have anything to do with a creep like that?'

'It's possible that it may not even be Fisher, in which case we're both overreacting.'

'Let's hope you're right. But I still think we should keep our eyes and ears open just in case either of us picks up anything that might explain the mystery.'

'Good idea. Because one thing's for certain, I don't want to get on the wrong side of your father.'

'And even if one of us does find out that for some reason there's bad feeling between our two families, it doesn't mean that we have to become involved.'

'I couldn't agree more,' said Sebastian as the speedometer climbed to sixty, another new experience. 'How many set books did your tutor expect you to have read by the beginning of term?' he asked as he moved into the outside lane to overtake three coal trucks driving in convoy.

'He recommended about a dozen, but I got the impression that I wasn't expected to read all of them by the first day of term.'

'I don't think I've read a dozen books in my life,' said Sebastian as he passed the first of the lorries. But he had to brake sharply when the driver of the middle lorry suddenly pulled out and began to overtake the one in front. Just at the point when it looked as if the driver would pass the front lorry and return to the inside lane, Sebastian glanced in his rear-view mirror to see that the third lorry had also moved into the outside lane.

The lorry in front of Sebastian inched its way forward allowing it to draw up alongside the lorry that was still on the inside lane. Sebastian checked his rear-view mirror again, and began to feel nervous when he saw that the lorry behind him appeared to be closing in.

Bruno swung round and waved his arms furiously at the man driving the lorry behind them, while shouting at the top of his voice, 'Get back!'

The expressionless driver just leant on his steering wheel as his lorry continued to move closer and closer, despite the fact that the lorry in front still hadn't quite overtaken the one that remained in the inside lane.

'For God's sake, get a move on!' screamed Sebastian, pressing the palm of his hand firmly on the horn, although he was aware that the driver in front wouldn't be able to hear a word he was saying. When he looked into the rear-view mirror again, he was horrified to see that the lorry behind him was now no more than a few inches from his rear bumper. The lorry in front still hadn't progressed enough to move back into the inside lane, which would have allowed Sebastian to accelerate away. Bruno was now waving frantically at the lorry driver on their left, but the driver maintained a constant speed. He could easily have taken his foot off the accelerator and allowed them to slip into the safety of the inside lane, but he didn't once glance in their direction.

Sebastian tightened his grip on the steering wheel when the lorry behind him touched his rear bumper and nudged the little MG forward, sending its number plate flying high into the air. Sebastian tried to advance a couple more feet, but he couldn't go any faster without running into the front lorry and being squeezed between the two of them like a concertina.

A few seconds later they were propelled forward a second time as the lorry behind them drove into the back of the MG with considerably more force, pushing it to within a foot of the lorry in front. It was only when the rear lorry hit them a third time that Bruno's words *Are you certain you're making the right decision?* flashed into Sebastian's mind. He glanced across at Bruno who was now clinging on to the dashboard with both hands.

'They're trying to kill us,' he screamed. 'For God's sake, Seb, do something!'

Sebastian looked helplessly across at the southbound lanes to see a steady stream of vehicles heading in the opposite direction.

When the lorry in front began to slow down, he knew that if they were to have any hope of surviving, he had to make a decision, and make it quickly.

◄o►

It was the tutor of admissions who was given the unenviable task of having to phone the boy's father, to let him know that his son had been killed in a tragic motor car accident.